NACH SCHEMA F
SHAUN STAFFORD

STREAK OF GENIUS PUBLICATIONS
Stamford, Lincs, UK

NACH SCHEMA F

First published in 2015 by Streak of Genius Publications

www.streak-of-genius.co.uk
www.shaunstafford.co.uk

Copyright © Shaun Stafford 2014

The right of Shaun Stafford to be identified as the Author of the Work has been asserted by him in accordance with the Copyright, Designs and Patents Act 1988.

Set in Minion Pro 9pt

ISBN 978-1505692884

All rights reserved. No part of this publication may be reproduced, stored in a retrieval system, or transmitted, in any form or by any means without the prior written permission of the publisher, nor be otherwise circulated in any form of binding or cover other than that in which it is published and without a similar condition being imposed on the subsequent purchaser.

This novel is a work of fiction. All characters in it are fictitious and any resemblance to real persons, living or dead, is purely coincidental.

For Tom

Who taught me the difference
between fascism and communism.

Shaun Stafford lives near Stamford, Lincs. He has two sons. By day, he leads a wholly bohemian and non-profitable existence – indeed, some say Shaun Stafford only exists in the mind of a very twisted individual. By night, and sometimes way into the early hours of the morning, he writes fiction. He has written numerous books, and has written and starred in a number of short films. *Nach Schema F* is his tenth novel, and is the sequel to his bestseller, *die Stunde X*.

Email: shaun@shaunstafford.co.uk

Website: www.shaunstafford.co.uk
Blog: shaunstafford.blogspot.co.uk/

Also available by Shaun Stafford

The Journal
die Stunde X
Blood Money
For the Love of the Devil
Putrid Underbelly
Journals
Peeling the Onion
Besotted
Maggie's Children

About the book

This sequel has been a long time in the making. I wrote its predecessor, *die Stunde X*, twenty years ago, in 1994. The mainstream publishers at the time, in their wisdom, decreed that it wasn't original, that books about the Nazis winning the war had been done a couple of times previously. They suggested I write something else. Now, twenty years later, the alternative history market is massive. It has a huge following. And *die Stunde X* remains my bestselling book.

Many people will see me now as a writer who produces work of transgressive fiction. That's true, of course it is, but I don't believe I should be pigeon-holed into any one particular genre. I enjoy writing transgressive fiction, but I also enjoy losing myself in a fantasy world such as the one which existed in *die Stunde X*. That world continues in this sequel. Some small changes have been made to correct errors made in the original book. I don't think readers will notice them.

I hope you enjoy it.

Acknowledgements

A massive shout out to my biggest fan (still) and one of my very good friends, **TOM GAFFIGAN**. Tom actually appears in this book, somewhere, and a couple of passages were inspired by him, either directly or indirectly. Indeed, I wrote a couple of scenes whilst I was sat at the bar in the pub Tom once owned. Any writer who says that he isn't inspired to create characters even loosely based on people he knows is lying. I hope, however, that if anybody recognizes anything of themselves in any of the characters in this book, they take it in good humour. None of you are Nazis!

1

Dougie moved quickly, pushing through the busy Christmas shoppers, making his way to the target. He checked his watch, saw that it was 4.15pm, and that spurred him on to push more vigorously. He had fifteen minutes to get there. Cursing himself for not leaving earlier, he contemplated what he would say to his superiors if he didn't complete his mission.

He could feel the SIG Sauer P226 pistol hanging in a shoulder holster, ready to be drawn. It contained seventeen rounds – sixteen in the magazine and one in the chamber. Enough ammunition to easily take out half a dozen unarmed people. The problem was, though his target might well be unarmed, the half a dozen men with him would be bristling with high-tech weaponry.

Dougie was under no illusions. His mission today was going to be one from which he would not return. He'd resigned himself to that. Suicide missions, it seemed, were all that Combat UK were capable of nowadays.

That thought was in his mind as he roughly shoved a German couple to one side. Ever since 1995, when the reprisal killings had taken place, London was a city dominated by Germans. One hundred thousand English men and women had been chosen at random and executed as punishment for the assassination of the Führer. The mass graves, just to the north of London, could be seen from Autobahn One, the road that linked London with Edinburgh. And as Engländers were murdered by the SS, so German immigrants came over to take the jobs that were vacant. The Germanization of the country was proceeding at a very speedy pace, and there wasn't a lot that Dougie or the combined – albeit miniscule – force of Combat UK could do about it.

All that was left for them were these type of missions. Ones from which the participant knew there was little chance of them returning. The men and women who carried out these missions were nonetheless proud to know that they were striking a massive blow at the German regime. Combat UK had seemingly become obsessed with carrying out suicide missions, people sacrificing themselves for the greater good.

Making his way through the crowds, Dougie shoved a middle-aged

German aside. You could tell the Krauts. Mostly, they all wore Swastikas on their right arms. They were all still good Nazis, loyal Party members. Hadn't they learnt what the Nazi regime was all about? The German glared at him, but Dougie gave him a look that told him to shut the fuck up. That in itself was dangerous – the Germans, the SS, the Gestapo, they were all looking out for terrorists. And to a suspicious, paranoid German, Dougie could've been classed as a terrorist based on his appearance alone.

He was early thirties, dark-haired, with a rough beard. He was so typically anti-Aryan that he stood out a mile. But the Aryan Germans that had emigrated to England rarely paid him any attention. After all, they were used to working with Engländers. Even when he shoved them, they didn't seem overly concerned. They'd been told before they had emigrated here that the native Engländers were rude and arrogant.

Dougie was still in a hurry.

He shoved another German out of the way and the German turned to him and swore, but Dougie didn't understand. He wasn't that bothered about learning German in school – even the swear words didn't appeal to him.

He just glared at the German, as if to tell him that it would be unwise of the Kraut to pursue the matter. The German shook his head, a look of distaste on his face, as though he'd been dealing with dog shit on his shoes

He was close now, and the pistol felt heavy, yet comforting, beneath his armpit. He could see that there were now more Germans in the area. A few Waffen-SS officers, their MP5 submachine-guns hanging in front of them. They didn't appear overtly threatening. They were just carrying out general police duties in what was a high security part of London.

He saw the restaurant sign now, and undid his jacket. He'd made up the lost time, and was so close now he could almost taste victory. He knew that it was a suicide mission. He knew that there was no chance of him succeeding in getting away afterwards.

But what did it matter, so long as he completed his mission?

He could see the entrance to the restaurant, the plain-clothed security detail officers – not Gestapo, but wearing casual clothes. They'd be carrying the MP5K, the machine pistol variant of the ubiquitous submachine-gun the SS officers were issued with.

nach Schema F

As he got ever closer to the restaurant, he saw his target. A smile crept across his face.

*   *   *   *   *

Reichsstatthalter Klarsfeld had eaten a good late lunch. He'd eaten a typically English meal. Steak and chips, with battered mushrooms. It had been exquisite, the steak cooked rare, the blood still dripping from the meat. He'd been in the company of a young Gestapo officer. It had been a business meal that Klarsfeld had been hoping would turn into pleasure.

The Gestapo officer was certainly attractive, young, and had spent the first hour of the meal talking business. Klarsfeld had listened intently. He had actually wanted to know what she had to say. He was, of course, concerned with the security of the *Deutscher Staat von Großbritannien*. But she was a beautiful creature to behold, and before long he'd asked her if she was single. He already knew she was – his own personal SS staff had provided him with plenty of intelligence about her.

He'd just wanted to know how honest she was.

She'd said, "I have no time for romance, Herr Reichsstatthalter." And she'd smiled at him in a way that he'd found so attractive. He had a thing for younger women.

"How old are you?" he asked her.

She seemed embarrassed, but she'd said, "I am twenty-five."

Klarsfeld smiled. For his age, he was still an attractive man. And he wasn't a predator. He tried to seduce younger women, and invariably he succeeded. But on the occasions where he failed – and there were plenty of those – he merely nodded and moved onto the next potential conquest. He was a Nazi, most certainly, but he was not an animal. He didn't abuse his power. Some women supplicated themselves before him, but that didn't turn him on. He wanted women who genuinely found him attractive. That was what turned him on.

He said to her, "SS-Untersturmführer Brauchitsch, you are a most delightful creature." They were now drinking coffee. She smiled at him demurely, and he was reminded of the report about her. Two years ago, she'd been working undercover, and the guy she'd been investigating turned out to be one of the men sent by Combat UK to kill the Führer. She was a very experienced Gestapo officer, in spite of her juvenile appearance. She had ordered the killing of the person she was supposed to have fallen in love with.

She was a ruthless Nazi.

Klarsfeld wasn't totally sure he was happy with that.

A couple of years ago, he'd been investigated by the Gestapo regarding his involvement in the plot to kill the Führer. As the Governor of the German State of Great Britain, he had been responsible for overall security. But that hadn't stopped Combat UK from carrying out their assassination. Even more problematic for Klarsfeld was the fact that he had been linked with Reichsführer-SS von Stauffenberg, who had been executed for attempting to implicate the then-Vizeführer. There had been a very in-depth investigation, but thankfully Klarsfeld had been absolved of all charges. He knew that it must've upset the new Reichsführer-SS, Schaemmel, but there was no way, legally, that Klarsfeld could've been charged with any wrongdoing.

Unfortunately, the same could not be said for the man in charge of the SS in Great Britain, SS-Oberstgruppenführer Röhm. Röhm had been arrested, and there was much evidence to link him to von Stauffenberg. He was seen as an ally to the disgraced Reichsführer-SS, and was executed a few weeks after the investigation had begun. Klarsfeld had never considered Röhm to be a friend, but he was a close colleague. He was, therefore, grateful that Röhm had been shot dead rather than decapitated as a common criminal.

He'd even been present at the execution.

Röhm had regarded him with a steely gaze, and then had grunted as the 5.56mm rounds from ten assault rifles had torn into his body.

Klarsfeld had been impressed that Röhm had refused to be blindfolded. He'd said, quite clearly, "I want to see the German traitors who want to kill me. I am a loyal German, and I am proud of what I have done. Heil Führer!" As the last word had left his lips, he'd grunted and sunk to the ground, blood pouring from the many wounds in his body.

So now here he was, standing with Fraulein Brauchitsch in the foyer of the restaurant. He had half a dozen plain-clothed Sicherheitspolizei officers with him. He knew that the young Gestapo officer was also armed. She looked up at him, and there was a smile on her face.

She'd done her duty for Germany.

She had no reason to pretend that she was in awe of him.

nach Schema F

"Might I call you Ellen?" he asked her.

"Of course, Herr Reichsstatthalter."

"I hope that you enjoyed the meal."

She let out a small laugh. "Mein Herr, I was honoured to be in your company today. I still am honoured."

He was intrigued. Part of him wanted to ask her how she could kill a man she'd supposedly been in love with, but this wasn't the time nor the place. Their lunch date was over. But he wanted to see her again.

He knew that if he asked her back to *Der Amtssitz des Reichsstatthalter*, the official residence of the Governor of the German State of Great Britain, she would probably oblige. Part of him wanted extend the invitation, but he knew that he would only want to make love to her and never see her again.

But Ellen, she was a different woman.

She had this streak of independence.

He wanted to see her again.

He said, "We will drop you off at your home, Ellen."

Now he was using her first name. She just smiled and said, "Herr Reichsstatthalter, I can get a taxi."

"Please," he said, "call me Erich."

She gave a little laugh. "Mein Herr, I am not worthy."

"Nonsense. You are a beautiful thing. I am flattered to have been in your company for the last few hours."

Then they stepped out into the cold.

And that was where things seemed to go wrong.

There was a loud flash, an explosion even, and Klarsfeld had felt pain in his left arm the likes of which he'd never experienced before. He was aware of Ellen throwing him to the floor, screaming out some command to the Sipo officers supposedly guarding him. There were more loud bangs. Klarsfeld was so close to pissing himself.

But Ellen said in his ear, "Do not worry, Erich. We will look after you."

There were more loud bangs, and Klarsfeld almost sobbed.

And then Ellen stood up.

She had a pistol in her hand, and she was looking at him. She said, "Please, Herr Reichsstatthalter, stay where you are. The ambulance is on its way."

And then he'd watched as she'd stepped up to a man who was lying five yards away.

*   *   *   *   *

Dougie saw the Governor step out of the restaurant. He had a woman alongside him, wearing a little black dress. His latest conquest, no doubt, some English whore who didn't care who she slept with to help herself and her family.

Dougie drew the SIG Sauer, and took aim at the Governor, Klarsfeld, the icon of Germanic rule in England. He'd wanted to say something monumental, something that people would repeat, even these German bastards. Something that would go down in the history books, and would be repeated again and again, and when German rule was ended, would be paraphrased by generations to follow.

But all he said was, "Die, you Kraut fucker!" before squeezing the trigger.

It had happened so fast. The whore with Klarsfeld had pushed the Governor to one side. The first three rounds Dougie fired seemed to hit nothing in particular, but the final one clipped Klarsfeld in the arm, sending him spinning to the ground.

And then Dougie had felt the heat of rounds tearing into him.

Screams, in German, demands for him to get to the ground, which seemed worthless, considering he was already falling, the pistol tumbling from his grip and spinning across the pavement, far from his reach. He hit the ground hard, and looked around for the gun, but it was gone.

He heard a woman say something in German, and turned to look at Klarsfeld, who seemed so close he could almost touch him. The woman was standing next to the Reichsstatthalter. She had a pistol in her hand, a Walther P99 if he wasn't mistaken.

He twisted his head to follow her as she moved, looking into her eyes as she stood over him.

Her pistol was aimed at him.

She said something in German, gave him a half-smile, and then opened fire.

And then, for Dougie, there was just blackness.

2

The Führer looked at Schaemmel. It had been a long time since he'd felt this angry, this pissed off. Leading the Reich was something that only certain people were capable of doing. It was a vocation. And the Führer knew that this was his vocation. His predecessor certainly hadn't been up to the job. He'd been looking to make peace with the Americans and the Russians.

The Führer had thought that was wrong. The Reich could never survive if the Russo-American Pact did not fear it.

So the Führer had planned the assassination of his predecessor, and the present Reichsführer-SS, Schaemmel, had been party to the plans.

Now the Führer could only look at Schaemmel and become concerned. Just like falling for a woman who was happy to have an affair, betraying her husband, so Schaemmel could not be trusted. He had happily agreed to plot the assassination of a former Führer. Could he be trusted to defend the present Führer? Where did his loyalties lie?

"So tell me, Schaemmel, what the hell has happened in Great Britain?"

"Somebody attempted to kill Klarsfeld."

"That *Arschloch*? Remind me again why he is still alive."

"We could not prove any link to the former regime," the Reichsführer said. "He is, after all, only a governor."

"Is he a good one though?" the Führer asked. He was standing at the library wall, looking at the thousands of books before him. His office, his residence, was in the Reich capital, Germania. Many years before, it had been called Berlin, but it had changed a lot since then, absorbed many of the surrounding towns and villages. Now, the buildings were huge, the roads straight. This was what the capital of the most powerful nation in the world should look like.

Schaemmel said, "Mein Führer, it is not for me to say. Your word is final, you know this."

The Führer frowned. He was sick of arse-licking juniors afraid to speak their minds. He said, "Tell me, Schaemmel, should I replace him? I want an honest answer." He looked out of the huge window in his office. He could see the plaza leading up to the Reichstaghalle, where his office was located. To his right, he could see the Volkshalle, with its huge dome dominating the skyline of Germania. Far beyond what he could actually see – the skyscrapers, the offices, the very expensive houses – he knew there were the lower-class businesses and residences, the ones that helped to keep Germania afloat.

"He has been loyal."

"So you keep saying," the Führer snapped. "But that is not an answer, Schaemmel." He turned and looked at the person who was essentially the second-in-command in the German Reich. "I expect honesty from my staff." It was an insult, but the Reichsführer-SS took it well.

He knew his place.

"The *Germanization* of Great Britain is continuing," he said. "I would envisage, from figures produced to me by my staff, that within two years, there will be virtually no wholly-British citizens still living in Great Britain. We have diluted their race. They are now perhaps seventy percent Aryan."

The Führer smiled. As a race could be diluted negatively through the intervention of foreign influences, conversely, as was the case with Germans fathering the children of British women, so a nation could also be diluted positively. The British – the English in particular – were almost Aryan, and in ensuring that the only children that were produced in England were half-German, it would not be long before Great Britain became wholly Aryan.

"You still have not answered my original question," the Führer said. "Should Klarsfeld be replaced?"

"It would be easy to replace him now," Schaemmel said. "He is in hospital. It is just a slight wound. But people do actually die from such wounds. Infections can be deep."

"You are not understanding me," the Führer said. He was feeling more angry now. He was sick and tired of this. All he wanted were advisors who would actually give him real answers instead of answers they thought he wanted to hear. "Should we remove him?"

Schaemmel seemed to get the message now. It was some moments before he actually replied. "Mein Führer, Klarsfeld seems to be popular in Great Britain, in spite of the reprisals policy in 1995. He seems able to stop the entire British population turning against us." Schaemmel gave a half-smile, and the Führer was reminded of how the Reichsführer-SS had

nach Schema F

been overly confident a couple of years ago. It was strange to see it resurface. People had a small amount of power, and they were confident. Schaemmel had to the potential to be a threat, but the thing was, without men like Schaemmel the Führer would not have his power.

He said to Schaemmel, "I need your support."

Schaemmel nodded. "I am here to do—"

"You are here to support me," the Führer said, quite clearly. "Do you want me to be candid, Herr Reichsführer?"

"I am your servant."

"Stop bowing down to me, or I will find somebody who will do what I ask of him without trying to lick my arse at the same time."

The Reichsführer-SS smiled. "Tell me, then, mein Führer."

"I think that our greatest problem comes from nations such as Great Britain," the Führer said. "They are a proud nation, and I know that they will never happily subjugate themselves to German rule. I am not sure that the Reichsstatthalter there is telling me everything I need to know." Schaemmel could only shrug. "Perhaps my predecessor was right. Perhaps we should modernize our rule in our outlying states. Make these people think that they are a valued part of Germany."

"I don't think they are that stupid, mein Führer," Schaemmel said.

"So tell me this, Herr Reichsführer. Why is it that the people of Poland, of France, of Belgium and Spain, have allowed themselves to become subjugated to German rule? What is so different about the Engländers? Why do they possess more pride in themselves than the rest of Europe who dropped to their knees in the 1940s and 1950s?"

"If I may be so bold, Mein Führer?" Schaemmel asked. The Führer nodded. "They are almost Aryan. They are an island nation, undiluted by non-Aryan influences." The Führer smiled – finally, his subordinate, his supposed right-hand man, was coming round to his way of thinking. "Perhaps we should be nurturing them, giving them more autonomy?"

"Perhaps you may be right," the Führer said.

"And Reichsstatthalter Klarsfeld?"

"Maybe we can used him."

"Yes, Mein Führer," Schaemmel said. "We have him under close supervision."

"Excellent," the Führer said. "You will keep me informed, Herr Reichsführer?"

"Yes, mein Herr," Schaemmel said, getting to his feet. He saluted. "Heil Führer!" The Führer returned the salute, and watched as the most senior member of the Schutzstaffel left his office. Then he got to his feet and wandered over to the window again. This was the Germania Hitler had wanted to build.

Albert Speer had seen most of the magnificent buildings erected before his death in the late 1980s, but even after then, the building work had continued. To the right of the Volkshalle, in the heart of the commercial district, a skyscraper was being erected that would not only be the largest in Germany, but in the entire world. Taller even than the American World Trade Centre. The Führer was determined that the tradition of building everything bigger and better than anywhere else should continue.

And why not?

Was not the *Großdeutsches Reich* the most powerful and wealthiest nation in the world? Did it not own the whole of the European continent, most of the Asian continent, the oil fields of Arabia? The Reich could sustain itself for many, many years to come.

But there were other issues to discuss.

Returning to his desk, he picked up a telephone and spoke to his secretary. "Anke, please would you have Herr Fleischer and Herr Bauer sent to my office."

Fleischer was his Foreign Secretary and Bauer was his Propaganda Secretary. What he had to discuss with them was far more significant than minor troubles with poorly-armed insurgents in Great Britain.

3

Marcus Dauny heard the alarm clock and sighed. It was early – this much he knew without even having to look at the time. And work at the Gerhard Fieseler Werke, on the outskirts of Peterborough began at 8am.

It was unusual for an Engländer to be taken on by a company which worked directly for the regime, but Dauny was a staunch English Nazi, proud to wear the Hakenkreuz on his right arm. Some fellow Englishmen spat in his direction, but only when he wasn't looking. Everybody feared English Nazis, even more so than German Nazis, because the English were more fervent in showing their support for the German Reich, in betraying those they saw as the enemy.

Dauny lived on the outlying reaches of Westhalz, a lower-middle-class estate that was inhabited predominantly by Germans, with the odd English family sprinkled here and there. Had he been a German national, his job would have afforded him a much bigger house in a more salubrious location. He would've had a Mercedes Benz, with a smaller BMW for his wife, if he were married. He would've had a cleaner and a cook.

But Dauny, by virtue of birth, was English, not German, and so his skills as a computer expert were utilized by GFW for rather less than they would've employed a German in a similar role. Not that he was bitter, he thought as he showered. His skills and his loyalty to the Reich put him in a better position than most other Engländers who had to work on farms, on building projects, or in factories and warehouses.

No, Dauny was happy. As happy as a man could be in a country where the majority of the native population still talked about the 'what ifs' of the Second World War. Dauny wasn't concerned with history. All that mattered was the future.

He looked at himself in the mirror.

His face was distinguished, with an authority that belied his true age of thirty-eight. His hair was grey, receding, but cropped short in a way that told people he was no longer happy to cling on to the past. He was a big man, tall, with a wide frame, and a paunch that betrayed the fact that he was well fed and undoubtedly wealthy. His well-made clothes also gave off that aura of financial well-being.

Satisfied with his appearance, he stepped out of his house and climbed into his car, a two-year-old BMW 3-series. So smug was he with all that life had to offer him that he failed to notice the BMW M3 that pulled out from a side road and began to follow him on his journey to work.

*   *   *   *   *

Harry Dean was a typical working class man, his hands calloused from days spent in the factory, his muscles tight and firm from all the hard labour and heavy lifting he did, and his belly round from all the beer he drank every evening.

He was forty-six, with a lined face that readily showed his age, and a sadness in his eyes for a wife who had been cruelly taken from him when they were both just twenty-three. He'd never got over the loss. There was a photograph of her that hung above the mantelpiece in his small, two-bedroom house in Nordbretton, a poor, working class suburb of Peterborough where most of the workers at the factories on the Bretton Industriegebiet lived.

The house was a stone's throw away from the RuprechtWerk, which manufactured small electronic components for computers. It took Harry all of three minutes to get from his front door to the factory gates. Once there, he worked a twelve-hour shift for RM200 per week, lugging heavy boxes around the warehouse. There was a one-hour break after five hours and thirty minutes. Sometimes Harry went home for lunch, but mostly, he stayed in the factory.

Most of his fellow workers were quiet individuals. Those who showed any signs of intelligence or interest in the arts were immediately highlighted as being different, and it wasn't long before the Gestapo started to show an interest in them. Those that did return to work in the factory after such an investigation never again showed any signs of intelligence or interest in the arts.

Arbeit macht frei, the slogan above the gate pronounced, and it was repeated at various locations within the factory itself. 'Work makes you free.' Harry always grunted a laugh whenever his eyes fell upon one of those signs. Mostly he chose not to look up, because that's when he saw the ominous Hakenkreuz emblems hanging from the ceiling, huge red

nach Schema F

flags, with a black hooked cross inside a white circle.

Everybody who had English blood inside them learned to fear that symbol.

Harry had learnt to fear it many years before.

But he tried not to think of the circumstances why.

It was a normal Monday morning as he walked into work. He fixed himself a coffee, before making his way to the warehouse, in preparation for the start of the conveyor belt. But there was much hubbub in the tea room, and Harry, who was never really one for watching the news, wondered what it could be.

He knew that somebody had tried to assassinate the Reichsstatthalter on Saturday, but surely that was old news. And then somebody turned to Harry, some woman he barely recognized – because he tried not to build up friendships with the people at the factory – and said, "There was talk of devolving more powers to the English people – they're putting an end to them, It was on the news."

Somebody else added, "The Führer himself spoke about it. He said that it was time to look to the future."

Harry nodded. He took a sip from his coffee. It was hot, but he wanted to get out of the tea room. And then, as though he'd read Harry's mind, the line supervisor came in and shooed them all away, saying that the managers at RuprechtWerk would probably not share the Führer's goodwill.

Harry kept the smile inside as he worked out his shift.

This was good news for him.

4

SS-Sturmbannführer Wolf Loritz read through the report with interest. There was much about Reichsstatthalter Klarsfeld that interested him. The Governor was currently in a hospital bed in the Goebbels Krankenhaus in the capital, recovering from a gunshot wound to the arm. By all accounts, he was enjoying being nursed by the young women there.

The report he was reading contained some background information on the would-be assassin, Dougie Hardcastle. He was in his thirties, a workshy individual, in and out of employment, never able to hold a job down for more than a few weeks. He'd been psychiatrically assessed by the *Reichsarbeitsdienst*, the Reich Labour Service, after he'd lost his last job two weeks before the assassination attempt.

He'd been assessed as being clinically depressed.

Loritz was not stupid. Of course the man would be depressed. He couldn't hold down a job, and there was the threat of being sent to a Konzentrationslager where he would be forced to work until he dropped. The obvious first question was, did the depression cause him to remain unemployable, or was it a result of being unemployable? More significantly, *why* was he unemployable? Even people so stupid they could only lick stamps all day were given a job in the German Reich.

Then there was the question of why, after having been assessed as being clinically depressed, his file was not passed onto the Aktion T4 group for consideration. As a routine, long-term, clinically depressed people were, for want of a better phrase, 'put to sleep' – they could serve no useful purpose within the Reich. Hardcastle, by all accounts fitted the criteria for Aktion T4 euthanasia. He made a note in his 'to-do' book for that oversight to be investigated.

He didn't bother to consider why the case had taken so long to go from the Reich Labour Service to the psychiatric assessment department, because he knew that labour shortages and backlogs were high.

Hardcastle appeared to have been a deeply disturbed individual with a grudge against the German Reich, and yet there was still something odd about the case. For a start, where did he get the weapon? A SIG Sauer

nach Schema F

P226, general Orpo issue, should never end up on the black market, but if it did, an unemployable man such as Hardcastle should not have been able to afford to buy one.

Loritz knew that the weapon was with the Geheime Staatspolizei's forensic team. They would discover from where the weapon originated, and then pass the information onto Loritz for further consideration.

Loritz had a feeling, an odd sensation he couldn't shake, that he was dealing with something far more sinister than a crazed individual who hated Germans. Something about this case didn't feel right.

He looked at the young Gestapo officer sitting on the opposite side of the desk. She was mid-twenties, very pretty, and had been through a lot during her brief service. Her father was some wealthy industrialist in London, but Loritz was not impressed with this.

SS-Untersturmführer Brauchitsch had rose rapidly through the ranks over the last couple of years, as had Loritz. Both of them had been involved in the operation to prevent the assassination of the Führer. Brauchitsch had been working undercover for more than a year, trying to infiltrate Combat UK. She'd made contact with one of their new recruits, and had subsequently learnt that he was part of the assassination plot.

Brauchitsch had admitted during her post-operation debrief that she had fallen for the young man. However, she'd shown her loyalty by having him killed before he'd had a chance to assassinate the Führer. Unfortunately, she had not been able to learn the whereabouts of a second assassin, who had gone on to complete his task.

All in all, her background was good. The psychological assessment conceded that she was indeed upset at the death of the terrorist, but that such a thing was to be expected after spending so long working undercover. She had, quite simply, gone native, but had still managed to retain her loyalty to the Fatherland. It concluded that she was able to return to active service.

And then, a few months later she'd arrived at Loritz's department.

The report she had submitted to him was detailed, well-written, and also pondered upon suspicions that he himself had – that Hardcastle was not a lone gunman, but was, in fact, working for either a resurgent Combat UK, or one of the many splinter groups that had sprung up in the midst of its original destruction.

Loritz said, "Frau Untersturmführer, this is an excellent report."

"Thank you, mein Herr."

He'd noticed her looking around his office as he'd been reading her report. Hung on the walls were half a dozen photographs of Loritz meeting various dignitaries. But none showed him meeting the Führer. He wasn't yet that important. Her eyes had lingered on the framed pencil drawings, and he could imagine what she was thinking. How could a man like him be responsible for such exquisite art? He decided to probe her on the subject.

"You like my art work, Frau Untersturmführer?"

Brauchitsch's eyes shifted to the nearest of the drawings, A4 size, depicting the face of a woman. She was crying. That was what the young Gestapo officer would notice – in all of the drawings, the people seemed upset. Loritz could remember the woman. She was such a pretty thing, but she had betrayed the Fatherland. He'd drawn her face as he'd sat in the courtroom watching her trial.

"They are very good, mein Herr."

"Thank you, thank you," Loritz said. "We all have hidden talents, do we not? Yes, that is why there is always a place for the Geheime Staatspolizei. Because some of us have hidden talents that are wholly undesirable."

"I am sure that your talent is one that should not be hidden, mein Herr."

"Oh, you will have me blushing, gnädige Frau." Loritz smiled tightly.

"You have been drawing for a long time, mein Herr?"

"Since I was a child," Loritz said, and his mind wandered back to those days, before his father had practically demanded that he give up such childish pursuits and prepare himself for a career in the Schutzstaffel.

Back then, he'd never drawn faces that were upset.

He sighed. "But enough of frivolities," he said forcefully. "Tell me, Frau Untersturmführer, how is your operation proceeding?"

"Reichsstatthalter Klarsfeld is proving to be a very courteous and polite gentleman."

"He is much the ladies' man. I am hearing tales of him in the hospital," Loritz said with a smile. "If half of what I am hearing is true, then he is getting a far better service from our health department than one should expect."

"I cannot comment on that, mein Herr. As I stated in my report, I only accompanied Herr Klarsfeld to the one meal."

"Yes, yes," Loritz said. "And he barely mentioned politics. Tell me, Frau Untersturmführer, do you think that he suspects?"

"I have not been given enough time to ascertain that, mein Herr. But this recent assassination attempt should provide me with ample opportunity to get to know him better. If you would make me his personal bodyguard?"

Loritz nodded. He was going to do that anyway, but this young woman had pre-empted that. "You are a very bright officer, Frau Brauchitsch. I think that you have a very long future with the Geheime Staatspolizei."

"Thank you, mein Herr."

"That will be all for now," Loritz said. The woman got to her feet and saluted enthusiastically. When she was gone, Loritz opened one of the drawers next to his desk and took out a drawing pad. With a pencil, he started to sketch out a face.

Ellen Brauchitsch's face.

He was determined to draw at least one more face where the person was not upset.

5

The Führer remained seated behind his desk as the Foreign Secretary and the Propaganda Secretary were shown into his office. The window to the side of him, made of bullet-proof glass, showed a view of the Großer Platz, a vast paved plaza that was the centrepiece of the capital. It was surrounded on all sides by the massive buildings of German government and commerce. Not quite what Speer had intended originally, but like most things in the Greater German Reich, there had been changes.

Herr Fleischer was a thin man, tall, dark hair, with an untypically German face that, years ago, would've seen him prejudiced against. He certainly would not have been working for the government. But this was the late 1990s, and sentiments were more modern.

In any case, it would've been unfair for the Führer to judge Fleischer on his appearance. As the Foreign Secretary, he did precisely what was asked of him, and he was also perfectly capable of offering the Führer sound advice. The Führer trusted him.

He also trusted Bauer, who was tall, powerfully built, and very young for a government secretary. He had just turned thirty-five, and over the last few years had quickly made a name for himself in the *Reichsministerium für Volksaufklärung und Propaganda*. He'd succeeded the previous incumbent after a hunting accident, and the Führer had been impressed with Bauer's ability to have even him half-believe that his predecessor's death *was* an accident.

Bauer also had a voracious appetite for women, and many junior ministers and admin assistants had succumbed to his wily charms. But what Bauer did professionally, he also did for his private life. His wife, mother to his two sons, was blissfully ignorant of his extra-marital activities.

The men saluted, then took up seats opposite the Führer. They waited for him to speak. It was his wont to make people wait. That way, he could look at their faces, read them, watch their eyes, see if they had anything to hide.

He didn't expect either of these two men to have anything to hide.

"Gentlemen," he said, "I would like to discuss today our relationship with the United States of America."

Bauer smirked slightly and looked at Fleischer. As far as he was concerned, this was a topic for the Foreign Secretary to answer.

Fleischer said, "Mein Führer, as you will be aware, we have withdrawn all of our diplomats from the United States. Similarly, we have expelled all of their diplomats. As you will also be aware, our two nations maintain something of a Cold War status."

"As you say, I am aware of these facts," the Führer said with a nod. "Would you say, Herr Fleischer, that it would be beneficial for us to open up fresh talks with the United States?"

"Given our current situation, mein Führer, with our Wehrmacht still fighting Russian resistance, I would say that it would be highly unwise to provoke the Americans."

"You feel they could be a threat to the might of the Greater German Reich?" the Führer asked quickly. He wanted to test Fleischer's honesty – the Führer was no fool, and he didn't like to be surrounded by 'yes-men'.

"I think they are undoubtedly a force to be reckoned with," Fleischer said. "It was a shame that attacking the United States was not really a viable option in 1995."

The Führer nodded. That much was true. Certainly, they could've used conventional missiles and bombers and rained down terror and violence upon America. But the sheer distance between the Greater German Reich and the United States of America made it virtually impossible to launch a land assault. Any troops would have to be sent over by sea, and would be extremely vulnerable to air attack. Dropping troops in by air was also fraught with danger, thanks to the hours it would take them to travel from the Reich to the US. However, those distances also prevented the US from launching a land attack on the Reich.

The two nations had reached something of an impasse.

"We have almost defeated the Russians," Fleischer went on. "Or so I am led to believe. I notice Reichsmarschall Zabel is not present at this meeting, mein Führer, but I will assume that you are more apprised of the military situation in Russia than I."

"You assume correct," the Führer said. There were small pockets of Russian resistance that were yet to be defeated, but essentially the Soviets had fallen. Moscow had been taken, and the Wehrmacht was so far east that it was almost touching Alaska. That in itself would be highly beneficial to any future invasion attempts."

"We have no reason, at the moment, to concern ourselves with the United States. They are as powerless as we are. The only slight concern is that Canada has given them free reign to move their troops, and as I understand it – and I'm sure somebody from the Sicherheitsdienst could confirm it – they are building up a force in Alaska to counter any attack from that direction."

"Do you think they will attack us in Russia from Alaska?"

"It is always possible," Fleischer said. "Which is perhaps why we need to reassure them of our peaceful intentions."

"And you think they would believe us?" The Führer let Fleischer cogitate on that question for a few moments, before he shifted his gaze to Bauer.

Bauer drooped his bottom lip, squinted, and nodded his head slowly. "Mein Führer, I'm sure we could have them believing that by the end of the week."

"Herr Bauer, please do not make promises you cannot possibly keep," the Führer snapped.

Bauer seemed unaffected by the Führer's hostility. "It is true. They will think that we have become militarily weakened by the prolonged conflict in Russia. And for sure, we have lost many good soldiers, loyal Germans, in that fight. They will believe that we will need time to lick our wounds. Perhaps we could consider opening up trade agreements with them. We have huge oil reserves."

"The Americans produce their own oil."

"They certainly do, mein Führer, but not in such vast quantities as our oil fields in Arabia. In return, we could consider importing certain consumer items from them. The fact we're willing to open up trade negotiations would imply to the Americans that our war efforts in Russia have cost us a lot of money."

The Führer nodded. Bauer's idea seemed to have some credence, but it would not be an overnight solution. "Perhaps we should send a high profile diplomat over there – an official visit." His eyes fell upon Fleischer, who visibly baulked at the suggestion. "Oh, come now, Michael, surely you are not afraid?"

Fleischer, recovering now, shook his head. "Not in the slightest, mein Führer." But the Führer knew what he was thinking. The SS had executed all of the American diplomats it had found at the US embassy in 1995. It might be possible that the Americans would still want their revenge.

"Gentleman, what we have just discussed, I shall leave in your hands, yes? I expect a briefing from you both within a week. It would be advisable for the pair of you to work in close proximity with one another."

The Führer nodded curtly, and the two men got to their feet, saluted, and left the office.

America was a huge problem for the Greater German Reich, but even it was not undefeatable. Once they had built up a fresh relationship with the US, he could then start pushing troops further into Russia, closer to Alaska. Alaska was the key. Once they had a footing on the American continent, it would be far easier to move troops across.

Then Canada would fall under the might of the Wehrmacht, and the United States would quickly follow.

6

Harry Dean parked his battered red NSU RO120 Wankel Spider in the car park of the Bretton football stadium and switched off the engine. 'Stadium' was perhaps too grand a title. It was an austere concrete building which served as the bar and function room tagged onto the back of a stand that ran down one side of the pitch and barely shielded supporters from the elements.

The stadium was home to three football teams, and Harry played for one of them – Bretton AFC. They were currently lying third in the Peterborough Second Division. Playing football, as well as other sports, was encouraged by the Nazi regime as a way of keeping the population fit and occupied. If the population was fit, it was less of a burden on the health service, and if it was occupied, people were less likely to cause trouble.

Harry wasn't a particularly good footballer – he was perhaps an average defender. His size frightened most attackers, and belied his ability to engage in short bursts of speed that enabled him to get to the ball first. He generally played football to stay in shape, fulfilling one part of the Reich's desires.

But if he were being honest, and in the Greater German Reich nobody was ever one hundred percent honest, he came here mainly for the company. There was no match for his team today, but two other teams were playing. A smattering of spectators cheered half-heartedly when one team had a shot on goal.

Harry made his way from the car park, pausing momentarily to watch the football match. His eyes scanned the small crowd, and then he walked into the Bretton Sports and Social Club, out of the bitter cold into a room that was only marginally warmer but was at least shielded from the wind.

There were perhaps a dozen people in the small bar, and the murmur of quiet conversation could be heard. Harry walked up to the bar and smiled at the landlord.

"Tom," he greeted.

Tom toyed with his glasses and said, "Mr Dean. Your usual, I take it?"

"A pint of German piss and an insult, yeah."

Tom began to pour the pint and said, "I see you made the effort to dress up for us." He nodded to Harry's attire. Harry was wearing jeans and a sweater, both of which were slightly grubby. He gave a little laugh.

"Car trouble on the way over," he explained.

"Ah, never buy a German motor."

"Your pearls of wisdom never fail to impress me, Tom," Harry said, handing over a Reichsmark and taking the pint of Doppelbock from the landlord. It was the strongest lager that Tom sold, running at 10%. "It's just a shame they always come *after* the mistake."

"You know why that is, don't you?"

"No," Harry said, shaking his head with a smile.

"The benefit of hindsight," Tom explained mysteriously. He smiled and moved onto the next customer. Harry picked up a copy of the *Volkischer Beobachter* and read the headlines. There it was again – the Führer announcing that his cabinet was considering devolving more powers to the British.

"You seen this?" Harry asked Tom.

"Oh yes," Tom said. "Oy vay, the Führer is a merciful leader, for sure, my son." He always did a bad version of a London Jewish accent, not that Harry or Tom had ever heard a real Jew speaking. There had been no Jews in England since the late 1940s, but there were plenty of impersonators who did sketches on comedy shows.

Tom finished serving his customer and came back over. "You know the problem with that though?" Harry shook his head and sipped his beer. "The missus will want to go shopping in London to celebrate!" Harry smiled. Black humour was all they really had now. "When she read that, she said to me, 'Can I have fifty Reichsmarks to take to London with me?' I said to her, 'Forty Reichsmarks? What do you want thirty Reichsmarks for?'"

The two men laughed heartily. The jokes were anti-Jewish, not anti-German. They were safe. Nobody paid them much attention, and nobody would report them to the authorities.

When they were alone at the bar, Tom said quietly, "You've been to the debrief?"

Harry nodded sombrely. "It could've gone better."

Tom pushed his glasses up his nose. "Well, I did have reservations. After all he'd been through ..."

"It was a one-way trip, Tom," Harry reminded his friend. "I didn't see many people volunteering."

"What did the Number One say?"

Harry said, "He wasn't pleased. We don't know whether it was a mistake or whether Dougie was actually trying to do that."

"So what next?"

Harry looked down at the headlines. "Well, what do you read into this bullshit from the Führer."

"Well, he's either being a very genial chap, or else he's lying through his teeth," Tom said.

"That much is obvious."

"I think he's lying through his teeth," Tom said. He wasn't talking loud, but he was animated. To the casual watcher who couldn't hear what was being said, it would appear as though they were chatting about something innocuous. "He's up to something."

"But what?"

"Well, the attempt on Klarsfeld's life should've resulted in a number of reprisal killings," Tom said. "We should be bathing in the blood of innocent people."

"So why aren't we?"

"What am I? A member of the Gestapo?" Harry gave a small laugh.

"Knock knock," said Tom.

"Who's there?" Harry said, resigned to another bad joke.

"Ze Gestapo."

"Ze Gestapo who?"

"Ve vill ask ze questions!"

Harry sipped his pint and looked at his watch. It was a little after two in the afternoon. The rendezvous was supposed to take place at two, so it was already late.

There could be many reasons why his contact was late, so he tried not to let his nerves overcome him. He carried a cyanide capsule, which he was determined to slip into his mouth and bite down upon should he ever be in danger of being captured. He knew precisely what the Gestapo were capable of in their torture rooms.

He just hoped that his contact had a similarly firm resolve.

It took a lot of guts to kill yourself.

Ever since the tragedy of 1995 which had effectively destroyed Combat

UK, the resistance movement had struggled to survive. Now they worked outside of London, where they carried out low quality attacks on soft targets – off-duty Orpo officers, civil servants and collaborators. The Nazis were concerned, obviously, but not enough to launch widespread counter-revolutionary measures. The English resistance was more of a small annoyance to them. But the resistance movement had modernized itself. It operated in small cells of no more than three or four people. Each cell's leader worked for a 'Number One'. The Number One knew the leaders of four cells. That way, each person only knew a handful of people. And through the torture procedures, it only took one man *not* to crack, and no names, no leads, were forthcoming.

The cyanide capsules were issued to every English Resistance Army volunteer. They were expected to choose suicide over capture, if at all possible.

Harry knew that Liam Lovett, Combat UK's leader, was still alive. There were rumours that he had died in the pogroms that had followed the assassination of the Führer two years ago, but then the legend had started to rise a few months later. Some said he was still in London, avoiding the SS round-ups for reprisal killings, slitting the throats of Gestapo officers as they ate meals with their wives. Others said he was in America, plotting the nuclear destruction of the Greater German Reich. And there were rumours he was in Scotland, being nursed back to health after escaping from a Konzentrationslager north of London.

Harry knew the truth.

Tom, on the other hand, knew Liam Lovett only as this mythical character whom people spoke of quietly, and never in the presence of either Germans or English Nazis.

Harry finished his pint. It was 2.20pm, according to his watch, and he'd waited long enough for the contact to arrive. The dilemma was, if the Gestapo had squeezed information from his contact and they knew about this location, they'd have it under surveillance. If Harry left now, so close to the rendezvous time, he was sure to be detained and questioned.

Better to forget about the meeting altogether. Make an afternoon of it. If the Gestapo, in their infinite wisdom, chose to raid the place in an hour or so, desperate to turn up a traitor, they'd find regular customers and Harry, who would be the token drunk. He held up his empty glass and Tom shook his head.

"It's not a session beer, Harry."

"I'm not gonna trash the place," Harry assured him. "Three pints of this, and then I'll move over to Becks." Satisfied, Tom took the glass and poured out another pint of Doppelbock. Harry, who hated Germans and everything German, actually quite liked Doppelbock. It had a very strong, sweet taste, and more than that, it got him drunk very quickly. The Doppelbock logo on the glass also told any potential idiots that he was not a man to be trifled with.

He was on his third pint when two Germans came into the bar. A hush descended upon the assembled Englishmen. Harry turned to look at the newcomers.

Of course they were German. You could tell just by looking at them. A young woman, no older than twenty-five, her hair short, casually dressed in jeans and a sweater, with Adidas training shoes on her feet. The man with her was slightly older, similarly casually dressed, but he was in no way the woman's boyfriend. The body language between them certainly did not imply that.

The woman was also in charge.

She led the way to the bar, and Tom wandered over.

"What can I get you?"

The woman looked Harry up and down, her eyes settling on the pint glass in his hand. "I will have a Becks for my friend," she said, "and a glass of water for myself." There was barely a hint of a German accent in her voice, but her polite delivery gave her away.

She paid for the drinks, and sat down on a bar stool. Her male escort remained standing. He made a show of watching the football match on the large screen TV as he sipped his lager. Harry looked at the reflection of the woman in the mirror behind the bar. She was looking around, taking in the faces of the people sitting at tables, huddled in corners. The conversation had started again now that the drinkers were reassured that these Germans weren't going to arrest anybody.

Not just yet, Harry thought.

These two newcomers were undoubtedly Gestapo. And the fact that they were here, in this bar, suggested that his contact had been arrested. It didn't appear as though the contact had given up the identity of the man he was supposed to be meeting, but he had clearly given up the location.

Harry said to the man, "Are you a Man United fan then?" On the TV, it was Manchester United versus FC Bayern München, playing in the European Cup knock-out rounds. The man gave a half smirk, and shook his head.

"I am afraid not, mein Herr."

"No, me neither," Harry said, turning his attentions back to the TV. The Germans were dominating the game.

"Then who do you support?" the German asked him.

Harry looked back at the young woman, who seemed irked that her partner was having a trivial conversation about football. "Peterborough United," he answered. "I'm a very loyal fan. Yourself?"

"Well, I must confess I have never been a fan of *Die Roten*," the German replied. "My team is Hamburger SV."

"Ah yes," Harry said with a nod. "They're not having a very fortunate season, are they?"

"Alas, this is true. I am sure we can expect a return to form perhaps next season." The German took a swig from his beer and looked at his companion.

"I'm sorry, gnädige Frau," Harry said. "I'm hijacking your partner and discussing football with him. You must think I'm pretty rude."

She smiled, but it never reached her eyes. "Regardless of ethnicity, you men are all the same. You think only of beer and football."

"Well, could I ask what brought you in here today, this being a bar in a football ground?"

Tom butted in. "Harry, can you stop harassing my customers. It's not bloody often we get new ones in here, and the old ones are all dying."

"It is fine, Herr Landlord," the woman said, still smiling. "I understand the curiosity of the Engländer. We are looking for somebody."

"Perhaps I can help. Who are you looking for?"

"We are looking for a gentleman by the name of Herr Harry Dean," the woman said, giving a smile. "Yes, perhaps you could help?"

7

Harry overcame the initial shock at hearing his name mentioned, and was hoping that his face hadn't blanched. He considered where the cyanide capsule was.

"I'm Harry Dean."

The woman's smile broadened. "The very man we are seeking," she said. "I am SS-Untersturmführer Brauchitsch, Geheime Staatspolizei. This is my colleague, SS-Untersturmführer Himmler. He is not a relation," she said, smirking conspiratorially.

Harry was aware that nobody was speaking in the room, and his heart seemed to be beating far too loudly in his chest. He said, "Geheime Staatspolizei? I am under arrest, Frau Untersturmführer?"

At that moment, the door to the bar opened and a tall, balding man stepped into the bar. Harry's eyes passed him over but showed no recognition, even though this was the contact he had arranged to meet.

"No," Brauchitsch said. "We would like to ask you a few questions about a man called Douglas Hardcastle."

So this plainly had nothing to do with the contact. It was still, however, a very dangerous conversation for Harry to become involved in.

He'd been taught the craft of counter-interrogation. If you have to lie, or cover something up, base it at least partly on something that was actually true. He had known Dougie. There was no sense in lying, because these Gestapo officers were not stupid.

"I know Dougie, yes," Harry said with a nod and a wry smile. Dougie had not been named in any of the newspapers as the attempted assassin of Klarsfeld. "Why, what's he bloody gone and done now?"

Brauchitsch said, "Is there perhaps somewhere quieter where we could talk?" She turned to Tom. "Herr Landlord?"

A couple of minutes later and they were sitting in an untidy office at the back of the building. Harry had moved some papers from two of the chairs, and dumped them on the floor. The man, Himmler (no relation) had a notepad in his hand.

"Were you a friend of Herr Hardcastle?" the woman asked Harry.

Harry shrugged. "Well, calling me a friend would perhaps be stretching it a bit. I worked with Dougie for a few weeks at my factory. He lives a few doors up from me – not that I've been round to his house. I see him in the odd pub, perhaps have a beer with him. He's always skint and trying to get guys like me to buy him a drink. I'd say we were nothing more than casual acquaintances." Harry did his best to look confused. "Look, what is this all about? Whatever that workshy idiot has got himself mixed up in, it's nothing to do with me."

Brauchitsch said, "We are trying to build up an account of Herr Hardcastle's background. The people he knew, who they knew, and so on. It would certainly go in your favour if you were to provide the Geheime Staatspolizei with all of the information you have to hand."

"I'll do everything I can to help you, Frau Brauchitsch, but can't you tell me what he's been up to?"

"This is a matter of State security," the woman said. "In these cases, we ask the questions, you answer them."

Harry was reminded of Tom's earlier joke about the Gestapo. He shrugged, sipped from his pint and said, "Ask away."

"Could you provide us with the names of any of Herr Hardcastle's other associates?" Harry thought about that for a few moments. Obviously the Gestapo had been given his name by somebody. The problem was, he could give this damn woman half a dozen names, but he had no idea if they had any connection with the resistance.

He knew why the Gestapo were digging around in Peterborough, eighty miles north of the capital. This was where Dougie came from. They'd thought they were being clever in sending an unknown agent down to the capital to carry out the operation.

But Dougie was fucked up, and as a consequence, he'd also fucked up. The fact that the Gestapo knew who he was proved that he hadn't been totally honest with his handlers. He'd said that he'd never been in trouble with the law before, but clearly his records were on file somewhere. The operation had turned out to be a bloody mess from start to finish. But as he'd said to Tom earlier, there weren't many volunteers for suicide missions.

Harry gave the woman five names, people he'd seen Dougie drinking with on a casual basis. He was just glad that the useless bastard hadn't been taken alive, or else Harry might've found himself on the wrong end of a Gestapo torturer.

He drained his pint. Right now, he fancied another strong lager. He intimated this to the woman, and she nodded. "Well, thank you, Herr Dean. We appreciate the information you have given us."

And then the minor interrogation was over.

The two Gestapo agents left the bar, where Harry sat down. Tom came over and poured him another Doppelbock, "On the house."

Then he said, "What's the difference between communism and National Socialism?" By this point, Harry wasn't sure he was in the mood for another of Tom's jokes, but he shrugged his shoulders. "Communisn is the exploitation of one man by another man, whereas National Socialism is the other way round."

Harry gave a wry smile and then downed half of his pint.

*   *   *   *   *

Himmler drove the car. He turned to look at Ellen. She knew that he had a soft spot for her, but that wasn't going to change her opinion of him. His ludicrous name, for a start. Most 'Himmlers' and 'Hitlers' who weren't related to the great men had changed their names in the 1960s. Clearly, Himmler's father hadn't. To most Nazis, particularly the Old Guard, it was considered to be a form of blasphemy.

"What did you think of Dean?" he asked her.

"Typical arrogant Engländer," she replied. "He clearly hates the Germans, and the German Reich too."

"A resistance fighter?"

"He is a drunk, and he works in a fucking factory, Willi," Ellen snapped. "What the fuck has he got to offer the so-called resistance movement? For sure, he can tell them how to pick packages from a shelf, but nothing more."

"There is no need to be so offensive, Ellen," Himmler said. He didn't sound hurt – he sounded pissed off. They were both the same rank, and she knew he felt as though she shouldn't be taking charge of everything. He was a little older, had more time in.

But therein lay the truth.

She was younger, less time served, and she matched him now in rank. She also had the ear of their leader, Wolf Loritz. She knew that she was impressing Loritz. The Sturmbannführer was not a man renowned for

nach Schema F

being impressed by his junior officers. But she felt some kind of affinity towards him.

"You know, sometimes you can be so arrogant," Himmler admonished her. "You think that tomorrow, you will be my senior officer."

"Maybe I will, Willi," Ellen said with a smirk.

"Fuck you, Ellen."

"Tell me, Willi, those names that asshole gave us, do you think we need to waste time questioning them?"

"They are leads, Ellen, of course we should question them. I recall that they all featured on Hardcastle's mobile phone."

"It's just this shit hole, this town, what is it called? Peterborough. It is so depressing. Full of Engländers and jaded German immigrants. Why the fuck would any German choose to come to this God-awful country?"

"Your father did, Ellen," Himmler said smugly. "And if it wasn't for your father moving to England, you probably wouldn't be in the privileged position you now find yourself in."

"Perhaps not," agreed Ellen. "Maybe I would be in a better position on the Sicherheitsdienst command."

"You really are fucking arrogant, Ellen."

Ellen gave a half smile. "Take me back to the HQ, Willi. I want to drink schnapps and forget what I do for a living." And she meant it.

Just over two years ago, she'd been in love with an Engländer. She wasn't supposed to be in love with him – she was just supposed to use him, nurture him as a potential agent. But over the year or so that she'd known him, he'd just been a regular Engländer – hard-working, innocent, seemingly unaffected by the resistance movement, Combat UK. And so Ellen had found herself falling for him.

But Jerome's father had been arrested by the Gestapo for an indiscretion and sentenced to death, and after that, Jerome had changed. If she were being honest, secretly she felt as though Jerome's father had been arrested just to force Jerome's hand, seeing as how she was so close to him.

In the event, he'd been involved in the plot to assassinate the Führer, and after torturing a young woman with whom Jerome had shared a brief liaison, Ellen had found the man she loved at a hotel in London, armed with a sniper rifle and a submachine-gun.

Jerome hadn't survived the gun battle. He had died in Ellen's arms, and although she'd remained loyal to the Fatherland, she had been deeply affected by his death. They'd sent her for psychiatric assessment, and after a handful of sessions the doctor had concluded that she was fit for duty, a loyal, if at one time emotionally disturbed, member of the Geheime Staatspolizei.

In the intervening two years, she'd worked hard to reassume her position as a graduate fast-tracker. She'd thrown herself wholly into her work, and had arrested many dissidents. She'd given evidence at their court trials, and she'd watched a handful of them being executed.

SS-Sturmbannführer Loritz had suggested she do that, to harden herself to the job she was doing. He'd said, "You cannot hide from the reality of your work, Frau Brauchitsch. You cannot see it as some kind of fantasy. You must know precisely what happens to the people you arrest, the people you testify against. You must know, so that you do not idly play with people's lives." If nothing else, Loritz was a fair man, one who could not abide corruption.

The journey to London didn't take long on the Autobahn One that ran from Scotland to the capital. A few chirps of the siren, and the M3 found it easy to weave through the traffic.

Himmler parked the car in a car park close to the newly built *Polizeipräsidium*. The police headquarters was an impressive structure, over 600ft tall, consisting of thirty-five floors above ground and another five floors beneath the ground. It was London's tallest building, and could be seen from practically anywhere in the city.

On top of the concrete and glass monstrosity, there was a Reichsadler holding a Hakenkreuz. At the foot of the building, surrounding the large, stone-pillared entrance, hung a dozen red flags of the Greater German Reich. The DSvG Gestapo had their offices there, occupying ten floors, including the subterranean ones. The work that was carried out beneath ground was of a less subtle nature than that carried out above ground.

Ellen climbed out of the car and approached the *Polizeipräsidium* with almost the same amount of dread she presumed interrogation subjects experienced. But hers was a dread at having become jaded with her work, and she would have that emotion over the other any day of the week.

As they approached the entrance, three black BMW M3s, red lights on their roofs flashing brightly, swept past, and down into a subterranean car park that was only used by high-ranking SS officials and Gestapo

nach Schema F

officers taking in suspects.

Ellen paused momentarily, and then said to Himmler, "You know, Willi, you ever wonder what Germany would have been like had we not won the war?"

"Ellen, that is something which would be too awful to contemplate for the German people," he replied.

And yet, still Ellen wondered.

8

Marcus Dauny noticed the dark BMW following him on the way back from the Bretton Sports and Social Club. He was supposed to have met somebody from the resistance movement at the club, but he'd heard two people introduce themselves as members of the Geheime Staatspolizei and immediately his bowels had loosened. The Hakenkreuz that usually adorned his right arm had been removed – the man he was meeting had told him it wouldn't be advisable to wear it to the club – and so Dauny had felt somewhat exposed in the presence of the Gestapo officers.

He drank a pint of real ale in the bar, Fuller's London Pride, and watched the football match on the TV. Dauny wasn't one for football, preferring cricket and rugby, two sports that the Germans didn't actually play with any great enthusiasm. The result of the football was expected, with Manchester United losing 3-1 to the German team but putting up a valiant effort. The commentators said that English teams needed to devote more money on scouting for local talent, but the fact was they just didn't have the money that the German teams possessed.

Dauny made idle chatter with the landlord, a decent enough chap whose name was Tom. It transpired that Tom had only just taken over the running of the club, and so was still learning about real ales, though Dauny had to concede, and was polite enough to tell Tom, that his London Pride was one of the best outside of the capital.

But all the time, he knew that the Gestapo officers were in another room, questioning his contact. Dauny couldn't leave without finishing his pint, because that would've looked suspicious to the patrons of the bar, but he actually felt felt terrified.

In the event, he managed to leave before the Gestapo agents returned, and was now driving home. As for the dark BMW behind him, he knew, as did almost everybody in England, that the Gestapo drove dark BMW M3s, renowned for their speed. Indeed, M3s were only sold to the Schutzstaffel, and when they were no longer of any use, they were scrapped, their engines destroyed so they didn't fall into the hands of 'ordinary people'.

Dauny was worried.

He pulled over to the kerb alongside a shop and hopped out, risking a glance back. The M3 had also pulled up to the kerb, perhaps twenty yards behind him. He could see the occupants, two large men, both regarding him with beady eyes.

He entered the shop, bought a newspaper, some milk and a bottle of wine, and then returned to his car. As he did so, he saw that the two Gestapo men were standing on either side of the driver's door.

Panic set in, but Dauny was from good English stock, and so retained his confident demeanour and his stiff upper lip. He stepped up to the car and smiled.

"Good afternoon, chaps. Anything I can do for you?"

One of them looked at his right arm, noting the Hakenkreuz armband. "You are a loyal Party member, Herr Dauny."

They knew his name. Dauny frowned. "Could I ask who you chaps are?"

"I am SS-Hauptsturmführer Huber," the German said. "Geheime Staatspolizei."

Dauny nodded. "Well, good day to you. I recall speaking to some of you chaps when I joined the Party many years ago."

"I believe you may have spoken to the Sicherheitspolizei," the German said. "They generally deal with such matters. Similarly, they usually deal with personal protection. It is not something the Geheime Staatspolizei usually gets involved in."

"I'm sorry? Personal protection."

"Your work is very important for the Greater German Reich, Herr Dauny. This you must know, yes?"

"Of course."

"We cannot allow anything to happen to you."

"Of course not."

"Can I ask you, Herr Dauny, what was your business at the Bretton Sports and Social Club? From our records, this is not one of your usual, how you say, haunts."

Dauny felt beads of sweat sprouting on his forehead. But he was an intelligent man, and he could think on his feet. "I wanted to see the football match. Furthermore, I'd heard that the Fuller's London Pride there was of exceptional quality. Turns out that was true. I complimented the landlord on his pint."

"Hmm," the German said, his eyes dropping to the armband again. "And you removed your Party armband?"

"Well, let's just say that some people aren't supporters of the Greater German Reich," Dauny said. "If I travel to a pub that I'm not sure about, I always remove it. I have no desire to be assaulted."

"It is unfortunate that other Engländers do not share your enthusiasm for the Reich, Herr Dauny."

"Quite."

"I would like to give you some advice, Herr Dauny, and it is this. You would be wise to choose where you drink in future. This bar has many subversives as customers. Your security could not be guaranteed if you continue to drink in such establishments."

"I will bear that in mind, Herr Hauptsturmführer," Dauny said.

"Additionally, there is always the risk that you might find yourself being approached by undesirables who may want to turn you away from the Greater German Reich."

Dauny laughed, but the Germans merely smiled at him. "That is ludicrous, Herr Hauptsturmführer. I am a loyal Party member. I was born as a citizen of the Greater German Reich. You call me an Engländer, but that, to me, is an insult because I'm a German."

The German nodded politely. "Well, Herr Dauny, we are here to make sure that no ill befalls you." He opened the driver's door and gestured for Dauny to enter.

"There really is no need."

"Nonsense. A loyal Party member like you, we are just civil servants doing your bidding."

Dauny climbed in and the door was closed behind him. Then the German knocked on the window. Dauny wound the window down.

"Herr Dauny, you have nothing to fear."

Dauny nodded and smiled. "Not with you gentlemen following me."

As he pulled away from the kerb, he noticed the Gestapo men climbing into their M3. Soon, they were right behind him. They had wanted him to know he was under surveillance. And that could only mean one thing.

They were warning him.

They wouldn't warn him if they thought he was about to involve himself with English resistance fighters. They'd simply arrest him.

That meant they knew nothing.

nach Schema F

Dauny smiled to himself.

A few years ago, his father, a very wealthy Englishman, had told him that one could make money out of the Germans, but never enough, and that one was English, not German. He'd told Dauny about Churchill, about how every Englishman had died inside when the Germans had captured and executed him.

He'd told Dauny that every Englishman should be ashamed for allowing that to happen, and that they should prepare for the future, when they could drive the dirty Hun out of England.

Dauny had been waiting for that moment for the last twenty-odd years. But he was an intelligent man, Oxford-educated. He knew that driving the Germans out of England was no longer a possibility.

He'd joined the Nazi Party because at the time it had seemed to be a good career move. When he was twenty-two, the only people the Nazis were taking on in the field of computing were either Germans or Party members.

But then one night, a few months ago, Dauny had a nightmare, where he'd seen what had happened to England in the 1940s. The beaches of Dunkirk, the massacre of the soldiers there, bombed from the air and then attacked by the German ground forces. More than one-hundred thousand men, killed in just a few days. British soldiers, turned into carrion for the French crows.

The nightmare had expanded itself to the German Luftwaffe, their Messerschmitt 109s shooting Hurricanes and Spitfires out of the sky, as though guided by some mystical force. The Heinkel and Dornier bombers dropping their massive payloads on airfields and aircraft factories, destroying them, before launching firebomb attacks on all major British cities.

Hundreds of thousands of British civilians blown to pieces, and those who were left had no homes to return to once they emerged from the bomb shelters. The British people had succumbed to the might of the German Luftwaffe, and before long the Wehrmacht was making its way across the English Channel, disgorging itself onto the southern beaches.

But this was no mere nightmare.

This had been the reality.

And when Dauny had awoken, he'd realized that he was just reliving the stories that his father, that his father's friends, had told him. This was not a history written in the books they'd taught him at school.

At school, they were taught that the English people were an Aryan race, and that it was only right that they should fall under the umbrella of the Greater German Reich. But Dauny had watched his friends disappear because they were not quite as Aryan as him. He'd watched the children of friends being taken away because they were handicapped. He'd watched this happen over the last twenty years, and he'd seen the number of friends he had diminish.

Either they disappeared, or members of their family did, and they hated the Germans and the Nazi Party as a result. In both cases, he lost friends. He had buried his father, and he'd remembered him saying about driving the dirty Hun out of England.

It was around the time of the nightmare that he'd been approached by an Englishman, who was clearly not as intelligent as him, who was uncouth, who swore like a filthy battlefield private, and who hated the Germans as much as his father had.

Dauny could remember that initial contact.

He was sitting in a pub alone, reading a book. He had no friends to drink with. His work colleagues were, for the most part, German, and they had no interest in drinking with an Engländer. And most of the English people he knew despised the Nazi armband he wore and would not be seen drinking in his company.

But this Englishman approached him and said, "You're a computer expert – tell me, the Messerschmitt or the Spitfire – which was the best fighter?"

Dauny was taken aback. He put down the book, some garbage written by a former Waffen-SS officer who seemed to have a large opinion of himself. The man, whose name Dauny still didn't know now, even now, smirked at the cover.

"Surely you don't think the 109 was better?"

Dauny, wearing his Nazi armband, said, "Well, neither possessed a computer, so I'm not sure I'm actually qualified to give an opinion. But the 109 had many good points."

"The Spitfire was faster, more manoeuvrable, and more importantly, it was British." The man fixed Dauny with a stare that he found disconcerting.

"It's nothing more than one fighter against another," Dauny said.

nach Schema F

"Does it really matter? It was more than fifty years ago when those two aircraft were dogfighting."

"One bore swastikas – the other the roundel of the RAF," the man said. He was sipping from a pint of lager – but not the usual German mix. This was something from a brewer called Sam Smith. It wasn't, apparently, as good as some of the German lagers, but it was British. If you still believed in the notion of Britishness.

"You know, Sam Smith ales are actually not that good," Dauny said, holding up his Batemans XXXB. "You should try this. It's strong though – perhaps you couldn't take it."

The man smiled, and then his eyes fell upon the Hakenkreuz on Dauny's arm. He nodded at it. "Do you wear that with pride?"

"I'm not actually sure what business it is of yours."

"None of my business at all," the man said. "But I believe that you have as much English blood running around inside you as I do." He smile and took a sip from his beer. "I'm surprised that doesn't burn on your arm."

"You know, I really must be going."

The man fixed his eyes and shook his head. "You're going nowhere," he said. "We're not stupid. We know what you're about. Some of us knew your father."

"You know, if I make a phone call—"

"You will bring the Gestapo here, sure," the man conceded. "But why would you do that? Would that make your father proud? Do you think he would want you to go running to the Nazis every time an Englishman spoke to you? I think not."

Dauny was hurt by that comment.

He said, "I find that insulting. What do you want?"

"It's not what *I* want," the man said. "It's not what the people I work for want. It's what *you* want, Mr Dauny." And there it was. He'd been called 'Mister' rather than 'Herr'. It had been a long time since he'd been called Mr Dauny.

And that had been the turning point.

And for the last few months, he'd lived a life full of fear.

Today had frightened him more than anything.

9

David Vermont had been elected President of the United States of America almost two years ago, just a few months after the last President resigned. The resignation has been a consequence of the break-up of the Russo-American Pact, and the fact that the Germans had been convinced that the US had, along with the USSR, been involved in the plot to murder the Führer of the Greater German Reich.

Vermont wasn't privy to the secret documents pertaining to that particular year, and nobody on his staff at the West Wing was telling him anything. In a way, Vermont was grateful for that. At least then he wasn't lying if he continually denied any American involvement in the plot.

Things had changed a lot over the last two years.

For a start, all relations with the Greater German Reich had broken down, and with them gone there was also no trade agreement. The Germans, after a successful campaign of invasions in the Middle East, now owned most of the oil fields. Qatar, Iran, Saudi Arabia, Kuwait, they'd all fallen after brief, but vicious, conflicts. Iraq had subjugated itself to the Reich, and in return its people had been richly rewarded. Baghdad, the region's capital, now resembled New York, with an abundance of skyscrapers. Its factories produced cars, trucks, aircraft, all destined for the far reaches of Germany, and the Iraqi people were as wealthy as any German.

The GGR exported oil to Canada, to Pakistan and India, to Japan and the Australian Republic. More than that, a gallon of petrol cost less than fifty Reichspfennig. The Germans were prospering, and the once-proud nations that had been swallowed up by the Reich – the French, the Spanish, the Italians, the Polish, and many, many more – were prospering in the same way.

And now the Nazis had taken over more than eighty percent of the once great nation of Russia. The Russians could not cope with the massive influx of troops, the aerial bombings, the threat of nuclear destruction. And that threat had also been delivered to the Americans two years earlier. The Americans had two choices – call the Germans' bluff, or stand down.

nach Schema F

Vermont's predecessor had, quite rightly, chosen to stand down.

For two years under Vermont, the GGR and the USA had been in a perpetual state of Cold War, their nuclear missiles trained on one another's cities, airbases, army barracks. Mutually assured destruction prevented either from starting a war.

But over the last week, something had happened and now Vermont was sitting with his closest advisors to discuss it.

The Secretary of State, Margo Wilson, was a powerful woman who'd been mooted America's first female President. But right now, she was Vermont's chief advisor on foreign matters. Her role was never going to be an easy one because of the situation between the US and Germany.

She had a proud face. Some might've described her as a handsome woman, few would've said she was pretty. But she carried with her an aura, an indefinable quality, that had many junior advisors fawning at her feet.

It was her who spoke first, and she barely glanced at the report she had open in front of her.

"I'm sure you all know who Michael Fleischer is, but just in case you've been buried away somewhere for the last two years, he's the *Großdeutsches Reich*'s Foreign Secretary, a man with whom I've had the displeasure to deal with on a small number of occasions." She looked around the room, and Vermont saw her eyes falling upon the faces of the three men also present. There was General Herve Goldstein, the Chairman of the Joint Chiefs of Staff, descended from a family of Jews who'd managed to escape Nazi Germany in 1939; Simon Patrese, the Secretary of Defense, a cautious man, second generation immigrant from Italy – his grandfather had come over from Milan in the early 1900s, before the rise of Mussolini; and John T Wright, the Director of the Central Intelligence Agency, whose own particular lineage could be traced right back to the first wave of immigrants to come over on the Mayflower. With backgrounds steeped in honour, hard work, tradition and bravery, they were tough men to impress.

Wilson said, "Yesterday, we received a communication from the German Foreign Office, purporting to have been signed by the Foreign Secretary himself."

"Are those bastards threatening us again?" Patrese drawled. "Don't they understand what MAD is all about?" He picked at some fluff on his jacket.

Wilson smiled tightly, politely, waiting until she had the Italian-American's full attention again. "The Germans are making overtures at peace."

"Peace?" scoffed Goldstein. "Those lying sons of bitches."

This time, Wilson was more curt. "Allow me to finish, General. They are willing to open negotiations to allow diplomats back into their country."

"We know what happened to the last ones who were based there," Patrese said.

Vermont watched Wilson's face. There was a hint of emotion, but it soon disappeared. Her fiancé had been based at the American Embassy in London. There were few survivors after the Germans had stormed the building, and her fiancé was not among them.

"Furthermore, they are willing to open trade negotiations, with a view to exporting to us some of their vast stockpiles of crude oil at, and I quote, 'extremely favourable prices'," she said. "With a view to importing goods from us."

Vermont digested this information, and for the moment his advisors were silent. He could see them all looking at him. They knew that his questions would come. With the exception of Wilson, they would all be on the back-foot, answering him without any prior knowledge. But that was what made them such good advisors.

He said, "Herve, what's the full situation in Russia?"

Goldstein said, "The Germans are close to Chukotka, which is the most easterly part of Russia. I'd say that they'll find the last few hundred miles pretty hard going, and there's a whole load of fuck all there for them to capture. Just Eskimo settlements and such like."

"So essentially, they have occupied all of Russia?"

"From our satellite photography, I would say that Russia is now practically part of the Greater German Reich," the General said. "But that's not without its cost. We estimate that there are around a million German soldiers in Russia. That's stretching their Wehrmacht way too thin."

"But the rest of the Reich is militarily secure?"

"Yes, Mr President."

"We estimate, Mr President, that the current number of soldiers in the

Wehrmacht alone is around five million." This from John T Wright. "Our intelligence would suggest that in spite of its massive commitment to the occupation of Russia, the German Wehrmacht is still a formidable force. However, as Herve says, there is a cost to the Germans, in the form of resupply. Russia is huge, and our satellite photos are telling us that there is a colossal commitment, both financially and in manpower, to resupplying the occupying force."

"Overstretched themselves a little bit," Patrese said. "Eyes are bigger than their belly."

"They didn't have much choice," Goldstein said. "If they didn't move on the Russians two years ago, it's possible that we could've capitalized on the Russian mainland to launch our own attack."

"We missed the boat," Patrese said.

"Something like that," the General said.

"So the Germans need money?" asked Vermont.

"They need time, Mr President," Patrese said. "They need to lick their wounds, maintain a stronghold on the Russian people. It wouldn't surprise me if they didn't offer the Russian people some incentive to work for them."

"Such as?"

"A bribe. Keep the Russians sweet, and they won't fight back or rebel against German occupation. Rebuild the infrastructure in a way that the Russian government never could. Let's not forget that the GGR is the wealthiest nation on the planet."

"But they still can't get to us," Vermont said.

"Mr President, if only that were true," Wright said. He was in his late fifties, a veteran of guerrilla campaigns in South America in the 1970s, when the US was trying to force those countries in the southern hemisphere to sign up to a Federation of America. Experienced in black ops, he'd managed to get Argentina and Brazil to agree, which gave the US a military foothold in the south. His hair was shaved so close to his head, it was difficult to see whether he was balding, receding, or would otherwise have a full head of hair. His eyes were blue, some said cold, but could shine warmly when needed. He wore his stubble at a permanent two days' growth.

He said, "Forgive me if I'm wrong, but the Chukotka Peninsula, isn't that just sixty miles off the coast of Alaska? It would take a few fast ships just three or four hours to sail across the Bering Strait."

Now all eyes were on Wright.

It was some moments before the President spoke. "That's why they want Russia so much."

"As the General said earlier, there's fuck all in that part of Russia, and lots of it," Wright said. "Now, it's pretty harsh terrain, and the Germans are having a bad time of it. We have satellite photos showing that they're building new towns perhaps two hundred miles from Chukotka. Without a doubt, these will be arms manufacturing facilities, to enable them to resupply quickly should they make a move on Alaska."

"How many people do we have stationed in Alaska?" Vermont wanted to know.

Patrese said, "Fifty thousand."

"We can triple that number within a couple of days," Goldstein said.

"Would be a bad move, Herve," Wilson said. "Mr President, the Germans have satellites, just as we have. If they see us building up our forces in Alaska, they may view that as a hostile act."

"You just want us to sign that goddamned trade agreement," Patrese snapped.

"It's a sensible move," Wilson said. But nobody seemed to agree with her. "Let's look at it this way. We can put a hundred thousand soldiers in Alaska, but that's just going to provoke the Germans. However, I'm sure we can have troops ready to be moved north and into Canada should the Germans launch an attack. And in the meantime, we'll be getting cheap oil from them, and we'll also be able to negotiate some good trade deals."

Vermont looked at his advisors. He wanted their honest opinions on this matter because if he made the wrong decision here, the American people would not forgive him, and neither would history.

"Herve?"

"Margo has a point," he conceded. "*If* we can strike up some kind of deal with the Canadians. They've not been very forthcoming with information or trade deals themselves. But if we can change that, then yes, we can move our troops and aircraft north almost as fast as the Germans can cross the Bering Strait."

"Simon?"

"I don't trust the Germans, Mr President," Patrese said. "And any deal they make will be biased in their favour. I think if we do strike up a deal with them, we need to prepare for a potential attack on American soil within the next couple of years."

Vermont nodded. "How about you, John?"

The CIA Director gave a little shrug. "They're buying time, but then I guess so are we. Just depends who gets the jump on who. But I think we still have some tricks up our sleeves. We have a handful of guys still working their balls off and risking losing their heads in the GGR."

With his advisors having answered honestly, Vermont turned to Wilson. "Set up a meeting with Fleischer. It happens on American soil."

Vermont was left alone with his thoughts and the photographs of his wife and three children. All four of them relied upon him, as the Commander-in-Chief, to keep them safe from the threat of the Greater German Reich. But then, so did 350 million other people.

It was a heavy burden to bear.

Vermont reached for the Prozac in his drawer.

He'd been taking them since the day he'd been elected.

10

Harry Dean walked across Ferry Meadows, a wide expanse of woodland, farmland and flood plains surrounding a large lake just to the north of Peterborough. He used to come here as a child to fish with his father. In the madness of the Greater German Reich, here the pair of them had found solitude. There were no Gestapo officers, no uniformed SS troops, no Orpo. Everything was out in the open, and if you chose your fishing spot well, you could see someone approaching you for miles around.

Marcus Dauny had called him from a phone box. He'd been sure not to mention his name. The shakiness that was audible in Dauny's voice was a big giveaway that something had gone wrong.

Harry had asked if he liked fishing.

And now here he was, walking through the bitter cold to a less popular fishing spot. All the same, two men fishing for carp here would not look suspicious. There would be no listening devices, nobody taking photographs of them – it was a very safe spot for a clandestine meeting.

Harry set up the fishing gear. Dauny had said that he had none, so Harry set up two rods. And then he waited. As he waited, he recalled the last time he'd come here with his father. His father couldn't remember the war – he wasn't born until 1944, by which time it was already over, and the Germans had invaded Britain.

Harry's father had been brought up as one of the first British children to be known as a German citizen. Paul Dean spoke German and English. But *his* father – Harry's grandfather – was a true Brit. He'd even fought against the Germans. Once the war was over, the soldiers who'd been prisoners of war were released, and urged to join the Wehrmacht. Harry's grandfather had initially resisted, but his wife had persuaded him to do what was asked of him, for the sake of his family.

The strange thing for Harry, when he was a young boy, was visiting his grandparents, seeing the Nazi regalia that decorated their front room. It had, as far as he could remember, been a bone of contention between his father and his grandfather. The good Nazi, and the English-German, or Engländer, which was the name given to all English people born after the occupation. The Nazi could only speak English, but worked loyally for

nach Schema F

the Wehrmacht, where he served as an *oberstabsfeldwebel* or sergeant major; the Engländer could speak fluent but he hated Germany.

It was from his father that Harry had inherited his rebellious streak. His father had taught him the true history of the 1930s and 1940s when they were on their fishing trips – the tales of the Nazis butchering the Jews, torturing and shooting prisoners of war, the inhumane treatment of political prisoners, of anyone who opposed the regime.

Harry had not forgotten any of it.

He wondered, as he saw Marcus Dauny walking across the field towards him, what kind of an upbringing the wealthy man had had. Dauny was wearing a flat cap, a long, green overcoat, and hiking boots.

There was no Hakenkreuz armband.

The two men stood facing each other.

Then Harry said, "Sit down. Let's fish."

They didn't speak for a few minutes. They just concentrated on their fishing. Fixing the bait, casting out their lines, watching the floats for any sign of movement. Harry didn't expect they would have much luck.

He said, "I don't know a lot about you, Mr Dauny."

"Really?" the other man said. He spoke with a posh accent, as one would expect from somebody with a privileged background. "It begs the question, why am I meeting you then?"

"You mean other than the guy who originally contacted you?"

"Yes."

"The resistance operates in small cells," Harry said. "The guy who set up the original meeting between the two of us, I have no idea who he is. He's just a voice on the end of a telephone line. And to him, I'm much the same."

"He gave me your number," Dauny explained. "That's how I was able to call you."

"I'm surprised you did," Harry said. He fixed his eyes on Dauny. "After what happened at the last meeting, I was expecting you to break off contact."

"I almost did."

"What changed your mind?"

"Part of me thinks that what you chaps are doing is right," Dauny said. He fed out some more line, watched his float bob a few feet to the left. "I look around at our society, and I think there is so much unfairness. I'm an intelligent chap, my grandfather was very wealthy. In another life, I would've been running my own business."

"Life hasn't been unfair to you, Mr Dauny," Harry said. "I do know that you live in a very nice house and you drive an expensive car."

"I'm still an Engländer," Dauny said. "I'm still treated like a second-rate citizen."

"I'd like to know what that makes me," Harry said with a wry smile. "Third- or even fourth-rate?"

"I know nothing about you," Dauny said. "I don't even know your name."

"Harry."

"Well then, Harry, call me Marcus." The two of them shook hands. "You know, lots of us just accept the fact that we are Engländers, part of the Greater German Reich. I joined the Nazi Party because it seemed like a good career move. There were also rumours that Engländers could get jobs in the civil service. Perhaps even become part of the policy makers in England."

"Like that would ever happen."

"What needs to happen, Harry, is for the Nazis to realize that we're happy to work with them so long as we're treated as German citizens, rather than as Engländers."

"You think it's right that we should consider working with the Nazis? After what they did in the 1940s?"

"You're talking about the so-called *Endlösung*? The Final Solution? Most of the Jews are in America, alive and well and making films in Hollywood and money in New York."

Harry shook his head at the other man's naivety. "I can't believe that you've actually been taken in by that rubbish."

"Fairy tales, Harry, dreamt up by British politicians, to turn us against the Germans," Dauny said. "Of course, back in the early 1940s, before we were occupied, such things were expected. Turn us against the enemy and all of that." Dauny looked at Harry. "Think about it," he said. "If you were a soldier, and you were ordered to butcher innocent people, would you do it? Could you do it?"

"I think, Marcus, you've forgotten about the reprisal killings," Harry said. He tossed some bait into the lake. "One hundred thousand innocent men and women, rounded up and butchered."

nach Schema F

Dauny nodded and shrugged. "It was unfortunate, certainly, but the Führer had been assassinated."

"You're a fool if you even attempt to justify that."

"Well, we'll have to agree to disagree on that one, Harry. But allow me to continue with what I was saying before I digressed. I want to help to change the Reich. Give more autonomy to the people in the satellite states. The Greater German Reich needs to be totally modernized if it's to survive. The Führer himself has intimated such a thing may take place."

"The people live in fear, Marcus. They won't attempt to change the regime." Harry reeled his line in a little. "Is that why you're here?"

"Well, tell me, Harry, why are *you* here?" Dauny asked. "Don't you want to change the regime?"

"I want to destroy it," Harry said.

The two of them fished in silence for a few more minutes, and then Dauny said, "So where do we go from here?"

"My job is to talk to you, test your resolve, and if I think you're safe, take you to meet somebody."

"Who?"

"I can't tell you that," Harry said.

"Why not?"

"For security reasons."

"Why do I have to meet this person?"

"I'm presuming that you have an influential position in the Nazi regime," Harry said. "Perhaps because you're a Party member, or maybe because of your job?"

"My job," Dauny said thoughtfully. "Oh my God."

"What?"

"That's it – my job."

"What's your job?"

"I can't tell you that," Dauny said.

"Why not?"

"For security reasons."

Harry couldn't help but smile.

"So, Harry, have I passed your 'resolve' test?"

Harry watched his float bob – once, twice …

"A fish," he said, and he yanked on the rod. It took him a few seconds to land it, a large pike, and as he clubbed it, he looked up at Dauny.

"Sometimes we get lucky," he said.

11

Ellen Brauchitsch slipped behind the wheel of the M3 and checked herself in the rear-view mirror. She knew she was attractive, in a very atypically German way. Her hair was a light brown – some had cruelly said ginger – and her eyes were too. She had a large nose that had caused some of the kids back at school in Germania to dub her *Juden Nase*, as if any of them had actually ever met a Jew. But she was most definitely German, even if she didn't possess the prerequisite Aryan features. Her family tree had been investigated way back before she was even born, in the late 1940s, when the Reich was trying to remove any hint of Jewish ancestry from its citizens.

Her unusual looks were occasionally beneficial in her career, because she could sometimes go undercover as an Engländer, though she had to concede that her clipped, if unaccented, English usually gave her away as being a German.

They'd decided, her superiors, that she was an excellent investigator. Tenacious, with a very bright and analytical mind, she was better at finding people rather than torturing them. She'd only ever tortured two people in her life, and she had confessed to her psychologist that she hadn't enjoyed it.

Loritz had explained to her afterwards that one was not supposed to enjoy torture. One used it to push a person just beyond the boundaries of their tolerance, and no more than that. It was taught at the Geheime Staatspolizei college that if you torture somebody in a way that pushes them way beyond their tolerance levels, any information gained from them is liable to be inaccurate.

In fact, Loritz had said, "If I were to torture you in such a way, you would confess to being the person who shot dead our last Führer."

Ellen had said, "I just don't think I have the stomach for torture, mein Herr."

Loritz had just nodded. "It is sometimes this way," he'd said. "And a few years ago, a Gestapo agent without the stomach for torture would find himself removed from service. But now there are so many more tasks that a person such as yourself can do."

And today, Ellen was performing one of those tasks.

Reichsstatthalter Klarsfeld was returning home from hospital, and Ellen was responsible for his security. That meant managing ten SS officers. But more than that, she was to question Klarsfeld, surreptitiously, to find out where his loyalties lay.

This, Loritz had told her, was an instruction that had come from the office of the Reichsführer-SS himself. He'd added that he was placing an enormous amount of trust in her and he hoped that she wouldn't let him down.

Ellen was certain that she wouldn't.

Thirty minutes later, the Reichsstatthalter was sat in the passenger seat beside her, with two plain-clothed SS officers in the back, and more security officers in the two other cars that were in front and behind.

"So, Frau Untersturmführer, the Geheime Staatspolizei has decided, in its wisdom, to put you in charge of my security," the governor had said.

"I know that it seems strange, Herr Reichsstatthalter, that someone as young as me should have such an important position," Ellen said, "but I can assure you that my service record is impressive. SS-Sturmbannführer Loritz would not have placed his trust in me otherwise."

"Ah yes, Loritz," Klarsfeld said, his face clouding over. "A very enthusiastic Gestapo officer. I'm surprised that he has not risen even higher through the ranks than Sturmbannführer. I did hear that he was offered a post in the Sicherheitsdienst back in Germania, but that he turned it down."

"I cannot speak for the Sturmbannführer, Herr Reichsstatthalter," Ellen said. "Perhaps he likes it in the DSvG?"

"Much as I do, my dear, much as I do."

The rest of the journey passed by quietly, and soon they were at the Amtssitz, the governor's official residence. Once there, Klarsfeld made a show of greeting all of his staff, passing the odd comment, even cracking a few jokes about his condition.

Then he invited Ellen into his library for a chat. Klarsfeld instructed his butler to bring in a bottle of red wine, assuring Ellen that it was of the finest quality, and barking, "Nonsense!" when she'd told him she was still on duty.

After the wine was delivered, Ellen took a sip, and decided she would not drink the entire glass. Klarsfeld, however, was gulping the wine down with much gusto.

He asked, "How long have you been in the DSvG, Ellen?"

"Since I was about eight, Herr Reichsstatthalter."

"So that is, what, sixteen, seventeen years ago?"

"Yes, mein Herr."

"Drop the formalities, Ellen. If you cannot call me Erich, then call me Herr Klarsfeld."

"As you wish, Herr Klarsfeld."

"Tell me, do you miss the Fatherland?"

Ellen pondered that question. The Fatherland was what Germans unofficially called the country of Germany, which formed just a part of the Greater German Reich. She thought back to her time at school, the bullying and teasing, and shook her head.

"I can only remember the school, and my time there was not good."

"Ah, why was that, my dear?"

"I was teased," Ellen said. Her hand instinctively went to her nose. It wasn't enormous, but it was not the cute button nose that adorned the faces of the blue-eyed, blond-haired girls. "They said I had the nose of a Jew."

"You have striking features, Ellen," Klarsfeld said. "Never forget that. It is the fact that you are so different from the run-of-the-mill German girls that makes you stand out from the crowd. We can't all look like the perfect Aryan specimen. My God, if we did, then it would be as difficult to tell us apart as it is to tell one Chinaman from another." He chuckled at that. "You have no other memories of Germany? Did you live in Germania?"

"Yes, Herr Klarsfeld. In the old part of the city, Berlin. My father had a large house there. He still has it, as a matter of fact, but it is rented out to the Reich. A civil servant lives there now."

"And what do you remember about Germania?"

"I remember the Volkshalle," Ellen said. It was virtually impossible not to see the huge building from anywhere in Germania. It wasn't just one of the tallest buildings, but also the widest. It adorned postcards that had been sent all across the globe. The great Führer, Hitler, had delivered a speech to 200,000 German citizens in 1950 in that very building. "My father took me there for one of the tours."

"It is a magnificent building," Klarsfeld admitted with a slight nod.

"But there are rumours that its foundations are crumbling. The Thousand Year Reich, and yet Speer's great *Volkshalle* probably won't last a hundred years."

"Is that true?"

"The old city was built on very soft ground," Klarsfeld said. "I think they unwittingly chose a particularly weak spot to build the Volkshalle." He smiled ruefully. "Of course, if the Volkshalle should fall, it will be a terrible thing for Germany, but I am sure it will be rebuilt somewhere else." He gulped from his wine. "Tell me, Ellen, what do you think of England, of Great Britain?"

"It is just a country," Ellen said. "If I am being honest, I rarely leave London." She wasn't lying there. Her recent excursion to Peterborough was probably the furthest north she'd ever travelled in the German State of Great Britain. "My work keeps me here."

"I did hear a rumour about you," Klarsfeld said.

"And what was that?"

"It is not worth discussing, Ellen, I should not have mentioned it."

Ellen thought about that for a few moments. Klarsfeld would know that she'd been involved in the capture of one of the Führer's assassins. And the gossip about her relationship with Jerome had been rife throughout the *Polizeipräsidium* a few months ago. Now, she had powerful friends, and that part of her life was, if not literally then in every other sense, written out of history.

She decided not to pursue the matter.

Klarsfeld said, "What made you join the Geheime Staatspolizei, Ellen? It is a difficult career choice."

Ellen smiled. She could give an intelligent answer, or one that was appropriate, but she chose to be at least a little bit honest with Klarsfeld. "I wanted to be a spy," she said.

"A spy?" Klarsfeld chuckled. "Is that what you are now?"

"The reality is nothing like the fantasy, Herr Klarsfeld."

"Perhaps, like your superior officer, you should consider the Sicherheitsdienst? Maybe then, you'd be working in America, spying on our enemies, rather than being sat here with me boring you."

"Herr Klarsfeld, you are not boring me," Ellen said sheepishly.

"I am sure that you are too kind," Klarsfeld said.

"If I may be so bold, what brought you to England?"

Klarsfeld moved his head back and stared at the ceiling. "Ah yes, my history. My dear, do you really have time to listen to an old man's reminisces?"

"I am sure your reminisces are very entertaining."

"Oh, I have many stories to tell," Klarsfeld said. "Little anecdotes which entertain the many dinner guests who come to the Amtssitz. But the story of why I am here, that is less interesting."

"So why are you here?"

"It seemed like an easy place to retire," Klarsfeld said with a sigh. "Reichsstatthalter in one of the Reich's furthest outposts. I thought, how dangerous can that be? And yet, look at what has happened here in the last few years. Look at me at the moment, shot by a would-be assassin."

"Do you regret being here, Herr Klarsfeld?"

"I love this country, Ellen," the old man said. "That is the truth of the matter. I love its diversity, its architecture and its landscapes. I even – though God knows why – love the people. They are proud, and they still haven't shaken that feeling of independence. In a way, it is very quaint."

"I get the impression, Herr Klarsfeld, that you consider yourself to be more English than German."

"I am not English, Ellen. That is a silly thought. I have been here a long time though. I am a politician, in the loosest sense of the word – there is no such thing as a politician in the Reich – and I see the DSvG as my own country. In a way, it is. The Führer is not concerned with what goes on here. You know, I tried for months to get him to the stop the reprisal killings. They have done untold damage to the German reputation in this State."

Ellen sipped from her wine. The Reichsstatthalter was now incriminating himself.

"You know, I was very surprised that I was not executed two years ago," he said wistfully. "I know that the Führer himself considers me to be something of a joke, and the Reichsführer-SS has no respect for me at all. I suppose that is why I am still alive – they do not consider me to be a threat to the Reich."

"And are you a threat?"

Klarsfeld smiled and took another gulp of wine. "You know, my dear, I am fully aware that you have been sent here to spy on me."

Ellen was taken aback, but her training kicked in. She looked stunned, and shook her head. "I have been tasked with protecting you, Herr Klarsfeld, that is all."

"Ellen, the Sicherheitspolizei looks after the security of people such as me. You are a member of the Geheime Staatspolizei. You are an internal spy. If you were really as good as you purported to be during the journey over here, if you were really as respected as I am led to believe, then you would not be doing this job. In charge of a security detail for a puppet leader? I think not."

Ellen didn't know what to say. She could feel her mouth drying out, and she took another sip of wine.

"I am sure you will report back to SS-Sturmbannführer Loritz precisely what I have just said," the Governor continued. "You will intimate that I have become jaded with the leadership of the Reich, and that my loyalty is in question. You may suggest that I be removed from my position as Reichsstatthalter. You might even, if you were feeling particularly vindictive, suggest that the death penalty would be advisable. You will do all of this, because you are a loyal German and a conscientious member of the Geheime Staatspolizei." Klarsfeld leant forwards and looked into her eyes. "You will do this, without knowing what I am all about. You see only traitors and loyal subjects – you do not see the people in between."

"Are there people in between?"

"I am no traitor, Ellen. I wish only to modernize the Greater German Reich. To stop brutalizing and terrifying the people." Klarsfeld stood up and walked to the nearest bookshelf. "We are the greatest country in the world, the most powerful, the most wealthiest. But humans do not have any rights. Not even Germans from the Fatherland." He picked up a book from his library, looked at the cover. It appeared well-worn, heavily read. He smiled at her. "You know, I have kept this library for years. I entertain guests in this very room, much as I have supposedly entertained you tonight. And yet none of them, much as you have not, look upon the spines of the books here." He held the book up. "This, do you know what it is?"

"I am afraid not, Herr Klarsfeld."

"This is a very well-thumbed copy of *War and Peace*." He put the book back and plucked out another. "And this? A book by an English author, George Orwell, written in 1949, some years after Great Britain was invaded. This one is called *Nineteen Eight-Four*. I do not imagine that they teach this book in the literature lessons at school. It is about an oppressive regime and the effects it has upon society as a whole. It is one of many books that the regime has forbade us to read. Indeed, Orwell paid with his life for writing it." He held the book up, as though he were encouraging Ellen to take it from him. Then he put it back, and pulled out another. "This one here, I am sure you must have heard of this, even though I doubt for a minute you have read it. *Das Kapital*?" Ellen nodded slightly. "Communist, subversive reading. Another banned book. And yet somebody once said to me that unless you read the works of the enemy, you cannot criticize them. The communists, the few who still exist, do you not think that they read *Mein Kampf*? It is imperative that they get into the mind-set of their enemy." Klarsfeld took another book out. This one looked old, thick. He held it up and compared that and the Karl Marx book. "One is communist, one is National Socialist. Ah, you see, this one, my dear, is a first edition of *Mein Kampf*, signed by Adolf Hitler himself. Given to my father many years ago. One is communist rhetoric and the other is fascist rhetoric. Which one do you believe in?" Ellen was about to say that it was obvious what she believed in, but Klarsfeld smiled. "You believe in Hitler's book – that much is apparent. But have you read Marx's book? Or the Communist Manifesto? I have a copy of that here also. You will find that no matter what you believe, there will be something to interest you in every book you read."

He pulled another book out of the shelf.

"This is the Bible. I am sure they still taught Religious Education at your school." Ellen nodded. "Do you believe that the Earth was created in six days and on the seventh, God rested? Do you believe that we are all descended from Adam and Eve? That the Earth is only 10,000 years old?"

"What is the point in all of this."

"Humour me, my dear. Do you believe that we are all descended from Adam and Eve?"

"No."

"But you recognize that some people believe this is so?"

"Of course. Naive fools."

"Why do you not believe it?"

"Because it cannot possibly be true."

"Because Cain and Abel must have slept with their mother in order for the human race to continue? They must have fathered their own brothers and sisters? And then *they* must have slept with one another. And so on?"

"If you put it down to basics, then yes, that was the way it must have happened."

"This book, the Bible, is full of incest, violence, murder, and a belligerent God who kills non-believers, and yet people believe that it is gospel. Why is that?"

"Belief is a strange thing, mein Herr."

"It is, yes," agreed Klarsfeld. "Is this book not full of hypocrisy and double standards? An ideology which people follow even though they know what is written in the book cannot possibly be true?"

Ellen shrugged, and then eventually nodded her head.

It was only after she'd done so that she realized when he was asking her the question, Klarsfeld was holding aloft *Mein Kampf*. He gave her a half smile.

"I am trying to change things for the better," he said. "If you *must* believe the rhetoric, then make sure that you have read the rhetoric of the other side." He tossed the book at her, and she grabbed it, felt its hard cover, worn somewhat softer through years of reading.

She opened it up.

It said, in an elegant scrawl, *To Herr Klarsfeld, a loyal Party member. Adolf Hitler.*

She looked up at the old man.

And for the first time in two years, she felt doubt.

12

Barry Rhodes had been in the German State of Great Britain for a long time. He was thirty-seven, but had spent the last seven working undercover. Prior to that, he'd spent ten years working in the United States of America with former Britons, learning their accent, adopting it, mastering it, until he was able to speak just like an Engländer. Then he'd been inserted into Great Britain, and had spent a further twelve months learning how to speak like an Engländer from the Fenland. There were subtle nuances which he had to adopt to sound like a true Fenlander, and he could only do that amongst other Fenlanders.

Now, it was as though he'd lived here all of his life.

Rhodes was American, but had been working for the Central Intelligence Agency for the last seventeen years. He hadn't even finished college before they'd recruited him, a young man with an unflappable personality, and the ability to adopt different accents, though back then he'd used that ability to impersonate famous people for a burgeoning stand-up comedy routine. He'd also spent two years working for an amateur dramatics company, and had been described by many of his contemporaries as a 'method actor'. He truly believed he was the person he was playing.

He'd been a 'sleeper' for the last seven years, but had just been awoken a few weeks ago. He'd taken a week's leave from his job on a farm to travel to Scotland. There he had met the legendary Liam Lovett, one time leader of Combat UK, and the man who, with the help of the United States government, had overseen the assassination of the previous Führer.

Rhodes had heard the stories in the local pubs where he drank. Engländers said that Lovett was responsible for the reprisal killings and that he had sank deep into depression as a consequence. Some said that he'd killed himself. Others than he was an alcoholic. But when Rhodes met him, he found him to be lucid, calm, and determined to strike a massive blow at the Greater German Reich.

Now Rhodes found himself in a sports club attached to a football ground in Peterborough, a glass of Bateman's XB in his hand, watching the match on the screen. Two German sides, and nobody in the pub seemed overly concerned to spectate.

The landlord came over, a guy in his forties with a smile and a shock of grey hair. He toyed with his glasses and said, "Not seen you here before, mate. I don't think the football brought you here, did it?"

"I'm afraid not," Rhodes said. "I've arranged to meet a friend."

"Late then, is she?" the landlord said, looking at his watch.

"It's actually a 'he'," Rhodes said. "I'd heard that he might have some work for me."

"All the best jobs are found in pubs, mate," the landlord said. He went over to the pub phone, which was on the far end of the bar, picked it up and dialled a number. Rhodes couldn't hear what he was saying, but the alarm bells began to ring in his head.

He looked around the bar. There were three old guys in one corner playing dominoes. In another corner, a middle-aged couple were having an animated and friendly conversation. In the middle of the room were four young guys, all dressed in tracksuits, and looking suitably sweaty as though they'd been playing football on the pitch outside.

He watched the people without actually lingering on anyone in particular. He was looking for furtive glances, suspicious movements, anything that could indicate that one of them was readying a gun or switching on a listening device or a video camera.

He did this for five minutes.

Rhodes sipped from his glass as the door to the pub opened.

He turned his head slowly, as though he were a man unconcerned with whoever was coming in, and saw a huge bear of a man enter. The man walked up to the bar and said, "Pint of the usual please, Tom."

The landlord, having finished his phone call, wandered over. He said, "A pint of German piss and an insult, Harry?"

"Make it a Doppelbock," this man, Harry, said. At that, Rhodes paid attention to what was being said. He'd been told to listen out for a particular conversation.

"You know, I get worried sometimes," Tom said. "I do have a social conscience, and I just think that one day, I'm gonna turn you into an alcoholic."

It was all happening as he'd been told it would, which meant that these two men were part of the resistance.

nach Schema F

Rhodes drained his pint, as the landlord poured the Doppelbock and put it down in front of Harry, who handed over a ten Reichsmarks note.

Tom said, "That's just ten Reichsmarks," smirked at his joke and then opened the till to get some change. He turned to Rhodes and said, "Another XB, mate?"

"Er no, I think I'll have a vodka."

Harry sucked in air and shook his head. Tom did likewise and leant in conspiratorially. "Are you sure you want a vodka? It is early in the day."

"Just one for the road."

"Well, even Hitler didn't drink vodka, you know," the landlord said, fixing the drink.

"Why not?"

"It made him nasty," Tom answered, putting the glass down.

Straightaway, the landlord walked off and then Harry turned and held out his hand. "I'm Harry," he said.

Rhodes nodded. "I figured." He shook the proffered hand.

Harry looked at his watch. "Our man will be here in five minutes. Then we'll take the seat in the corner there. All the other speakers in the bar will be turned up, apart from the one right above our heads. Nobody will be able to hear what we're discussing."

Rhodes nodded again. He took a sip from his vodka.

* * * * *

The man, Dauny, was just as Rhodes had expected. Well-educated, well-spoken, a little bit on the fidgety side, but clearly at least partway committed, if he were here after meeting with the man called Harry a few days ago.

Harry said, "Marcus has a few ideas which you might find peculiar, but his heart's in the right place."

Rhodes was back on the XB, and he raised his pint to Dauny. "I see you have a love for real ale – not like this peasant sat next to us."

Dauny raised his own glass. "Yes, I do try to taste as many different ones as I can."

"Well, let's not waste any more time," Rhodes said. "We'll get straight down to business."

"Yes, Harry here was saying that it's either my position in the Nazi

Party or else my job that you're interested in."

"We don't have any need for a Nazi Party member," Rhodes said.

"That's what I thought."

"It's your job."

Dauny breathed in deeply, took a swig from his pint, and then looked at Harry. As far as Rhodes was concerned, Harry's involvement in this discussion was over. He'd served his purpose in introducing the two of them, but he had no idea who Rhodes was, or what part they wanted Dauny to play in the resistance. There was a very good chance that Dauny, if he were as intelligent as he was rumoured to be, would not even have told Harry where he worked.

Rhodes contemplated in his mind the right time to ditch Harry. If the Gestapo had agents on any of them, one of them leaving before finishing a drink would look suspicious.

He glanced across, saw the fruit machine, and caught Harry's eye. Then he shifted his gaze back to the machine.

Harry got the message.

Rhodes heard the landlord, Tom, mention something about the machine only just having been emptied, but wasn't concerned. He was just bothered that he now knew the names of three people who were connected to the resistance. This was information which could potentially be plucked from him under interrogation.

He looked at Dauny.

"Your work is very important to you."

"I know," the Englishman said. "Or I wouldn't be here."

"You know, many agents have been lost approaching men like you," Rhodes said. "They make the contact, and they're never seen again."

"What you're saying is that men like me report them to the authorities?"

"Possibly."

"What's your name?"

"You can call me Barry."

"First I meet Harry, then I meet Barry. I presume you're going to introduce me to somebody named Garry next?"

"I am the final person from the resistance you will meet," Rhodes said. "We're very careful now. Very."

"You know, the other day I was stopped by the Gestapo," Dauny said.

nach Schema F

"They told me they had me under surveillance. I think they got bored when I went for a walk at Ferry Meadows the other day, but I don't think they're very bored today."

"You were followed?"

"I'm always followed."

Rhodes considered the implications of that. "You've been here before?"

"Once. I was sampling the ale here."

"And you liked it?"

"It was very nice," Dauny said. "So much so that I had to return, in spite of the rather lower class clientele."

"Do you think they'll believe you?"

"If they don't, I'm dead."

"If they don't, I'm dead as well," Rhodes said.

"You're saying I'd give you up?"

"I'm saying that if the Gestapo were truly suspicious of you, everybody in this pub at the present moment would be interrogated," Rhodes explained. "Some of us would be tortured."

"And how many names can you give up?"

"I'm higher up the tree than some people. I can give up some very important people. But they won't torture me."

"You're certain of that?" Dauny asked.

Rhodes just smiled. "We need you to perform a task for us."

"It's possible I may be able to help you."

"I have been told that you are a computer expert," Rhodes said. "A programmer. Some have said that you've been involved in the programming for the missile launch control systems."

"In a very small way."

"Is it true, Mr Dauny, that programmers build in, what do they call them, *back doors*? Ways into the computer systems they program which allow them to bypass any of the password security systems?"

"If I was programming a system for you, and you were just a small businessman, but with information that I might potentially wish to access – such as the bank account details of your customers – then it's conceivable, were I unscrupulous, that I might program a 'back door' into your files, yes."

"A logon ID and password that can never be removed from the software, because it's been hardcoded in?"

"Certainly. The logon code checks for the hardcoded password before it checks a list of passwords created by the users. It's perhaps two or three lines of code. Ten seconds additional work. I would say that almost every computer programmer does it, just on the off-chance that they may need to get into the computer system."

"Tell me, Mr Dauny, does such a facility exist in the software for the launch systems?"

"Most of that software came from Germania," Dauny said. "I really had very little input in the implementation. You could say I'm just responsible for debugging what already exists."

"Well then, perhaps you can't be of any use to us," Rhodes said. He smiled wryly and raised his pint to his lips. He had showed out to this person, but it had all been in vain. Seven years of undercover work lost.

But then Dauny said, "Ah ah, don't be so quick to dismiss me, old chap."

"Go on."

"I debug the software. On the rare occasions that I do find errors in the code, it is my job to rewrite the code, reassemble it, and upgrade the computer system."

Rhodes could feel a smile creeping across his face. He said, "So tell me more, Mr Dauny, about this back door access."

Dauny smiled and raised his empty glass.

nach Schema F

13

SS-Sturmbannführer Wolf Loritz was puzzled. He was reading through the eye-witness reports, statements and information documents concerning the assassination attempt on the DSvG governor a few days earlier, and he'd uncovered a few discrepancies. Ordinarily, he would not bother himself with such mundane work. Those tasks fell to his subordinates. But something about it was really bugging him, and Loritz was nothing if not tenacious. That was how he'd managed to continually get promoted over the last few years.

He read through the biography on the would-be assassin, Dougie Hardcastle, and frowned even more. Hardcastle hailed from a city called Peterborough, which was more than eighty miles north of the capital. Without a doubt, he'd been sent down to the capital to carry out the assassination. It was a long way to send somebody just on the off chance that they might bump into the governor.

It implied that Hardcastle had been told where to go and when to go there. Indeed, the eyewitness reports also stated that Hardcastle had been pushing his way through crowds to get to the restaurant, which suggested that he knew that Klarsfeld was present.

That in itself implied that there was inside information.

Some kind of collusion.

The worrying thing was that none of his subordinates appeared to have picked up on it. In particular, he'd expected Brauchitsch to have spotted it. She was on the scene, she'd even killed the would-be assassin, but not until after he'd managed to shoot Klarsfeld in the arm.

He picked up the telephone and called for his assistant, who arrived within a couple of minutes from his own office on the floor below. After the usual preliminaries of saluting, Loritz asked the man to sit down.

"Herr Obersturmführer, I presume that you've read the report on Reichsstatthalter Klarsfeld's unfortunate incident?"

SS-Obersturmführer Schmid nodded. He was a very capable adjutant, and his eyes fell upon the open files on Loritz's desk. "I have, mein Herr." Loritz waited a few moments. Initially, it appeared as though even the experienced Schmid had failed to notice the discrepancies. But no, the

Obersturmführer hadn't finished speaking. He said, "I am compiling a report, Herr Sturmbannführer, which details a number of issues with the information we have been provided."

Loritz nodded. "Continue, Herr Obersturmführer."

Schmid smiled. "I am sure, mein Herr, that you have reached similar conclusions to me."

"Indulge me."

Schmid shrugged, though it was not disrespectful. "I have noticed that Hardcastle, the would-be assassin, came from a city eighty miles north of London. My research, based upon reports from some junior officers who looked into his background, suggests that there must be an active cell of terrorists operating from this city."

"Peterborough?"

Schmid nodded. "It is, of course, speculation, borne out of facts and assumptions. But if we can speculate that something is happening, then it is also safe to assume that the terrorists are doing it."

Loritz smiled at that. Speculation and assumptions, when used by intelligent people, enabled the Geheime Staatspolizei to reach conclusions that were invariably correct. It was the sign of a good Gestapo officer who could speculate and assume, and then deliver results.

"You need to elucidate," Loritz said.

Schmid shrugged again. "Hardcastle was not in London on the off-chance that he might bump into the Reichsstatthalter. He was armed with a SIG Sauer pistol, which implies that he was in London for a purpose. The purpose of assassination. A SIG Sauer pistol fetches 800 Reichsmarks on the black market. Hardcastle did not have that kind of money. Searches into his bank accounts have shown that there were no significant deposits or withdrawals. Furthermore, I have discovered that there are a number of people with whom he is connected to in the city of Peterborough, all of whom require further investigation."

Loritz agreed. "Can I trust you to arrange for this to happen?"

"Of course, mein Herr. As I said, my report is almost complete, and I was going to suggest that you put me in charge of this investigation."

Loritz smiled. Schmid was a very enthusiastic officer, not at all obsequious or competitive, and Loritz had high hopes for him. He was also a very impressive interrogator. In fact, Loritz could see a lot of himself in Schmid.

"The other issue, mein Herr," Schmid went on, "is that somebody must have informed these terrorists of Klarsfeld's movements for that day."

"It would appear so, wouldn't it?"

"It is worrying," Schmid said. "I can delegate the Peterborough work to some very capable officers. However, I would like to investigate the leak myself. I would prefer not to involve any other officers."

Loritz smiled tightly. "You are suspicious that the leak may well have come from our department?"

"If I am being honest, mein Herr, the leak could have come from anywhere. Security is the most likely source, but we did have one of our officers in the restaurant."

"You are talking of Untersturmführer Brauchitsch?"

"Unpalatable though it may seem, it is not entirely unheard of for a Gestapo officer to turn."

Loritz said, "Investigate her first. I want her either ruling out or interrogated."

"If I may speak out of turn, mein Herr?"

Loritz frowned, but nodded in agreement.

"I get the impression that you have a certain amount of respect for this particular officer."

"She has proved to be a very able investigator," Loritz said. "Her work a couple of years ago was admirable. And she has been passed by the psychology department as being fit for duty. I have spoken to her on a number of occasions, and I have always felt she is trustworthy. I would be ... disappointed, mostly with myself, if my judgement of her was incorrect."

"If it were the case that she was untrustworthy, then the only people at fault are those who prepared the psychiatric report on her."

Loritz appreciated that. Schmid was not toadying, and neither was he gloating. He was just stating facts. "If you can eliminate her from the enquiries, Herr Obersturmführer, I would appreciate it. If there are ... discrepancies, then she should be eliminated, period."

Schmid was clear with what Loritz, and he got to his feet and saluted.

14

Ellen awoke with a hangover. It was unusual for her to drink heavily, but her conversation with Klarsfeld the previous night had had a profound effect on her. He had known exactly what she was up to. He had seen straight through her, and then he had tried to turn her.

That was her conclusion. He was corrupt, he was disloyal, and he wanted her to follow in his footsteps. When she'd got back to her apartment, she'd cracked open a bottle of Schnapps and had downed half the bottle as she'd watched a sad film and thought about her life.

Though the psychiatrists had concluded that she was fit for duty, deep down, she wasn't so sure. Jerome had been a gorgeous young man, an Engländer, but kind and thoughtful. And going undercover, she'd felt almost English herself. Even her parents didn't know what her job entailed. They'd seriously thought that she'd become a nurse after initially having been recruited by the Geheime Staatspolizei at university. It came as something of a shock to them when she'd finally revealed the truth.

Not that they were disappointed. Her father was a major industrialist, a good German, and he'd sat her down and told her that he was proud with her choice of career, and proud of her role in the attempt to prevent the assassination of the previous Führer.

He'd also intimated that he'd never really approved of her 'relationship' with Jerome Varley, and so was pleased that it was nothing more than work for her.

But he was wrong. It wasn't just work for her, and that was the problem. She didn't consider herself to be overly manipulative, but she'd been able to tell the psychiatrists exactly what they wanted to hear. She didn't trust them enough to be totally honest with them. She felt that if she had told them the truth, she'd probably end up in a Konzentrationslager – and by now, she'd be dead.

Last night, she'd gone to bed severely drunk, and she'd thought of Jerome as the room had spun around heavily before her eyes. The spinning had got even worse when she'd closed them, and it wasn't long before she'd rushed to the bathroom to rid herself of the excess. At the

nach Schema F

Geheime Staatspolizei academy, they'd been warned about drinking heavily. It was frowned upon, which probably explained why Ellen couldn't take alcohol in any great amount. She'd never been one to use alcohol as a crutch or a coping mechanism, but last night had been different.

Even though Klarsfeld was obviously convinced she'd be writing a damning report about him, he'd not attempted to hide his true opinions. She had a feeling that he'd had access to her personal file, knew everything about her, and probably considered that she was weak because of her relationship with Jerome – pliable, easy to manipulate.

Last night, bitter, drinking Schnapps, she'd been convinced he was wrong.

Now, waking up, she wasn't so sure.

She'd thought she was a loyal German citizen, but all those thoughts of Jerome were now firmly at the front of her mind. All of Klarsfeld's talk about wanting to modernize the Reich, wanting to make things better for the people – well, that actually made perfect sense.

She couldn't imagine living in a country without fear. It dominated the lives of everybody, even those who actually worked for the regime. High-ranking SS officers were not exempt from perusal by the regime. She'd been told that in the United States of America, people had freedom of choice. There was no such thing as *untermenschen* – everyone was treated equally, irrespective of race, religion or handicap. There was no Aktion T4, weeding out the sub-humans, those the regime considered to be a burden on the state.

Fixing herself a glass of water, she contemplated that as she stared out of the kitchen window of her apartment. She could see the car park below, where her BMW 330i was parked. The regime had been kind to her though – it had enabled her to lease this expensive flat, whereas most women her age could only afford much smaller places. She had a nice car, almost top of the range. She had a personal computer, a large screen TV. Her fridge and freezer were stocked up with expensive foodstuffs. In her wardrobe hung designer label clothes.

She wanted for nothing.

But she was still afraid.

Her eyes found a BMW M3 as it turned into the car park below. She was off-duty today, so she knew that it couldn't be Himmler coming to pick her up for work. And yet, only the Gestapo drove M3s.

She frowned as she watched two men climb out.

One of them was Schmid, Loritz's adjutant. He was dressed in a suit, a long overcoat, his shoes impeccably polished. He looked upwards at the apartment block, and then, with his colleague who was carrying a briefcase, made his way towards the entrance below.

Ellen's heart began to race in her chest. But there were fifty other people living in this apartment block. It didn't necessarily mean that they were coming here to visit her.

And then somebody rang her buzzer.

nach Schema F

15

Schmid had an air about him that told all who met him that he wasn't a man to be lied to. Ellen had heard all about his reputation – the man was, like his boss, an accomplished interrogator. And now here he was, on her doorstep.

Ellen tried not to sound concerned. "Herr Obersturmführer Schmid, this is an unexpected surprise."

"May we come in, Frau Brauchitsch?"

Ellen noted that he wasn't referring to her by her Gestapo rank. She stood aside, and Schmid and the man with him – a beast who was probably six foot five, with blond hair and blue eyes – stepped into her apartment.

She followed them as they made their way into her front room, where she saw Schmid looking around at the decor.

"Understated and tidy in the way that only a woman's home could be," he said, giving his appraisal. Then he smiled as his eyes locked onto hers. "This gentleman with me is SS-Sturmscharführer Keitel." Ellen blinked and looked at the big man. She'd heard the name Keitel before. He had a reputation for being a brutal torturer. "Shall we sit, Frau Brauchitsch, and then we can get down to business."

Ellen sat down on one sofa, and Schmid sat down opposite her. The big man, she noted, remained standing by the window. He was looking out, but she knew that he'd be listening to every word that was spoken.

"How can I help you, Herr Obersturmführer?" she asked. She truly had no idea why Schmid was here. Though she'd started to have doubts about the regime, that only stemmed from last night, and as far as she was aware the Geheime Staatspolizei could not yet read minds.

"There have been a few concerns raised about the events surrounding the attempt on Reichsstatthalter Klarsfeld's life."

Ellen frowned. "Concerns? I did everything I could to prevent his assassination. If it wasn't for me—"

Schmid raised a hand. "Allow me to finish, gnädige Frau." He paused momentarily, smiled, and then continued. "Without boring you with details, some of which, I hasten to add, you should have spotted yourself during the course of your investigation, I believe that the assassin had inside information concerning the whereabouts of the Reichsstatthalter."

Ellen blinked again, and then the realization of what Schmid was doing here, in her flat, hit her. "You think that I betrayed him?"

"We are speaking to the entire contingent of security officers on duty that evening," Schmid said. "And SS-Sturmbannführer Loritz himself was keen to eliminate you from the enquiries at an early stage." He smiled tightly.

"Well, I did not betray him," Ellen said indignantly.

"As we speak, your telephone records are being accessed," Schmid said. "I am hoping that no discrepancies are uncovered. Do you have your mobile phone with you?"

"Yes," Ellen said, fumbling in her pocket and holding it up.

Schmid took out his own phone, pushed a couple of buttons, and then Ellen's phone started to ring. Satisfied, he cut the connection and pocketed his phone. "We have a search team waiting," he said. "Once our chat is concluded, they will be conducting a full search of your home."

"You are looking for another mobile phone?"

"Well, I can see that your investigatory skills are not quite so bad as I first thought," he said with a smirk. "Yes, we are. But we are also looking for any correspondence. Your bank accounts are being accessed also, to see whether any suspicious payments have been made to you."

"You are wasting your time, Herr Obersturmführer. That much I can promise you."

"Hmm." Schmid didn't sound convinced. "It is rare for any SS officer to assist the terrorists, but it does occasionally happen. Naturally, it is viewed upon with the gravity one would expect. However, sometimes we discover that the SS officer concerned has been blackmailed or otherwise coerced – threatened, even. We cannot forgive the officer, but we can show a degree of leniency."

"I have no idea why you are telling me this."

"I am giving you the opportunity to talk to me," Schmid said. "Confess, provide me with information, before our search team uncovers something which could condemn you."

"I promise you that they will not," Ellen said defiantly.

Schmid got to his feet as the buzzer sounded again. Keitel went to answer it. It was obviously the search team. "There is something about you, Frau Brauchitsch, something which I cannot yet put my finger on." He wagged his finger at her, and instantly, Ellen found herself feeling guilty. "But rest assured," he went on as the door opened and uniformed men from the *Suchmannschaft* entered, "I will find out what you are up to."

Two hours later, the search was concluded, and nothing untoward had been discovered. Schmid also received phone calls, presumably from officers looking into her bank accounts and phone statements. They also came back clean.

Schmid seemed a little bit disappointed, but gave a subtle shrug at the door as she showed him out.

"Remember, there is nothing you can hide from the Geheime Staatspolizei," he said, and then he and Keitel disappeared, leaving Ellen to look around her ransacked apartment.

The men from the *Suchmannschaft* were professionals. They didn't linger over her underwear drawer, and they viewed her photograph album, with a few holiday snaps of her in a bikini with resolute disinterest. But they also did not tidy up after themselves. Things had been removed from drawers and left on the floor in piles. Books and CDs had been taken from shelves, and placed in heaps on the floor. It would take her as long to tidy up as it had taken them to disassemble the place.

Cursing, Ellen replaced the cushions on the sofa which, thankfully, they hadn't sliced open. She'd have received compensation if they had, but that always took a few days to come through. She flopped down on the sofa and gave out a heavy sigh.

This, she thought to herself, was the way that the Nazi regime treated everyone. Not just Engländers, the French, the Spanish, the citizens of all the provinces of the Greater German Reich – but Germans too. Even her position as a young, vibrant officer in the Gestapo did not protect her.

Klarsfeld was right.

But what could she do about it?

16

The press coverage was huge as the black Focke-Wulf FW90 airliner bearing the Nazi insignia dropped from the clouds some ten miles out of Dulles International Airport. On either side of it were three F-15 Eagles from the United States Air Force, each of them bristling with air-to-air missiles.

The Americans were taking no chances. Any deviation from its directed course and the Nazi airliner carrying the German Foreign Secretary, Michael Fleischer, would be shot out of the sky. That had been made perfectly clear prior to this monumental meeting taking place.

The FW90 had been accompanied from Germany by six Messerschmitt MF440 advanced jet fighters from the Luftwaffe, to a point midway across the Atlantic Ocean, where its security was handed over to the USAF. From that point on, it had followed the agreed course and had given no cause for concern.

Now as it dropped down low, following the ILS glide slope to the main runway at Dulles, journalists jabbered into their microphones in front of their cameras, eager to be the first to deliver the news of an unprecedented moment in history.

After taxiing to a halt, the Foreign Secretary and his wife were the first to leave the airliner. They didn't wave at the waiting crowds; the crowds weren't here to offer support or a friendly welcome, and that was apparent om some of the banners they were carrying. Instead, they made their way quickly down the steps, accompanied by their entourage of civil servants, and were whisked away in the motor cavalcade that had been patiently awaiting their arrival.

Within an hour, the cavalcade was parking up in the car park beneath the Whitehouse, and Michael Fleischer was climbing out, picking at his suit as he looked around the dull, grey, but well-lit, interior. His wife stood beside him. They spoke in German.

"When will they take us to our accommodation?" she asked him. Fleischer glanced at his wife. He hadn't wanted to bring her here. He felt that it was possibly too dangerous, and in any case, she should be at home with the children. Truth be known, he hadn't wanted to come here at all, to the hostile United States of America, where the politicians and the people despised him and his nation.

He said, "Have patience, my dear."

His advisor stepped up to him. "Herr Secretary, are you ready?"

There was an entourage of suited Americans standing near what Fleischer presumed was the elevator leading up to the Whitehouse. He nodded at his advisor and followed him to the elevator doors.

The elevator was large enough to hold twenty people without any of them being cramped. Fleischer presumed that since nobody had spoken directly to him that the Americans present were merely Secret Service agents and low-level officials not worthy of his attention.

The elevator ground to a halt and the doors opened onto a large room, opulently decorated, with walls that bore impressive framed photographic portraits of US Presidents from the past. A young man stepped up to Fleischer, his hand outstretched. The German Foreign Secretary shook it curtly.

"Herr Fleischer," he said in almost perfect German. "I am Jeremy Ramey. I have been assigned to you as your assistant during your stay in the United States of America." Fleischer merely nodded. "In a brief moment, you will be introduced to the President and the First Lady. There will be a short photo opportunity, and then Frau Fleischer will be taken to the hotel where you will be staying. I will accompany her. You will be taken to see the Secretary of State, Ms Wilson. She is eager to speak with you."

Suitably informed, the German couple were led into another room, where the President and his wife were waiting. There, the two men shook hands and their wives kissed one another on the cheek, as the photographers and newsmen recorded the event.

As they were being led into another room, away from prying eyes, the President turned to Fleischer. "I will speak with you tomorrow, Herr Fleischer, after your meeting with the Secretary of State." And with that, he and his wife disappeared through another doorway.

Fleischer turned to his aide. "These Americans," he snapped. "They show us no respect. He dismisses me as though I am nothing more than a mere civil servant." His aide shrugged in agreement.

Ramey said, "The President is a very busy man, Herr Fleischer, and I'm sure you can understand that you will be dealing with the Secretary of

State regarding the purpose of this visit. She will debrief the President later."

Fleischer scowled. "Tell me, Herr Ramey, your German – it is good. Do you have German blood in your family?"

"My mother. She left Germany thirty years ago. She never stopped speaking the language."

"Why did your mother leave Germany?"

"My father is a banker. He had dealings in Germania. He and my mother fell in love, and when he returned to the United States, she came with him."

"I see."

"You do not approve, Herr Fleischer?"

"Of Germans leaving the Fatherland?" Fleischer shrugged. "Our nation is large and powerful enough to sustain such emigrations to other countries. But one must always question why a loyal German would choose a foreigner over a fellow German." The young man didn't seem to know how to respond. Fleischer, for the first time, smiled and added, "But then, I suppose one cannot help who one falls in love with." He glanced at his wife, and she smiled at Ramey.

Fleischer subsequently found himself in a large boardroom, sat at a huge table with chairs for thirty people. He was on one side, with his closest advisors next to him. He was kept waiting for half an hour before the Secretary of State entered with her own bank of advisors. The Germans all stood politely as she walked up to the table. She sat directly opposite him, barely giving him a glance.

The Germans sat down.

"Herr Fleischer," Margo Wilson said, speaking in English. "Allow me to welcome you to the United States of America. It has been some time since a leading Nazi official has set foot on our shores."

Fleischer smiled tightly. "Frau Wilson, we prefer to be called Germans, rather than Nazis. You are referring to us by our political party, rather than our nationality." He outstretched his hands. "To you, this may seem a pedantic point, but it is, nonetheless, very important to a proud German such as myself, and indeed, my loyal colleagues on either side of me."

Wilson nodded. "I concede that point, Herr Fleischer, and I wish it to be known that I did not mean to insult you or your colleagues." Fleischer

nach Schema F

nodded back at her. "Now, if we can get right down to business? I'm led to believe that you have a proposition for the American people."

Fleischer raised an eyebrow. These Americans, they were so impatient. They just wanted to get right down to it. He turned to his closest advisor in the Foreign Ministry, Odell Kohl, who probably knew more about the intricacies of the trade deal than he did. Kohl opened up a folder to a relevant page and pushed it in front of Fleischer.

And Fleischer detailed the proposed trade deal.

17

The Reichsführer-SS listened to what the Foreign Secretary had to tell him over the telephone, and took the contents with a pinch of salt. He knew that Fleischer would not be telling him anything confidential. Both of them were fully aware that the Americans' CIA would be listening in on the telephone call, making notes, interpreting not only the German language, but the subtle nuances of what was being said, desperate, in their paranoia, to find something inflammatory.

As far as he could ascertain, the meeting had gone well. Fleischer had said that the American Secretary of State – a woman, for God's sake! – had seemed pleased with what he'd suggested. But Schaemmel knew that she would also be suspicious. The Americans were no fools, and they would be looking for anything to suggest that the Germans were up to something.

Which, he thought with a smile as he put down the telephone receiver, they were. But the Americans would undoubtedly agree to the trade deal, financially beneficial to them and the Germans, in spite of any suspicions they held.

As he left his own office, on his way to brief the Führer, he contemplated whether or not the Americans knew what the Reich's ultimate plan was. A delaying technique to prepare for a push across the Bering Strait and onto the American continent. There was a very good chance that they'd considered this as being a possibility.

Schaemmel had a vested interest in protecting the Reich. Since the Führer had removed the post of Vizeführer after his accession to the leadership, Schaemmel was second-in-line to the ultimate power should the Führer succumb to illness or assassination. Almost twenty years the Führer's junior, he had no doubt he would soon accede to the throne.

One thing he knew about the Nazi regime was that it was a ruthless place in which to work. Since Hitler's death, the Führers had protected their position through assassinations, murders, and inserting non-threatening people into key positions. Schaemmel was in a key position in the regime, and whilst the Führer had needed him a couple of years ago so that he could initially assume power, Schaemmel was in little doubt that the Führer would soon see him as a threat. Hitler's acolytes had loved and adored him. Nowadays, the Führer's acolytes saw only power in the hands of their leader, and it was a well-known fact, if not often spoke of, that they also coveted that power, much as Schaemmel did.

The Führer's plans for the future were daring. To spread the massive army of the Reich across Russia, and then cross over to the American continent to invade from the north, through Alaska, down into Canada. It would be a masterstroke if they could pull it off. A few tactical nuclear strikes on US airbases, and opposition would be quickly eradicated. But what they needed was time to prepare for such a massive conflict.

In the Führer's office, Schaemmel sat down and briefed his leader.

When he'd finished, the Führer nodded his head, steepled his fingers and rested his elbows on his desk. "Tell me, Schaemmel, what do you think of this plan of ours?"

"It is bold, mein Herr."

"It is," the Führer conceded. "It is indeed." He pondered on that for a few moments. Schaemmel knew better than to interrupt him. "Perhaps it is a step too far?" His eyes met those of the Reichsführer-SS, and Schaemmel felt as though his loyalty were being tested.

He decided not to offer an opinion one way or the other.

The Führer seemed satisfied with that response – or lack of.

He said, "How are things in Great Britain proceeding?"

Schaemmel had received information from SS-Sturmbannführer Wolf Loritz, who was heading the up the investigation into the British Reichsstatthalter.

He said, "I am assured that a very competent Gestapo officer is keeping him under close observation, but has yet to compile a detailed report."

"He is out of hospital?"

"Yes, but he is not yet back at work."

The Führer's eyes turned to slits. "I see the benefits of keeping Klarsfeld in his post, but I'm also seeing the benefits of removing him."

"Perhaps you could recall him to Germania? Question him personally. Sometimes, one can get a better perception of an individual's loyalty by speaking to them face to face."

"You have a point there, Schaemmel."

The Reichsführer-SS looked at his leader. The Führer was staring contemplatively at the papers in front of him. This was arguably the most powerful man in the world, and he'd expressed a moment of uncertainty, perhaps even a moment of weakness. This was something that nobody else would ever witness.

Schaemmel knew now that the Führer regarded him as both a valued ally and a potential threat. All at once, he felt powerful and yet vulnerable.

18

Rhodes looked at the computer screen and frowned. To him, it was just a meaningless jumble of letters and numbers interwoven with the occasional word. He looked at Marcus Dauny and frowned.

"So what is this?" he asked.

They were sat in a disused factory in a rundown part of Peterborough. The phone line was still working – that was something Dauny had asked for. A working phone line. Into this working phone line he had plugged one end of a short cable. The other end went into the *tragbarer rechner*, a portable computer with a screen that could be folded down over the keyboard to allow it to be easily transportable. The *Trag* was a relatively new invention, and most Germans hadn't been given access to them. Rather, they had to use a *rechnerarbeitsplatz* – RAs – a clunky desktop workstation.

He said, "Have you heard of the *breitnetz*?"

Rhodes shook his head. He was not a computer expert.

"This is the wide network," Dauny explained. "The *lokalennetz* is what we use in the office – a small, local network of computers. However, most *lokalennetze* can be accessed by anybody with access to the *breitnetz*. Are you following me?"

Rhodes frowned. "No, but does that really matter?"

Dauny sighed. "Essentially, we can go onto the wide network, which is accessible via the phone line," he said, pointing to the portable computer and then to the phone junction box, "and then by entering a local network name and a password, we can access a local network – essentially, other computers – which can be hundreds or thousands of miles away."

"My God. You can do that here?" Dauny nodded, seeming quite proud of himself. "That's amazing. You can access everything you can at work, right here in this shitty old factory?"

"Everything." But there was a look of irony on the Englishman's face. "However, whilst I can, theoretically, access all of the files I am able to access within my work place, I don't have all of the software to open those files."

"Software?"

"The computer programs," Dauny said. He was struggling to give an easy to understand definition. "It's like the tools we use on the computer to access the files."

"I see," Rhodes said. But he didn't, not really. As he'd previously said, he didn't really need to. All he needed to know was that Dauny possessed the skills to complete the task they had for him. He had worked on the computer system responsible for the Germans' missile launch control system. That meant that the resistance could break into that particular system and cause untold damage. With regards this 'software' Dauny was discussing, he said, "That sounds like a problem."

"It could be. But software, computer programs, they can be copied." He tapped the portable computer. "I don't have it on this *Trag*, and to be honest I wouldn't really want to install it on here – these things are checked by security regularly to ensure we're only using them for work – but it's possible I could get it put on the RA I have at home. But therein lies another problem."

"Which is?"

"I don't know if they security team are able to monitor access from the *breitnetz*. For example, I'm presuming it's possible they could log all telephone numbers used to access a local network via the wide network. And from that, it's a small leap for them to be able to log all activity during that access period."

"So ideally you'd want your access to be ... hidden?"

Dauny nodded. "Something like that." He sighed. "We'd need a network expert to carry out that type of work. I'm a computer programmer, not a network expert."

"Do you know a network expert?"

"I know lots of them. Do I know one we can trust?" He shrugged. "Other than you and the people I've recently met, I don't know anybody who's opposed to the current regime – certainly not amongst my work colleagues."

Rhodes said, "Give me some names. We can persuade people to join us."

"And put me at risk?" Dauny's head shook. "Not bloody likely."

"He doesn't need to know anything about you – we can keep you separate." Rhodes could sense the doubt on Dauny's face. The computer programmer shook his head again. "Marcus, we need you to get into this system. We need to know how it works. We need to use this system."

Dauny typed away on the keyboard and the screen changed to show an image of the German flag, red, with a white circle inside which of was the hakenkreuz or hooked cross. On this screen, in the red portion of the flag, were two white boxes. One was labelled '*Verbraucher*' and the other '*Kennwort*'.

"We're now at the access screen to my own personal workstation," Dauny said. "If I enter my user name and my password, I could access my files."

Rhodes nodded. "Let's see."

Dauny did more typing, and the German flag disappeared to be replaced by a grey screen upon which were placed rows of small squares, pictorial representations of things which Rhodes did not understand.

"This is the *Betriebssystem*," Dauny explained. "It's what we use to work with the files. Each of these small boxes, if I click on them, they will open up software applications or files." To demonstrate, he clicked on one of the boxes and the screen was filled with text. "This is a document – a report I'm working on."

"And you can work on this document anywhere in the world?"

"Anywhere there's a phone line, yes."

"That's amazing," Rhodes said. Dauny clicked something on the screen and the document disappeared.

"In order to access the software for the launch systems, I need a programming application. I can probably lay my hands on one, but as I say, I cannot install it on this laptop. For security reasons, we're only allowed to work on the launch system software while we're at work. If I access it when I'm not at work, using my user name and my password, well, let's just say that it wouldn't be advisable for me to return to work. That's why we need a network expert."

"And that's why you need to give us some names."

Dauny closed down the portable computer.

The room in which they sat was on the mezzanine level. The empty factory space lay beneath them, visible through a large window. Dauny took the portable computer from the dusty table upon which he'd placed it and put it in a large bag. The pair of them were sat on grubby office chairs on wheels.

"So tell me, Barry, what's the plan?"

Rhodes shrugged. "Not sure I can tell you that."

"Oh, come come, if you're involving me, I have a right to know."

Rhodes stood up and wandered over to a window that looked out onto a moderately large, but deserted, car park. The pair of them had walked here. He wondered how much he could tell Dauny.

"Sabotage," he finally said.

"Sabotage? What, destroy the missile launch system? To what end?"

"Without the capacity to launch their nukes, the Greater German Reich would be exposed."

"To attack? From the USA? Certainly they're the only country capable of launching a nuclear strike. But that would result in the deaths of millions."

"Millions of Germans," Rhodes said. "Cut off the head and the monster will die."

"You want us to sabotage the launch systems so that the USA can launch missiles at Germania?" Dauny shook his head. "That's not something I want to get involved in."

"You're already involved, Marcus."

"I'm involved, but I can walk away."

Rhodes gave a wry smile and shook his head. "Not now, Marcus. I don't think your conscience will allow that. You know that this is the only way to bring an end to the Reich. Remove the Führer from power. Remove the entire hierarchy. Replace it with something else. Do you realize how happy people will be – not just Engländers like us, but Germans too. Do you think they like living in such an oppressive regime?"

"It's not as bad as people suggest, Barry."

"It is. You know it is." Rhodes fixed his gaze on Dauny. "Do you think that the Führer will ever modernize the Reich, make it a good place for everyone to live? Come on, Marcus, you know that's never going to happen. Look at you. Intelligent man, scrabbling around for scraps in a cage full of true Germans. And even they're not happy with their miserable existence."

Dauny was still shaking his head. He looked up at Rhodes.

"Marcus, we have to do this. I can't say what the USA will decide to do once we sabotage the launch system, but we have to give them that opportunity. We give them that opportunity, and other people make that judgment call. Other people who aren't us."

He left Dauny for a few moments. The Englishman was softening. Rhodes was speaking about the USA as though it wasn't his country of birth. Did he consider himself to be American anymore? He'd been living here for so long.

Dauny said, "I suppose you're right. It's just ... I'm struggling to countenance my involvement in the massacre of millions of people."

"It might not come to that."

"There is also the fact that we have no way of knowing how long our system sabotage would remain active."

Rhodes frowned.

Dauny continued. "We have no way of knowing if they have contingencies in place, some way of overcoming our sabotage."

"Is there any way of finding that out?"

Dauny sighed. "I guess that one falls to me as well then?"

"You're our expert."

"I'll think of some guys you can approach—"

Rhodes held up a hand. He'd heard something. He turned and looked out the window. A BMW M3 was pulling into the car park, its powerful engine just about audible. No siren was sounding, but red lights flashed from behind the front grill.

"Fuck."

"What?"

"We have to go," Rhodes said, looking at Dauny's bag. "Grab that, let's get out the back."

He practically pushed Dauny in front of him, out of the office, and then down the stairs. He dragged the Englishman across the empty factory floor, because he feared Dauny was not that fit. The rear door was padlocked shut, but Rhodes kicked it a few times. On the fourth kick, it flew open with a bang. Rhodes shoved Dauny outside.

They started to run across the grassy area to the rear of the property. Only one M3 had pulled into the car park, so it was safe to assume that it wasn't, as yet, a full-scale operation. But then, as they reached a tall fence that was rotting away in places, the sound of distant sirens, getting closer, filled the air.

Dauny looked panicked. Rhodes just heaved himself against the fence in a place where it looked particularly worn and one of the panels gave way. A few hefty kicks and the panel splintered. He pushed Dauny through. The sirens, the vehicles to which they belonged, were close now. If the Gestapo had arrived in silence, then the sirens meant that the Orpo – the order police – were turning up. When they turned up mob-handed, a van load of them could mean anything up to a dozen officers.

Rhodes glanced back at the factory. He could see the door through which they'd exited, open like a flashing beacon, pointing almost accusingly at the hole in the fence he'd just created. They probably had about 20 seconds before somebody realized the route they'd taken.

Rhodes hopped through the hole in the fence.

On the other side there was a row of trees, masking a road beyond.

They stepped between the trees. On the other side of the road were more industrial units. The nearest one was a car salesroom. Rhodes nudged Dauny and signalled that he should go there. As they parted, both crossing the road, Rhodes headed off in the opposite direction. He wasn't the only pedestrian on the street. He was hoping to mingle in amongst them.

As he walked, he didn't look back. Cars drove by, but he paid them no attention. In his head, he was trying to come up with an answer to the inevitable question he'd be asked if the Gestapo or the Orpo stopped him.

Ahead, he could see a bus stop with people waiting. The buses ran every ten minutes. A glance at his watch told him one was due in just a couple of minutes. They were always punctual. He relaxed slightly.

And then he heard the roar of an engine as a car approached.

It pulled up alongside Rhodes with a squeak of its tyres.

The window of the M3 wound down and a hand came out.

"You, halt!"

Rhodes stopped and looked at the car. He wasn't the only person to do this. Three men climbed out, but at that moment, Rhodes wasn't sure who they were after. He was just one of half a dozen people who were now standing about nervously.

"Your papers," one of the Gestapo officers said. None of them had showed any form of identification. They didn't need to. The black M3, the red flashing light, the arrogance of the men, all of these things told everyone that they were officers from the Geheime Staatspolizei. Rhodes fumbled for his own ID and held it up. One of the men snatched it from

nach Schema F

him.

"Herr Rhodes, what is your purpose here?" This was the inevitable question. "You are far from your residence."

Rhodes said, "It's a beautiful day, mein Herr. I just thought I'd go for a walk."

"A walk?" A frown crossed the Gestapo officer's face. "Through an industrial estate?"

"My house is along this bus route," Rhodes explained. "Behind, from where I've come, is Flag Fen. I often walk out there." He gave a sheepish smile. "It's a way of keeping fit."

The Gestapo officer frowned. He didn't look particularly old. Early twenties, new to the job, probably new to the area. He glanced down at the ID again, and then he reached in his pocket and pulled out his notebook. He jotted down some details from the ID, and then handed it back.

"Well, I hope you enjoyed your walk, Herr Rhodes."

Then he moved onto the next person.

Rhodes tried not to heave a sigh of relief. Instead, he walked up to the bus stop. He arrived just as the bus did, and he climbed on, found a seat and closed his eyes, thankful for his lucky escape.

19

SS-Obersturmführer Mann sat in the passenger seat as a junior officer drove the BMW M3. It was unusual for somebody of his rank to turn up for what at first would appear such an insignificant matter – normally, a file written by a junior officer would arrive on his desk, and then he could decide whether or not to personally intervene.

But this was different.

This was potentially a case of industrial espionage.

As the car pulled up outside a derelict factory, Mann took one more drag from his cigarette, opened the door, and tossed the cigarette onto the pavement. He stepped out.

He was casually dressed. Jeans, sweater, a leather jacket. Indeed, it was rare that Mann ever wore a suit. As a member of the *Breitnetzsicherheit*, the department in charge of computer security, Mann and his team spent much of their time sat at desks in front of computers.

He strolled up to one of his juniors.

"What is it?"

He followed the junior officer inside. Their conversation continued as they climbed the stairs.

The junior, Vogel, said. "Somebody was tapping into a *lokalennetz* from this location. As soon as it was flagged, we informed the local Gestapo team. I was just up the road so I came here myself." Mann coughed as they entered the dusty office. Forensics had already done their job, dusting for fingerprints.

"What do we have then?"

Vogel walked across to the desk, bent down and lifted up a telephone cable. At the other end was a connector for a computer. "This, hooked up to the telephone line."

"Hmm," Mann said. He flung himself down on one of the chairs in the office. "The phone line, presumably, was active?"

"Businesses here are transient. They come and go. Phone lines aren't disconnected when the business closes down or moves on, because usually another business takes its place shortly afterwards." Vogel tossed the cable back on the ground.

"Perhaps that practice should be reviewed," Mann said. He made a mental note to suggest that in his report to his senior officer. "Tell me more, Vogel. They tapped into a *lokalennetz*. Which one?"

"The Gerhard Fieseler Werke."

"GFW, eh? Software company."

"Yes, mein Herr."

"And what did they do during this access? Did they attempt to access any software files?"

Vogel shook his head. "They merely opened a report. No work was completed on the report in question. The access lasted just a few minutes. I'm led to believe that the first Gestapo unit arrived just a minute or two after the access was closed down."

"And I am presuming, judging by the lack of any suspects before me, that this Gestapo unit arrived too late?" Vogel shrugged and rolled his eyes. Mann poked a finger in his ear, gave it a good wiggle. His ears were always giving him trouble. He made another mental note to book an appointment with his doctor.

"A search was made of the area," Vogel said. "We have a list of names of people where were seen in the vicinity."

"Hmm." Mann stood up and walked across to the window. "And have any fingerprints been turned up?"

"Lots," Vogel said. "As you would imagine for a place like this."

"Okay. How about this access. Who was it made by?" Mann turned to look at Vogel.

"The identification credentials used belong to a member of staff at GFW. Marcus Dauny."

"Hmm."

Mann looked out of the window again. This place really was depressing. He couldn't wait to return to London. More than that, he couldn't wait to return to Germania.

"Then I suppose, my geeky little friend, we must pay Herr Dauny a visit, yes?"

20

Marcus Dauny considered himself to be a moderately intelligent man, more intelligent than most, certainly. It took a certain level of mental agility to work through university, to get a degree in computer science, to become a computer programmer. Dauny, however, was starting to realize that there was one thing he actually lacked.

Common sense.

Accessing the local network using his own user name and password, that was just reckless. He'd assumed that the security team who undoubtedly monitored network access would only be checking for things such as access to the software he'd been working on. He knew that was forbidden. Clearly they were monitoring all access – and accessing the local network from an abandoned factory would definitely be defined as suspicious activity.

Dauny sat and went through the financial figures for a new Audi A4 with the salesman once more, and was almost seriously taken in. He'd been thrown in here by the resistance contact, Barry Rhodes, but he'd listened to everything the salesman had told him, and he wondered whether it was indeed time to trade in his BMW for a shiny new Audi. His interest was now logged on the computer system, and he hoped that would give him a genuine reason for being in the vicinity should the Gestapo stop him when he left the showroom.

But that was only part of the solution to his problem.

He left the showroom an hour later, the portable computer, or *Trag*, in the bag slung over his shoulder. He needed to erase any evidence of his recent log-on to the works' network from the *Trag*. He found a telephone kiosk and stepped inside. Unlike residential and business phones, kiosk phones cost money. He fumbled around for some Reichspfennige and dumped them on the small shelf in front of him.

He dug out his pocket diary and searched through the contact list. He'd made many contacts at university, some of whom he'd stayed in touch with. One in particular had proven helpful in the past.

He dialled the number.

"Hello?"

nach Schema F

'Owen, it's Marcus, how are you doing, chap?"

"Oh, mustn't grumble," the voice on the other end said. "But I'll wager that you can, judging by the fact that you're calling me."

"Ah yes. You recall that software you installed on my *Trag* a few months back?"

"The word processing stuff? Yeah. It's still working?"

"It is, yes, but I want it gone. And I want any evidence of its existence gone."

"I can do that. I can uninstall it."

"And any evidence that it has been used?"

"Well, that's possible, sure, but it might take some time. Better to do a full reinstall of the BS." Dauny smiled. The *Betriebssystem*. If that was reinstalled, all history of the *Trag*'s use would be gone as well. "But you'll lose your files unless you back them up to CD."

"I can do that. How soon can you reinstall the BS?"

"It takes a couple of hours to do," Owen said.

"Yes, but can you do it today?" Dauny looked at his watch. It was a little after 2pm.

"Sure, if you can get over to mine."

"That'd be perfect."

"Should I be asking why you want to hide the fact that you've been using unauthorized software?"

"Security check at work," Dauny explained. "All *Trags* are going to be checked for any discrepancies. If they see I've got that word processing software on there, it could cost me my job."

"What about the version on your RA?"

"That's fine. They won't be checking that one."

"Okay. How soon can you get here?"

Owen lived in Leicester, a city some forty miles away. Dauny couldn't risk going home to fetch his car. The Gestapo could be waiting for him. And he didn't even want to chance using the rail network, despite there being regular trains to Leicester. He had phone numbers for a number of taxi firms. He decided he'd give one a call.

"Couple of hours," he told Owen, and after saying goodbye, Dauny hung up and phoned one of the taxi firms he used regularly. "A party," he explained. "In Leicester. Can't risk taking the car, old chap." He was giving them far more information than they needed. He told them he wanted to be picked up from the coffee shop just up the street. They said they'd be there within quarter of an hour.

He spent an anxious ten minutes nursing a cup of hot coffee before the taxi arrived. He didn't bother to finish the drink. He jumped in the back of the taxi. Thankfully, the driver was English, which meant that even if he did have any suspicions, he hopefully wouldn't pass them on.

Dauny took a handkerchief from his pocket and mopped his brow.

This subversive malarkey was getting to him.

nach Schema F

21

The Reichsstatthalter did not appear to be in his usual good humour as Ellen entered his office at the Amtssitz. The expression on his face most definitely was not welcoming. One of Klarsfeld's assistants hurried past Ellen on his way from the office.

Klarsfeld looked up at Ellen and shook his head.

"Herr Klarsfeld, is there something wrong?"

"This!" he said, holding up a fax. Ellen could see the insignia at the top, the Reischsadler holding the hakenkreuz in its talons. The emblem of the Office of the Führer.

"What is it?"

"I am being summoned back to Germania, my dear. The Führer himself wishes to speak with me, and of course the Führer cannot speak on the telephone!"

Ellen walked up to the desk.

"Sit down, sit down," he told her impatiently. She did as she was instructed. "Here I am, recuperating after being shot in a failed assassination attempt and our Führer demands that I pay him a visit. I am not a well man, Ellen, as you can plainly see." Ellen didn't know how to respond, but that didn't seem to matter because the Reichsstatthalter continued nonetheless. "He also knows how much I abhor flying, and yet he will not even permit me to travel by land. This, apparently, will take too much time."

There was a knock at the door and Klarsfeld's secretary, Helga, poked her head in the office.

"Herr Reichsstatthalter, we have coffee for you."

"Bring it in then," Klarsfeld snapped impatiently.

A tray was brought into the office and placed on Klarsfeld's impressive desk. He ushered the secretary and her assistant away with a wave of the hand.

As he poured himself a cup of coffee, Klarsfeld cast a glance at Ellen. It was as he was pouring a second cup, presumably for her, that he said, "My dear Ellen, have you submitted your report to Loritz?" He put down the jug of coffee and began to stir his own.

"Mein Herr, I have submitted no report as yet." Ellen decided to be honest. There was no point in continuing the lie that she was here only to assure the Reichsstatthalter's security. He'd already worked out that there were other reasons as to her presence.

Klarsfeld took a sip from his cup.

"Are you writing one?"

She shook her head. "No, Herr Klarsfeld."

Klarsfeld's eyes continued to stare at her for perhaps half a minute. Ellen held his gaze. To look away would smack of guilt.

He took another sip and then put his cup back on the saucer.

"Will you write one?"

"Mein Herr, it is part of my duty that I must write—"

"Yes," he stopped her. "Your duty." He looked back at the fax from Germania. "Much as it is my duty to return to our capital." He gave a sigh. "Ellen, I must apologize to you. This is out of character for me to be so rude, and in any case, you did not deserve to bear the brunt of my frustration and anger."

"There is no need to apologize."

"That is very gracious of you," the Reichsstatthalter said, getting to his feet. "I fear we must waste this coffee which was so lovingly prepared for us. I would like to go for a ride to the countryside, and then for a walk. If you would accompany me?"

"Herr Klarsfeld, it is my duty to accompany you anywhere you travel outside of the Amtssitz."

"Ellen, my dear," Klarsfeld said, walking to the door of his office, "you must refrain from discussing your 'duty'. We each of us are aware of our duty. There is no need for you to endlessly mention it."

An hour later, the Governor's black Maybach was pulling to a halt in a small car park in the Chilterns. Five black Audis, each containing four members of the Reichsstatthalter's security team, spread out around the Maybach. Klarsfeld hopped out and Ellen felt compelled to follow him.

"Come, Ellen," he said, and then he began to walk. His security team fanned out. Ellen was his close personal protection officer. The rest of them were there to seen incoming threats and deal with them or otherwise alert her. She was wearing an earpiece so she could hear what was going on around them.

They walked for perhaps two miles before they came to a picnic bench.

nach Schema F

Klarsfeld sat down and signalled for her to be seated alongside him.

"Over there, my dear," he said, pointing a hill in the distance, "is Ivinghoe Beacon. Its summit is 750 feet above sea level. Were we to climb to the very top, we would have a line of sight of perhaps sixty miles." He folded his arms and sighed. "Such undefiled beauty in a country where such a thing is a rarity."

"It is a magnificent view."

"It is more than that, my dear. This – this is England. This is where I come when I want to forget bureaucracy and wholesale death. But do you know what? The Engländers, they will not come here. They are afraid to. They think that if they come to a place like this, we, the Germans, will be suspicious."

"Because of its isolation?"

"Precisely. Why would anybody want isolation? For sure there is only one reason why anybody would want isolation."

"Because they have something to hide."

Klarsfeld snorted a laugh. "When you return to your apartment at the end of an arduous day, Ellen, would you invite everybody at work to come home with you?"

"Of course not!"

"Why not?"

"Because ..."

"Because you want isolation perhaps?"

Ellen couldn't help but smile.

"Tell me, Ellen, did you give any thought to what we spoke of the other night?"

Ellen frowned. She looked at the large, imposing hill in the distance. It was nothing like the mountains back in Germany.

"The next day," she said, "I was subjected to a search. My colleagues saw fit to see whether I had anything to hide. I felt as though I were being molested."

Klarsfeld didn't look at her. He didn't respond immediately. Finally, he said, "My dear, this is the Greater German Reich. This is what happens. Nobody trusts anybody else. Tell me, do you have friends?"

Ellen thought about that for a few moments. Did she have friends? Of course she didn't. They were not encouraged to get drunk in the Geheime Staatspolizei, and socializing amongst staff was definitely not the done thing. And then there was the fact that nobody in the Gestapo trusted any of their colleagues.

In fact, the last time Ellen had a friend was back in school. And when they'd left school, they'd also lost touch.

Ellen gave a small laugh. "I suppose, Herr Klarsfeld, I do not have any friends. In fact, all of the people I know, these are just people I work with."

For the next couple of minutes, Klarsfeld didn't say anything. In fact, he just had a happy smile on his face. Ellen looked at him a few times, but still that expression remained there.

He broke the silence.

"We are not encouraged to have friends, Ellen. In the Greater German Reich, our loyalty lies not with our family, and it certainly does not lie with our friends. For we must be prepared, if needs be, to report these people to the representatives of the Fatherland."

He turned to her.

"Could you do that, Ellen? Frau Untersturmführer? Could you report your family, your friends, to your superiors? Is this what drives you on? To see people tortured, executed?"

Ellen closed her eyes.

Klarsfeld said, "What I am saying to you, this is having an impact?"

"You know it is."

"What would you like to say to me, gnädige Frau?"

Ellen squeezed her eyes shut.

"You do not like torture, do you?"

"No."

Klarsfeld gave a brief laugh. He said, "And here you are, having been sent to investigate me. To find my flaws. And yet you have flaws of your own."

"You are being unfair, mein Herr."

"I am? Well, I am not about to write a report about you, Frau Untersturmführer. I am not about to condemn you to a life, albeit briefly, in a konzentrationslager." As he turned his head, his eyes met Ellen's. "Is that what you are going to do, Frau Brauchitsch? Condemn me to a konzentrationslager?"

Ellen looked away. She stared at the hill in the distance. The fact that she was here, with twenty members of Klarsfeld's personal security, it

nach Schema F

made her nervous. Were they loyal Nazis or were they loyal to Klarsfeld? And therein lay another question. Was she a loyal Nazi, or was she succumbing to Klarsfeld's way of thinking?

She finally said, "Mein Herr, you are asking me questions you should not ask me."

The Reichsstatthalter laughed.

"You are fearful. I can understand that." He paused. "This ... this country. Essentially, this is mine. You know, the Reichsstatthalter can pass laws, he can organize his security forces however he sees fit. These men who surround us, they are loyal to me. Many of them have spent very little time in the Fatherland. To them, I am the leader, I am the Führer. Blasphemy, yes, to compare myself to the Führer?"

"Perhaps."

"I have no desire to be the Führer of the Greater German Reich. Here, in England, I am the leader. But I am also tasked with representing the office of our Führer, which means I must ensure the laws he decrees are obeyed." Klarsfeld choked back a laugh. "Do you think that I wanted these reprisal killings to take place? Do you think I enjoyed watching thousands of my citizens being butchered? I was helpless, powerless to do anything. I could not intercede to prevent these from happening, though I did appeal to the Führer's office. I couched my protest in the terms of it being counterproductive, that this terrorist group, Combat UK, was virtually destroyed."

"It is not though," Ellen said quickly. "The recent attempt on your life is evidence of that."

"But of course. I put that down to the fact that we have been butchering English men and women, rather than as a personal attack against me." Klarsfeld turned to her. "Look at me, Ellen." She did as he asked. He was a handsome man for someone his age, dapper, warm. She could smell his aftershave from here. "The assassination of our last Führer, the one you could not prevent from happening, the one where you had to order the shooting of your boyfriend?"

Ellen felt herself visibly blanching.

"My dear, there is not much I do not know about you. The Gestapo, the Sicherheitsdienst, they may well be masters of security, but I too have my own team. Loyal to me. However, let me return to the assassination." His eyes were still on hers. "Though it was planned by Combat UK, the plot's existence was known to Schaemmel, our current Reichsführer-SS, and also to our current Führer who was, at the time, Vizeführer. They colluded to have the Führer assassinated."

"But why would they do that?"

"The thirst for power knows no boundaries," Klarsfeld said. "And the old Führer's plans for the Greater German Reich were not in keeping with Adolf Hitler's ideology for a 'Thousand Year Reich'." He shrugged. "Your paymasters are not to be trusted, my dear."

Ellen digested the information.

"But von Stauffenberg—"

"He suspected such a plot," Klarsfeld said with a sigh. "He went to confront the Vizeführer. And the rest, as we know, is written in history."

Ellen spotted a man walking up to the bench.

She said, "How can you be sure that von Stauffenberg suspected this plot?"

Klarsfeld turned and smiled at the man as he drew closer.

"Ah, Herr Scholl."

Ellen looked this man up and down. He was wearing a suit, although he stood in the fashion of a former soldier, bold and upright.

"Herr Klarsfeld."

"It is good to see you again, old friend. I trust you are keeping well, in spite of the circumstances preventing you from venturing permanently from your hiding place?"

"I am alive, Erich. That is all I can say."

"Sit down." Klarsfeld turned to Ellen. "This is former SS-Oberführer Scholl, of the Waffen-SS. He was Reichsführer-SS von Stauffenberg's right-hand man. Herr Scholl, this is SS-Untersturmführer Ellen Brauchitsch, part of the team which attempted to prevent the assassination of our last Führer."

"Frau Untersturmführer," Scholl greeted with a curt nod of the head. "In spite of your team's failure, it was a valiant attempt. However, we must all share some burden of that guilt."

"I have heard of you," Ellen said. "You went on the run shortly after the Führer was assassinated. You were linked to the plot, along with von Stauffenberg and Röhm."

"Ah yes, Röhm. I heard that he had a good death."

Klarsfeld nodded. "Defiant to the last. Refused to wear a blindfold."

"Frau Untermsturmführer, what you have been told by your superiors, these are all lies," Scholl said. "You were lied to back then and you have been continually lied to. This existence of ours – of yours, for mine is somewhat more secretive – it is not right. We deserve more freedom. The Reich needs to be modernized. Our last Führer intended to bring about changes which would've seen the German people, the citizens of the Greater German Reich, given more rights."

"This is tantamount to talk of a Putsch."

Scholl shook his head. "What happened before, the assassination of the Führer, that was a Putsch. And now we are all living with the consequences."

"My job is to maintain the security of the Greater German Reich," Ellen said, but even she knew that she was repeating parrot-fashion the mantra which had been forced upon her during her training.

"If we do not do something, Ellen, there will be a war," Klarsfeld said. "A world war unlike the first two world wars. Our Führer will not rest until he has brought the USA to its knees, until the Greater German Reich spreads across to the American continent. Unlike our allies, Japan, and our protectorates such as Australia, the USA will not succumb to the German way of thinking. Our Führer will always see the USA as an enemy."

"But there is talk of a new trade treaty—"

"A way of buying time, gnädige Frau, that is all."

"You have an answer for all of my arguments," Ellen said.

"Perhaps that is because an answer exists for all of your arguments."

Deflated, Ellen said, "What am I to do?"

22

Dauny flopped down on his sofa. He felt sleepy. It hadn't just been the journey to Owen's, the seemingly eternal wait as the *Trag*'s operating system had been reinstalled, nor the journey home, though all of those had contributed to his exhaustion.

But Owen also brewed his own beer, and Dauny had partaken of a few samples of the different ale's in the shed in which they sat as the *Trag* was slowly brought back to life. The problem with drinking in such a fashion, from smaller glasses, was that it was difficult to keep track of how much you were drinking, particularly when the ales are all of different strengths. Dauny had no idea how much he'd consumed. He wasn't exactly legless, but he'd drunk enough to make him sleepy.

He'd dozed off on the taxi ride back home, and now he was desperate to continue his nap.

He closed his eyes and found himself in that halfway house between sleep and consciousness.

A knock at the door brought him back to his senses.

Still half-asleep, he went and opened the front door.

Standing there were two men, both casually dressed, one of them wiggling a finger in his ear, a frown on his face.

"Yes?"

"Herr Dauny?" the finger-wiggler asked.

"Yes."

"Ah, Herr Dauny, I am SS-Obersturmführer Mann, Geheime Staatspolizei," he said. He produced his ID. "Breitnetzsicherheit, to be precise. This is my colleague, Vogel." The other man gave a slight nod. "May we come in?" The question was asked in such a manner that Dauny knew he could not refuse them.

He led them into his living room.

"What is this about?"

"You are a difficult man to track down, Herr Dauny," Mann said. "Vogel and I have been trying to find you for the last few hours. Ach, but never mind, you are here now."

Dauny looked Mann up and down. He had a young face, a beaming smile. His eyes, blue, never left Dauny's face. Glancing at the other Gestapo officer, Vogel, Dauny noticed his eyes darting around the room.

"May we sit, Herr Dauny?"

"Of course."

The three of them sat down, Dauny in the armchair, the two Gestapo men on the sofa.

"What is this about?" Dauny asked again, though he knew perfectly well why these men were here.

"You work for the Gerhard Fieseler Werke, yes?"

"I'm a software engineer, yes."

"And as such, you have the authority to connect to your employer's lokalennetz from anywhere, yes?"

"Occasionally I can work from home, yes. Sometimes I'm sent electronic letters which require urgent responses. I generally check for electronic letters two or three times a day at the weekends, and perhaps once before I go to bed during the week."

"Hmm." Mann took out a packet of cigarettes. He lit one, shook out the match, placed it on the coffee table in front of him. He retrieved the ashtray which Dauny used whenever he smoked cigars, put it on the arm of the sofa. "Tell me, Herr Dauny, when was the last time you accessed your works' lokalennetz?"

"Last night."

"Last night? Not today at, when was it, Vogel?"

"Eleven-forty-three, mein Herr."

"Not today at eleven-forty-three then, Herr Dauny?"

Dauny frowned, shook his head. "Most certainly not."

"Hmm. Tell me, Herr Dauny, where were you at eleven-forty-three?"

"I was here, at home."

"But of course, you went out? When we first came here at, when was it, Vogel?"

"It was around one o'clock, Herr Obersturmführer."

"When we came here at one o'clock, you were not here." Mann looked around the living room, holding out his arms expansively. "We did return on numerous occasions, did we not, Vogel?"

"Yes, mein Herr."

"We have travelled up from London, you see, Herr Dauny, and that is quite some journey, even travelling in a very fast car on the main autobahn. I felt it prudent to conclude our investigations while we were up here, rather than have to return at a later date, you know, file an expense claim for more accommodation and meals. This would be a waste of our time and a waste of the Reich's money."

"Of course."

Mann flicked some ash in the ashtray then took a long drag from his cigarette. It had the word '*juno*' embossed on its body.

"I am curious now. Tell me what you have done today, where you have been?"

"Well, firstly I went to a car showroom. I'm thinking of trading my BMW in for an Audi."

"An Audi, you say?" Mann smiled. "Of course, Audis are my favourite also, but our employers buy us BMWs." He shrugged. "Of course, they are both very good German car manufacturers. Difficult to choose between the two. Did you cut a deal?"

"No. I prefer to consider all options before I make a decision."

"Wise," Mann said with a nod and a frown. "Very wise. Tell me, this car showroom. Where would it be? Which salesman did you speak with?"

Dauny stood up and went to his bag, which also contained his *Trag*. He found the quote from the dealer and brought it back, handing it to Mann as he sat down.

"Ah yes," the Gestapo man said, passing the quote to Vogel, who took a note of it. "This dealership, in Fengate, it is a long way from here. Is there not one nearer to where you live?"

"You're not from Peterborough, so you wouldn't know," Dauny said. "Most of the dealerships are in that particular area of the city."

"Hmm." Mann took another drag from his cigarette. "I am curious, so you must enlighten me. Curiosity, it is a fact of life when you work for the Geheime Staatspolizei. You did not take your car with you to this dealership. You chose to walk?"

"It was a lovely day, and as I say, I had no intention of making a decision there and then. My BMW is only a couple of years old, it's in excellent condition, and the salesman would have no reason to inspect it, not until I was ready to sign any paperwork."

"Hmm. And after this showroom visit, where did you go then?"

"I went to see an old university friend of mine, Owen Dunne. He brews his own beer, and he has quite a selection at the moment." He gave

nach Schema F

Owen's address and Vogel jotted it down.

"Ah, so you are, how you Engländers say, slightly worse for wear, yes?" The German gave a conspiratory laugh. "This is why you look sleepy."

"I'm afraid so."

"Well, we shall not detain you much longer, Herr Dauny. Tell me, does anybody else have access to your user name and password at GFW?"

Dauny frowned. "The guys who run the lokalennetz would, but nobody else."

"Ah, of course, the *netzspezialisten*. We must speak with them next." Mann took one final pull from his *juno*, stubbed it out in the ashtray and then stood up. Vogel did the same, as did Dauny. "Well, we shall be on our way, Herr Dauny, and many thanks for your time."

"Glad to be of help."

"There is just one other thing. Your *Trag*. Do you have it?"

"Yes, it's in my bag."

"Ah, good. If you would not mind surrendering it to Vogel." Mann smiled sheepishly. "Security checks. You understand? We shall return it the moment we are finished with it."

Dauny handed the *Trag* to Vogel and the two men left.

He closed his eyes and let out a long, deep breath.

Right now, he needed a stiff drink.

23

As they travelled south towards London, Vogel driving, Mann contemplated the conversation he'd just had with Marcus Dauny. Much of what the Engländer had said had aroused suspicions, but then it was natural for a member of the Geheime Staatspolizei to be suspicious.

Juno cigarette in hand, he went over every aspect of the conversation, dissecting each question asked, each answer given, trying to spot obvious flaws. But there was nothing. Dauny had answered each question without hesitation. Either he was not lying or he was one cool customer.

Throwing the stub of his cigarette from the window, he said, "Vogel, what was your impression of Herr Dauny?"

"Typical Engländer."

"Lying?"

"That is not what I meant by 'typical Engländer'."

"Oh? So what did you mean, my nerdy friend?"

"I meant he displayed some arrogance, defiance. I also felt that he answered all of your questions without pause."

"Of course, you are right. But something ... something does not smell right with this case."

"The car dealership was close to the factory."

"Yes. Yes it was."

"He had an answer for everything."

"He most certainly did, Vogel."

"And I dare say that his *Trag* will have a freshly installed copy of the operating system."

"I dare say it will."

"Herr Mann, do you think Dauny will crack under interrogation?"

"I feel that he might," Mann said. He sighed, lit another cigarette. He tutted and gave off the aura of someone who was bored. "However, he is a Party member, so we would need very good cause to arrest him. And I feel that he would also know very little of consequence."

"Perhaps all of this is merely a coincidence."

"Tell me, Vogel, how long before the results on the fingerprints come back to us?"

nach Schema F

"A week perhaps."

"And this list of names, the people who were stopped in the vicinity by the local Gestapo, perhaps we should put some investigation into this?"

"I will task somebody with looking into that the moment we arrive back at the Polizeipräsidium," Vogel assured him.

"Hmm."

Mann stroked his chin thoughtfully.

"Tell me, Vogel, is it right to be suspicious of everybody, of everything that everybody says?"

"So long as you're not suspicious of the things I say, mein Herr."

"Hmm."

24

Erich Klarsfeld did not trust the Führer. He also did not trust Reichsführer-SS Schaemmel. And yet here he was on a plane about to land in the Reich's capital, Germania, on his way to meet the pair of them.

Of course he was nervous. It was not unheard of for leading officials to be summoned to Germania never to return home. Although it would be possible to have Klarsfeld killed in the DSvG, the Führer apparently liked to be up close and personal with those he ordered to be assassinated.

Klarsfeld had brought Ellen along, though she would not be much use should the Führer decide to have him killed. In fact, she would end up sharing a similar fate. The Führer would not like to have witnesses.

Klarsfeld gripped the arms of his seat as the airliner dropped beneath the clouds to reveal the Adolf Hitler Flughafen situated in the commercial district of Germania. He could see skyscrapers behind the airport, and beyond them the magnificent Volkshalle, its 500 foot high dome atop a 200 foot high plinth dominating the skyline of the city. Once used by Hitler to deliver speeches to masses of adoring citizens, it now held concerts. The acoustics of its massive interior were poor, but it was still the premier venue where orchestras from around the Reich performed. Occasionally rock bands also played there.

Klarsfeld did not like to fly. At this moment in time, as the aircraft lurched lower on its final approach, he feared the prospect of crashing even more than he feared the wrath of the Führer. He glanced at Ellen. She was reading a magazine, seemingly uninterested in their impending doom. He couldn't help but smile.

She was starting to come round to his way of thinking. All the same, it was very dangerous for him to bring her here, to the capital, when she knew so much which could destroy him. For starters, he knew that bastard Loritz was looking for the opportunity to bring him down. Loritz was a loyal Party servant, unswerving in his support for the Further, for the regime. Ellen, she was still malleable, and there was just as much of a chance that she would fall into line behind Loritz.

As the Maybach swept through the streets of Germania, on its way to

Der Parlamentstrasse, the escort vehicles to the front carving a path through the busy traffic, he helped himself to a brandy from the drinks cabinet. He didn't offer Ellen one. Officially, she was on duty. The ice chinked in the glass as he leant back.

"So, Ellen, how do you like our capital? It has been some time since you have been here."

"For you too, Herr Klarsfeld."

"Yes. It has been a long time. And yet, it has not been long enough."

The hakenkreuz flags still hung from the tallest buildings, much as they had the last time he'd been here. They were a constant reminder of an oppression that really was no longer needed. All of the undesirables Hitler had spoken about – the so-called *untermenschen* – were now dead. The Jews, there were none of them within the Reich. Those who had managed to escape the clutches of the concentration camps were living in the US. The gypsies, none of them had survived. Back in the 1940s, no countries wanted to take them in. Even now, under Aktion T4, those who did not conform to the ideal of the Aryan specimen – the disabled, the infirmed, the mentally unsound – were euthanized. Now, of course, the method used was painless and humane – a lethal concoction of drugs designed to send the person to sleep – but the outcome was still barbaric.

There were no more demons for the Nazi regime to vilify.

Once the demons from society were gone, what was left to terrify the public with?

Klarsfeld let out a sigh and downed the brandy. He could see the Reichstaghalle in the distance. It had been many years since he'd seen that building. It sent a shiver down his spine.

"Have you ever been to the Reichstaghalle, my dear?"

Ellen shook her head. "I was too young, I think, for my parents to consider taking me on the tour. " He looked at her face – her expression was one of fascination. This was all essentially new for her. And Germania, the bulk of Germany in fact, was wholly different to the *Deutscher Staat von Großbritannien*. Here, yes, there was an undercurrent of oppression, but almost everybody had it good. They were all native Germans, after all, the true German Aryan master race. In comparison to the DSvG, this was a relaxed atmosphere. Well, relaxed for those not on their way to visit the Führer himself.

"I would presume that while I am being spoken to by our Führer, you will have a chance to tour the building. It is magnificent. I was a guest of Adolf Hitler's many, many years ago. Of course, he did not spend much time in my company – there were many of us there. Loyal Party members. By this point, he was old, he was ..." Klarsfeld pondered how he should word this. "He wasn't well," he said diplomatically. He wondered whether the interior of the Maybach was under surveillance, whether people from the Sicherheitspolizei were listening in on every word he said.

As the small cavalcade approached the Reichstaghalle, Klarsfeld put the empty brandy balloon back in the drinks cabinet.

He said, "I often wonder ..."

After a pause, Ellen said, "Wonder what, Herr Klarsfeld."

He shook his head. "Nothing," he said. "I wonder too much sometimes."

He often wondered whether Hitler, the beloved Führer, had been assassinated.

The lobby of the Reichstaghalle was huge, the ceiling over 150ft above them. Ellen was in awe, Klarsfeld could see that. German flags hung down in the places between the tall windows. A large mural of Hitler was against the back wall. Men from the Leibstandarte-SS *Führer*, the regiment in charge of the Führer's security, stood on guard everywhere he looked.

On a spot between two wide staircases was the reception desk. Armed guards ensured that nobody ascended the stairs without the prerequisite permission. Five young women were behind the desk, dealing with small queues of people. Also behind the desk was a man in a suit. He saw Klarsfeld approaching and immediately rushed over.

"Herr Reichsstatthalter," he said, holding out a hand. Klarsfeld shook it. "I am Kleinmann. I have been instructed to take you directly to the Führer's quarters." He looked at Ellen.

"This is Untersturmführer Brauchitsch," Klarsfeld said. "Head of my security detail." Kleinmann's left eyebrow raised slightly. "Ha, I see that you are curious because of her age. I can assure you that the Frau Untersturmführer is quite capable of leading my security."

"I do not doubt that, Herr Reichsstatthalter," Kleinmann said. He bowed his head slightly. "Frau Untersturmführer," he said, clicking his heels slightly. "You may accompany the Reichsstatthalter up to the

Führer's antechamber, but you will not be permitted to enter his office. Unless, of course, the Führer decides otherwise."

They were led to some elevators behind the reception desk. Klarsfeld's security team were directed to a waiting area on the ground floor. The elevator was spacious. It took them smoothly up to the upper levels of the Reichstaghalle. Here, they found themselves in another lobby. In comparison to the main lobby, the ceiling here was only forty feet over their heads. Paintings adorned the walls, and the German flag hung from the ceiling. There were more guards here, MP5 submachine guns in their hands.

Opposite the elevator were huge double doors that led into the state room, a vast area where the Führer would meet visiting dignitaries. It was perhaps a hundred feet square. Towards the left was a huge banquet hall, beyond which were the kitchens.

They followed Kleinmann to a wide archway on the right that led through to a corridor. On either side of the corridor were offices, some larger than others, all of them crammed with men and women working on computers. Kleinmann turned to Klarsfeld and said, "The Führer does not use the state room that often. We are going to the office next to his personal quarters."

Klarsfeld had never been here before. The Führer's main residence was in the Reichstaghallehalle, though there were other homes throughout the Fatherland where he could choose to live. This particular Führer, however, rarely left Germania. Klarsfeld had heard rumours that he hadn't left the Reichstaghallehalle in months.

At the end of the corridor they found themselves in a small reception area where a secretary busied herself on a computer. Kleinmann smiled at her, and then turned to Ellen.

"I am afraid you will have to wait here," he said.

Klarsfeld was led through some impressive double doors and into the Führer's private office. Kleinmann did not stay. Klarsfeld walked up to a desk that was so large it could surely have doubled as a conference table. The Führer sat behind it. A painting of Hitler hung on the wall behind him.

"Ah, Reichsstatthalter Klarsfeld," the Führer said. "It has been some time since I last clapped eyes on you."

Klarsfeld didn't salute. He said, "Heil Führer."

"Yes, quite. Take a seat."

Klarsfeld looked to his left. Reichsführer-SS Schaemmel was already seated. His uniform was black, crisp, the silver braiding almost dazzling. His cap had been placed on the Führer's desk. In a way, that demonstrated the close working relationship he had with the Führer.

"Herr Reichsstatthalter," he greeted. His voice was still as shrill as Klarsfeld remembered.

"Herr Reichsführer." Klarsfeld sat down.

"So Erich, are you recovering well from the attempt on your life?" The Führer leant back in his chair, which creaked beneath his weight. He was over six feet tall, a bulky man.

Klarsfeld could hear a clock ticking noisily in the otherwise quiet room. The windows were closed, their glass bulletproof. Nothing could be heard of the busy plaza outside.

"I am almost one hundred percent fit, Mein Führer. It was nothing more than a flesh wound."

"Good. And things in *der Deutscher Staat von Großbritannien*, they are good?"

"They are better now that the reprisal executions have been stopped," Klarsfeld answered candidly.

"Well, I felt that it was time to show some benevolence towards the Engländers. After all, we cannot damn an entire group for the ills of a handful of individuals." The Führer's eyes dropped to some paperwork on his desk. Between him and Klarsfeld there had to be at least eight feet of polished oak. "Tell me, Erich, how goes the fight against the Engländer terrorists?"

"I feel they are not so much of a problem, mein Führer, but you would probably glean more information from Oberstgruppenführer Mittendorf. This does, after all, fall within the realm of his responsibility."

"But Erich, you are the man in charge of Great Britain, are you not?"

"Yes, but—"

"And of course, that makes you ultimately responsible for what happens there."

"With respect, mein Führer, I do not have any say in the selection of the staff in charge of our security." Klarsfeld was aware that he was treading a fine line. Schaemmel was responsible for selecting the oberstgruppenführern in charge of the SS contingents in the various provinces. In a way, Klarsfeld was directing criticism at the Reichsführer-SS, a bold move to make in Germania.

Schaemmel visibly bristled.

"I fully recognize that Röhm had to pay for his crimes against the Reich," Klarsfeld went on. He felt a twinge of guilt in betraying his former colleague in such a way. "But Mittendorf is, in my opinion, far from being capable of heading security in a province such as Great Britain."

The Führer almost smiled. Klarsfeld saw the smile reach his eyes, but his mouth didn't twitch.

"You would question the ability of an oberstgruppenführer of the Reich? One who has attained the highest level possible with the SS?"

"It is not meant to be criticism of the Schutzstaffel, mein Führer. But Great Britain has special challenges, one which most SS officers do not face until they are stationed there. As a consequence, there is usually a settling in period. Röhm had been there many years."

"And he had questionable loyalty," Schaemmel reminded him.

"I do not doubt the veracity of the evidence against him, Herr Reichsführer. I am merely saying that in the ten years he had been in charge of our security, he gained an intimate knowledge of the security problems we faced."

"More than intimate," Schaemmel snapped. "Oberstgruppenführer Mittendorf is a fine officer—"

"Were he based elsewhere – France, perhaps, or Spain – I am sure he would have no problems adapting. But, Herr Reichsführer, I think you will agree that the DSvG has its own unique problems, ones which SS officers who have served their entire careers elsewhere within less challenging provinces have not experienced."

"Well, I for one, appreciate your candour, Erich." The Führer was smiling. Klarsfeld had just stabbed a colleague in the back, and he knew that the Führer would like that. "Herr Reichsführer, what would you suggest as a solution to Erich's problem?"

"Mein Führer, I was not aware that there was a particular problem within the DSvG. I am sure that the Reichsstatthalter is merely fussing like an old woman." Schaemmel shot a look at Klarsfeld. "No disrespect," he added with a tight smile. "SS-Oberstgruppenführer Mittendorf has not been in his post long enough to have adapted fully to conditions in the province. In any case, I have no intentions of discussing staff performance and appraisals with a civilian."

"I concede that, Herr Reichsführer," the Führer remarked. He turned to Klarsfeld. "Rest assured that in the interests of security, not only for Great Britain, but for the Greater German Reich, I will be paying particular attention to Oberstgruppenführer Mittendorf's performance."

At that point, there was a knock at a door to the Führer's left.

"Come."

The wide door opened and two females entered the office, one of them pushing a trolley. They served coffee for the three of them, left cream cakes on a platter, and then scurried away.

The Führer stirred some sugar into his drink. Schaemmel picked his coffee cup up and took a sip. Klarsfeld did likewise.

"Erich, I have been having these concerns about you."

"Mein Führer?" Klarsfeld felt his stomach lurch. He was fully aware of the fact that Schaemmel's holster was on show, that the leader of the SS had a Heckler und Koch pistol close at hand. He wondered whether that was a same pistol which had been used to kill the previous Reichsführer-SS.

He felt his mouth dry up.

The Führer tapped his spoon on the top of his coffee cup and lay it down on the saucer.

"I feel that you have been out in the wilderness for too long. How long have you been in Great Britain? More than twenty years?"

"It has been a long time, mein Führer."

"I am thinking that perhaps it is time for you to come home?"

"Come home?"

"Your work for the Fatherland has been much appreciated, Erich—"

"Mein Führer, my work is not yet at an end."

"It is time for you to contemplate retirement," the Führer said. "You have an impeccable and unblemished service record."

"I am but a loyal Party member."

"Quite." There was something in the way he said it which made Klarsfeld suspect the Führer didn't mean it. "And now it is time to put up your feet and relax."

"I have no desire to retire, mein Führer. I wish to continue serving the Reich."

"Your loyalty is impressive, Erich. Faultless." The Führer appeared to ponder on something for a few moments. Then he looked down at one of the folders on his desk. He frowned, then raised an eyebrow as he opened the folder. "It is not for me to be revealing this information just yet, but there is an opening within the Reich which may interest you."

"Mein Führer?"

"Tell me, Erich, is not Great Britain a dim and miserable place, beset with thunderclouds and miserable, cold skies?"

"The weather certainly leaves something to be desired."

"Precisely. I think it is time that the Reich rewarded you for your service."

Klarsfeld had no idea where this was headed.

"I serve the Reich not for rewards, mein Führer."

"Of course not. And yet it is only right." The Führer tapped the folder he had been looking at. "There are things which must be organized before I can reveal all to you, Erich. But in the meantime, you shall be Germania's guest." As if on cue, the doors to the office opened and Kleinmann entered the room with Ellen. "Ah, Kleinmann, you will see the Reichsstatthalter to his accommodation?"

"Certainly, Mein Führer."

"Excellent. We have put you up in the Berlin Kaiserhof. I am sure it is even finer than it was the last time you visited Germania. You have the penthouse suite. The adjoining rooms have been given over to your security team." The Führer's eyes fell upon Ellen. "And this must be SS-Untersturmführer Brauchitsch, the young Gestapo officer who saved your life."

"Heil Führer!" Ellen barked, offering a salute.

The Führer smiled and turned to Erich.

"Erich, you will leave myself and the Reichsführer in the company of this fine young officer. I wish to commend her personally for her bravery."

Klarsfeld's eyes widened. He looked at Ellen. She appeared just as anxious as him.

25

Ellen watched as Kleinmann ushered Klarsfeld out of the Führer's office. She felt distinctly underdressed and overwhelmed. Here she was wearing jeans and trainers in the presence of the world's most powerful man.

The Führer chuckled.

"You look as though you are terrified," he said. He frowned at the Reichsführer-SS. "Tell me, Schaemmel, could this really be the woman who saved the life of one of my governors?"

Schaemmel just shrugged. He looked Ellen up and down and she felt uncomfortable under his gaze, as though she wasn't just underdressed, she was entirely naked.

"Sit, Frau Untersturmführer." Ellen did as she was told. "So, you were with Herr Klarsfeld the night he was shot?"

"Yes, Mein Führer."

"You shot the terrorist?"

Ellen's mind slipped back to the night in question. In a way, those sequence of events had made her think of Jerome, the young Engländer she had almost fallen in love with, the man who had defiantly died in her arms singing some insulting song about Hitler.

She said, "I did, mein Führer. He had already been injured."

"Summary execution then?" The Führer looked at Schaemmel wearing a bemused smile. "Do we still allow that, Herr Reichsführer?" And then he laughed. To Ellen, he said, "I like that in a person, particularly in one of my SS officers. The ability to make a decision and to carry it out."

"It is ... unconventional, mein Führer," Schaemmel said. "Field executions are not routinely carried out if an arrest can be made." His eyes fell upon Ellen. "It is better to interrogate a suspect, a criminal, before they are executed."

"I reacted instinctively. The man had shot the Reichsstatthalter. There were witnesses. I did not want any Engländers to get the impression that officers of the SS were weak and indecisive." At the time, Ellen could remember thinking that. She was setting an example.

Now she wasn't convinced that the example was a good one to set.

"You have spent some considerable time in the company of Herr

Klarsfeld, have you not?"

"I suggested to SS-Sturmbannführer Loritz that it might be prudent to step up the security for the Reichsstatthalter."

"And then, of course, there was also your little mission for the Sturmbannführer, was there not?"

Ellen should've expected this. Nothing was ever a secret in the Reich.

She said, "I have been monitoring Herr Klarsfeld's activities."

"To determine his loyalties?"

"That was part of the mission parameter, mein Führer."

"And tell me, Ellen," the Führer said, disarming her with his use of her given name. "What conclusions have you drawn?"

"I have not been working on the mission long enough to—"

"Your suspicions then, your beliefs, your initial appraisal with regards to Herr Klarsfeld's loyalty to the Reich."

All of the things that Klarsfeld had spoken about over the last few days, the meeting with the fugitive, Scholl, the fact that Klarsfeld's own security team seemed to be more loyal to him than to the Führer, all of these things shot to the front of her mind. She considered the fact that the Reichsstatthalter thought of himself as more English than German.

She cleared her throat.

"I cannot question his loyalty, mein Führer, not yet."

"Not yet? This would imply that you have doubts."

"Not at all," Ellen said quickly. The room in which they were sat was huge, but she felt a claustrophobic heat descend upon her. "I merely want to explore all possibilities before I come to a conclusion. I would not like to suggest any wrongdoing where is none. Nor would I want to declare him loyal if there was any doubt I had overlooked."

The Führer pondered this momentarily. He lifted his coffee cup, took a sip.

"Frau Untersturmführer, you are a diligent and perceptive officer. See, Schaemmel, these are the officers we need in command. Ones with foresight and perception. And of course, loyalty."

"Indeed, mein Führer."

Ellen thought it was remarkable that the Führer was calling the Reichsführer by his surname in her presence. Ordinarily, such a thing could be deemed disrespectful. In a way she felt flattered to be treated to such a display of banter between the two most powerful men in the

Greater German Reich, in the world even.

Then she considered the fact that perhaps she was being lulled into a false sense of security. But then, was she important enough to be deceived by such powerful men? Particularly when they could just have her thrown into an interrogation room.

"There is no need to look so concerned. I just wanted to speak with a loyal member of the Geheime Staatspolizei." The door behind Ellen opened, and Kleinmann stepped back into the office. "Kleinmann, would you see to it that the Untersturmführer is provided with transport to the Kaiserhof?"

"Of course, mein Führer."

And Ellen was led out of the office. Kleinmann didn't speak to her until they were down in the underground car park, where a BMW M3 was waiting, its engine running.

"Good day to you, Untersturmführer Brauchitsch."

The journey to the hotel took no longer than five minutes. Ellen was dropped off outside. This was the first time she'd been to Germania since her childhood. It seemed as though everywhere she looked, she could see the Volkshalle.

And there was something else she noticed as she entered the hotel. Everybody seemed happy. A total contrast to the people back in Great Britain.

Everybody, that was, except for Klarsfeld, who was waiting for her in the lobby.

26

The car was a Mercedes 4x4. As Klarsfeld climbed in alongside her, he said, "This is a hire car." A member of his security team was driving, and another sat in the front passenger seat. Behind this Mercedes was an Audi A4 saloon, in which sat four more members of his security team.

What they were doing wasn't illegal. Klarsfeld was perfectly entitled to choose his own security team, and his security team were also perfectly entitled to choose their own transport. But this could potentially be seen as an act of defiance towards the Germanian Sicherheitspolizei, the local security specialists.

As the Mercedes pulled away, Klarsfeld said, "Those hotel rooms – bugged. The Maybachs and BMWs they supplied us with, those too."

"But why the need for such secrecy?" Ellen asked.

"Well, of course the locals will follow us. That is not much of a concern. Where we are going, well, we have permission to travel there. But I have no wish for my private conversations to be under surveillance as though I am a common criminal."

"Or a terrorist?"

Klarsfeld looked at Ellen with a raised eyebrow, and then his face cracked into a slightl smile. "Or a terrorist, yes. Speaking of which, what did our Führer say to you? Undoubtedly my name cropped up, yes?"

"He asked me a few questions about you, Herr Klarsfeld."

"That *Arschloch*, Loritz. I am certain he covets a much elevated position than the one he already possesses."

"Your position?"

Klarsfeld choked back a laugh. "My dear, I am merely a neutered politician, a diplomat with no powers at all. Loritz would not want my position. No, I feel Loritz wants to return to Germania, but in order for a mere Gestapo sturmbannführer to ingratiate himself amongst the Party elite, he needs to do something big."

"Such as finding evidence that the Reichsstatthalter of *der Deutscher Staat von Großbritannien* is a dissident?"

Klarsfeld smiled. "Yes, Ellen, that would do it. Tell me, what did you tell our beloved Führer about me?"

Ellen's felt her face clouding over. "For a moment, I almost told him everything that I know."

"What stopped you?"

"I just told him the truth, Herr Klarsfeld, that I had not yet completed my investigations."

"Ah, you are but just a loyal Party servant?"

"Something like that."

"Well, my young dear, you will soon find out exactly what the Party does to its loyal servants."

The car sped through the streets of Germania, occasionally flashing a red light on the dashboard to make its way through traffic. Even in the heart of the Reich, people knew to respect the flashing red light of the Gestapo. Soon, they were on the main autobahn leading out of the city. Germania was a massive city, almost forty miles in diameter, but closer to the outskirts the house and buildings grew smaller and more sparse. Finally, they reached the countryside. They travelled for perhaps twenty minutes, the Mercedes keeping a steady 60mph. A turning ahead was marked KZ Katerpow, and the Mercedes steered down it. The Audi followed. The road narrowed to just two lanes. In the distance, Ellen could see a tall fence, and beyond it some large warehouse-sized buildings in amongst smaller, single level buildings. Two of the larger buildings had large chimney stacks, perhaps a hundred feet tall.

She knew instinctively what this place was.

A konzentrationslager.

She wasn't naïve.

She looked at Klarsfeld. "What are we doing here?"

Klarsfeld just smiled. The Mercedes was slowing as they approached the small gatehouse. A handful of men from the *SS-Totenkopfverbände* stood around, two of them smoking. They all stood more upright as the Mercedes came to a standstill.

One of them walked up to the driver's window.

"What is your business here?"

The driver explained that the Reichsstatthalter had an appointment with the camp's commandant, SS-Obersturmbannführer Bischoff. The officer turned to one of his subordinates, who disappeared into the gatehouse. Moments later he came back out and nodded.

"May we see your papers?" the young officer asked, looking beyond the

nach Schema F

driver, his eyes falling first upon Klarsfeld and then lingering questioningly on Ellen. Everybody in the car dug their papers out – Geheime Staatspolizei badge for Ellen and Sicherheitspolizei IDs for the two guards. Klarsfeld showed his Party ID. The officer saluted casually, and directed the driver to the car park of the administration block.

The administration block was a short, wide building, with many windows that looked out onto the busy car park. A wide entrance was a hive of activity, as civilian and SS staff passed through. It seemed as though a shift change was underway.

Klarsfeld and Ellen walked into the administration block and were taken by one of the receptionists to SS-Obersturmbannführer Bischoff's office. A door designated him the Lagerkommandant.

He was much younger than Ellen expected him to be, perhaps in his early thirties, handsome, with a friendly smile. He shook her hand and gestured for them to be seated. A secretary took orders for drinks – coffee all round – and returned moments later with their refreshments.

"Well, it is certainly an honour to have one of our Reichsstatthalter visit the camp," Bischoff said. "We do not have many visitors. Well, not willing ones anyway." Ellen noted that the window to the right of Bischoff's desk looked out onto the camp itself. Internees were moving from one area to another, urged on by uniformed men from the Totenkopfverbände, the branch of the SS charged with camp security. The internees wore striped uniforms and hats.

"Well, I would like to thank you for your hospitality, Herr Obersturmbannführer. This is SS-Untersturmführer Brauchitsch. She is in charge of my Close Personal Protection team. She has spent many years in Great Britain. Naturally, we have konzentrationslager there, but I should like her to see how they differ from those within Germany."

"Ah, Frau Untersturmführer, you will find that the camps here are very different to the ones we have in the provinces. I know that the people of the Greater German Reich consider the camps in the provinces to be nothing more than so-called extermination camps, *vernichtungslager*. I cannot vouch for the veracity or otherwise of such claims. But here at Konzentrationslager Katerpow, we like to think of it as being a *Rehabilitations-und Umerziehungslager*. Rehabilitation and re-education of German criminals and dissidents. Of course, we have our execution facilities. It is perhaps unfortunate that all konzentrationslager must have such a place. But some individuals are beyond redemption, unable to be rehabilitated."

Ellen tried to imagine this young, handsome man, with a kind and friendly face, ordering the deaths of former criminals and political dissidents. He was wearing a wedding ring. She wondered if he had children. There were framed photographs on his desk, but they faced him, so she was unable to see who they were of. She wondered whether his wife knew the details of his job. She wondered whether he confessed to her on those days when he ordered someone to be beheaded by the *fallbeil*. She wondered whether he actually watched such executions.

"Tell me, Herr Obersturmbannführer, do you also have torture facilities here?" Klarsfeld asked. Momentarily, the young man's face cracked, the warmth left his eyes. He blinked more quickly than was natural.

"It is unfortunate that such a facility is required, but yes, we do have an area devoted to interrogation."

"May we view that area?"

"Herr Reichsstatthalter, almost all of the konzentrationslager is available for you to visit. Virtually nowhere is out of bounds."

"How many internees are here at present?"

"Katerpow is a medium-sized camp. We have almost 3,000 internees. Perhaps ninety percent of them are dissidents." Ellen knew that the term 'dissident' was a catch-all. People who spoke out against, or otherwise criticized, the Reich were branded as dissidents. In the provinces, non-Germans were interrogated to ascertain whether or not they were members of anti-German factions before being summarily executed. It appeared as though here in Germany, 'dissidents' were sent to camps such as this to be punished and re-educated. Ellen wondered whether the dissident's family was also sent here. She knew such things happened in Great Britain. She knew, for example, that when Jerome had gone on the run after murdering a security officer, his family had been sent to a konzentrationslager. She knew nothing of their fate, but presumed that they did not survive long.

"Tell me," Klarsfeld said, "dissidents – are their families also arrested?"

"I cannot speak for the processes of arrest that are operated by the Geheime Staatspolizei. We merely deal with the people who are sent to us. I can see if SS-Sturmbannführer Hackenholt is available to see you.

nach Schema F

He is in charge of the interrogation area. A Gestapo officer, naturally. He would be better placed to answer such questions." Bischoff clasped his hands together and rubbed them. "Now, we will have a tour of our camp, I will show you each area, and then we will return here for a late lunch."

Ellen had never been to a konzentrationslager before. She had never wanted to face this side of the Reich. The knowledge that it existed was enough for her, without having the harsh realities presented to her.

They viewed the accommodation for the internees. This was a long, wide building with bunks for fifty people. At the foot of each bunk was a small chest, presumably where people could store their belongings. Ellen stepped up to one, lifted the lid. Inside were a handful of books, a teddy bear, a spare change of clothes.

"We do encourage our internees not to keep personal items," Bischoff said. "Theft is, naturally, quite rife, and my staff do not have the time nor the inclination to investigate such trivial matters."

Towards the other end of the dormitory was a doorway marked Waschraum. The showers and toilets.

"This is a female dormitory, ages fourteen and upwards. Under fourteens – juveniles – are held in separate areas with their mothers."

"So if an under-fourteen is decreed to be a dissident, his or her mother is arrested also?" Klarsfeld asked.

Bischoff shrugged. "As I said before, I cannot comment on arrest policies. I merely operate the camp."

On the opposite side of the dormitory to the washroom were a handful of table and chairs, presumably where people could socialize after their day's work before the lights went out.

They left the dormitory and went to a large, tall building. Inside were perhaps a couple of hundred people working. Sewing machines clattered noisily. Some people were ironing. All were female, from teenagers to women in their sixties.

"Here, the internees work," Bischoff said. "They begin at 7am, they take lunch at midday for thirty minutes, and then they work until 5.30pm. A ten-hour working day. There are breaks mid-morning and mid-afternoon for them to use the toilet facilities. This they do six days a week. On a Sunday, there is rest. As you can see, the work is productive and meaningful. Work makes one free."

"And what do the men here do?"

"We have a wood mill on the other side of the camp where trusted internees are sent to work. Some men work within the Sonderkommandos. Most of our male internees work in the brick factory. It is hard work."

"How long are these people held here?" Klarsfeld asked as they were led out of the sewing shop.

"Indefinitely. Who can say how long it takes to rehabilitate or re-educate an individual? Some, they will spend the rest of their lives here."

"Herr Obersturmbannführer, are you happy with your work?"

The three of them stopped walking. To the left, twenty internees walked past on their way to some work detail. With Bischoff within the perimeter of the camp, the machine guns on the towers were pointed at anything that could prove to be a direct threat to him. In addition, out of earshot but maintaining a watchful guard on their leader, a dozen SS officers encircled them.

"Things have changed a lot over the last few years, Herr Reichsstatthalter. I do not deny that in the past, there might well have been extermination camps. That was right for the time, however. Their existence was required to make the Reich strong and powerful. Now ... well, you see the people here. Do they look undernourished? Do they look poorly treated? Oh, to be sure they are not happy. Who would be when faced with internment? But the people here, they are not like you or I. They have broken the rules. They must first be punished and then they must be re-educated."

"And as you say, if they cannot be re-educated ..." Klarsfeld didn't finish his sentence.

Bischoff held out his hands in a helpless gesture.

"This is how it is. Am I happy in my work? Yes, insomuch as I am doing a job which protects the security of the Reich and the loyal German people."

"And those two buildings there," the Reichsstatthalter said, pointing to the two large buildings with chimney stacks attached to them. "Those would be the crematoria?"

Bischoff nodded. "When people cannot be re-educated, well, they must be disposed of."

"May we look?"

"You may." They walked across the camp towards the crematoria. No smoke was billowing from the chimneys. As if to emphasize that fact, Bischoff said, "It is not often that we have to dispose of undesirables."

"And yet the crematoria are large."

"They are."

They entered the nearest one. Men from the *Sonderkommado*, internees who worked within the camp regime, were sweeping and cleaning the large area where the furnaces were.

"There are twenty furnaces in each crematorium," Bischoff said. "The dead are cremated separately and, if requested, their ashes are returned to the relatives."

"How are undesirables ... executed?"

"As with all konzentrationslager, we employ the *fallbeil*. Internees are beheaded. It is cheap, efficient, and it is less distressing for the SS officers working on execution detail."

"May we see the execution area?"

Bischoff lead them to the other end of the crematorium, past the *Sonderkommandos*. They went through a set of double doors and were in a large room. Ahead, two wide doors faced them. They were locked shut. On the right side of each door was a control panel. An SS officer took a set of keys and unlocked them both. He opened both doors outwards and revealed a *fallbeil* within each of the small rooms beyond.

Bischoff led them into the one on the left. The *fallbeil* was basically a bench with a guillotine at one end. Beneath where the blade would fall was a large trough which obviously caught the head and blood from the decapitated corpse. The floor was stainless steel, and curved down slightly to where a drain was located. Similarly, the walls and ceiling were lined with steel. Alongside the *fallbeil*'s bench was a gurney. A hosepipe on a reel was located on the other side. The room stank of disinfectant.

"The internee will come through that door," Bischoff said, pointing to a door on the other side of the *fallbeil*. "Beyond that door is the waiting area. Two officers will accompany the internee. The internee is placed on the *fallbeil*, face down, and the neck clamp is locked in place. The officers come through this door, the door is closed, and then one of the officers will use the control panel. A few seconds later, Sonderkommandos are sent in to retrieve the body which is taken to the furnace room. The trough is emptied, the room is washed down. This takes perhaps five minutes. And then the next internee is brought in. In effect, ten internees can be executed within an hour in each room. Then, of course, the furnaces are full. It takes perhaps three hours to cremate a body."

Ellen was doing the maths in her head, but she needn't have bothered.

"If we were a fully functioning *vernichtungslager*, working twenty-four hours, working very efficiently, we could perhaps fully dispose of three hundred and twenty people in one day." Bischoff shrugged his shoulders. "But we are not."

"How many people have been exterminated here?"

"That information would be classified, Herr Reichsstatthalter. But KZ Katerpow has never been a *vernichtungslager*. This here, this *fallbeil*, this execution room, the furnaces beyond, the tall chimneys that cast long shadows over the konzentrationslager, they all stand as a deterrent to the people in the camp, to the people outside the camp, living in society. A warning that if they do things which are un-German, they might end up here, in this room, strapped to that bench, seconds away from the end."

Ellen involuntarily shuddered as she contemplated the falling axe that efficiently removed the head from a body. She imagined the head tumbling forwards, clattering into the trough, blood squirting from the carotid arteries in the exposed neck stump. She imagined what the Sonderkommandos had to deal with, removing the body, lifting the head from the trough, washing the blood down the drain.

"It is a sobering thought, Herr Obersturmbannführer," she said.

"It probably gives you a different perspective on your job," Bischoff said. "The people you arrest, they end up here, or in a place like this. The consequences of you getting it wrong are serious. You see, the people who refuse to conform, the people who end up here, some of them may be innocent. How can you re-educate somebody who feels that they have been wrongly imprisoned?" Bischoff took out a mobile phone and dialled a number. There was a brief conversation that Ellen didn't pay much attention to. Then he ended the call and said, "SS-Sturmbannführer Hackenholt is free to see you. As you would imagine, the Geheime Staatspolizei administration block is close to this facility."

Bischoff led them through the doorway leading to the waiting room beyond. A long bench that could hold perhaps twenty people was on one side of the wall. A desk was along the other side. They went through another door at the end of this room and were in a lobby area. Through a set of double doors and they faced the other crematorium. To the left was a single storey building. Bischoff took them there.

He left them in the company of a stern-looking man he introduced as SS-Sturmbannführer Hackenholt. Hackenholt was dressed in trousers, a shirt, a blue tie. He led them through to a small office on the other side of a large one where half a dozen smartly dressed people sat.

They sat down.

"Herr Reichsstatthalter, Frau Untersturmführer, I welcome you to KZ Katerpow." Hackenholt gestured to the large pile of files on his desk. "As you can see, I am a busy man, but if I am being honest I appreciate the opportunity to put my work to one side every now and again."

"And I appreciate you giving us some of your time to answer a few of my questions," Klarsfeld said.

Ellen looked around the office. There were certificates on the wall testifying to Hackenholt's attendance on numerous training courses. There was a photograph of his graduation from the Gestapo Training Centre. Another photograph showed him with a group of armed men. A window behind his desk showed a view of a large field where internees were exercising. On another wall, a hakenkreuz flag hung, alongside a lifelike painting of Hitler. Next to that hung two smaller paintings, one showing Heydrich, the other of Himmler.

A framed certificate on the other side of the flag proclaimed that he was a loyal Party member. Ellen had a similar certificate, though hers was in a box in a cupboard in her apartment back in Great Britain.

"So, the Obersturmbannführer tells me that you have a few questions about the legal aspects of dissidents who are spending time in this camp?"

Klarsfeld gave the Gestapo man his warmest smile. "You must understand that things are different here, in the heart of Germany, to the way they are back in the provinces. The Frau Untersturmführer here, and I, were curious as to what constitutes a dissident, how they are arrested, what happens to their families. Back in *der Deutscher Staat von Großbritannien*, naturally we get dissidents, but none of them are of German birth. They are dealt with differently."

Hackenholt nodded. "I understand. Yes, it must seem peculiar to you the notion that true Germans would become dissidents, terrorists even. But it happens. I suppose in the DSvG, true Germans have chosen to live there. Loyal Party members working for the good of the Reich. Here in

Germany, however, we have people who are opposed to the regime. Democrats," he said, almost spitting the word out. "People who refer to our Führer as a dictator, as though a dictator is a bad thing. These people seem to think that a life in the United States would be better. But tell me, what do they get there? The opportunity to vote for a leader. Is that a good thing? Give people a choice and they will always make the wrong one." He shrugged. "Here in Germany, you never see a poor man. You never see somebody struggling to provide for their children. Certainly, some people work harder than others, some people spend their days in physical labour, but they are rewarded. Have either of you been to the United States?"

Ellen's face fell into a questioning expression. Travel to the United States was not forbidden, but it was definitely discouraged. And members of the Schutzstaffel, which included those in the Geheime Staatspolizei, were not allowed to travel there for fear that they would become compromised.

"Let me tell you about it," Hackenholt continued. "There are ghettoes, places where *untermenschen* live. Entire suburbs of cities. The people who live there are unable to work, to provide for their children. Their children starve to death. But you might say, ach, should we concern ourselves with the children of negroes?" Hackenholt shook his head. "It is worse than this, even. There are Aryan people in the United States who cannot afford to provide for their children, even though they are working. They work for a pittance while the *jüdischen Schweine* prosper. There is such disparity of wealth that it is obscene." Hackenholt paused, glanced at the painting of Hitler. "Of course," he went on, "there is a disparity of wealth within the Großdeutsches Reich. We cannot dispute this. Some people are paid more for what they do. For instance, a surgeon, he earns much more than I do. And I, I earn more than the man who sweeps the rubbish from the streets. And yet our street cleaners, they can afford to provide a home and food for their family. They can afford, even, to drink beer, to smoke cigarettes, to buy for themselves a car. These are the people who are the lowest paid in our country, and yet they are far more wealthy than the lowest paid in the United States of America." Hackenholt shook his head and said, "Ach, but enough of my politicizing. This is merely a backstory to the reason behind this konzentrationslager. We have dissidents who are opposed to the regime, who speak out against the Führer. Certainly, we are all entitled to an opinion. But there are some things which are sacred, are there not?" His eyes turned to Ellen. She wondered how much he knew about her. She felt paranoid.

"One must never hold a negative opinion of the Führer, nor of the Reich," Klarsfeld said. "So tell us, please, about an average dissident, if such a thing exists."

"The average dissident ... hmm, how to define such a thing. There are many people who share un-German sentiments, who criticize the regime. After interrogation to ensure that they are not affiliated to any proscribed organizations, it might be decided that they can be re-educated in a facility such as this. Some of them may be here for just a few months, others may be here for a couple of years. Of course, the rehabilitation and re-education process is something which SS-Obersturmbannführer Bischoff is concerned with. My team and I, we deal with people when they first arrive. We are here to ensure that this is the right place for them."

"What happens if you decide this is not the right place for them?"

Hackenholt held up both hands and pointed the forefinger of each in the direction of the two crematoria.

"They end up there. Sometimes a person is beyond redemption."

"That must be a tough decision to make?"

Hackenholt shrugged. "I have been here for six years. I have learnt not to get emotional about such things."

"And a dissident's family? They end up here?"

"Sometimes, yes. Sometimes it is safer that way. You remove the father from a household, it is possible that his wife, his children, will also become dissidents. If they atone for their father's crime, if they spend a couple of years being re-educated, then it is less likely to happen."

Ellen thought about Jerome's family, his mother, his brother and sisters, in a place like this. And yet back in Great Britain the camps were more harsh. She hadn't been to one, but she knew they were more like the extermination camps Bischoff was talking about earlier.

"Bischoff, he was telling us that there are children in the camp, that their mothers are with them," Klarsfeld said. "Are children capable of being dissidents?"

Hackenholt shrugged. "It is rare that a juvenile is sent here, but it does happen. And nobody wants to execute a child. At least, not an Aryan child. If they have been sent here to be re-educated, then their mothers will come with them. Once they reach fourteen, their mothers are released, and the young person's re-education continues in the adult quarters. However, most of the juveniles are here because their whole family has been interned. I understand it's very much different in the provinces – but then, in the provinces you are dealing with individuals who are not true Aryans."

"Yes, there is a huge difference between here and the camps back in Great Britain," Klarsfeld said. "Tell me, are there frequent interrogations?"

"We have four interrogation rooms, two attached to the rear of each of the crematoria. Believe me, dragging a prisoner to the crematoria is enough to instil fear in them. But we primarily interrogate people when they first arrive. After that, they are in Bischoff's hands."

"Are any executions scheduled for today?"

Hackenholt laughed. "You have been reading too much fiction, Herr Reichsstatthalter. This is not a death camp. Though of course executions do occur. But generally, when that happens the internees are taken directly from the main part of the camp and executed. We do not have a 'death row' as such. But we are now getting into the realms of camp operations, and Bischoff knows more about this than I do."

"You must forgive me, Herr Sturmbannführer, but I am still curious as to the full definition of a dissident. For example, and please humour me here, what kind of things have the dissidents here at KZ Katerpow done to earn their place in a *Rehabilitations-und Umerziehungslager*?"

Hackenholt considered this question for a few moments. "Well," he said, glancing at the files in front of him. He lifted the top one. "Today's intake, thirty-eight people. Let me take a look." He started to read down a list. "Number one, he was arrested for being drunk and disorderly, but he was also criticizing the Reichsführer-SS. He referred to him as a toadying *Schleimscheißer*." It was apparently the first time Hackenholt had read this file because even he gave a chuckle at that one. "Okay ... well, I dare say there will be little for my team to glean in the way of intelligence from that one. What else do we have?" He scanned down the list. "Ah, yes, this individual was distributing pro-democracy leaflets in a public library. These people, we have to be careful of. Some of them – perhaps even all of them – are either members of, or otherwise affiliated to, the *Deutsch Antifaschistische Liga* or even the Vierte Reich. Of course, they might not have perpetrated actual acts of terrorism, but we can sometimes get useful information out of them."

"You will interrogate him?"

"Her," Hackenholt corrected. "Of course."

"And then what?"

"If we discover no evidence of any other crimes committed, then she will be sent to the main camp. Even members of the DAL or the Vierte Reich can occasionally be re-educated. But information taken from her could be used to arrest terrorists. Terrorists, they do not come to a konzentrationslager such as this."

"Well, I thank you for your time, Herr Sturmbannführer, but I fear we must let you get on with your important work," Klarsfeld said. They all shook hands, and then a young SS-Totenkopfverbände officer came to escort them back to the main administration block. As they were walking, Klarsfeld pointed to a large two-storey building on the other side of the camp.

"That building there," he asked. "What is it?"

"That is the *Medizinische Forschung Block*, mein Herr," the young officer explained. Klarsfeld nodded his head.

They shared a fine late lunch with Bischoff. Towards the end, as the Obersturmführer poured brandies for the three of them, Klarsfeld said, "I noticed the *Medizinische Forschung Block* as we were walking back from the Gestapo offices."

"Ah, the Medical Research Block. Yes, that is where we treat the infirmed."

"And ... research?"

Bischoff sniffed his brandy. It was a fine cognac, even Ellen could tell that. He said, "That part of the camp is beyond my control, out of my jurisdiction, and cannot form part of your tour." He did not look at either Klarsfeld or Ellen as he said this.

"I sense some ... disapproval?"

Bischoff smiled, but it wasn't a happy smile. "As I am sure SS-Sturmbannführer Hackenholt explained to you, criticism of the regime is not tolerated." He held out his hands. "And if you have any particular ... criticisms of your own, then I would suggest that this is not the place for them, and I do not wish to hear them. Speaking as a loyal Party member myself."

"I apologize. I meant no disrespect."

Twenty minutes later, Klarsfeld and Ellen were back in the Mercedes on their way to Germania.

Klarsfeld said, "What did you think of the German konzentrationslager?"

"I have nothing to compare them with."

"But you know that the ones back in Great Britain are much, much worse."

"I am led to believe that, yes."

"And yet you can see that life at KZ Katerpow is no bed of roses."

"They are dealing with dissidents and political prisoners."

"Yes, they are. You think that it is right for people to be imprisoned for having a different opinion to you?" Ellen didn't answer. "That woman the Gestapo man Hackenholt spoke of. The one distributing pro-democracy leaflets. What do you think will happen to her?"

"She will be interrogated and re-educated."

"You have never interrogated anyone, have you, my dear?"

Ellen's mind slipped back a couple of years, to the one occasion when she had personally interrogated somebody. A member of Combat UK, a woman who had also been sleeping with Jerome, the man she had started to fall for. Ellen had been leading a small Gestapo team.

She had also tortured the woman.

She clenched her teeth as she thought about what she'd done.

She thought about sending jolts of electricity through the body of a young woman who had been sleeping with the man she was falling in love with.

She remembered that after she'd got all of the information from this young woman, she had taken out her pistol and shot her in the head.

Angrily, she turned on Klarsfeld.

"Yes, I have interrogated somebody. I tortured them as well. I have also shot people. I am not so pure and white as you would believe."

Klarsfeld smiled. "Then you will know that this woman, this distributor of pieces of paper, she has very little to look forward to. Tell me, Ellen, did you enjoy torturing somebody? Did it make you feel important, powerful?"

"Stop the car," Ellen said. The driver glanced in his rear-view mirror. He looked first at Ellen and then at Klarsfeld, who shook his head. "I said stop the fucking car!"

They were on the autobahn, there was nowhere to pull over

Klarsfeld said, "Some people, they cannot torture. It makes them ill. It is not something I could do. I do not think it was something that you enjoyed doing. I think that you were caught up in the moment."

Ellen looked at him. She felt a rage inside of her, but also a sickness. Guilt as well. She could even remember the fine spray of blood that had splattered against the wall when she had shot the woman she'd been torturing.

"You think that I know nothing, Ellen, but I know everything. I would not have drawn you into my world if I didn't know everything about you. If I didn't know how you felt."

Ellen started to cry.

27

SS-Obersturmführer Mann looked up at his adjutant, Vogel, as the young, bespectacled officer rushed into his office. In Vogel's hand was a piece of paper.

"Ah, Vogel, you look like the cat who has got the cream."

"Herr Obersturmführer, we have the fingerprints from the warehouse."

"Remind me again, which warehouse is this?" Mann asked, lighting up a *juno*.

"The one in Peterborough."

"Ah yes, our Mr Dauny, the Engländer, and the strange case of the breitnetz incursion. Sit down, tell me more."

Vogel sat down and said, "After the incursion, as you are aware, the local Gestapo stopped and questioned a few individuals." Mann shrugged. He would've expected nothing less. In truth, he had dealt with a few more cases since they'd begun this particular investigation. "One of those individuals, a man by the name of Barry Rhodes, his fingerprints were found at the warehouse."

Mann leant forwards on his desk. "Hmm. Now that is intriguing. Tell me more about Mr Rhodes."

"He works as a lorry driver."

"So, he is no computer expert then?"

"Not much need for a computer in a lorry, mein Herr."

"You are definitely right, my loyal *Schwachkorb*." Mann took a few drags from his cigarette. "And this Mr Rhodes, is he friendly with our Mr Dauny? I know such a thing would seem unlikely, and yet these Engländers seem to drink their disgusting real ale in eclectic social circles."

"I can find no connection between the two of them, Herr Mann." Vogel consulted his notes again. "The curious thing is that Barry Rhodes has existed, so to speak, for the last seven years. Prior to that, I can find no record of him."

"Seven years. And for security checks, most organizations only go back five years. Personal IDs only last five years."

"He has a National Security number."

"And yet that is possibly easy to forge. After all, much as we all love the Großdeutsches Reich, we must concede that we are not exactly overwhelmed with illegal immigrants."

"He appeared out of thin air seven years ago, mein Herr. And unless we had been investigating such a serious matter, his deception might not have been uncovered. But there really is only one reason why a person would appear within the Greater German Reich out of thin air."

"Hmm." Mann sighed. "I am hoping, my geeky little friend, that you are about to tell me that Mr Rhodes is currently in the custody of the Geheime Staatspolizei in Peterborough."

"This is our investigation," Vogel said. "I did not want it to be fucked up by those provincial idiots."

Mann clapped his hands slowly. "Spoken like a true spoilt child of Germania." He stood up, dragged greedily on his cigarette and then stubbed it out in the ashtray on his desk. "Well, come, my angry little friend. Let us visit Mr Barry Rhodes and give you the opportunity to rid yourself of the frustration you feel at having been bullied as a small child at school."

28

Marcus Dauny wasn't too sure he wanted to be involved in the English resistance anymore, not after his meeting with the men from the computer security branch of the Geheime Staatspolizei.

The problem was that the Gestapo had clearly seen that his user ID had been compromised, and it was natural that they would suspect him of accessing the GFW local network from an unauthorized location. He was now a suspect. He was even toying with the idea of coming clean to the Gestapo men. After all, he hadn't actually committed a serious crime. Just accessing his works' network from an unusual location wasn't against the law, surely?

He had arranged to meet Rhodes at the bar at the Bretton Sports and Social Club. As he walked through the car park he glanced around at the other cars, looking out for the distinctive M3s of the Gestapo. Of course, the Gestapo also employed less significant vehicles from time to time, if they were working undercover.

Nevertheless, satisfied he wasn't currently under direct surveillance or immediate threat, he wandered to the bar's entrance. Inside, a football match was playing on the large TV screens. Dauny walked up to the bar, nodded a greeting to the landlord, the jovial bespectacled guy, and asked what he recommended.

"Don't ask me, mate," the landlord said. "I never touch that filthy stuff. Now, if you asked me about lagers …" He toyed with his spectacles.

"Sadly, I'm not a lager man, old chap."

"What about a Batemans Victory? How's that for irony?"

Dauny nodded and watched as the beer was poured. He sat at the bar and after paying for the beer, turned to the TV screen. He had no idea who was playing – football wasn't really his sport – but he allowed himself to become almost hypnotized by the sight of tiny men running around on a green background. In a way, it made him seem to fit in with those around him, these working class people who viewed the Germans and the English members of the Nazi Party as oppressors.

Dauny had worn his Party armband to work. As soon as he left the office and climbed into his car, it came off. It was no longer because he feared the reactions of those around him – in the past he had removed it on occasions when he went shopping or if he was travelling in areas where it was likely to draw unwanted attention. Now he removed it because he no longer felt comfortable with it on his arm. He no longer felt like a loyal Party member.

Dauny thought about his job, about the way he was treated there. Sure, he was better paid that most Engländers, but he still wasn't properly respected by his German co-workers. They barely even considered him to be a colleague, and he certainly wasn't viewed as their equal.

Rhodes had mentioned disabling the nuclear missile launch system, which would leave Germany – and Germania in particular – vulnerable to attack from the US. That would cost millions of lives. Men, women, children. Collateral damage? He wasn't sure he could live with that. He was, after all, a man of peace.

He finished his pint, checked his watch. He'd got here forty-five minutes early. It was still fifteen minutes before Rhodes was due to arrive. Dauny signalled for the landlord, asked for another pint of Batemans Victory.

"Be careful with that stuff, me old duck," the landlord said. "That's six percent." Dauny shrugged and the landlord poured him another.

As he sipped the dark beer he contemplated what life would be like in the United States. Whilst travel was permitted to the US, both US customs and Germany customs would question why such a visit was being made. A person had to be interviewed by US diplomatic staff in order to obtain an entrance visa, and then they had to be interviewed by Sicherheitsdienst officers before they were given an exit visa. People in sensitive positions were always denied exit from Germany. Dauny figured that the SD would consider his position to be sensitive. He had information he could give to the Americans, after all.

He chuckled at the irony of that.

On the TV, one of the teams scored and some of the men in the pub shouted and cheered. There was a brief discussion between a group of them appraising the quality of the goal. To the side of the bar was a newspaper, and he gestured to the landlord, asked if he could have a read.

The problem with newspapers was that they were heavily censored and heavily biased. No news story ever criticized the government. During the period of the punishment killings, the media didn't mention them. A proclamation was announced just before they began. And when they ended, a further announcement was given. No mention of numbers killed, just rumours and conjecture in hushed whispers.

This news, all of it was sanitized. As he turned the pages, all he could see were stories about crimes and murders, gossip about celebrities, hard luck tales of people who had lost something or someone precious to them.

The sports pages had coverage on cricket and rugby matches, but there was a heavy bias towards football. Unsatisfied, he put the newspaper down and turned to look out of the window. A car was pulling into the car park. It looked like Rhodes was driving it. He parked it up. Dauny took a sip from his pint.

And then a black BMW pulled into the car park.

The landlord leant against the bar. "Gestapo," he said.

Dauny felt the colour drain from his face.

29

Rhodes wondered whether Dauny's resolve would remain firm or whether the fact they'd almost been caught by the Gestapo would get to him. This was a risky business, the stakes were high, but so were they gains if they succeeded. For one thing, he'd be able to leave this godforsaken country and return to his homeland. He hadn't seen his brother, his sister nor his mother since he'd left all those years ago.

If this plot, which was very much still embryonic, should succeed then Germany would be a much different place. The leadership removed, their capital destroyed, a defenceless state. The US could demand its surrender. The people of Germany, of the Greater German Reich, would finally be free.

But so much relied on luck.

This meeting with Dauny, the computer programmer, would either make or break the plot. If Dauny had lost his nerve, if Rhodes couldn't convince him to stay on board until the end, then all of this would be for nothing. As he pulled into the car park of the Bretton Sports and Social Club, he looked around for Dauny's car but it wasn't there. It was possible, of course, that Dauny had walked here, but at the back of Rhodes's mind was the suspicion that Dauny was a no-show.

He switched off the engine, looked at the football ground's bar, the social club, a real part of England in amongst the hell of the Greater German Reich. Here, there were no Germans, there were no English Nazis, there were just Englishmen and Englishwomen.

Taking the keys from the ignition, he was about to open the door when it was abruptly opened from the outside. Rhodes looked up to see a casually dressed man standing there. He presumed the man was German. He was tall, had that look about him, and in any case he was holding his Geheime Staatspolizei badge.

"Herr Rhodes?"

"Yes."

"I am from the Geheime Staatspolizei. Would you mind stepping out of your car?"

Rhodes did as he was told and saw another German standing near the rear of his car. This one was shorter than the first.

"I am SS-Obersturmführer Mann," the first German said. "This is my assistant, Vogel." The second German didn't offer any greeting.

"What's this about?"

"We'd like you to come with us," Mann said.

Rhodes considered the fact that Dauny might be in the bar, watching all of this unfold. If these Gestapo officers entered the bar, that would leave Dauny hopelessly exposed. Rhodes, he could be replaced, but Dauny, with his skills, with his knowledge, with his security clearance, he was irreplaceable.

Rhodes smiled at the German.

And then he ran, darting beyond Mann's grasp, dodging Vogel, running across the car park. He launched himself across the bonnet of a parked car which was in his way, and then he was on the football pitch, running past the goalposts. One hundred metres to the other end, to a possible escape route.

He knew the Germans would be following him, and he assumed that both of them were fit. It was going to be a question of who ran out of steam first. The Germans were shouting at him to stop, but of course Rhodes had no intention of doing that. At the halfway line, he was aware of the fact that the Germans were closing in on him. Their shouts were louder, though breathless. As he reached the penalty area on the other half of the pitch, someone grabbed his jacket and Rhodes was slowed momentarily. He shrugged the hand away, but another grabbed him, and this time he was pulled to the ground and his arm forced up behind his back.

He was breathing heavily and so were the two Germans. They were all out of breath. He felt them putting handcuffs on him and then he was pulled to his feet.

Mann was smiling.

"A bit of exercise, eh, Herr Rhodes?" He let out a chuckle. "You should know that I am not as fit as once I was." He wagged a finger. "Please do not do that again."

Rhodes said nothing.

As he was led back to the Germans' black BMW, he just hoped that Dauny had got away.

30

Dauny watched as the Gestapo men opened Rhodes's car door.

A hand rested on his forearm, and he turned to look at the landlord.

"Go to the hallway where the toilets are. At the end of the corridor is an emergency exit. Take it, and then go to the left. There's a passageway to the side of where the old barrels are stored. Follow that to the end, and you'll come out on Kaiser Street. From there, you're on your own."

Dauny nodded his appreciation, drained his pint and left the bar.

He strode towards the emergency exit, pushed the bar and stepped outside. He was in a small yard, fenced off. He knew that to his right would be the football pitch. To his left was a narrow passage, the fence on either side over six feet tall. He walked quickly down this for perhaps fifty metres as it curved around the rear gardens of houses on Kaiser Street. Finally, he came to a tall gate. This too had a bar to open it. Dauny did and pushed the spring-loaded gate open. He stepped out into the street and the gate swung shut behind him.

This was a road with terraced houses on one side, semi-detached properties on the other. It was a long walk to his house, but he could take a bus. He found a bus stop in an adjoining street, and only had to wait five minutes before one arrived. This was the wrong route to take him directly home, so he had to go first to the main bus station in the city centre to catch a connecting bus. In a way, it was eye-opening, mixing with regular Englishmen and Englishwomen. These were factory workers, shop workers, people he wouldn't ordinarily associate with. He looked at their faces, on the bus, at the bus station. There were few smiles, but occasional looks of fear, uncertainty, suspicion.

This was the real England, the one he didn't see. These people didn't have the same privileges as he did. These were the oppressed of whom Rhodes and Harry had spoken. The ordinary people. These were the people who had probably lost relatives in the reprisal killings.

The buses stank of sweat, of dirt. People around him swore under their breath. He had to sit next to somebody. The bus weaved its way through the streets for half an hour before it reached a road that was close to where he lived. He got off. He walked home.

He opened a bottle of wine and poured himself a large merlot. Then he stepped out into his garden, sat down at the garden table and contemplated what had just happened.

He'd been asked to betray the Greater German Reich for the resistance, for people affiliated to Combat UK. He had been seriously contemplating helping them, and at this meeting today with Rhodes, he'd intended to offer them his commitment. But watching the Gestapo arresting Rhodes, he had to consider the fact that he'd be making a huge mistake. There really was only one reason why the Gestapo had arrested Rhodes, and that was because they had, somehow, connected him to the incident the other day at the factory. And if they'd done that, then it wouldn't be a leap of faith to connect Rhodes to him. And he'd already attracted the attentions of the Gestapo officers – incidentally, the same Gestapo officers who'd just arrested Rhodes.

Mann and Vogel.

They would be taking Rhodes to an interrogation suite. They would interrogate him. Torture him. Rhodes would talk, Rhodes would reveal Dauny's name. They would arrest him, they would torture him, and then they would execute him.

Dauny necked the wine and considered his options.

As he did, there was a knock at the door. He almost jumped out of his skin. But the knock wasn't loud and imposing. It was just a regular knock. Not the kind that Gestapo officers would use. He put down his glass and stepped back into the house, into the hallway that led to the front door. His heart pounding in his chest, he reached for the handle, opened the door.

31

Rhodes sat in the back of the car, his hands cuffed behind him, strapped in, unable to move. Vogel was driving, Mann was in the passenger seat. He occasionally looked back at Rhodes and smiled. They left Peterborough, turned south on the main autobahn, heading towards London.

Mann had said, "We're taking you to the Polizeipräsidium." The police headquarters. The Gestapo headquarters. The main one, not the provincial one that every town, every city in England possessed. This was bad news.

As they reached the outskirts of London, the skyscrapers visible in the distance, Rhodes said, "What have I been arrested for?"

Vogel's eyes looked at him in the rear-view mirror. Mann turned and said, "All will be revealed. And hopefully you will also be able to help us with our enquiries."

Rhodes sighed. He knew what was coming. He'd never thought he'd actually end up in this situation. He wondered how strong he would be, whether he'd crack, and if so, how quickly. He wondered whether he would give up Dauny's name, the names of people he knew in the organization.

At the police HQ, they helped him out of the car. On his feet, he felt his legs go weak. Mann patted him on the shoulder.

"You seem nervous, friend," he said. "My mother, she would always say to me, 'If you have done nothing wrong, you have nothing to fear.' She was quite right."

They entered a lift which took them from the subterranean car park to some floor in the tall building. Rhodes didn't know which floor it was. He was just looking down at the ground. He felt dejected. Back in the US, they'd told him about torture, they'd tried to prepare him, but how can you prepare a person for that? They'd told him all of the methods that were used. They'd demonstrated a few of them, the ones that didn't leave people permanently disfigured. Waterboarding. It had felt like he was drowning.

They'd said, "That won't be the worst, but it might be what they start with."

They'd also said, "Depending on what they suspect you of doing, they might start with something far more serious."

Far more serious.

Like pulling out his fingernails, his teeth, enucleating an eye. Beating him with sticks, breaking his legs, his arms. Weakening him. All of these and more.

"People eventually succumb to pain," they'd told him. "It's inevitable. The question is, how long can you hold on before you succumb? Can you hold on long enough to protect assets?"

They'd also said, "Give up a name before you give up the details of a mission. People can be replaced. The mission cannot be."

Rhodes, he was replaceable.

The lift doors opened and he was led out into a corridor. They took him to a room, sat him down at a table.

Mann and Vogel sat opposite him.

Mann took out a packet of cigarettes. He offered one to Rhodes. Rhodes shook his head.

"You do not smoke?" Mann shrugged as he lit one and puffed on it. "Ach, it is a filthy habit, of this there is no doubt. But we all must have a vice, yes?" Rhodes didn't speak. This room, it didn't look like a torture suite. It just looked like a regular interview room. "Tell me, Herr Rhodes, why did you run from us?" Rhodes shrugged. "It made you look guilty. What are you guilty of, Herr Rhodes?"

"I've done nothing wrong."

"Hmm." Mann frowned, stuck a finger in his head and waggled it. "If you have nothing to hide, then why would you run? This is what I cannot understand." Rhodes remained silent. "Tell me, Herr Rhodes, do you recall a few days ago being stopped by the Gestapo?"

Rhodes knew this was coming. "Yes."

"Do you recall the answer you gave to the Gestapo officer when he asked what you were doing there?"

"I was going for a walk, so that's what I would've told him."

"Tell me, Herr Rhodes, do you know a man by the name of Marcus Dauny?"

Rhodes tried to remain calm. He didn't want to give any emotions away. He shook his head. "I don't recall anybody who goes by that name."

"The bar you were about to visit – were you going to meet anyone there?"

"I was just going for a beer."

"Hmm."

Vogel stood up, walked to the wall on the other side of the room. He made a show of looking down at his running shoes.

"Tell me, what do you know of computers, Herr Rhodes?"

"Computers?"

"Yes. I know that with your work you probably do not use one. But are you familiar with computers?"

"I've heard of them, yes, but that's about the sum total of my knowledge. Not interested in them."

"Hmm."

Mann leant back in his chair and clasped his hands behind his head.

"Do you know that all I seem to be doing at the moment is driving up to Peterborough and then returning back to London. Of course, with our autobahns, it does not take too long, but all the same, I hate being cooped up in a car for an hour." Mann took a drag from his cigarette. "So, computers. Vogel, would you tell Herr Rhodes about our computers, please?"

"Certainly, Herr Obersturmführer." Vogel remained where he was. Rhodes turned to look at him.

"I should warn you," Mann said. "Vogel is something of a geek."

"Essentially, our computer system enables us to collate evidence, details and facts pertaining to an investigation. For example, once the Gestapo officer who questioned you in the street returned to his desk, he placed your name on our computer system. So when we were searching for suspects for our investigation, all we had to do was see whether anybody had been stopped and questioned on this particular day, at this particular time, in that particular location. Our computer database is quite extensive. For example, with just a few clicks of a computer mouse, I can discover who is under investigation in Germania. I can find out a person's criminal record. I can learn where they have lived in the past, what job they have, what qualifications they attained and at what establishment."

"Listen, Herr Rhodes, because it gets interesting here," Mann said.

Rhodes felt his heart pounding in his chest, because he had an idea of what what was coming.

Vogel said, "The curious thing is that you do not appear to have worked anywhere prior to 1990. I can find no former addresses for any periods prior to that year. Now, of course, perhaps you were out of work and homeless up until 1990, though it is unusual for any of our citizens to lead an indolent and wasteful existence for such a long time." Vogel pushed himself away from the wall and walked up to the table. Rhodes had to raise his head to look at him. "What is more likely is that you weren't actually born in England. What is more likely is that seven years ago, you were sent to England."

"That's absurd."

"Of course, computers do make mistakes. But this is so rare that on the balance of probabilities you simply did not exist in England prior to 1990."

"Let me tell you, Herr Rhodes," Mann said, "when we discovered this about you our investigation took on a whole different slant. You see, we thought that you had, for some reason, tried to access a computer network to which you are not entitled to have access. But this, this means something far more serious. This is spying. Spying is out of our jurisdiction." Mann took one last drag from his *juno* before stubbing it out. He got to his feet. "Come, Herr Rhodes. We must take you to the basement levels, where you will meet a couple of my colleagues."

As he stood up, Rhodes realized that his world was going to get a lot worse over the course of the next few minutes.

32

Dauny opened his front door to see Harry Dean standing there. Though Dauny was a big man, Harry was bigger. He looked up and down the street and then entered the house. Dauny visibly heaved a sigh of relief.

"So the Gestapo have arrested Barry."

"He tried to get away," Dauny said.

"So I heard."

Dauny led Harry through to the lounge, offered him a seat.

"What does this mean for me?"

Harry took a deep breath, let out a sigh. "Well, it's possible you may be compromised, but I can virtually guarantee Barry won't give them your name."

"How can you be so sure?"

"Barry is American. CIA. He's a spy. If he has to give up anything, it won't be anything which compromises the mission."

"Is there any need for me to get involved now?"

"We will still need your skills, Marcus. I'm taking over as your handler. I've been fully briefed on the mission parameters. We continue as if Barry hasn't been captured."

"Earlier, you said I may have been compromised. In what way?"

"The mission is the only suspicious thing Barry is involved in. There's no other reason for him to have been arrested."

Dauny nodded his head. "They came to the warehouse when we were accessing the computer system."

"Yes, Barry told us."

"I was questioned. They took my *Trag* away with them." Harry frowned. "My portable computer. They took it away. The men who arrested Barry were the same ones who came to question me."

"They didn't arrest you."

"I'm a Party member," Dauny said. "I suppose my answers seemed plausible to them."

"Let's hope so."

"So what now?"

"When are you due back at work?"

"Tomorrow."

"You need to go in, act as if nothing's happened."

"That's not exactly going to be easy," Dauny said. He didn't relish returning to work with the threat of arrest by the Gestapo hanging over him.

"You have to. The only alternative is that we smuggle you out of the country. But then that's an asset wasted. Not to mention the actual financial cost of getting you out of the Reich." Harry stroked his chin. "Barry said something about you getting some computer security expert on board."

"There are people I went to university with," Dauny said. He was thinking about Owen. Owen always flew beneath the radar, bending and breaking many laws. But then the crimes he committed were not crimes against the State. You couldn't be executed for stealing computer software.

"You need to think of a solid one and introduce him to me. And you need to do it quick. I'm not convinced we have much time."

"Surely it's madness to proceed with this mission of yours."

"It's madness if we don't," Harry said, getting to his feet. "You need to arrange a meeting with one of these computer experts. I will question them and assess whether or not we can trust them."

"And if you think we can't trust them, what then?"

"They disappear and we move onto the next computer expert."

Dauny finally realized that he was dealing with men who had the capacity to be as ruthlessly lethal as the German security forces they were fighting against.

Harry patted him on the arm and then held his arm. It was a firm grip.

He said, "We cannot fail."

33

They travelled in the lift down to the fifth floor below ground. Rhodes felt the air becoming more chilly the further down they went. The doors opened and he was led out into a lobby. A desk was against one wall. Ahead was a barred gate. To the right, a corridor, and to the left, some offices.

They weren't alone in the lobby. There were two men, plain-clothed, and three uniformed officers from the Waffen-SS. Mann shook hands with one of the Gestapo men.

"Heil Führer, Schmid. This is Herr Rhodes."

"Heil Führer," Schmid said. He looked Barry up and down. "Good day to you, Herr Rhodes. You and I are going to have a little chat."

"Vogel, sign the paperwork," Mann said.

Forms were completed, the men shook hands, and Mann and Vogel left the lobby. Schmid nodded to the man with him, a huge beast squeezed into a tight suit. This man grabbed Rhodes and led him down the corridor. Schmid opened one of the many doors that lined the left side of the corridor and stepped inside. Rhodes was practically dragged into the room.

There was a table, two chairs, and to the rear of the room, another doorway.

Rhodes was forced to sit. Schmid sat opposite. The bear stood in the corner nearest the door.

"Where are you from, Herr Rhodes?"

"I come from Fenland—"

Schmid said, very slowly, "You can stop with the bullshit." He shouted the last word. He took a deep breath as though composing himself. "Now, I will ask you the question again. Where are you from, Herr Rhodes?"

Rhodes shook his head. "I'm English. I—"

A shadow moved in the corner of his eye and then there was a ringing in his ears accompanied by a sharp pain running up the side of his face. He turned to see the bear standing over him.

"We could do this all day, but I presume that you would keep relling me that you are from England, that you are from the Fenlands. This would be a waste of my time." Schmid looked at the big man. "Keitel, take him through to the back."

Keitel dragged Rhodes effortlessly from the chair and took him to the other door. He opened it and flung Rhodes into the room beyond. Rhodes skidded on the steel floor. He looked around. The walls were steel too, as was the ceiling. There was a drainage grid in the floor. Next to the door was a table with a single chair. On the other side of the room was a steel door.

Rhodes looked up. Eight feet overhead a bar ran from wall to wall. Two pairs of handcuffs hung from it.

Schmid came into the room.

"Get on your feet," he said. Rhodes stood up. "Strip."

"What?"

"Strip," Schmid commanded, sitting down at the table. Rhodes proceeded to undress. As he did so, Keitel opened the steel door and brought out a pedestal, placing it beneath the handcuffs. Rhodes was dragged onto the pedestal and Keitel locked him into the handcuffs. His arms were bent slightly at the elbows. Keitel jumped from the pedestal and dragged it from beneath Rhodes's feet.

He dropped a few inches and the cuffs bit into his wrists. He cried out.

Schmid looked up at him.

"Now, Herr Rhodes, I will ask you questions and you will answer them."

They'd told Rhodes during training that the fear would get to him. That he would feel his teeth chattering, that he would piss and shit himself. They'd said he'd do all of this before the torture even began. They'd warned him that even in those very early stages, he'd be tempted to talk, to give up some information, anything to stop them from continuing.

They'd told him not to do that.

They'd said, "When you give them a piece of information, they believe they've opened the flood gates. And they won't stop until you're empty."

Rhodes could feel his bowels loosening, his stomach churning. He felt vulnerable and dehumanized. Already, he could feel the strain in his arms, his shoulders. Behind him, he could hear the bear man, Keitel, moving something, picking something up.

Schmid took out a pen and opened the file he was carrying. He jotted

nach Schema F

something down and then looked up at Rhodes.

"So, am I to presume that you are American? CIA?"

"No."

Almost before he'd finished speaking, he felt something strike his lower leg with such ferocity it made him howl out in pain. He swung back and forth with the momentum of the blow. His leg felt like it was broken. He looked down. His shin was split open, a bone protruding, blood dripping onto the floor. Keitel stood near him with a baseball bat in his hands.

"I'm going to continue asking you questions, Herr Rhodes," Schmid said, "and I will write down your responses. However, if I think you are lying, SS-Sturmscharführer Keitel, here, will strike you."

"I'm not lying." Keitel swung the bat against Rhodes's backside, and again Rhodes cried out.

"Why were you in the factory in Peterborough eight days ago?"

"I wasn't."

The bat struck Rhode's broken leg. The pain was excruciating. He was finding it difficult to breath. He vomited, most of it spewing out onto the floor, but some splattering his own body.

"Your fingerprints were found there," Schmid said. "Tell me, how do you know Marcus Dauny?"

Rhodes didn't answer. He saw Keitel about to move. "No, no! Wait!"

"Well?"

"I don't really know him." Keitel swung the bat backwards. "No! Listen! I don't really know him. He's just some posh guy who comes into the pub. That's all. I know he's a Nazi. I've seen him take his armband off before he gets out of his car."

"And what is your relationship with Herr Dauny?"

"I stole his wallet," Rhodes said. "A couple of weeks ago. It's obvious that he's well paid. I figured he'd have a lot of cash on him."

"I see. And did he?"

"A couple of hundred Reichsmarks."

"Do you know whether Herr Dauny reported this theft to the police?" Schmid asked, jotting something down.

"He was very drunk at the time. He probably figured he lost it."

"Was there anything else in the wallet?"

"I was looking for a PIN number for his debit card," Rhodes said. "I didn't see one. And there was a works pass, with something like a password on it."

"And what did you do with this works pass?"

"I sold it."

"You sold it? Who to?"

"It's a guy I know, he does things with computers. I don't know what. I don't really know anything about them."

"This guy's name?"

"Look, please, I don't know what his name is—"

The baseball bat was swung into his other leg. This time, Rhodes felt the bones crack. Immediately, he retched again, but mostly they were just dry heaves. He blacked out from the pain momentarily. When he came to, he was aware of his bowels opening. The shit poured from him. It wasn't solid.

They'd told him this would happen.

They'd said that the priorities during interrogation were to a) protect the asset, b) protect the mission objectives and c) give up the cover name. He'd protected the asset, he'd protected the mission objectives, and all that remained was for him to give up the cover name. If the procedures had been carried out correctly, somebody would right now be on a boat to Ireland and then from there to the USA.

Rhodes gasped, tried to get air into his lungs, trying desperately to catch his breath.

"You are wasting my time, Herr Rhodes," Schmid said.

"Williams," Rhodes gasped. "Michael Williams."

Schmid jotted this down. "You have his address?"

"No. I met him at the Bretton Sports and Social Club. He's one of the regulars."

"And he is a computer man?"

"I don't know what he does, only that he bought the works pass from me."

Schmid squinted. "So, if I send some of my people to this Bretton Sports and Social Club, someone there will be able to identify this Michael Williams?"

"Yes."

For a few moments, nobody spoke. Rhodes could smell shit, piss, vomit and the sickly sweet stench of open wounds. Both of his legs hurt like hell, a kind of pain he never imagined could have existed.

nach Schema F

"Well, I thank you for that information, Herr Rhodes," Schmid said. "However, there is still the question of you not existing prior to 1990. I want you to tell me where you came from and how you got into this country."

"I was born in Fenland," Rhodes said.

The baseball bat was swung into left knee and at that point, Rhodes blacked out.

34

SS-Unterstrumführer Willi Himmler parked the BMW up outside the Bretton Sports and Social Club in Peterborough. He had been here before, with Ellen Brauchitsch, who had since gone on to better things. Today, he was here with SS-Unterstrumführer Zimmerman, who had only very recently been promoted.

"I have been here so often, I think I've become one of the fucking locals," Himmler said as they got out of the car.

"I hate travelling from London," Zimmerman said. "Everywhere north of London is full of Engländer pigs. *Untermenschen.*"

Himmler shook his head. Zimmerman was old school. He'd worked for a month on the reprisal killings. Lots of people did a few shifts, but Zimmerman seemed to relish it. Himmler had seen him torturing suspects, and though he himself had a strong stomach, some of the things Zimmerman did left a nasty taste in his mouth.

They entered the bar. Football was playing on the TV screens. There were perhaps twenty people sitting at tables drinking, eyeing the action. The barman, a grey-haired, bespectacled man, was wiping down the bar. Himmler remembered him from the last time he'd been here.

He and Zimmerman walked up to the bar.

"All right, squire, what can I do you for?"

Himmler smiled. These Engländers, with their odd way of talking.

He said, "We are from the Geheime Staatspolizei. We are looking for somebody."

"Well, maybe I can help?"

"What is your name, mein Herr?"

"I'm Tom," the barman said. "Tom Flannigan."

"Well, Herr Flannigan, it is possible you could help us. We are trying to locate a gentleman by the name of Michael Williams."

"Michael Williams?"

"Yes. You know of him?"

"Everybody knows Michael Williams," Flannigan said. "Bit of a dodgy geezer."

"Dodgy? How so?"

"Troublemaker," the barman went on. "God knows what kind of things he's mixed up in. He sometimes tries to sell knock-off gear. I don't permit that in my establishment."

"Quite. Where does he work?"

"Works for himself," Flannigan said. "Officially, something to do with fixing computers." He shrugged. "I can barely use the TV remote, let alone a computer."

"I see. And where does he live?"

"Eastfield Road. At least, he used to."

"Used to?"

"He did a runner about a week ago."

"A runner?"

"Had it away on his toes," Flannigan said. "Word was that he'd trousered some bunce from a deal and then didn't deliver."

Himmler frowned.

"Ripped somebody off," Flannigan said. "The bastard still owes me almost fifty Reichsmarks for his bar tab. I'll never see that again, especially if you blokes are after him as well."

Himmler frowned. He had been sent on a fool's errand.

"Does anybody know where he is?"

"Scotland, Wales, Ireland," Flannigan said. "Could be anywhere, mate."

Himmler pondered for a few moments. "Did he have any associates?"

"Associates? No, mate, he just had people he tried to swindle. Victims, rather than associates. Oh, I tell a lie. He was good mates with … oh, what's his name. Barry. Barry Rhodes. Always had some kind of scheme between the pair of them." Flannigan swung his tea towel over his shoulder. "Of course, Michael Williams was the brains out of the pair of them. Well, relatively speaking. Neither of them are bright."

"And where is Barry Rhodes?"

"Well, I would've thought you'd know. Two of your guys nicked him yesterday, from that car park outside. In fact, that's his car there, the red one."

Of course, Himmler knew that.

"Tell me, Herr Rhodes and Herr Williams, were they friendly with a man called Marcus Dauny?"

"Who?"

"I was told he drinks in here. He is, how you say, posh."

"Posh." Flannigan looked up to the ceiling, frowned and then nodded his head. "Ah, yeah, Posh Knob."

"Posh Knob?"

"My nickname for him," Flannigan said with a shrug. "Drinks real ale. Nasty stuff."

"Was he an associate of either Barry Rhodes or Michael Williams?"

"Nah, mate. From different classes, weren't they? I won't say they never spoke – it's a pub, people talk – but that's about it. The posh guy comes in here randomly, usually when we've got a new ale on." Flannigan tapped one of the beer fonts.

Himmler decided they weren't going to get any more useful information out of the barman. He gave his thanks, and he and Zimmerman left the bar. Once they were back in the car, Himmler called up the local Gestapo office and asked for an address for Michael Williams in Eastfield Road. He keyed it into the sat nav and they drove round there.

Williams' house was a mid-terrace which fronted the path. Himmler knocked on the door while Zimmerman looked through the solitary downstairs window. It wasn't a big house. This was something pre-1940s, left in place after the Germans had started to expand Peterborough.

Zimmerman said, "I cannot see anything."

Himmler cursed under his breath. Zimmerman took a pouch of small tools from his pocket, got to his knees and picked the lock. They stepped into the house. It had a musty smell. They searched every room but found no-one. Upstairs, in the main bedroom, the wardrobes were virtually empty. In the kitchen, they found letters addressed to Michael Williams, some unopened.

"He has gone," Zimmerman said.

"So it would appear. The question is, did he go before or after Barry Rhodes was arrested."

"The guy from the bar said he left a week ago."

"Did you believe him?"

"Why would he lie?"

Himmler gave a half smile. "Why would anybody lie, Zimmerman?" He patted Zimmerman's face. "Because they have something to hide."

35

Dauny went to work as normal. At lunchtime, he phoned Owen Dunne, told him he might have a bit of work for him. He didn't elucidate. He invited him down that evening, said he wanted to introduce him to somebody. Owen seemed interested. He phoned Harry Dean, told him he wanted to meet him that evening after work. They arranged to meet at the Sports Club.

Harry was already sat at the bar when Dauny arrived. The landlord was stood with him. He came over and locked the door.

"What's happening?" Dauny asked. The landlord poured him a Victory ale.

"The Gestapo were round here earlier," the landlord said.

"Have you two been formally introduced?" Harry asked. "Tom, Marcus." Dauny shook the landlord's hand.

"The Gestapo?"

"Barry's given up his cover name," Tom said. "They were asking after Michael Williams."

"Who's Michael Williams?"

Harry took a sip from a particularly strong looking lager. "Operatives working on an active mission are given a cover name. A partner, if you like, someone whose name they can give to the Gestapo during interrogation. The idea is when they get arrested, the partner, the cover name, goes to ground. We do our best to make sure they get out of the country. It's preferable to the arrested guy giving up the mission details."

"So he's cracked?"

Harry frowned. "You'd crack as well, Marcus."

"I wasn't being critical," Dauny said. "I was just wondering what that meant for me."

"They asked about you as well," Tom said. "I told them you barely knew one another. Just the odd chat in here at the bar."

"Shit," Harry said. "So they've connected the pair of you."

"Because of the computer access," Dauny said.

"Right, the chances are that Barry has coughed to the computer access along with Michael Williams," Harry said. He rubbed his fingers together as though contemplating something. "Right, we need a reason as to how Barry had your access details."

"He stole your computer?" Tom suggested.

"No good. The Gestapo have my portable computer. They know it wasn't stolen."

"Fuck."

"How about …" Harry and Dauny both looked at Tom. "How about, right, listen to this. How about Barry nicked your diary with all of your passwords in it?"

"I do have a diary but I don't write my passwords down."

"They don't know that."

Harry looked Dauny up and down. He shook his head. "No," he said to Tom. "It's too clichéd. What have you got in your pockets?"

Dauny took out a handkerchief, some change and a wallet. He put them on the bar. Harry and Tom looked at one another.

"What?"

"Wallet," Tom said.

"Somebody stole your wallet," Harry said.

"No, not stole," Tom said. "They'd want to know why he didn't report it."

"You lost your wallet."

"And it had your logon details written down somewhere," Tom said.

"That's what you tell them."

"They questioned me the day we broke into the factory."

"You didn't know then," Harry said. He picked up Dauny's wallet, looked inside, took out the banknotes. "I mean, what's fifty Reichsmarks to a guy like you? You didn't even realize it was gone till a few days later."

Dauny looked between the two of them. Tom straightened his glasses. "If we're thinking how it could've happened that Barry got your access details, you can bet that Barry was thinking how it could've happened as well."

"You can guarantee they're going to question you," Harry said. "But as a loyal Party member, they won't haul your arse down to London and throw you in an interrogation room. You might just end up at the Gestapo HQ in town."

"Well, I must say that makes me feel a hell of a lot better."

"The Polizeipräsidium in London has its own crematorium," Harry said.

"There's a good chance that Barry is now smoke," Tom said. "In the Smoke." Dauny couldn't believe these guys were making light of Barry's fate. "Gallows humour, mate. If you didn't joke about it then you'd have to think about it. And nobody wants to think about it."

"When you give up the information about the wallet, don't make it obvious," Harry said. "You've got to sneak it into the conversation. They're bound to mention Barry. And you say something like, oh, I dunno, 'I thought there was something dodgy about him – I think he was the one who stole my wallet.' Something like that."

"I'm not sure," Dauny said. "What if they torture me?"

"There's a good chance that if they really thought you were a suspect, you'd already be in London getting your legs and arms broken," Harry said.

"But if they do torture me? I know you. I know Tom now."

"I have a cover name," Harry said. "But in any case, I'm *your* cover name. You have to give up a name, you give me up."

"So when they arrest me, you're going to disappear?"

"I'm going to disappear, but I'm not going to leave the country," Harry said. "Not until I'm certain I'm compromised. When you're released, you come here for a drink. Tom will get in touch with me."

"What if they make me give up Tom's name?"

Tom raised an eyebrow. "Then you're fucking barred."

Harry said, "If you give up one name, that's all they expect. In this game, most people only know the name of one other person. If you give up a second name, they will beat you to death to get more and more names out of you." Harry patted him on the arm. "But this, it's all speculation. I can pretty much guarantee you'll have a very polite interview with some fine Gestapo men."

"Knock knock," Tom said.

Dauny frowned. Tom gestured for him to respond. "Er, who's there?"

"Ze Gestapo," Tom said in a ludicrous German accent.

"Ze Gestapo who?"

"Ve vill ask ze questions!"

Dauny laughed in spite of the situation he was currently in.

Harry said, "That joke doesn't improve with age, Tom." Then he seemed distracted by something out of the window. "Who's this?" Dauny turned and looked, and saw a VW Golf pulling into the car park. He recognized the man behind the wheel.

He said, "This is Owen."

"Your computer security guy?"

"Yes." Harry reached inside his jacket, pulled out a pistol. He checked it was loaded. "What the hell is that?"

"I told you," Harry said. "If I feel he can't be trusted, then he has to disappear. For all of our sakes."

Dauny watched as Owen got out of his car, thinking that he was coming to some business deal. He wouldn't know that his life was about to be changed completely over the course of the next few minutes. Tom let him in. Dauny shook his hand, introduced him to everyone. They sat down at one of the tables. Tom brought them all drinks over.

Owen said, "This all looks very secretive."

"It is," Harry said. "Marcus tells us that you're an expert with computers."

"Well, yes, but then so is he?"

"But you're a security expert."

Owen frowned, looked at Dauny. "What's this all about, Marcus."

"Tell me a bit about you, Owen," Harry said. "Your background. Tell me about your mum and dad."

"What's this? Therapy?"

Harry smiled. "Indulge me."

"My mum and dad are English," Owen said. "My dad has his own business. Microchip production. His company is based in Germany. He sent me to university in England. That's where I met Marcus."

"Is your father a Nazi?"

Owen looked at Dauny and he spread out his hands. "What the fuck?"

"Just answer his question, Owen," Dauny said.

"No, my father is not a fucking Nazi. He's just a regular Englishman who works with the government to produce microchips."

"Do you consider yourself English or German, Owen?" Harry asked.

"What is this?"

"Please."

"I'm English. I was actually born in England. My mother lives in England. My father flies back from Hamburg every weekend. Marcus, I thought you said you had a business deal for me."

"This is to do with computers," Harry said. "We need your help."

"Computer security?"

Harry looked at Dauny.

Dauny sighed. They hadn't even told Owen who he'd be working for. Were they leaving that up to him?

Owen shook his head. "Get the fuck out of here, Marcus."

"What?"

"You're working with ... with terrorists?"

Dauny looked at Harry. This didn't seem to be going well. He wondered whether Harry would shoot Owen.

"One man's terrorist," Tom said, "is another man's freedom fighter."

Owen took a sip from his drink and regarded the three of them suspiciously. He looked at Dauny. "What the fuck have you got yourself mixed up in, man?"

"It all made sense a few days ago."

"And now?"

Dauny took a deep breath. "And now, it still makes sense."

Owen leant back in his chair. "I'm not a fool, you know. You guys, I know that if I tell you I'm not interested in what you're telling me, you're just going to kill me. So what then? Do I pretend I'm interested, and then when you let me go, I walk straight to the nearest police station and tell them all about you?"

Harry smiled and leant forwards, onto the table. He downed a mouthful of lager. "I'm going to make it very easy for you, Owen. If you don't want to work with us, then yes, I will have to make you disappear. As for you telling us that you want to work with us, that you're interested, well, it's not as simple as that. You have to convince me. And me, I'm a sceptic."

Owen looked at Dauny.

"Fucking hell, Marcus. Why couldn't you have just come to me? What's this shit all about? These threats?"

"I don't know you well enough to know whether I can trust you, Owen. Not over something like this."

"I knew when you brought your *Trag* round, I knew then that something was going on." Briefly, Dauny considered that he had betrayed his old university friend. But he knew deep down that Owen had no love for the establishment, for the government.

"Are you a Nazi, Owen?" Harry asked him.

"No, I'm fucking not. I dislike politics. I'm neither a Nazi nor am I an English separatist. I don't care. My life, it's simple, it's easy. No problems or issues."

"You're happy with your life?"

"I'm moderately wealthy, I don't get any hassle from the police." Owen looked at Dauny. "Well, apart from the visit from the Gestapo asking whether you'd been round to my house the other week."

"Marcus, tell him what we need him to do," Harry said.

"I need to be able to access the computer network at work," Dauny said. "And I need to do it from an untraceable location. Is such a thing possible?"

Owen raised an eyebrow. The thing with Owen was that he was unable to resist a challenge, particularly one to do with computers. He leant back in his chair, picked up the glass of Riesling Tom had poured him and took a sip. "Marcus Dauny, you are an utter bastard." Dauny smiled. "You know how to hook me, don't you?" He looked at Harry. "Right, I'll tell you this now. I don't give a shit about your cause. It means nothing to me. And that's me being very honest. I hope you appreciate my candour." Harry gave a nod. "But I cannot turn down a challenge like this." He turned back to Dauny. "Is it possible to access a *lokalenetz* from an untraceable location? There are ways to make such a thing possible, most definitely. It depends on the security, of course. I've hacked into other computer systems before. But nothing linked to a government company. I'll have to research this."

"How long will it take?" Harry asked.

"You don't know much about computers, do you, Harry?"

"Nothing at all."

"One day, Harry, everyone will have a computer in their house, and they'll be able to connect to any computer in the world. But not yet, not for many years. In answer to your question, it could take me a week, it could take me longer. Hacking into a system isn't an exact science." Owen looked at Dauny. "Are you going to tell me what part of the system you want to hack?"

"I want to alter the missile control launch software."

"Fuck."

"I can access it through my own sign-on using a back door."

nach Schema F

"Dauny, you put a back door into a government computer system? You're a bad man."

"Every programmer does it."

"Maybe. But at Uni, you were always so straight-laced."

"I have my moments, chap."

Owen looked between Dauny and Harry. "Okay, you've got me. I'll need to know as much about the system as you can find out. And once I've sorted the access for you, I don't want to know what you intend to do. It doesn't interest me."

Harry held out his hand and Owen shook it.

"So, did I pass your test?"

Harry smiled and nodded.

36

Rhodes woke up and found himself lying on what appeared to be a hospital bed. He felt light-headed, but there wasn't much pain. He glanced down at his legs. Metal pins were holding his bones in place. The split skin had been sewn up. Even the blood had been washed away.

He frowned.

He had been expecting them to just summarily execute him, not provide him with healthcare. Why would they go to all this trouble if they were intending to execute him? A nurse came into the room, but she didn't say anything to him. She checked his blood pressure.

"Where am I?" he asked her. She didn't reply. She left the room.

Ten minutes later, the door opened again and the Gestapo man, Schmid, came into the room. He stood by the side of the bed.

"Herr Rhodes, how are you feeling?" Rhodes didn't feel like responding. The German just smiled. "You have been trained well. I admire your defiance. Right now, I would say that you are wondering why we have fixed up your legs, yes?" Schmid sat down on a chair next to the bed. "Well, I believe that you are not Barry Rhodes from Fenland. I believe that your name is something completely different. And I believe that you're from America. But I do not think you want to admit that, do you?" The German shrugged. "No matter. There are ways to get you to talk to me without putting you through pain. Sometimes pain, torture, it is not effective. As I say, you have been well trained." Schmid sighed. "Your friend, Michael Williams, he was not at home when my men went to his house. But I expected that he would have left the moment you were arrested. Criminals, they are like this. Spies also."

"I'm not a spy."

"You have been in England for seven years, and effectively you have just been working in a manual job. There are no state secrets there." Schmid tapped his chin thoughtfully. "So I can only presume that you are here as a sleeper, to be activated when there is a specific task for you to do. Now, I am wondering whether you have been activated. Whether you were in the middle of a specific task when you were arrested." He shrugged. "Well, I dare say you do not want to tell me. We could, of course, torture you again. Put electrodes on your genitals, remove your fingers, your eyes. But once we start to do that, you will realize that we will not be letting you live. And once the pain has reached a crescendo, you know that it will not get any worse. You will give up. But giving up does not necessarily mean that you will *give up* information. Giving up could mean that you have simply given up on life. Torture, sometimes, is counterproductive, particularly when used on trained men. So let us disregard the use of torture. We could of course arrest and interrogate every person who knows you. It is doubtful that these people would be as well trained as you. Whatever they know, they will give it up once we start to beat them. But then, do they have any useful information to give us? Indeed, some people will say anything when they are being tortured. They will tell lies about their friends, their neighbours, their work colleagues, just to make us stop. Again, torture is counterproductive, especially when used on people who have nothing worthwhile to tell us." Schmid looked at his watch. "We have this thing called a 'truth serum'. Now I know you will be thinking that such a thing cannot exist. Can I really give you a drug which will make you reveal all?" He shook his head. "No, it is not this sophisticated. We will give you a cocktail of barbiturates, together with a drug called midazolam. What this will do is relax you. Once you are relaxed, you will start to talk. It does not always work, of course. It is still in the experimental stages. But this is how we will proceed with you, Herr Rhodes." Schmid stood up. "Of course, even if this does not work, we will keep you in protective custody. You are what I would describe as a high-value suspect. We will find some use for you, Herr Rhodes." The German walked to the door. "Make yourself comfortable. You will be our guest for quite some time."

Rhodes watched as Schmid left the room, and he wondered what the future had in store for him. He wondered about this so-called 'truth serum', and he wondered whether it would work.

37

Ellen followed Klarsfeld into his office, shutting the door behind them. He immediately sat behind his desk and she sat down opposite. They had just flown back from Germania. They hadn't spoken much during the flight. The memory of the konzentrationslager was still at the front of her mind.

Klarsfeld took out a bottle of Schnapps and two glasses. He poured them both generous measures, and slid one across the desk towards Ellen.

"Do not tell me that you cannot drink because you are on duty. You are working for me, and I say that it is okay for you to share a drink with me."

Ellen picked up the glass.

"You know, I do control this province. The SS here, they work for me. Theoretically, I can have any investigation stopped. Of course, I cannot control that puppet Mittendorf, the *Arschloch*, but that does not matter. I know that he thinks this room is bugged, but the people who are supposed to be bugging this room, they work for me."

"So we can talk freely?"

"Of course." Klarsfeld sipped from his drink. "The Führer thinks that he can muzzle me. He thinks he can take me away from DSvG, but that is not going to happen. He wants to retire me off but I shall not leave here."

"I am sure that the Führer can make it happen if it is his will."

"This is possible, of course. But perhaps the Führer will not be able to make this decision."

"I do not understand, mein Herr."

Klarsfeld stood up, walked to the window and looked at the view beyond. He said, "The assassination attempt on me was audacious, was it not?"

"It certainly was."

"There was always a risk that it could have gone wrong."

"How do you mean, Herr Klarsfeld?"

Klarsfeld swirled his drink around in the glass. "You think that I did not know it was going to happen?"

Ellen frowned. "I do not understand."

"It was necessary to prove that I am still a loyal Party member," Klarsfeld said. "An attempt on my life. And you, my dear, you stepped in even before my security detail could react. My security detail, they knew all about it." He turned to look at her. "I had words with them, naturally. They were supposed to stop the assassin before he even opened fire. Any bullets he did managed to shoot, they were supposed to miss me. It all could have been so different, so catastrophic."

Ellen still couldn't grasp what Klarsfeld was implying. She shook her head. "You knew there was going to be an attempt on your life?" He nodded his head. "So you know who was responsible for it?"

Klarsfeld smiled. "Of course, my dear. The man who sent somebody to *kill* me, he and I have a similar agenda."

"But they are terrorists, Herr Klarsfeld."

"They want the same things I do, Ellen. How do you think that this assassin knew where I was going to be?"

"My God."

"And now the Führer thinks that I am as hated in the DSvG as he is." Klarsfeld came back to the desk and sat down. "Tell me, Ellen, can I trust you? Or do you still have an undying love for the German Reich? Are you still a loyal Party member?"

Ellen considered how her life was proceeding. She was still very young. She could barely remember living in Germania. Did she even consider herself to be German? When she was undercover, she'd spoken English more than she'd spoken German. Even when she was conducting interviews, more often than not she spoke English because it was the first language for virtually every suspect. She was under no illusion that most of the people here in the DSvG hated her because they thought of her as German. But really, deep down she was almost as English as they were. She just happened to work for the German Reich. She worked in the most hated department as well. The Geheime Staatspolizei was a law unto itself. There were rules, of course there were, but they could quite literally get away with murder.

She thought about Jerome, the man she had fallen in love with. He had been a member of Combat UK. He was, essentially, the enemy. And she had treated him like an enemy at the end. She had had him killed. And it had affected her more than she liked to admit.

The Nazi regime had made her kill the man she loved. To say that she was becoming disenchanted was an understatement.

"Things are happening at the moment," Klarsfeld said. "Big things. Things that will change the status quo. I need to know whether I can rely on you, Ellen."

Ellen blinked. "I think you can, Herr Klarsfeld."

The Reichsstatthalter smiled, nodded his head. "I think SS-Sturmbannführer Loritz likes you, Ellen. He is a powerful man in the SS. Now, you may well think that Mittendorf would be the most powerful man in the SS here, would you not?"

"He is the oberstgruppenführer in charge of the SS in the DSvG."

"He gives orders to people," Klarsfeld said. "It is those people who carry out the investigations. And it is those people who are more valuable to a person like me. Loritz. Tell me about him."

"He is a good officer," Ellen said. "Well respected. I look up to him."

"What I find, Ellen, is that the longer an SS officer works in the DSvG, the more likely they will become native. Loritz, he has worked here for a long, long time. He is ruthless, of that I have no doubt. He is also powerful. As you say, he is respected. But the question is, do you think that he could be turned?"

"No," Ellen said. She was positive that Loritz could not, and mostly definitely would not, be disloyal to the Reich.

"That is disappointing. His men are investigating something I would rather they were not investigating."

"Who are the investigating officers?"

"One of them has ludicrously kept the name Himmler."

"Willi," Ellen said with a smile. "He used to be my work partner, until I was assigned to you."

"And what is he like?"

"He is basically a non-entity," Ellen said, and then shook her head. "I am being disingenuous. Judgemental. I have always found him to be a bit idiotic. Plus he has come on to me a couple of times. And he is also jealous of the way I came through the ranks."

"Can he be turned?"

"He is not significant enough."

"He is the lead investigator. How well do you know him?"

"As a work colleague," Ellen said. "That is all."

"Could you talk to him?" Klarsfeld raised an expectant eyebrow.

"What can I say to him? That I am a disloyal German?"

Klarsfeld gave a half smile. "I do not think you can be that candid, Ellen. I am sure you will play it by ear. But if he can be turned ..."

Ellen recalled Willi Himmler. What did she actually know about him, aside from the fact he was jealous of her success? They'd only ever spoken about work.

She said, "Who is he investigating?"

"A man has been arrested. His fate, well, we cannot ascertain what that might be. And in truth it is of no real concern. But this Himmler is looking into known associates. This could lead to some very valuable people being arrested, being interrogated. People who may well crack."

"I am not sure that I can persuade Himmler to break the rules. The most effective way you can use me, Herr Klarsfeld, is to allow me to go back into the field. To be partnered with Himmler again."

Klarsfeld seemed to consider this for a few moments. He nodded his head. "I can speak with Loritz. I could say that you want to return to active duty. My security is assured, so I no longer need your specialism. Of course, I do not have to tell him that I require your services elsewhere."

"What is the big plan, Herr Klarsfeld?"

"It is best if you do not know, Ellen."

Ellen picked up her drink and had a sip. "I just wonder what I am getting myself into, mein Herr."

Klarsfeld smiled at her.

38

Dauny stepped into the poorly lit pub. They were up in Scotland. Harry had said that they were here to meet somebody important. He'd added that this certain person would reveal the full mission objectives. That was enough to entice Dauny into a visit far up north.

The pub was located down a side street in a small town to the west of Aberdeen. They'd passed a police station on the way here, but Harry had assured him that in this town there wasn't a massive police presence.

The door was shut and bolted behind Dauny. He looked around. The bar was staffed by a single barmaid. Two people were playing darts. A group of men sat on one table chatting quietly. In the corner of the room, a man was reading a newspaper.

Harry led them across to the bar. He ordered a lager for himself and Dauny perused the limited selection of ales and chose the one which looked the least offensive. Harry led them with their drinks over to the man reading the newspaper. They sat down. The man lowered his newspaper. There was something vaguely familiar about his face.

"Mr Dauny, welcome to Scotland." The man held out his hand and Dauny shook it. "I'm Lyle Lovett."

Dauny raised his eyebrows. "I thought you were dead."

"For a while, I felt I was. I bore a heavy burden. But we have regrouped and we're ready to take the fight to Germania." Lovett took a sip from his whisky. "I'm glad that you've chosen to join that fight."

"I wouldn't say I've joined the fight."

"Well, you're helping us," Lovett said. "And I appreciate that."

"Harry said that you were going to tell me what you expect from me," Dauny said. "How you want to utilize my skills."

"All in good time."

"Are we safe here?"

Lovett smiled. "We're very safe here."

"I'm curious how you got my name. Harry spoke of my father."

"I knew your father. He wasn't quite ready to make the commitment, but he considered himself English. I knew that he would instil the same level of Englishness into you. We keep an eye on all possible assets. When

I learnt that you were working for GFW, I knew we had to approach you."

"My computer programming skills."

"And the possibility that you'd worked on something we could use."

"The missile launch control system."

Lovett nodded his head. "I will tell you now, Marcus, that we're working with agents from the United States of America."

"Barry Rhodes was one."

"Yes he was. He will be remembered by us all." They fell silent for a few moments. "Let him not have died in vain."

"So the Americans want access to the missile launch control system?"

"Initially, the idea was to disable the capabilities of Germany to launch its missiles," Lovett said. "But how long would that last before they could repair it?"

"A couple of days. Maybe just a few hours even, depending on what resources they throw at repairing it. They could probably have a backup system online within two or three hours. Of course, it depends whether they discover the fault."

"Well, America does not want to take the chance that Germany will regain the ability to launch a counter-strike. A new plan has been decided."

"Which is?"

"They have an asset in France, someone who works at one of the missile bunkers. He is prepared to launch the missiles in his bunker at Germania. A strike on the capital from within the Greater German Reich, destroying the German leadership."

"My God."

"The Germany that awakes the day after the attack will be a totally different Germany."

"The system won't allow target coordinates to be altered without going through the proper chain of command. Each missile is aimed at a particular strategic target in America, in Canada, in the South American states. Missile Command has the option to initiate launches from any particular silo depending on which targets they want to attack. Silo operators cannot launch independently without Missile Command having authorized the launch."

"And that's where you come in," Lovett said. "Can you change the targets of this particular bunker so that all missiles head for Germania? And can you let the bunker commander launch the missiles without authorization from Missile Command?"

Dauny pondered this request. Firstly, he knew that it was possible he could alter the target database. He also knew he could remove the failsafe for the silos in question. And he knew that he could disable the rest of the system to prevent launches from other silos. But the question was did he want to be responsible for the deaths of millions of innocent people?

He said, "There are twenty million people living in Germania. In the event of a nuclear strike, they would all die." Lovett shrugged. "Not every German is the enemy."

"Germany *is* the enemy," Lovett said. "Therefore all Germans, by default, are the enemy."

"I cannot countenance the murder of twenty million people."

"How many people has Germany killed, put to death in its concentration camps? Men, women, children, innocent people who, by virtue of their ethnicity, Germany has determined had no right to life."

"That doesn't mean that we have the right to condemn innocent Germans to death."

"Marcus, what did you think was going to happen here? Did you think that nobody was going to die as a consequence of your actions?"

Dauny sighed. Of course he knew people were going to die. But twenty million? The realization of that almost crushed him.

"It's just hitting home now."

"I can tell you now, Marcus, that the German Reich is making plans to invade the Americas. They've been pushing their way through the barren wastelands of Russia. Why do you think they're doing that?" Dauny looked at Lovett. "The Bering Straits – mostly ice during the winter, but a narrow piece of water over which they quickly move forces into Alaska. And from there, down through Canada and into the US. The Germans are preparing for war, Marcus. A conventional land war, because neither side will want to launch nuclear missiles. There is this concept—"

"MAD," Dauny said. "An acronym which describes the consequences of the launching of nuclear missiles by either the German Reich or the United States of America. Both sides would be destroyed. Even the Führer isn't crazy enough to launch nuclear weapons at the US."

"And vice versa," Lovett said. "So the war for the Americas will be fought by troops on the ground, by fighters and bombers in the air, by naval forces on the sea. And right now, the German Reich has an army, an air force and a navy almost twice that of the US. The only thing which has prevented the Reich from launching an attack has been the almost insurmountable distance between the two countries. But with the Germans about to gain a springboard from the Asian continent to the Americas, the concept of an invasion of America is tangible. The US can only defend, because they won't be able to get troops onto the European mainland. Bombers, perhaps, but not ground forces." Lovett stared intently at Dauny. "The real fear is that once the Germans start to take over parts of the US, the only response left for the Americans will be to launch nuclear weapons at Germany."

"Mutually Assured Destruction," Dauny said quietly.

"Mutually Assured Destruction," Lovett repeated. "And I can guarantee, Marcus, that a lot more than twenty million people will die if that happens. Much of Europe, much of America, will be a barren wasteland. We have the opportunity to prevent that."

Dauny had to concede that Lovett had made a valiant case for this particular sabotage, but that still didn't make him feel any better about the consequences of what they were asking him to do.

"And here's the bonus. Because the missiles will have been launched from within Germany, initially the German leadership – if any remain – will think that this was an act of rebellion, and the German Reich will be plunged into chaos. Some of the provinces – Britain, Ireland, Spain, Portugal – will declare their independence. The provinces in the Middle East, oil rich states, will declare their independence. The Germans in the provinces will be leaderless and will lose the will to fight. For the deaths of twenty million people, the world will be an entirely different place."

Dauny considered his options for a few moments. Then he said, "How many people were killed in the Reprisal?"

"A hundred thousand," Lovett said.

"And how did you feel about that?"

Lovett looked down at his drink. His face contorted as he struggled with his emotions. "I was almost suicidal, Marcus. It was my fault. I made a huge error."

"Imagine how you will feel after the deaths of twenty million people."

"I will be doing my best not to think of the individuals. The Reprisal was something wholly different. For a start, these were British people. They were being chosen randomly on a daily basis. They were being executed, sometimes in public, as a punishment. When we destroy Germania, it will not be for punishment. It will be because we want to destroy the German Reich."

"Have you lost your resolve, Marcus?" Harry asked him.

Dauny shook his head. "No, I haven't lost my resolve. I'm just trying to reconcile the deaths of twenty million people."

"They will all die instantly," Lovett said. "They won't suffer. The chances are they won't even know what is about to happen to them. The missiles will take twenty minutes to reach Germania. There will be panic at Missile Command, but it's unlikely the people of Germania will be given any warning."

"Twenty minutes? That's enough time for the Führer to escape."

"By helicopter, perhaps. A helicopter can travel at one hundred and eighty miles an hour. It will take a few minutes for Missile Command to clarify that a missile has been launched, that it's not an error. That will then be relayed to the Führer's office. A helicopter will be fired up, the Führer and some cabinet members will board it. They will have a little under ten minutes, maximum, to get out of the blast zone. Ground zero in the centre of Germania will mean an effective blast zone radius of twenty-five miles. For a thirty mile radius, any aircraft in the sky will be knocked down. Add to that the fact that there will be five missile launches, we can ensure that the blast zone radius will be more than forty miles from the centre of Germania."

"That will kill even more people."

"It most certainly will," agreed Lovett. "But it will also kill the Führer."

"A lot of people sacrificed to bring about the death of one man."

"This Führer is undoubtedly the most dangerous leader of Germany since Adolf Hitler," Lovett said. "Some have suggested that he is even more dangerous than Hitler. This is a man who no longer has any internal enemies. He cannot preach to the German people about the bogeyman within. He can only present to them the idea that the Americans are dangerous, that they must be eradicated."

"I've heard this rhetoric before," Dauny said.

"Then you must understand that it is true. How quickly can you complete your objectives?"

Dauny took a deep breath, let out a sigh. "You should understand that the code for the missile launch control system was completed by perhaps fifty different programmers, each working on a different module. We're talking about thousands of lines of code. There is a lot of work involved in altering different procedures. Then we have to hope that I can replace the previously assembled code with what I create. I can't replace code that's running. Essentially, the system has to be closed down, replaced and then rebooted. That would take fifteen minutes, perhaps. It won't go unnoticed."

"So we would need a diversion?"

"I suppose. But what kind of diversion?"

"Could we knock out the power to wherever this computer program is held?"

Dauny smiled, shook his head. "It's not as simple as that," he said. "The program is run from Missile Command. Even if there was a power cut, Missile Command runs on its own independent power. Each of the silos are networked – connected – to Missile Command. Each of those would report a system outage. This isn't something which can be done unnoticed."

"So you're telling me it's not possible for you to replace the computer system?"

"It is possible," Dauny said. "But it will be noticed. It depends how Missile Command responds. It's not unheard of for a system to crash, but to my recollection it's not happened recently."

"What happens when you have to do a software update then?" Lovett asked. Dauny was impressed. This man had done his research.

"The system is duplexed," he said. "There are effectively two versions of the software running. The current one – the live site – and the one which contains updates – the test site. Effectively, a switch is flicked, and the test site becomes the live site and the live site becomes the test site. For a few minutes, both software programs are running at the same time. The test site is booting up, and until it's online the live site remains online. Usually, these occur when there's a scheduled software update."

"When is the next scheduled software update?"

"In two weeks," Dauny said.

"Can you be ready by then?"

Dauny raised an eyebrow. "It would mean working twenty-four hours a day for two weeks."

"Think of the holiday you can have afterwards," Lovett said with a smile.

39

SS-Hauptsturmführer Schottel had been a member of the SS since leaving college. He had served as a loyal soldier in the Waffen-SS, fighting skirmishes against the Muslims in the Middle East when he was in his twenties. There, he had lost his right leg after his unit was ambushed by the Mujahedeen. He'd been rewarded for his bravery with the Order of the Iron Cross 2nd Class together with a Gold Wound Badge.

They'd asked him whether he wanted to be medically retired, but Schottel refused. So they transferred him to Missile Command, where initially he was in charge of one silo. Five years ago, after promotion to hauptsturmführer, he was put in charge of Raketenbunker Grenoble, which housed five silos.

Schottel wasn't married, and that made those around him suspicious. He was, after all, in his late forties. He'd been investigated twice by the Gestapo over accusations of homosexuality. In fact, Schottel was straight, but painfully shy around women. He'd been in just one relationship, when he'd been in his early twenties, before his unit was stationed to Iraq. After his leg had been blown off, his girlfriend left him. Since then, he'd got his sexual fulfilment from whores.

He'd been approached by a volunteer from Vierte Reich just three years ago. He'd been on holiday in Spain. The man who'd approached him had been either brave or stupid. He'd asked Schottel how he'd lost his leg. Something in Schottel's voice must've made him sound disillusioned, because the volunteer had invited him along to a meeting.

Schottel's response had been, "You do know I'm an officer in the Schutzstaffel?" The volunteer had just smiled.

"Of course," he'd said. "You wouldn't be the first SS officer to come to one of our meetings. Though most of them come undercover."

Schottel had not attended the meeting. He had lost more than one colleague to those terrorists. Car bombs, assassinations, brutal beatings. He could not condone such actions. But on the other hand, he had become jaded with the German Reich, with its oppressiveness, its secrecy, with the fact that people he knew had simply disappeared. Though he considered himself to be a loyal German, he did not consider himself to be a Nazi.

Two years ago, he had taken to drinking in one of the more partisan bars in Grenoble. There he had witnessed a young couple dishing out leaflets which detailed the ideology of democracy. He'd followed them outside, asked them to stop. They'd looked terrified. He'd taken them to his car and then sat in it with the engine running.

He'd explained that he wanted to speak with someone in charge.

Over the course of the next six months, he went to clandestine meetings with volunteers from Vierte Reich. They were, naturally, suspicious of him. At the early meetings, he was told that a sniper was watching him. They constantly checked him for surveillance devices. They presented him with the details of members of his family, inferring that they could be killed if he proved to be untrustworthy. But his persistence eventually paid off.

He'd been introduced to an American, an undercover agent from the Central Intelligence Agency. This guy had seemed to know a lot about Schottel, and was very interested in the fact that he commanded a missile bunker.

The American had asked him, "If you could push that button and destroy Germania, would you do it?"

It had been a tough question to answer.

"The Germans want war," the American had said. "They won't stop until they control the entire world. The only way to prevent that is to destroy Germania and kill the Führer and his cabinet. A lot of people will be killed in the process, but compared to the amount of people who will die as a consequence of another world war, it's a small price to pay."

"You want me to kill Germans?" Schottel had said.

The American had nodded his head. "It's possible that's what we will want you to do. It will be a big sacrifice. Are you prepared to do that? To sacrifice twenty million people to kill the Führer and prevent a war?"

Schottel could not truthfully answer. It was true that in the event of a war, in the event of the use of nuclear missiles being authorized, he gave the order to his silo commanders to launch their missiles, to send them on to their targets, where they would take the lives of millions of people. He had said before, to his superiors, to the psychologists who assessed him and his men annually, that he would not think about the individual casualties. He could think only of the target cities, the target bases.

In the case of war, the millions of people he would be killing by launching the nuclear missiles under his command would be on the side of the enemy. But they were still people.

Schottel had looked at the man, had nodded his head.

"Yes. I could do that."

And then, today, he'd received word from his contact in Vierte Reich. A date had been provisionally set. Two weeks. Fourteen days. And then he would have to press the buttons to launch five nuclear missiles at Germania.

There were thirty officers working for him at the bunker. They worked in pairs, in eight-hour shifts, ready to follow his command. None of them knew the targets for any of the missiles in the bunker. That information wasn't necessary in order for them to carry out their job.

Even Schottel didn't know the missiles' targets, just that they would fly across the Atlantic and destroy five places in the United States of America. At least that was the plan for the missiles, until Vierte Reich managed to change the target for each of the missiles to Germania.

Germania, five hundred miles away.

Schottel left the park where the meeting with the Vierte Reich contact had taken place and made his way to his car. He was certain the Gestapo didn't have him under surveillance. They'd have pulled him in by now were that the case. And would the Gestapo really be that interested in a lowly, disabled hauptsturmführer from one of the provinces? After all, what harm could he do? Missiles could not be launched without authorization from Missile Command. He was a neutered officer. Most of the men who worked beneath him sat at their stations reading books or watching television. System checks were carried out on every shift, but they took only an hour to complete. It was not unheard of for his men to drink alcohol at their posts. Nobody was expecting a nuclear war.

Schottel drove to the bunker. There was a detachment from the Waffen-SS on guard duty. Schottel did not have any command responsibilities for them. There were never any more than four guards on duty at any one time. The heavily fortified bunker could only be unlocked either from within or from Missile Command.

Schottel waved at the guards as they let him into the complex. It was rare that they ever bothered to check his credentials. Aside from the gatehouse and the huge circular doorways of the five silos, the only other building was a concrete cube which doubled as an office and rest room for officers going off duty and coming on duty. Occasionally, meetings were held there. The office also housed the sealed doorway behind which was a steel staircase which descended twenty feet below ground. Schottel accessed the intercom and asked for permission to enter. The heavy door slid open. The stairwell beyond was brightly lit. Security cameras were everywhere. Schottel stepped into the stairwell and the door slid shut behind him. At the bottom of the stairs, he reached another door. This one led to the elevator. At this one, he had to use a key-card to access the intercom. Again, he asked for permission to enter. The staff within the bunker would be viewing him on camera. They would also be checking for any unauthorized personnel within the stairwell.

The heavy door slid open to reveal a pair of elevator doors. Schottel used his key-card again on the control panel, and the doors parted for him. He stepped into the elevator. As it descended the fifty metres down to the concrete bunker, Schottel contemplated his future.

He very much doubted he would live to regret being the man responsible for killing twenty million Germans. Missile Command would immediately question the launching of the missiles. His men would question his actions. One of them would undoubtedly shoot him. They were all loyal officers of the Schutzstaffel. The Waffen-SS would be allowed to enter the bunker. If his own men hadn't shot him by them, they would either arrest or shoot him. If they arrested him, he was sure to be tried for treason and executed.

He closed his eyes.

The elevator halted and the doors slid open. He walked into a small room which had a set of double doors opposite the elevator. Once again, he spoke into an intercom before he was granted access. The doors opened for him and he stepped inside.

Immediately, he was in the bunker office. A corridor led to each of the five silos under his command. Video monitors displayed what was happening in each of the silo offices. The door leading into each silo office could only be opened from the inside or from Missile Command.

Schottel peeled off his jacket and hung it on the coatrack. He sat down at his desk and looked at the monitors. Some of the ten men on shift were sleeping. Others were reading or watching TV. He could see bottles of schnapps on desks in each of the offices. Nobody here took their job seriously.

Schottel spoke to each of the silos, asked them how their shifts were going. The responses were noncommittal and uninterested. It wasn't that his men didn't respect him. It was just that this wasn't like a combat unit. None of them seemed to think that they required discipline. None of them ever expected to have to launch a missile.

Schottel switched on the air conditioning and the stifling heat in his office seemed to blow away, to be replaced by a cold chill.

His eyes fell upon the map of the Greater German Reich on one wall of the office, and the chill seemed to ascend his spine until he had no choice but to shudder.

40

SS-Sturmbannführer Loritz put down the report and looked up at Schmid, his junior. In a way, the contents of the report had been soothing to him. It meant that his judgement was still sound.

"So she is clean?"

Schmid nodded. "Yes, mein Herr. There are no financial irregularities in any of her bank accounts. There was nothing in her apartment, no seditious material, no contentious books. Her telephone records do not cause any suspicion. She lives alone. She seems to live a simple existence. No overt displays of extravagance. She has not been socializing since her secondment to the Reichsstatthalter's security detail. The untersturmführer seems to be dedicated to her job."

"Good. I would not have liked to see her arrested. That would imply that I was placing trust in people undeserving of it."

"I would not expect you to make such an error in judgement, mein Herr."

Loritz closed Schmid's report and opened another. "This one, Schmid, is Brauchitsch's report on Reichsstatthalter Klarsfeld. Her assignment, it would seem, is over."

"Her verdict?"

Loritz smiled tightly. "She has a similar opinion of Klarsfeld as you have about her. The Reichsstatthalter has requested that she be returned to active duty. He says that her appointment as his head of security is hindering her career. He suggests a promotion."

"A promotion?" Schmid raised an eyebrow. He seemed put out, and Loritz knew why. Promoting Brauchitsch would put her on an equal rank to Schmid.

"She has proven to be a resourceful and effective investigator, though I have to say that she is not a good interrogator." Loritz shrugged. "But then we all have our faults and we cannot all be good at everything. I myself tried to learn to play the guitar when I was in my twenties. I gave up after three weeks. The guitar, sadly, passed away when I gave up trying to learn." He smiled at the memory. He'd smashed the acoustic guitar to pieces and thrown it in the trash. "I am going to put her in charge of Himmler and Zimmerman." He looked at Schmid and raised a calming hand to forestall any protests. "Of course that was initially your investigation, but you have Barry Rhodes to deal with now. I will send the three of them back up to Peterborough to investigate fully all of the potential contacts to Rhodes. In the meantime, I want you to continue questioning him. He is undoubtedly an American spy and he knows a lot more than he is letting on."

"My next step will be to use the truth serum."

Loritz snorted a laugh. "Well, if it works, I will be impressed. You know, however, that I have my doubts as to its effectiveness. But I agree with your initial assessment after your first interrogation. Rhodes will not succumb to further torture. That in itself would suggest CIA training. I shall give you another week to gather any further useful information. After that, I will suggest to SS-Oberstgruppenführer Mittendorf that he be tried as a spy. Undoubtedly he will raise this with the Reichsführer, who will then, naturally, consider all of the diplomatic implications." Loritz shrugged. He was becoming cynical about the current leadership. Political motivation seemed more important to the Führer and the Reichsführer. Of course, he would never voice such opinions to anyone, much less a junior officer. "It might be that our leaders will decide that it is better for Rhodes to just die."

Schmid said, "That would be a shame, mein Herr. He could be a valuable source of information."

"If you could break him, then yes, yes he would be a valuable source of information. But I rather think that would be an unlikely outcome." Loritz placed Schmid's file in a tray on the left side of his desk. "I shall keep you from your duties no longer, Herr Obersturmführer."

Schmid stood up and saluted. "Heil Führer!"

Loritz raised a languid arm. "Heil Führer," he said, and watched as Schmid left his office.

As he waited for his next appointment, Loritz took out his sketchpad and opened it onto a sketch he'd been working on. This one depicted Ellen Brauchitsch reclining naked on a sofa. Of course, it was created from his imagination. He had no idea what her body was like. But he had given her average sized breasts and slender legs. However, it was her face which he had so accurately captured. Her expression, again created from his imagination, was one of innocence. A half-smile, one eyebrow slightly raised.

Loritz worked on her face, redefining her nose, putting in a subtle shadow to imply that the light was coming from her right. He played with her hair, adding more bangs until it was more a fantasy view of the subject rather than an accurate portrayal.

His intercom buzzed.

Loritz put the sketch pad in one of the drawers in his desk, locked it, and put the key in his pocket. He told his secretary to send in his next appointment.

SS-Untersturmführer Ellen Brauchitsch entered his office. She wore a smart trouser suit. She offered a salute and Loritz responded in kind. He gestured for her to be seated.

"Frau Brauchitsch, how was Germania?" he said.

"It is a beautiful city, mein Herr. Much changed since I was last there."

Loritz smiled. "And your meeting with the Führer and Reichsführer-SS Schaemmel?"

"Daunting."

"I can imagine, though I did hear from the Reichsführer's office that both he and the Führer were impressed with your comportment." Loritz opened the report on his desk. "I have read your report on the Reichsstatthalter with interest, Frau Brauchitsch. And on this I must surely trust your judgement. You will, of course, be aware that your investigation was initiated from the Reichsführer's office. I have sent a copy of the report to them. I am sure that they will be happy with what they read."

"Thank you, mein Herr."

"And of course, Reichsstatthalter Klarsfeld was similarly impressed with you," Loritz said. "He told me that regretfully he must dispense with your services as he felt that you would be better placed back in active service." Brauchitsch nodded. It was highly likely that Klarsfeld would already have discussed this issue with her. "He also recommended that you be given a promotion."

"A promotion?"

Loritz smiled. He retrieved a letter from the tray on the right side of his desk. He scanned through it. It was addressed to Brauchitsch. It was confirming her promotion to obersturmführer and her new pay grade. Loritz took out a pen and signed the letter. He handed it over.

nach Schema F

"Congratulations, SS-Obersturmführer Brauchitsch." She flushed, read the letter, then held it tightly. "I have a new assignment for you. You will, of course, remember your old partner Willi Himmler."

"Of course, mein Herr."

"He is now partnered with a somewhat zealous young officer called Zimmerman." Loritz grabbed another file from his in-tray. He handed it over. "They are investigating Combat UK links in Peterborough. I am sure you can remember Peterborough."

"Yes, mein Herr."

"You are to be the lead investigator. Get yourself up to speed tonight and then meet up with Himmler and Zimmerman tomorrow morning. I want the three of you to travel back up to Peterborough and go hunting."

Brauchitsch stood up and saluted. Loritz watched her leave his office.

He took out his sketchpad and looked at the nude he had drawn.

He wished he had contemplated using colours. Had he done so, he could've shown her flushing cheeks.

41

Ellen hadn't been expecting the promotion. Were she not in the situation she found herself in – working for the enemy of the Reich – she might well have been pleased, felt proud of herself. She most certainly would have contacted her parents to let them know.

But she could hardly celebrate.

That evening, she read the file Loritz had given her, whilst curled up on her sofa listening to Wagner. There were the personnel files for Himmler and Zimmerman, together with their own reports of their investigations into Barry Rhodes's background.

Rhodes had apparently been a regular at the Bretton Sports and Social Club in Peterborough. The man who had attempted to assassinate the Reichsstatthalter, Dougie Hardcastle, had also drank at the Bretton Sports and Social Club. Ellen could remember interviewing a man by the name of Harry Dean, an associate of Hardcastle and also a regular at the club. Rhodes had apparently stolen the security pass of a man called Marcus Dauny, another drinker at the club.

Every single fact seemed to point in the direction of the Bretton Sports and Social Club.

Ellen was surprised that nobody had yet seemed to connect all of the dots. Of course, on Klarsfeld's instructions she herself was not meant to connect all of the dots. Indeed, she was emphatically supposed to persuade Himmler and Zimmerman *not* to connect all of the dots. And yet there was that natural investigative instinct within her that wanted to learn the truth.

She wanted to know what Klarsfeld's plan was.

When she arrived at the Polizeipräsidium the following morning, Ellen immediately accessed the computer system. Information about Barry Rhodes was restricted, and though she'd been promoted, her access level had not yet been altered. She keyed in the name Marcus Dauny and did a search. Dauny had been subjected to a routine stop and questioning some weeks ago. The report specified that he'd been seen leaving the Bretton Sports and Social Club, and had been warned by SS-Sturmbannführer Huber of the Peterborough Geheime Staatspolizei that he risked being approached by undesirables if he frequented such establishments.

Ellen wondered what kind of work Herr Dauny was involved in. The man was an Engländer, but a Party member. He drove a BMW, so he was moderately wealthy. She looked up his occupation. Software engineer, working for Gerhard Fieseler Werke. She researched that company and discovered that they created applications for government computer systems, much like the one she was currently accessing.

She could see now why Dauny was considered to be at risk from undesirables.

And Rhodes had stolen Dauny's work pass and had apparently accessed the GFW computer system from a location within Peterborough. He'd been investigated by SS-Obersturmführer Mann of the Breitnetzsicherheit, before being handed over to Schmid for further investigation. That's where the information stopped.

Everything continued to point towards the Bretton Sports and Social Club.

Himmler came into the room trailing another man with him.

"Ah, Frau Obersturmführer Brauchitsch," he said. "Must we both salute you like underlings?"

"Don't be an arsehole, Willi," Ellen said, getting to her feet. She shook Himmler's hand, and then Zimmerman's. Zimmerman was tall, thin, with a ferret-like face. "Who is driving?"

"I will," Zimmerman offered.

They made their way down to the car park.

"So, Frau Obersturmführer, what is our plan of attack?" Himmler asked.

"I want to visit the Bretton Sports and Social Club," Ellen said. "All of the recent suspicious activity in Peterborough seems to emanate from that particular place."

"It is just full of Engländer louts," Himmler scoffed. "Myself and Zimmerman visited there a few days ago."

"Yes," Ellen said as they reached the black M3. "I read your reports."

"You sound like you are questioning," Himmler said from over the roof of the car.

Ellen smiled courteously. "Think of it more as a colleague offering a second opinion." The three of them got into the car, Zimmerman behind the wheel, Ellen in the passenger seat and Himmler in the rear. Ellen had the reports from the two of them in her hands, together with some printouts about Marcus Dauny, Barry Rhodes, Dougie Hardcastle and Harry Dean.

Her main problem was how to investigate the connection between all of them without alerting either Himmler or Zimmerman to whatever plot Klarsfeld was hatching. Satisfying her own curiosity could ultimately lead to the plot being revealed to the Gestapo.

Within ninety minutes, they were pulling into the car park of the Bretton Sports and Social Club. From the rear of the car Himmler said, "They will be offering me an honorary membership at this rate."

Ellen instructed Zimmerman to stay with the car. She didn't know him and she didn't trust him. She led Himmler into the club. Sport was playing on the large TVs dotted around the bar, but the sound was down. A jukebox was playing 1960s music. Engländer bands, of course.

Ellen caught the attention of the man behind the bar and he wandered over, adjusting his glasses.

"What can I get you, me duck?"

Ellen smiled. "We would just like to ask you a few questions."

"Me? I'm flattered."

"You are Tom Flannigan, yes?" He seemed surprised. She'd read his name in Himmler's report. Flannigan nodded his head. "I would like to talk to you about some of your customers."

Flannigan looked around the empty bar. "Gerry's out the back having a fag," he said. Ellen smiled.

"It is not Gerry we want to talk to you about."

Flannigan looked at Himmler. "Your mate here, he's already spoken to me about Barry Rhodes and Michael Williams. A right dodgy pair, that's all I can say about them."

"I am sure. But there are two other gentlemen I would like to ask you about."

"Okay."

"First, can you tell me about Harry Dean?"

"Well, you questioned him yourself a few weeks ago," Flannigan said. "He's a huge guy, works in a factory – I think it's RuprechtWerk. Drinks Doppelbock mostly, but I only let him have two or three pints of the stuff. Loopy juice, that is, ten percenter."

Ellen nodded. Flannigan was telling her stuff she wasn't interested in. She said, "Who does he associate with?"

"Well, he'll have a drink with anybody in here," Flannigan said. "This kind of pub, it doesn't matter if you actually know anyone. Everyone's friendly."

"Does he come in here regularly?"

"Two or three times a week."

Somebody entered from a door to the rear of the club, some old guy, who wandered over to a table where a dirty looking ale was waiting for him. This was, presumably, Gerry the smoker.

Flannigan was being deliberately evasive. Ellen was reminded of the pub Jerome used to drink in, one which was a meeting place for Combat UK terrorists. The Pig and Whistle. This club, it bore similarities to the Pig and Whistle insomuch as it set alarm bells ringing in Ellen's head.

"Tell me, does Herr Dean associate with a gentleman called Marcus Dauny?"

"The posh guy?" Flannigan looked at Himmler. "As I told your mate, he'll chat with anyone, Dauny. He likes the real ale here. I don't drink that muck myself."

"So Herr Dean and Herr Dauny are associates?"

"I wouldn't go that far. They're occasional drinking buddies."

"Does Herr Dauny come here often?"

Flannigan shook his head. "Maybe once a week. We show the football here a lot and I get the impression he's more of a cricket or rugby fan. Like I say, he seems to like the ale, and I suppose that once in a while he likes to mix with the hoi polloi, what with him being a posh bloke and all that."

Ellen looked around the club. A couple of England pennants were hung from the top of the bar, but that in itself was not illegal. Most provinces in the Greater German Reich were allowed to display some form of national identity, particularly when it came to sports. There was an English football team, just as there were teams for all of the provinces in the Reich. They competed in the Reich Cup every two years. The old man sitting in the corner quietly sipping his ale was reading one of the State-approved newspapers. Ellen could almost guarantee that if she brought a search team in here, and they ripped the place apart, they'd find nothing of interest.

"How long have you worked here, Herr Finnegan?"

"A couple of years," the landlord said. "I've worked in the catering industry all of my life. Worked down in London for a few years, but I've come back home."

"You are originally from Peterborough?" Finnegan nodded. "I see." Ellen knew that she should now be prying into this man's background, sourcing every tiny detail about him, trying to find something to haul him in for interrogation. The Gestapo officer inside her was bristling. She didn't like the way this man was being so evasive.

She had to bite her tongue.

He knew something, that was for sure.

She thanked him and then she and Himmler left the club.

Back in the car, Himmler said, "What do you think?"

"It is the same as the last time we were here, Willi. Just obnoxious Engländers who secretly despise us. That man back there, he is just a fool. He pours beer and liquor for drunken Engländers." She leant her head against the side window. "He had nothing to offer us," she said, and she felt terrible because she knew she sounded lackadaisical and unprofessional.

"Where to?" Zimmerman asked.

"To Herr Dauny's address," Ellen told him. "Let us see what a loyal Party member has to tell us."

42

There was a car parked on Dauny's driveway, so Ellen presumed he must be at home. Zimmerman parked the M3 lengthways across the entrance to the driveway. Usual Gestapo tactic to prevent an easy getaway. Ellen presumed that Dauny would have something slightly more valuable to offer her. She turned to Himmler.

"You stay here, Willi," she said. "Let us give Zimmerman some experience of my methods."

"Your methods suck arse, Ellen," Himmler said, shaking his head.

"Insubordination, Willi," Ellen said with a smile as she climbed out of the car. As she walked past Dauny's BMW, she took a look inside. There was nothing of importance on show. Just a scarf on the passenger seat and a pair of driving gloves on top of the dashboard.

She rattled the door knocker. Moments later, Dauny opened the door. She showed him her badge.

"Herr Dauny, I am SS-Obersturmführer of the Geheime Staatspolizei. This is my colleage, SS-Untersturmführer Zimmerman. May we come in?"

"Yes, of course," Dauny said. He was dressed in slacks, a shirt, a pair of brown brogues. They went into his front room. "Please, take a seat." They all sat. "I'm presuming this is about my *Trag*? Obersturmführer Mann assured me it would be returned to me."

Ellen smiled tightly. "I wondered if I might ask you a few questions about your work."

"Certainly."

"You are a member of the Nazi Party, yes?"

"Of course," Dauny said, beaming brightly.

"Of course, yes. This much I know. I am a little curious as to the nature of your work. You work for Gerhard Fieseler, yes?"

"GFW, yes. I've worked there since leaving university."

"You are a software engineer?"

"Yes, computer programmer. It isn't as glamorous as it sounds." He said this with a charming smile.

Ellen raised an eyebrow. "I would not have considered it glamorous in any case, Herr Dauny." The Engländer's smile dropped. "Presumably you work on a particular government computer system, yes?" He nodded. "Which system is that, Herr Dauny?"

Dauny frowned. "Frau Obersturmführer, I have signed the Official Secrets Act. I cannot reveal the exact nature of my work. Alas, not even to a member of the Geheime Staatspolizei."

Ellen cursed herself. Of course he wouldn't tell her. It would be improper of him to do so. And right now he was probably thinking that she was trying to catch him out.

She smiled as though he'd passed her test.

"Of course not. You are, however, a valuable asset, and I am concerned about the fact that you have been linked to subversive elements."

"Subversive elements?"

"Barry Rhodes. He is currently in protective custody."

"I don't know him," Dauny said. There was a barely concealed look of panic on his face. "Not personally. I mean, I understand he drinks sometimes in the Bretton Sports and Social Club, but I'm only vaguely acquainted with him."

"It is believed that Rhodes accessed GFW's computer system using your access details, Herr Dauny."

"Yes, I have been thinking about that. My wallet went missing a few weeks ago. I was quite disappointed when I discovered its loss because it was a present from my late father. I keep my works pass in my wallet. I can only presume that Rhodes stole it."

"When did you notice your wallet was missing?" Ellen knew that his story matched that given by Rhodes, but all the same she suspected Dauny was lying.

"It was a few days later."

"A few days later? Did you not need your pass in order to access your place of work?"

"The security there know me," Dauny said. "It's rare that I've been asked to show my pass. Of course, when I noticed that it was missing, I reported it to the security team, and I believe it has since been deactivated. In any case, whoever stole it would not be able to get inside the GFW building. As I say, the security team know pretty much everyone who works there by sight. And of course, my user name and password have since been altered." Dauny looked sheepishly between

Ellen and Zimmerman. "And naturally, I have received a reprimand for losing my pass."

"Naturally," Ellen said. "I notice that you have not yet purchased the Audi you were interested in a few weeks ago."

Dauny frowned. "I'm sorry?"

"You visited a showroom the day your logon details were used," Ellen said, hoping that her change in subject would discombobulate Dauny. "I just note that you have not yet changed your car."

"No, I didn't change my car. I changed my mind instead."

"Tell me, Herr Dauny, what is your opinion about the so-called English resistance?"

"Is there still such a thing?" Dauny asked her. "Wasn't Combat UK eradicated over a year ago?"

"The attempt on Reichsstatthalter Klarsfeld's life would seem to suggest otherwise."

"There are always lunatics who still want to fight for a lost cause."

"So you think English resistance is a lost cause?"

"Isn't it? It's been over fifty years since England became part of the Greater German Reich. Most people can only remember being a citizen of the Greater German Reich. I can only remember that. Those who can remember the United Kingdom were either very young at the time or else are very old now. It's time for them to give up the fight."

Ellen smiled. She thought, but didn't say, *spoken like a true Party member*. She turned to Zimmerman, as though asking him whether he had anything to add. The untersturmführer shook his head. Ellen got to her feet and the two men did likewise.

"Well, Herr Dauny, I must thank you for your time." At the door, she turned to the Engländer. "You will, of course, get in touch if ever any subversive elements should try to approach you?"

"Of course."

"Good day, Herr Dauny."

Back in the car, she gave Himmler the general gist of the conversation.

"So he has nothing to hide?" Himmler asked.

"Oh, come on, Willi," Ellen scoffed. "Everybody has something to hide, including you."

"I have nothing hide, Ellen."

Ellen laughed. "If you say so, Willi. I, for one, know that you have a thing for that young rottenführer, Frau Raubel." She looked at Himmler and he blushed. "We all have something to hide, but some of us have no secrets."

"Whatever, Ellen. Where to now?"

"To Gerhard Fieseler Werke," Ellen told Zimmerman. If Dauny wouldn't tell her what he did for GFW, she was certain his boss would.

43

The truth serum was ready. Of course, SS-Obersturmführer Schmid was not fully convinced it would work, but he believed that not even the infamously brutal SS-Sturmscharführer Keitel could torture the truth out of Rhodes, so he would have to employ other methods.

Loritz had given him limited time to interrogate Rhodes further, and it was apparent that he did not believe that Schmid would succeed. It wasn't so much a lack of faith in Schmid's abilities. Rather, it was more indicative of Loritz's suspicious of Rhodes.

Schmid was certain that Rhodes was an American spy, and Loritz clearly concurred, but he felt it unlikely that he would be used as a political bargaining point. At the moment, for instance, Schmid knew that the Foreign Secretary, Michael Fleischer, was brokering a trade deal with the USA, and declaring Rhodes to be an American spy would undoubtedly create a diplomatic incident which would jeopardize relationships between the two countries.

Politics.

Schmid despised politics. Secretly, he thought that the leaders of the Greater German Reich should never engage in any political discourse with the USA. To Schmid, it was a sign of weakness. Eventually the American countries would be consumed by the Greater German Reich.

Schmid was in his office, preparing to descend to the interrogation block where a doctor would administer the concoction of barbiturates which would hopefully loosen Rhodes's lips. The phone call from the block had come through just moments ago, disturbing his quiet contemplation about Ellen Brauchitsch. In a way, he had been desperate to uncover some evidence of betrayal. She had a reputation as being an arrogant investigator, perhaps even immature, but when he'd had her apartment searched and had questioned her, she seemed a different person. What perturbed Schmid was that Loritz seemed to favour her, and her promotion was a frustrating turn of events. She was now the same rank as Schmid. She was also ten years younger than him. As far as Schmid was concerned, she'd just been in the right place at the right time.

In any case, he didn't trust her. She had a chequered history.

Infiltrating Combat UK, together with the rumours that she'd fallen for one of the terrorists. Those kinds of rumours, they could destroy a career. They should certainly have destroyed hers.

Schmid shrugged off thoughts of Ellen Brauchitsch and made his way down to the interrogation rooms. There, he met Keitel, the huge German who had, at one time, been SS-Sturmbannführer Loritz's right-hand man, but now belonged to Schmid. Keitel barely spoke, but seemed to have developed a form of telepathy with those he worked for, understanding, without prompting, precisely what was required of him during interrogation sessions. He was smoking a cigarette as he stood outside the room where Rhodes was located.

"Is the doctor here?" Schmid asked him.

Keitel gave a curt nod, and gestured with his head to a group of people stood in the reception area. There were a couple of Waffen-SS officers, and a female SS officer bearing the insignia of obersturmführer, together with a red cross, denoting her as medical staff.

"Frau Doktor?" Schmid said loudly. The woman turned, saw Schmid, and then said her goodbyes to the Waffen-SS men. She wandered over.

"Obersturmführer Schmid?" Schmid nodded. "I am Doktor Corcilius."

"Good day, Frau Doktor," Schmid said, bowing slightly.

Corcilius looked at Keitel. "You know, Herr Sturmscharführer, smoking will one day kill you. And believe me, it is not a good death." Keitel just smirked and took another drag from his cigarette before tossing it to the floor and crushing it beneath a heavy boot.

The doctor was carrying a medical bag. She gestured to the door. "He is in there, I presume?"

Schmid turned to Keitel. "Is he strapped down?" The big man nodded. The three of them entered the room. Rhodes was lying down on a gurney, his arms spread outwards, the skin exposed. He was strapped in place. Schmid stepped up to him so the spy could see him.

"Herr Rhodes, I hope you are not too uncomfortable."

"Fuck you," Rhodes said. He spoke quietly. Schmid was, however, impressed by his show of defiance.

He said, "They have trained you well, Herr Rhodes, the Central Intelligence Agency. But allow me to introduce you to Doktor Corcilius." Rhodes's eyes fell upon the female. She was in her forties, her SS uniform finished off by the knee-length skirt and the small black heels. She was opening her medical bag, and displayed no interest towards the prisoner. "How are your legs, Herr Rhodes? I understand you have been given painkillers?" The prisoner didn't respond. As a person trained in interrogation techniques by his CIA masters, he ought not to have even sworn at Schmid. But Schmid knew that emotions could overcome training.

Corcilius took out a syringe, together with three vials of what Schmid presumed were the barbiturates she was going to administer. She filled the syringe with one of the drugs and stepped over to the gurney.

"This is sodium thiopental," she explained, more to Schmid than to the prisoner. "It will make the patient more talkative." She injected the drug into Rhodes, who flinched when the needle was inserted. Then she stepped back.

Rhodes blinked nervously and lay his head back on the gurney. He started to breathe heavily. Schmid stepped up to him and looked down at his face.

"Herr Rhodes, are you with us?"

Rhodes fixed his eyes on Schmid.

"What do you want?"

Schmid smiled. "Just a little chat."

"I don't know anything."

"I am sure you do not. However, we can just talk, can we not?"

"What about?"

"About you, Herr Rhodes. Tell me about yourself."

"I work on a farm. I drive tractors. Lorries sometimes."

"You are a farmer?"

"A farm hand."

"A farm hand. That is interesting. You like working outdoors, Herr Rhodes? In the sunshine, yes?"

"There's not much sun in the Fens," Rhodes said. "It's cold and windy sometimes."

"I imagine it is, being right on the coast. Tell me about your house, Herr Rhodes."

"It's nothing special," Rhodes said. He squeezed his eyes shut. "It's nothing. It's nothing to do with you."

"Ach, come on, Herr Rhodes, you are with friends."

"You're not my friends, none of you."

"Who are your friends, Herr Rhodes?"

"Nobody. I don't have any friends."

Schmid noticed that Rhodes's accent had changed slightly. His words were slightly slurred, so he would've expected that, but the accent was shifting away from what he would describe as one belonging to an Engländer.

"Then I feel sorry for you, Herr Rhodes. We all need friends."

"Friends are trouble," Rhodes said.

"Yes, yes they can be trouble. They sometimes expect things from us that we are not prepared to give. Sometimes they want us to do things which would get us into trouble."

"I have no friends," Rhodes said. "Just associates."

"Associates?"

"Acquaintances." He struggled to get the word out. His eyes were closed now. He said, "I'm not saying another word to you."

"Tell me about your house, Herr Rhodes."

"It's just a small cottage on the coast, nothing special."

"I bet you have lovely views?"

"Yeah, I want to go back there."

"Go back? Back home?"

"Yeah, go back home."

"Where is home?" Schmid asked.

"On the Fens."

Schmid shook his head. "Tell me about the house you grew up in."

Rhodes opened his eyes and looked at Schmid. He seemed to be fighting with some internal torment. He shook his head. "I don't remember," he said.

"Oh, come, you must remember. The house where I grew up, it was not in England. It was in Bavaria. My parents, they had a smallholding. They used to tend chickens. My father, he worked as a lecturer. He is retired now." Schmid smiled at Rhodes. "Tell me about your parents' house."

"It was a big house. With a view of the sea."

"You like to live on the coast then?"

"It makes me feel free," Rhodes said.

"Do you not feel free then?"

"Not here, not in England, not in the Reich."

"When did you last feel free?"

"A long time ago," Rhodes said. "I can't remember. It's so long ago."

"Was that when you were living with your parents?"

Rhodes nodded. "I want to go to sleep."

Schmid looked at Corcilius who shook her head slightly, as though this was of no concern.

"You can sleep soon, Herr Rhodes. Tell me why you are here."

"You brought me here."

"I mean here, why you are in England."

"I'm working here."

"What is your work?"

"It's a secret," Rhodes said and then shook his head. "Fuck. It's farm work, that's all. Farm work." He closed his eyes. "I need to sleep." His breathing started to become heavy.

Corcilius went over to Rhodes, checked his pulse. She raised his eyelids, looked at his pupils.

"It is not an exact science," she said. "He is asleep." She turned to Schmid. "Too much of the drug and he will fall asleep, too little, and he will not talk. We have to get the balance right. It never works the first time." She gave a shrugged. "Sometimes, it does not work at all. But this was a promising first session."

"He did not tell us anything worthwhile," Schmid said.

"Did he talk more than he did when you interrogated and tortured him?" the doctor asked.

Schmid had to concede that Rhodes had been more loquacious during this session than he had when Keitel had broken his legs. "He spoke more, certainly."

"The key thing, Herr Obersturmführer, is to ask the subject leading questions. Lull him into a false sense of security." Corcilius started to pack her stuff away. "He will be out of action for the rest of today. Tomorrow, I will give him a slightly smaller dose. You should be able to talk for longer. In the meantime, think of how you can get the best information out of him without asking him direct questions." She walked to the door. "I should advise you, however, that it may be possible that he will not reveal anything of consequence. Be prepared for disappointment." And with that, she left the interrogation room.

Schmid turned to Keitel, who was wearing a sceptical expression.

"I know that you do not believe this will work, Herr Sturmscharführer, but even you must concede that breaking his legs achieved nothing." Schmid let out a sigh. "I believe that even if you cut off this man's balls, he would tell us nothing of consequence."

Keitel took a packet of cigarettes from his pocket, lit one and took a languid drag. He gave a shrug, but something in his eyes told Schmid that irrespective of whether Rhodes would talk or not, he was keen to cut the man's balls off.

44

The man sitting behind the desk was in his fifties. He spoke in the accent of a man who'd been born and brought up in Germania. Ellen already knew that Herr Heerwagen had only been in the DSvG for six months, that he'd transferred here from the main Gerhard Fieseler Werke offices in the Reich's capital. She'd read up on him before her and Himmler had come to the office in Peterborough. Heerwagen was short, stocky, his hair long and grey. His moustache, in contrast, was a deep black. He smelt of expensive cologne and cheap deodorant. When he'd shaken her hand, his grip was firm, and his wrist seemed weighed down by the expensive Rolex watch he was wearing.

The desk between him and the two Gestapo officers was fine oak, and was home to a computer workstation and two telephones. Three framed photographs were alongside an in-tray, angled so that Ellen could see they were of him and his family together. Heerwagen was a loyal Party member, had been a member of the Hitlerjugend before signing up to the Party when he'd turned eighteen. A hakenkreuz hung from the wall to the side of his desk and there was a framed print of Adolf Hitler on the wall opposite. Though he wasn't wearing an armband, Ellen put that down to the fact that he was in his shirtsleeves, his jacket hanging on the coatrack just inside his office door.

She said, "We are here to discuss one of your employees. Marcus Dauny."

"Ah, Herr Dauny, yes," Heerwagen said with a smile that was perfunctory rather than genuine. "He is one of our Engländers. We were obliged to take on a number of English workers many years ago. Some are more effective than others. However, Herr Dauny is a trusted worker and a loyal Party member."

Ellen nodded. "I understand that Herr Dauny recently received a reprimand for a breach of security."

"Regrettably so," Heerwagen said. "A blot on his personnel file. He lost his works pass, which resulted in our system becoming compromised. I understand that the Breitnetzsicherheit became involved, but I am sure that you are already away of this, Frau Obersturmführer."

"What can you tell my colleague and I about the security breach?"

"Herr Dauny's works pass was used to access our lokalennetz. No files of consequence were accessed, but the unauthorized access was brought to the attention of the Geheime Staatspolizei."

"And Herr Dauny," Ellen said. "What can you tell us about him?"

"Up until this incident, we had no concerns about him," Heerwagen said. "Indeed, I would say that this whole thing is nothing more than a moment of stupidity. We are all vulnerable to moments of stupidity. Herr Dauny is an Engländer, and I am led to believe that he likes to drink alcohol on occasion, as all Engländers do. He has been reprimanded and advised to moderate his drinking and to drink in more suitable establishments."

"You are still happy to employ him then?"

"Of course. His work ethic is unquestionable. He is a valued member of the team."

"I am curious as to how Herr Dauny was permitted to enter your offices without his works pass," Ellen said. Heerwagen seemed to squirm uncomfortably in his otherwise comfortable leather chair. "This would suggest, of course, that your office's security practices are in doubt."

"Naturally, once this was brought to our attentions, we ensured that our security efforts were improved. The fact is, however, that Herr Dauny has worked here for many years and is known to all of our security staff, and so naturally he was allowed to enter the building without anybody asking to view his pass."

"Your company supplies computer software to the government, does it not?"

Again, Heerwagen squirmed. "Yes, we do, Frau Obersturmführer."

"It would seem that your security is rather lackadaisical for such a facility," Ellen said with a tight smile. "Though it has to be said that Herr Dauny would not provide us with any information as to the nature of his work, which would suggest that he is at least able to abide by the Official Secrets Act." Ellen glanced at Himmler and then said, "What particular computer system does Herr Dauny work on?"

Heerwagen frowned. "Frau Obersturmführer, I must respectfully decline to answer that particular question, in the interests of State security."

"Of course," Ellen said. "Though you must also understand that I am concerned that State security has been breached due to Herr Dauny's negligence and your lax security procedures. It is my duty to report this breach to my superiors."

Heerwagen stirred the cup of coffee that was on the desk in front of him. He hadn't offered either Ellen or Himmler a drink. From behind Ellen came the sound of a cuckoo clock striking the hour, all eleven of them. The head of GFW's English subsidiary picked up the cup of coffee and took a sip.

He said, "The nature of our work is sensitive. This is something which I cannot deny. However, I can assure you that no sensitive data were accessed and that the compromised user logon details have been updated to prevent any future breaches from occurring."

It was apparent that, like Herr Dauny, Heerwagen was not overly keen to pass on any information as to the nature of business that Gerhard Fieseler Werke were involved in.

"You can rest assured, Frau Obersturmführer, that we take the security of our work very seriously."

Another dead end reached. She looked at Himmler, but he just shook his head. He had no additional questions. They said their goodbyes and returned to the M3. The three of them – Ellen, Himmler and Zimmerman – stood outside the car as Zimmerman smoked a cigarette.

"What are you thinking, Ellen?" Himmler asked.

"None of us are privy to the full Rhodes investigation. That implies that Rhodes is a very serious asset. I am curious as to what Herr Dauny's part is in all of this. I want to know what work he is doing for GFW which makes his works pass such a valuable item."

"GFW supply software to governmental departments."

"Yes, but which ones?"

Zimmerman frowned. "Could it have something to do with Geheime Staatspolizei? Combat UK would love to get hold of a list of our informants."

"Maybe," Ellen said. She looked back at the GFW offices. It was a modern building, on two floors, with a glass frontage and an impressive sign with the company logo rising from ground level. A hakenkreuz was painted on the side wall. She felt that this company did something more significant for the Reich than just maintaining a database for the Gestapo.

"Well, it seems like we are not going to find out, Frau

Obersturmführer," Himmler said. Zimmerman nodded his head and tossed his cigarette away. "Where to now?"

Ellen sighed. "The only person left on our list is Harry Dean. You remember him, Willi?"

"That Engländer Arschloch we spoke to a few weeks ago," Himmler said. He looked at Zimmerman. "He is a big man. We may need your help."

Ellen laughed and climbed into the M3. In a way, she felt part of the team once more, a Geheime Staatspolizei investigator. But she knew that she was only playing a part. Her life, her future, the very nature of who she was had been irrevocably altered.

She was no longer Ellen Brauchitsch, Gestapo officer.

She was Ellen Brauchitsch, supporter of the resistance.

Traitor.

45

SS-Sturmbannführer Loritz did not like loose ends. Loose ends implied sloppy investigative work, and he did not like to see that in the officers who worked for him. He certainly did not like to see that in himself.

He was reading through the files on the Klarsfeld assassination attempt, trying to find the leak. It was true that he had asked Schmid to look into this, but then, after clearing Ellen Brauchitsch of any wrong-doing, Schmid had been moved onto a different investigation, that of Barry Rhodes, and the Klarsfeld investigation had been put to one side.

Somebody had given information to the terrorists, to the person who had sent Dougie Hardcastle, the would-be assassin, to kill Klarsfeld. Someone had told them where and when Klarsfeld would be most vulnerable. Whoever that person was, they were a valuable asset for the terrorists. And yet the terrorists had not sent their top man to carry out the assassination.

Of course, any such assassination was always going to be a one-way trip for the person involved. A suicide mission. This was a close-up shooting, with very little planning given to escaping afterwards. Perhaps that was why they'd sent a worthless man such as Hardcastle. He was expendable. And yet he wasn't really up to the job.

Loritz opened up his computer system, checked the aerial photography for the location where the assassination attempt was carried out. This was an exclusive restaurant in a salubrious part of London. Klarsfeld, when he left the restaurant, would have to walk twenty yards to reach his car. Ten or fifteen seconds where he would be vulnerable.

Vulnerable to a sniper.

Loritz was now a manager of people. He rarely got involved in the day to day activities of an investigator. He merely assigned staff, read reports and reached conclusions. But the bug was still inside him. He pulled on his jacket, left his office, booked a car from the garage and drove to the restaurant, Claridges.

He stood in the precise spot where he believed Klarsfeld had been shot and looked around. As he did so, the restaurant's doorman wandered over to him.

"Can I help you, sir?" he asked. There was a trace of suspicion in his voice. The man was an Engländer.

Loritz smiled, flashed his ID at the doorman. "This is nothing for you to worry about, mein Herr."

"Is this about the governor getting shot?"

"Yes," Loritz said. "I am just tying up some of the loose ends."

The restaurant was in a moderately narrow street, terraces on either side of the road. Cars belonging to the restaurant's customers were parked in a long row, their chauffeurs sitting behind the wheel, ready to pull up to the entrance when their clients left the restaurant. This was why Klarsfeld would've been standing out in the open, vulnerable.

Loritz looked at the buildings on the other side of the road. Four and five storeys high, more than a few locations for a sniper to secrete himself. A shot from a rifle perhaps a couple of hundred yards away, and then the assassin would have ample opportunity to escape in the panic.

No, this was a suicide mission, that much was apparent.

But that being the case, the assassin should at least have managed to get at least one bullet into Klarsfeld's chest, unless he were a complete amateur. Which, by all accounts, he was. Loritz frowned, leant against the BMW and pondered momentarily, before he beckoned the doorman over.

He instructed him to stand in the position where Klarsfeld had been standing when he'd been shot. Then he traced Hardcastle's movements right up to the point where he'd shot the Reichsstatthalter, even going so far as to draw his SIG Sauer and aiming it at the doorman.

There was no way that Hardcastle should've missed.

He thanked the doorman and got back into his car.

Even an imbecile like Hardcastle could've done more than shoot Klarsfeld in the arm.

Loritz drove back to the Polizeipräsidium and returned to his office. There, he fired up his computer and accessed the CCTV footage from the day of the assassination attempt. The quality was poor and didn't really provide any good angle of the shooting, but it was apparent that Hardcastle was in a good position to shoot his target. The Reichsstatthalter's security team, with the exception of Brauchitsch, did not appear on high alert. They were caught unawares, certainly, and Loritz had already ensured that each of them had been reprimanded. But

nach Schema F

all of that made it even more unlikely that Hardcastle should've failed in his attempt to kill Klarsfeld.

Brauchitsch had pulled Klarsfeld to the ground, shielded him, but even taking into account her possibly lightning quick reactions, the bullets Hardcastle had fired from that proximity should've hit the governor's central body mass.

Hardcastle would have to have been incredibly inept to have failed.

Unless his attempt had been a deliberate failure.

But why?

What possible reason would there be for the terrorists of Combat UK to have the governor of the *Deutscher Staat von Großbritannien* in their sights but to fire only warning shots as opposed to lethal ones? To waste the life of a would-be assassin on nothing more than a warning?

Loritz picked up his telephone, called through to his secretary.

"Book me an appointment to see the Reichsstatthalter," he told her.

He was determined to get to the bottom of this.

46

The Engländer, Harry Dean, had not been at home when Ellen and her two untersturmführers had paid him a visit. By that time, it was late in the day, and she suggested they stop in Peterborough rather than travel back to London just for the evening. Himmler was slightly put out, but Ellen had it on good authority that he was supposed to be meeting the young rottenführer, Raubel, for a drink, so she could understand his annoyance. Zimmerman, however, was relishing the idea of drinking in the company of the Peterborough Gestapo at the local SS club.

Ellen left her hotel room shortly after 7pm, made her way down to the restaurant. There, she and Himmler enjoyed a meal together. He congratulated her on her promotion.

"I did not get the chance earlier, Ellen, with Zimmerman being there," he said. "I could not sound sincere."

"It is not a problem," she assured him. "And I am sorry that you are stuck here in this hell hole, missing out on the opportunity to bed that beautiful young SS officer."

Himmler smiled, shook his head and waved a dismissive hand. "Ach, I am probably too old for her anyway. And I am hardly a catch."

"You are a very handsome man, Willi."

"Ellen, I was not fishing for a compliment, and I really do not need your bullshit." But he grinned as he said it. "How about you? Is there nobody special in your life?" Ellen shook her head. "You keep your personal life so private."

"I guess that comes with the training, Willi."

"Nonsense. I have been through the same training and yet everyone seems to know all about my private life."

"Rumours and speculation," she said. "It is what we in the Geheime Staatspolizei thrive on, Willi. And Gestapo officers do seem rather inclined to gossip about one another like old women."

"I suppose we do." Himmler poured himself another glass of wine and offered to top up Ellen's glass. At first she resisted, but after some gentle persuasion, she relented. They both took a sip from their glasses. "So tell me, Ellen – and you can also, of course, tell me to mind my own business – but why are you single?"

"It is just the way it is."

"Can I be honest, Ellen?" She raised an eyebrow. "Candid."

"We are in the Gestapo, Willi, we do not have time for lies."

He smiled. "You know, there are lots of young officers who would relish the thought of taking you out on a date. But you have this ... this way about you."

"A way about me?"

"You are very career motivated."

"And this is a bad thing?"

Himmler shrugged. "I suppose not. But some men, they see ambition in a woman as a turn-off."

"Then that is their problem."

"Perhaps." Himmler was fiddling with his glass. The waiter came and cleared their plates away. The both of them thanked him.

"You looked as though you were about to say something, Willi."

"I was. But perhaps it is none of my business and not my place to say it."

Ellen gave a little sigh. "You are curious about my previous assignment."

"I think everybody is, Ellen."

Ellen picked up her glass, stared at the red liquid, at the way the light reflected from it. This was a topic of conversation she did not like to discuss. The last time she'd spoken about it was many months ago, when she was under investigation by the psychology team.

She wasn't sure whether it was the wine or whether the time was just right, but she felt ready to open up to somebody. And in her sad existence, Willi Himmler was about as close as she could get to a real friend.

She said, "Have you ever worked undercover, Willi?" He shook his head. "It is not easy, believe me, to be become a completely different person. Of course, it helped that I was young, that nobody in London really knew me, that I could actually use my real name. It also helped that the person they wanted me to target was a young man, inexperienced, trusting."

"Was he a terrorist? A member of Combat UK?"

Ellen gave a half smile. "No," she said, shaking her head softly. "No, Jerome was not a terrorist. At least, he was not at the start."

"Then why was he a target? His family? His father was a terrorist?"

"His father was just an innocent man," Ellen said. "But we suspected that people he knew, people Jerome knew, were terrorists. Back then, anyone who did not completely conform was under suspicion." She took a sip of wine. "I got lucky. That is all. It could so easily have turned out that Jerome had nothing whatsoever to do with Combat UK, and my time undercover would have been wasted."

"But he turned out to be a terrorist?"

Ellen put her glass down. "It is complicated, Willi, and I am not sure you would understand."

"Try me."

"Willi, I am not going to sleep with you."

Himmler grinned, shook his head. "If I were that transparent, Ellen, I would be tremendously disappointed. I am sorry if this hurts you, but you most certainly are not my type. I am asking you this because ... well, because we are kind of like friends."

"*Kind of like friends?*"

"Who can really be friends in the Reich, Ellen?"

Ellen chuckled. "You are right, of course. And I appreciate what you are saying. I appreciate your candour."

"As you said earlier, Gestapo officers do not appreciate lies."

"You want to know about Jerome?"

"You fell in love with him?"

Ellen closed her eyes, gave a little nod. "It was like that, I suppose. But unless you have worked undercover, you would never understand."

"What happened?"

"I was getting nowhere. There was nothing to report on. Jerome was just a regular Engländer, a bit resentful of the Reich, but certainly not a terrorist. And then the Gestapo arrested his father." She choked back a laugh. "Herr Sturmbannführer Loritz arrested him. Tortured him. Charged him with treason. At the court, he was found guily. *Todesstrafe.*"

"Executed? What did he do?"

"He said things he should not have said apparently, said something like he wished the Führer were dead."

"Stupid thing to say."

"Of course," Ellen agreed. "But tell me, Willi, can you really condemn someone to death for having a different opinion to you? Is that justification for executing someone?"

nach Schema F

"Ours is not to reason why, Ellen."

Again, Ellen let out a wry laugh. "I suppose you are right. But after his father was executed, Jerome went off the rails. For me, for the Geheime Staatspolizei, for Sturmbannführer Loritz, it was a wish come true. Jerome made contact with Combat UK. And the rest, as they say, is history."

"Is it true you shot him?"

"No," Ellen answered. "I was in charge of the assault team. Lots of us opened fire. I did not actually shoot him. He died in front of me." Ellen thought back to that moment. She'd demanded to know where Jerome's partner in crime was, and Jerome had laughed at her and sang a song. A song about Hitler. And then, as she'd been distracted by one of her officers, he had died.

She'd cradled his bloody, bullet-ridden body in her arms, but he was already dead.

"I cannot imagine what you went through, Ellen." Himmler actually sounded sincere. He reached across the table, squeezed her hand, held it momentarily and then withdrew. He looked sheepish, but Ellen appreciated his gesture.

"It is okay," she told him. "I am over it all now."

"Are you?"

Ellen frowned. "I think so." It was the most honest answer she could give him under the circumstances.

"It must have had an effect on you though? Made you question yourself, your job, what you are doing now?"

"I am a loyal Party member," Ellen said, "and a loyal investigator for the Geheime Staatspolizei, Willi. Nothing will change that."

"I was not questioning your loyalty."

For a few moments neither of them spoke. Ellen looked around the restaurant, these people eating in the company of two Gestapo officers. She knew that most of them would be Germans, working in the DSvG. What Engländer were here would either be well-respected Party members or else serving staff.

The serving staff in such establishments – frequented by high-ranking Germans and SS officers – were paid well and had good working conditions, to ensure they remained loyal. Money was a big motivator in an individual's loyalty. All the same, Ellen knew that it would be relatively easy for Combat UK – what remained of it – to place one of their agents in a place like this, to overhear conversations, to identify targets, to plant bombs, to assassinate people.

She thought about the attempt on Klarsfeld's life. The Reichsstatthalter had known it was going to happen. She wondered whether the assassin, Dougie Hardcastle, knew that he was going to die for no reason. But then, he had to have known. He was so close. He should have shot Klarsfeld from that distance, and Ellen now knew she couldn't take all of the praise in having saved Klarsfeld's life.

Hardcastle had deliberately missed.

He had died to make Reichsstatthalter Klarsfeld seem like a loyal German. He had made the ultimate sacrifice. Ellen resolved to question Klarsfeld about that the next time she spoke to him. Did the old man think that he had the right to bring about the deaths of people just to sway opinions about him? Did he think that made him different to the very people he opposed?

"Ellen?" She looked up at Himmler. "I said, what are our plans tomorrow?"

"Tomorrow? Tomorrow we pay Harry Dean a visit."

"We are getting nowhere just questioning people, Ellen," Himmler said. "At some point, we are going to have to bring one of them in for interrogation."

"Who would you suggest?"

"Everything seems to revolve around the Bretton Sports and Social Club," Himmler said. "I would suggest we arrest that obnoxious barman."

"Tom Flannigan?"

"He knows something is going on. We should beat it out of him."

Ellen shook her head. "I am not convinced he knows anything worthwhile, Willi."

"Well, let us arrest Herr Dean," Himmler said. "His name has been hanging around this investigation like a fart in a chemical warfare suit. Both him and the landlord, they are at the centre of all of this."

"We will question Dean, and then we will put them under surveillance."

"There are only three of us, Ellen."

"Flannigan does not appear to leave the club," Ellen said. "I suggest we follow Herr Dean and Herr Dauny."

"I just want us to achieve something, Ellen."

"I know," Ellen said. And in a way, she agreed with him. But she was treading a fine line between satisfying her own curiosity and screwing up Klarsfeld's plan, whatever that was.

She knew that if they pulled Dauny in, he would undoubtedly crack, but she felt that he was the lynchpin in whatever the plan was, and the plan would fall to pieces as quickly as he did.

She was going to have to be very careful.

47

Klarsfeld did not actually want to meet SS-Sturmbannführer Wolf Loritz. He had always found the Gestapo officer to be a dislikeable character, loyal to the Reich, unbendable. Of course, he had asked Ellen Brauchitsch's opinion as to the man's loyalty, and she had given him the answer that he had suspected. That Loritz would never be swayed, would never turn from the Reich.

But Loritz was one of the new breed, an officer in his thirties who had spent much of his working life in the *Deutscher Staat von Großbritannien*. There was every chance that he, like Klarsfeld, like many German immigrants in fact, had become partially Anglicized, preferring England to their native Fatherland. Many of the children of immigrants knew only England as their homeland. In a way, it was the direct opposite to the policy of Germanization, where the seeds planted by the Fatherland turned states into an extension of the Reich. Here in England, it was having exactly the opposite effect. The Engländers were a strong, proud people, and the Germans seemed to appreciate that.

Klarsfeld wondered what men like Loritz would do should the resistance plan succeed. When Germania was no more, when the Führer was dead, where would Loritz stand? Would he still be a loyal Party member? Would he still consider himself to be German? Would he still worship the Thousand Year Reich? Or would he adapt to the changes and become a loyal citizen of Great Britain?

Klarsfeld wondered how the changes brought about by the destruction of Germania would affect himself. Though he was effectively colluding with Combat UK, it would be apparent that there would be an uprising in the DSvG in the immediate aftermath. The SS, under the leadership of Mittendorf, would undoubtedly be mobilized, though some of the men and women would question their orders. Some Engländers would launch reprisal attacks against German citizens, German soldiers and German politicians. It would, for some time, be an unstable situation. And it was less than two weeks away, if all went according to plan.

What Klarsfeld didn't need right now were complications, and the appointment with SS-Sturmbannführer Loritz was potentially a

nach Schema F

complication. There was only one reason why Loritz wanted to see him – it was something to do with the assassination attempt.

Klarsfeld's phone buzzed and he grabbed the receiver to be told by his secretary, Helga, that Loritz was waiting to see him. Klarsfeld asked her to send him in, and then ensured that his desk was clear of anything which would attract the prying eyes of a Gestapo man.

Loritz was wearing a light grey suit, crumpled, as though he'd slept in it. He wore a red tie, but the top button of his shirt was undone. The collar was also slightly grubby. Klarsfeld stood and greeted him, shaking his hand. He offered Loritz a seat and they both sat.

"Herr Sturmbannführer, it is some time since I have seen you. You are looking well."

"I am looking tired and haggard, Herr Reichsstatthalter, this we both know," Loritz said with a smile. His grey eyes threatened to pierce Klarsfeld's mind. "But I have been working hard, so this is to be expected."

"I am sure you have. Can I get you a drink? Coffee, tea?" Loritiz shook his head. "How about a cognac?"

"If you do not mind, Herr Reichsstatthalter, I would rather not. I make it a habit never to drink alcohol on duty. In all honesty, I am not much of a drinker."

Klarsfeld took a bottle of cognac from the cabinet next to his desk, together with a snifter. He poured himself a glass and took a sip, then leant back in his chair.

"In diplomacy, many decisions are made after a cognac and a cigar," he said with a chuckle. "Perhaps it would be better if the masses did not learn this?"

"Perhaps."

"So, Herr Sturmbannführer, to what do I owe this pleasure?"

"I have been investigating the attempt on your life."

"Ah, that was many weeks ago. I am still alive, I am fully recovered, the man responsible is dead." Klarsfeld shrugged. "Must we pick away at old scabs?"

Loritz smiled, looked down at his hands as though inspecting his nails. He gave a sigh, looked around Klarsfeld's large office, and then fixed his gaze upon the Reichsstatthalter. "I am one of those people, mein Herr, who does not like to leave loose ends. If nothing else, I find it difficult to sleep at night if a crime I have been investigating remains unsolved." He scratched his head. "Perhaps it is a psychological deficiency on my part – but naturally, I would not care to admit such a thing to my own superiors." He smiled. "Though to be fair, if it is a deficiency, it is one with worthwhile qualities. An investigator should, for want of a better phrase, endeavour to get to the bottom of things, do you not think?"

"It is an admirable quality, Herr Loritz." Klarsfeld took another sip from his cognac. "But I am slightly puzzled. You imply that the attempt on my life is a crime which remains unsolved. However, we know that the attempt was made by a man who represented English partisans. The man himself was killed during the attempt by one of your officers – Frau Brauchitsch. I am forever in her debt, and yours too, for it was you who put her in charge of my care. In short, I am not sure what there is left to investigate."

Loritz smiled. It was quite a disarming smile. Klarsfeld wondered what it would be like to be interrogated by this man, a man with a ruthless reputation that overwhelmed the soft side he was rumoured – perhaps maliciously – to possess.

"I am wondering, Herr Reichsstatthalter, why you are still alive." Klarsfeld was genuinely taken aback. Loritz had said it in quite a confrontational manner. The Gestapo officer's smile dropped. "You see, the assassin was standing just a few feet from you, probably around the distance between you and me at the moment, with this beautiful oak desk between us. Even a partially-sighted man would have no trouble in managing to shoot somebody at that distance."

"But Brauchitsch managed to get me out of the way."

"Yes, and you were shot as you were pulled to the ground," Loritz said. "Shot there, in your arm. And what I cannot quite understand is this. You were pulled down, to your left, and yet the assassin managed to hit you with a glancing shot from his pistol – in your left arm. This would imply that even before you were pulled to the ground he was already aiming to your left, whereas most assassins, they would aim right just there." Loritz made a pistol shape with the finger and thumb of his right hand and aimed it at Klarsfeld's chest. "Bang, bang, bang. He fired three shots, he missed, and the fourth hit you just there." He moved his 'pistol' so that it was aiming at Klarsfeld's arm. Loritz shook his head. "I am struggling to work out how that happened. Unless Hardcastle's eyesight

nach Schema F

was seriously defective, it just does not make sense."

Klarsfeld sniffed the cognac, took another sip. He tried his best not to look guilty. He said, "What are you implying?"

Loritz shrugged. "At the moment, I can only make assumptions, and I would prefer to keep those to myself. But the attempt on your life, I would have to say that it was more of a warning."

"A warning?"

"As though the terrorists were telling us that they can strike at anyone at any time. I would say, Herr Klarsfeld, that you are very fortunate to still be alive. At the very least I would have expected you to have been seriously injured. A bullet to the chest at the very least. Luck was certainly on your side on that day. Luck, or ..." Loritz smiled and looked away.

"Or?"

Loritz smiled, shook his head, got to his feet. He said, "At the moment, I cannot say. But rest assured, Herr Klarsfeld, I am determined to get to the bottom of this." Klarsfeld stood up, walked to Loritz and shook his hand.

"Heil Führer, mein Herr," the Gestapo man said. He did not salute.

"Heil Führer, Herr Sturmbannführer."

Klarsfeld watched as Loritz left his office, and he wondered whether the man's tenacity would be the downfall of the mission.

48

Ellen made her way to the offices of the Breitnetzsicherheit, the Gestapo department in charge of computer security. She was back at the Polizeipräsidium in London. Harry Dean was still not at home, and a neighbour explained that she thought he'd gone up to Scotland for a holiday. A quick check at Dean's employer, RuprechtWerk, confirmed that he was away on annual leave, though nobody knew precisely where. There had seemed little point in hanging around in Peterborough, so she'd detailed Himmler and Zimmerman to put Dauny under surveillance and then had returned to London.

The offices here were dishevelled, the desks placed in haphazard locations, with computer screens on top of them, sometimes two or three to a desk. Casually dressed men and women – wearing jeans, teeshirts – seemed entranced by whatever was on the screens in front of them. Ellen walked up to the nearest of them.

"I am looking for Obersturmführer Mann," she said.

The young officer at the desk pointed to a doorway at the far end of the room. "He is in there," she said. Ellen nodded her thanks and made her way to the door in question. It was slightly ajar. She knocked on it, pushed it open.

The man sat behind the desk was smoking. He wore a sweater, his hair was dishevelled, and he was plunging a finger vigorously in and out of his right ear. He looked up at Ellen.

"Yes?"

Ellen stepped into the office. "I am Obersturmführer Brauchitsch. I am investigating an Engländer by the name of Marcus Dauny. I believe you have spoken to him previously?"

Mann smiled, gestured for her to sit down. As she did, Ellen noticed another man leaning against a filing cabinet in the corner of the room behind the door. He was a short man, not a typical Gestapo officer.

"That is Vogel," Mann said. "He is, for want of a better description, my assistant." Ellen nodded a greeting which Vogel returned. "Ah, so you are investigating Herr Dauny. Sadly, we got nowhere with him, did we Vogel? Even though the both of us know that he is most assuredly up to no good."

"I have my suspicions also," Ellen said.

"Sadly, we were pulled off the investigation when Barry Rhodes was handed over to one of your colleagues. SS-Obersturmführer Schmid?"

"Yes, so I understand. What can you tell me about Barry Rhodes?"

"I am presuming you have read my report, Frau Obersturmführer, in which case, sadly, there is nothing else of consequence I can tell you." Vogel coughed and Mann shot him a glance. "Forgive my assistant. He sometimes forgets his place. He is just your average computer nerd. However, he is, like me, rather chagrined by the fact that this case was taken out of our hands."

"Why was that?"

"Well, it was no longer just a computer security issue," Mann said. "I feel that once we discovered that Rhodes seemed to have appeared in the *Deutscher Staat von Großbritannien* just seven years ago, and prior to that no record of his existence could be found, the case became something more complex and sinister." Ellen raised an eyebrow. This was all news to her. Mann smiled and shook his head. "Oh, that is right. This information was redacted from my report. National security and all that."

Ellen smiled. Mann was a cynic. The old Ellen might've taken exception to him, seen him as a potential traitor. "So Barry Rhodes – what do you think he is?"

"Assumptions and speculations, Frau Obersturmführer."

"These are what we thrive on in the Geheime Staatspolizei."

Mann rubbed the side of his face. "Hmm. Well, consider the fact that Rhodes did not exist eight years ago, and what conclusion would you draw?"

"That he only came to the DSvG seven years ago?"

Mann clapped his hands. "Precisely. But, of course, this is nothing to do with myself and Vogel. We just investigate computer security."

"And Herr Dauny is a computer expert."

"Herr Dauny is a computer programmer," Mann said. "He works on a governmental system."

"Which one?"

"That is the question." Mann shrugged. "But Barry Rhodes wanted access to whatever computer system Dauny works on. And Barry Rhodes … well, he is more than your average terrorist."

"A spy?"

"An American, would be my guess."

"So the Americans are trying to gain access to one of the Reich's computer systems," Ellen said. "But which one? And why?"

"These are questions that perhaps only Herr Dauny or Herr Rhodes can possibly answer. Herr Rhodes is currently unobtainable to the likes of us."

"And Herr Dauny isn't talking."

"Hmm." Mann nodded his head. "But I am sure that he could be persuaded to talk. He is, after all, just a regular person. He is no spy and he is no terrorist."

"He will have to be interrogated."

"Most certainly. But he is a loyal Party member and you would need more than a tenuous link to a potential spy in order to have him arrested."

"At the moment, he is under surveillance."

"This is a start, of course."

"Could you even hazard a guess as to what might be happening here?" Ellen asked Mann. The computer investigator dug his finger in his right ear and scratched.

"You have to ask yourself this question. If America could gain access to any of the Reich's computer systems, which would they choose? Which computer system would provide them with the most valuable source of information?"

Ellen was none the wiser. She knew she'd have to give this more careful consideration. She thanked Mann and then made her way down to the garage. On the way, she put a call through to Klarsfeld's office, asked if she could see the Reichsstatthalter. He had a free slot later that morning. Ellen hopped into her M3 and drove across town. Near to the *Amtssitz des Reichsstatthalter*, she found a coffee shop and parked up outside. She had time to kill.

She ordered a cappuccino and rang Himmler.

"Ah, Frau Obersturmführer."

"How is it going, Willi?"

"He has gone to work," Himmler said. "We are currently sat outside his office playing 'I Spy'. I spy with my little eye something beginning with M."

nach Schema F

"M?"

"Monotony, Ellen. If he is like every other tedious little office worker, he will stay at work until five o'clock. He will not even leave for lunch. Rather, he will sit at his desk eating hideous, home-made sandwiches. Which means I will have to remain in this car sniffing Zimmerman's farts for the next six hours. Also, he smokes like a cancerous chimney."

"It is a hard life being a Gestapo officer," Ellen said with a smile. "Perhaps you can take some time off if you think he will be at work all day. I want him putting under surveillance the moment he leaves work. I want to know where he goes and I want to know what he does."

"Of course, gnädige Frau," Himmler said. Ellen cut the call and looked down at the copy of the *Volkischer Beobachter* which was on the table in front of her. The headline spoke of a trade deal between the Greater German Reich and the United States of America. Oil to America, and cars and trucks, clothing and fast food restaurants to Germany. There were even photographs of some of the cars which would be imported. Fords and Chevrolets. The newspaper said that cars such as the Corvette and the Mustang would be seen as fashion symbols to affluent Germans. The article praised the Führer for his progressiveness in bringing such imports to Germany.

Ellen skimmed though the newspaper, found another article which spoke of the Wehrmacht's advance through Russia. They were now at the Chukotka Peninsula, and all traces of Russian opposition had been destroyed. Even Ellen could see the strategic importance in the Wehrmacht occupying Chukotka. The American mainland was less than a hundred miles away.

Perhaps Rhodes and the Americans wanted to know something about the Reich's plans. Perhaps they were considering launching an attack on German forces in Chukotka. But why would they need to access a computer system in order to do that? Satellite photography would show the build-up of the Wehrmacht in Chukotka. It would show their precise locations. And Chukotka was suitably located for long-range bombers from the American mainland to reach.

And in any case, would America really launch an attack? Of course, they might be able to overwhelm the weakened forces in the far east of Russia, but they would not be able to target Germany direct. Not unless they used nuclear weapons. And if they used nuclear weapons, then

Germany was sure to retaliate. What was the term? Mutually assured destruction. No one can ever be victorious in a nuclear war because if you launch an attack, the other side will retaliate and both countries will be obliterated.

Unless …

Ellen put the newspaper down.

Unless one side were incapable of launching its own nuclear missiles.

49

Schmid looked at Corcilius and said, "So you think you have the right dose this time?"

The doctor looked at him impatiently. "This is not an exact science, Schmid, as I explained previously. Too much and he will fall asleep. Too little and he will tell you nothing. We need him relaxed. Last time, he was too relaxed."

"He was on the verge of opening up."

Corcilius nodded. "He was. I have reduced the dose only very slightly. But you must remember not to ask such direct questions. You must signpost him to the topics you wish to discuss. If you ask him a direct question, his mind will object. He will not answer a direct question that he would not ordinarily answer whilst not under sedation." She opened her case and took out a syringe and a vial of the drug. "I would also suggest you wait out here," she said, "until the drug has taken effect. You being in the room beforehand will only serve to antagonize him."

Schmid waited while the doctor did her thing. She opened the door and gestured for him to enter the interrogation room. He walked up to the gurney where Barry Rhodes lay. The spy looked up at him and frowned, confused, as though he didn't recognize Schmid.

"Mr Rhodes," Schmid said. "How are you feeling?"

"Good. Who are you? I remember your face."

"I am a friend, Mr Rhodes. I am probably one of your closest friends."

"I don't remember your name," Rhodes said. "Just your face."

Schmid smiled, tried to make it look as sincere as possible. "You have many friends though, Mr Rhodes. Are you sure you do not remember my name?" Rhodes shook his head. "Other friends then – do you remember their names?"

"Harry ..."

"Harry Dean?"

Rhodes squeezed his eyes shut. "I remember Harry."

"Who is Harry?"

"A friend. We drink together." Rhodes looked up at Schmid. "We ... we just drink together."

"And talk. All friends talk, Mr Rhodes. Just like you and I are talking now. What do you talk to Harry about?"

"Work."

"Work? What is your work?"

"It's ... it's secret."

Schmid gave a frustrated sigh and looked at Corcilius. She gestured for him to carry on.

"Tell me about other friends," he said. "About Marcus Dauny."

"Dauny. He's posh."

"He is, yes."

"He's not German."

"Do you not like Germans?"

Rhodes looked at Schmid. "You're a German."

"I am, yes. Do you have any other German friends?"

"German friends?" Rhodes frowned. He seemed to be trying to recall something from his memory. He said, "Schottel."

"Schottel? Who is he?"

"I don't know," Rhodes said. He was rolling his head from side to side. "I can't remember. The enemy. The enemy."

"Your enemy?"

"A traitor. A fucking traitor." Rhodes glared at Schmid. "A fucking traitor," he said again, almost shouting it.

"He betrayed you?" Schmid was confused. Schottel was a German name, and yet Rhodes had called him a traitor. Had this Schottel promised something to Combat UK and then failed to deliver?

"Disloyal," Rhodes muttered. Schmid looked at Corcilius. The spy seemed to be falling asleep.

"We're losing him again," he said.

Corcilius checked Rhodes's pulse. She patted his face. Rhodes looked at her, stunned, and then turned to Schmid.

"Fuck you," he said. "Fuck you and your questions."

That accent. It wasn't an accent from Fenland, not anymore. It was distinctly American.

"Fuck you!" Rhodes shouted. "Fuck you!"

Schmid backed out of the interrogation room and Corcilius followed. She closed the door. They could still hear Rhodes shouting at them.

"He fought through it," Corcilius said.

nach Schema F

"This shit is not going to work," Schmid said. He was disappointed. For a moment, he'd thought they were going to get something worthwhile out of Rhodes.

"Who is Schottel?"

Schmid shrugged. "I have no idea. He is obviously German."

"We can try again in a couple of days," Corcilius said. "I can dose him up tomorrow, but we won't ask him anything. If we keep him sedated, it may loosen up his mind even more."

"I do not have much time, Doktor Corcilius. Something big is happening here, and Rhodes knows what it is."

"We can give it one more try."

Schmid scowled. Was it really worth the effort? He gave a sigh, nodded his thanks at her and then left the interrogation suite. As the lift took him up to the 12th floor, he thought about what Rhodes had said. Firstly, him and Harry Dean were engaged in secretive work, but he wouldn't elaborate on that. Secondly, there was the name he'd mentioned. Schottel. Who was Schottel? Clearly, he was a German. But what did he do? The name would obviously require further investigation, even though Rhodes had described this Schottel as a traitor. There were more than a million Germans in the DSvG, but each one of them was recorded on the computer database. All of their personal details, a photograph of them, their DNA. Nobody had any secrets in the Reich. This Schottel, Schmid would find him.

50

Ellen stepped into Klarsfeld's office. He was sitting behind his desk, a concerned expression on his face. He was drinking cognac, and it appeared as though he'd had one too many. Ellen wondered why he'd allowed himself to get in such a state, particularly as he must've known he was due to see her.

"Frau Obersturmführer Brauchitsch, come in, take a seat." As she sat down, he said, "You are the second Gestapo officer to visit me today. I must say that I am starting to get a complex. Am I under investigation?"

"What do you mean?"

"Your boss, Loritz, he was here earlier, making subtle implications."

"What implications?"

"He wondered why the assassin failed to shoot me," Klarsfeld said. "He wanted to know why I was merely wounded in the arm when the assassin's bullets should have hit me squarely in the chest." The Reichsstatthalter drained his cognac and poured himself another. "He knows something."

"What does he know?" Ellen hissed.

"That is just it, Ellen. He does not know what he knows. He just knows something."

"I am starting to know how he feels," Ellen muttered.

"What is that supposed to mean?"

"What is going on here, Herr Reichsstatthalter?" Ellen asked. She didn't feel comfortable calling him Erich, or even Herr Klarsfeld. Right now, she thought it best to remain formal. "What is this 'mission'? What am I supposed to be preventing my colleagues from uncovering?"

"You do not need to know this, Ellen."

"I fucking do," Ellen said firmly. "I need to know for two reasons. Firstly, I need to know because how else am I going to steer my colleagues away from uncovering the truth? And secondly, I want to know exactly what I am getting involved in."

"As I told you before, Ellen, it is best if you do not know."

Ellen shook her head slowly. "I think you do not understand, mein Herr. You have asked me to betray my country, to ignore all of my training. You have not told me why and you have not told me what is going to happen. At the end of all of this, what is to be my fate? Will you cast me aside, leave me exposed to my colleagues in the Geheime Staatspolizei? Or will you have me killed before I am tortured, before I betray you?"

Klarsfeld gave a little laugh.

"You are being melodramatic, Ellen."

Ellen stood up. "You know what, I have had enough of this. You tell me that Sturmbannführer Loritz was here earlier, that he suspects something was not quite right about the attempt on your life? Well, I too suspect something was not quite right about the attempt on your life. Of course, I have inside information – information you gave to me. And yet, even about that you lied."

"I did not lie."

"You told me Dougie Hardcastle did not know he was going to be sacrificed," Ellen said. "You told me that your security detail were supposed to shoot him before he shot at you. Tell me, is your security detail that ineffectual that they actually allowed Hardcastle to draw his weapon, to open fire, before they managed to shoot him? And in any case, if Hardcastle had not opened fire, then the attempt on your life would not have been taken seriously. No, you needed Hardcastle to open fire. You needed those shots to be fired at you. You needed him to miss you."

"What are you saying?"

"What I am saying is that Hardcastle knew he was not supposed to kill you. He was being sacrificed to bolster your standing, to make you seem loyal and vulnerable. To ensure that you remain distanced from Combat UK."

Klarsfeld sipped his cognac.

"Oh, bravo, Ellen," he said. "I am surprised that it took you this long to work it out."

"So why did you lie to me? Did you not want me to know that you were prepared to sacrifice other human beings for absolutely no reason other than to improve your reputation? You did not want me to see how little you value life."

"Ellen, you have it all wrong."

"No," Ellen said with a sorrowful shake of the head. "No, I do not."

Klarsfeld looked troubled. He got to his feet, wandered over to the huge window and surveyed the view of London. He lifted his snifter up to his nose as though savouring the scent of his cognac.

"This plan, this mission, it is much bigger than just you or I, Ellen. It is much bigger than Dougie Hardcastle. It may well change the very fabric of the entire world. It will certainly alter the balance of power in this small state of ours. And I am the only one who can hold it all together. For the good of the British people here, the Engländers, the German immigrants, I have to remain here, in this position of authority, to at least try to make sure that the DSvG does not destroy itself."

"Herr Klarsfeld, what is going to happen?"

"You really do not want to know, Ellen."

"This is something to do with nuclear missiles?"

Klarsfeld turned to her, and the smile he wore was weary, sad. He sipped from his drink, wandered back to his desk and sat down.

"Do you think anybody wants a war, Ellen?"

"I do not know."

"This is about removing the head of the snake."

"Herr Dauny, he works on the computer systems which control Germany's nuclear weapons," Ellen said. The pieces were all falling into place now. "You want to disable the Reich's nuclear weapons? So that America can launch an attack?"

Klarsfeld shook his head.

"Do you think I want to kill hundreds of millions of Germans? Innocent people? Do you think that it is necessary for that many people to die when really the death of just one man can bring down the Reich?"

"The Führer? But why do the Americans want to access our nuclear weapons just to kill one person?"

Klarsfeld shook his head sadly.

"Oh, Ellen ..."

51

At home, Ellen poured herself a large schnapps and downed it in one. Then she poured herself another. She wandered across to the window in her sitting room and looked down on cityscape which greeted her. London, a city with almost 10 million inhabitants, her neighbours, some Engländers, others German. One of the largest cities in the Greater German Reich, but less than half the size of Germania.

This city, London, was her home now. She didn't know Germania, she didn't know Germany, not anymore. She wasn't even sure that she actually considered herself to be a true German. She had spent so long in the *Deutscher Staat von Großbritannien* that she truly considered herself to be more … more English? She spoke German a lot of the time, but she also spoke English too, and she spoke the language well, with barely a hint of an accent.

She closed her eyes and leant her head against the coolness of the windowpane. She had gone to Klarsfeld seeking answers, and though he hadn't spelled it out to her, the nature of the mission she was endeavouring to conceal for him was becoming all too apparent.

Two years ago, she had attempted to prevent the assassination of the previous Führer by men from Combat UK, one of whom she had fallen in love with. Now she found herself once again in the midst of a plot to assassinate the Führer, but this time she was on the other side. This time, she had been asked not to prevent it but to help to facilitate it.

She thought about her parents. Her father, the industrialist, her mother the faithful *hausfrau*. They were proud of her when she'd joined the Geheime Staatspolizei. As a German living in the DSvG, she had automatically, after her training, been assigned to Department D, which worked in the so-called occupied territories, the outlying states of the Greater German Reich. When she had been working undercover, she hadn't told her parents the scope of her work, hadn't revealed to them that she'd been ordered to get in a relationship with Jerome Varley, the young Engländer. Thinking the relationship was genuine, both of her parents had quietly disapproved, with her father telling her that she could potentially ruin her career in the Gestapo. Of course, once the truth had come out, they'd both been so proud of her, particularly after she'd been awarded the Order of the Iron Cross 2nd Class for her bravery.

Ellen walked to her bedroom, still carrying the schnapps. She opened the drawer of her bedside cabinet and took out a small box. Inside was her medal. She held it in her hand, inspected it, recalled the moment when it had been awarded to her. The ceremony. Herself and a number of other officers who had tried, in vain, to prevent the assassination. For each of them it had been a bittersweet moment. They were being honoured for their bravery and determination and yet they had failed in their task.

Also, Ellen had seen the man she had fallen in love with die before her, bleeding out from numerous bullet wounds.

She had worn the medal only once, on that day, dressed in her grey uniform with the *totenkopf* on one lapel and the word *Gestapo* embroidered in white on a green background on the other lapel. Dress uniforms were rarely worn by Gestapo officers – only during training or on ceremonial occasions. The Iron Cross had been pinned to her uniform, and a red, black and white ribbon was sewn onto the front pocket. After the ceremony, Ellen had put away the medal and the jacket, and had not looked at either again.

The medal felt heavy in her hand. When she had been presented with it, she had found it difficult to feel proud of her achievement. Now as she looked at it, she still could not muster up any pride. She could feel only shame because this medal was one of the greatest honours a person serving the Fatherland could receive, and she was now working towards betraying the Fatherland. Betraying and destroying.

In order to kill the Führer, the Americans were prepared to destroy an entire city, killing millions of people in the process. Klarsfeld was seemingly happy to go along with this and he expected Ellen to feel the same.

Ellen finished her schnapps and lay down on her bed, clutching the Iron Cross to her chest.

There had to be another way.

52

Ellen spent three days off work. She visited a medical officer and explained that she felt stressed, something which in itself was a dangerous thing for a Gestapo officer to admit. Work-related stress was invariably considered to be a sign of weakness, and officers were given limited time to 'pull themselves together', before they were removed from their post.

Individuals who continued to suffer with stress and who could not work as a consequence were subject to investigation by the *Reichsarbeitsdienst*, the Labour Service. The RAD ensured that feeble people were not a drain on society. They could assign such individuals to a konzentrationslager or recommend them for *Aktion T4*, the euthanasia programme which dealt with mentally and physically disabled people. Generally, *Aktion T4* worked to euthanize babies or young children before they became a financial burden to the Reich, but where adults suffered injury or illness which resulted in them being considered *lebensunwertes Leben* – life unworthy of life – then *Aktion T4* would euthanize them. When news of the existence of the *Aktion T4* policy filtered out to the population, the *Reichsministerium für Volksaufklärung und Propaganda* worked tirelessly to explain that euthanasia under such circumstances was considered *Gnadentod* – a mercy killing.

It certainly wasn't unheard of for previously healthy people to succumb to severe depression, be designated as incurable, and subsequently euthanized. As she'd left the medical officer the day after her visit with Klarsfeld, Ellen was determined that such a fate would not befall her.

She'd walked the streets of London's city centre, pausing occasionally to look around at the buildings, at the people, at the Nazi regalia. She paid a visit to the Denkmalhalle, the memorial building to Adolf Hitler which had, at one time, been a Christian cathedral. Inside, there was a virtual altar to the founder of the Thousand Year Reich. A huge tapestry hung on the back wall, a hundred feet by forty, a portrait of Hitler pensively stroking his chin. The ceiling and the interior of the magnificent dome were adorned with beautiful murals showing not just Hitler but moments in his history, his rise to power, his victory over the countries of Europe. Beneath the dome was a statue of Hitler standing a hundred feet tall. Engraved upon the black marble plinth upon which the statue stood was the quote, 'Without law and order, our nation cannot survive.'

Ellen looked up at the face of the man many considered to be not just the first Führer, but the only Führer of the German people. The passion of his convictions was etched onto his face. This was a man whom Ellen had looked up to in the past. The history lessons had enforced upon her, upon her fellow students, Hitler's greatness. He was not just a brilliant military tactician, he was also a man who loved the Fatherland, who loved the German people, who wanted only the best for the people of his country.

But now, Ellen's mind was in turmoil. Should she believe some of the criticisms of the Reich, of the regime, which she had heard of in the past? Was Germany really such a great country to live in? Were the German people truly happy? Did the Reich look after each and every one of them?

She spent two days trying to sleep, the telephone off the hook, her mobile phone switched off. She didn't want to think about work and she didn't want to think about the mess Klarsfeld had dragged her into. As she forced herself out of bed on the fourth day, determined to go to the Polizeipräsidium, she turned on her mobile phone and was greeted by a torrent of messages from Willi Himmler.

She ignored them. He could wait.

She still hadn't decided what she was going to do next. Did she really want to be involved in a plot where potentially millions of people were going to be sacrificed in order to assassinate one man.

"Not just one man," Klarsfeld had said. "The entire cabinet. It has to be everyone. We have to wipe out all traces of the Nazi leadership. It is the only way we can be sure a new, fresh, modern regime will take over."

Ellen dressed and left the house, travelled to the HQ in her BMW.

In her office, she reviewed the evidence, the information that had been gathered about Barry Rhodes, Harry Dean, Paul Dauny and Tom Flannigan. The four of them were linked. Rhodes, the American spy; Dean, the Combat UK leader; Flannigan, the facilitator or collaborator; and Dauny, the computer expert, the mass murderer.

He had to be stopped. He couldn't be allowed to proceed with whatever mission he'd been tasked.

There was a knock at her door and she looked up to see SS-Sturmbannführer Loritz looking at her. There was a pained expression on his face.

"Frau Brauchitsch, how are you feeling?"

"I feel better, mein Herr," she answered. "I also feel ... ashamed."

"Ashamed?" he asked her, stepping into her office. He sat down opposite her. "Why would you feel ashamed?"

"Taking time off because of stress."

Loritz frowned. It was like he didn't know where to look. His eyes fell on her. "I suppose we all need time away from work. You could have taken a leave of absence."

"I cannot lie, mein Herr," she explained. "It seemed better for me to tell the truth. We were taught honesty at the academy."

"Indeed we were. We were also taught it in the Hitlerjugend. I cannot think of a solitary German who was not a member of the Hitlerjugend. And a belief in honesty was foisted upon us when we were children. When we were young men and young women."

"Of course."

"And yet there are people who choose to lie," Loritz said. Ellen felt the blood leave her face. She knew she looked pale. Adrenaline had begun to course through her veins and her limbs felt shaky. The Sturmbannführer looked at her. "Do you know of whom I speak?"

"I am not sure."

"You are a very skilled investigator, Ellen, and yet I removed you from the investigation out of fear that perhaps you were involved." Loritz sighed. "I was wrong. I should have kept you on the investigation into the attempt on Klarsfeld's life."

"I see."

"Do you? Do you see the problems, the inaccuracies, the suspicious activities?"

"I am not sure I do, Herr Sturmbannführer."

"Klarsfeld was hit by one single bullet," Loritz said. "A stray round which caught him in the arm. The first three bullets, they all missed him. And yet Dougie Hardcastle was perhaps just six feet away. Even a child who has never before fired a pistol could manage to hit someone from that distance. It is illogical and unthinkable for any would-be assassin to miss from six feet."

Ellen thought about what Klarsfeld had told her. He was worried that Loritz was getting close to the truth. For a very brief moment, she wanted to be open with her commanding officer. She opened her mouth, but then paused.

"But ... why would the assassin miss?"

"This I cannot say." Loritz shrugged. "For some reason it was viewed as better to have Klarsfeld alive rather than dead. And I cannot even come up with a guess as to why that should be. I suppose you are curious as to why I have come to you with this."

"Perhaps ..."

"You were close to Klarsfeld. I know you gave an accurate report of him based upon the time you spent in his company, but is there anything about him you could have missed? Anything suspicious at all?"

"I cannot think of anything," Ellen said.

And her betrayal of the Reich was complete.

53

Zimmerman turned to Himmler. The frustration and annoyance was evident on his face. He was smoking a cigarette. Himmler wafted the smoke away and wound down the window.

"You should fucking step outside if you want to smoke, Zimmerman, you fucking pig."

"Himmler, why are we sat here doing nothing? I feel uncomfortable from all of this sitting with my thumb up my arsehole."

They were, once again, outside the offices of Gerhard Fieseler Werke, waiting for Herr Dauny to complete his day at work. They'd already checked at Harry Dean's house, but the Engländer was still away on holiday. They were wasting time and growing bored and their investigation wasn't proceeding in any positive direction.

"This is the work of an investigator," Himmler said, though without any conviction.

"Your ex-partner, our leader, what is she doing? She is sick and we are pissing around watching an office."

"Well, what would you suggest?"

"We need to interrogate somebody."

"Ach, you are just desperate to torture someone," Himmler said with a dismissive wave of the hand. "There is more to investigation than that."

"Dauny would crack—"

"Dauny is a loyal Party member and we have little grounds to interrogate him," Himmler said.

"Then the landlord, Flannigan. He will talk."

"Oh, you think, do you?"

"Everybody talks in the end, Himmler."

Himmler had to admit that their current line of investigation did seem to be a waste of their time. Dauny got up, went to work, left work, went home and then went to bed. Perhaps Dauny was not actually connected to Combat UK. Perhaps the key personnel were Rhodes – already in custody – Harry Dean and Tom Flannigan.

But Dean was away. Away where? A couple of years ago, Scotland was the place where Combat UK terrorists received training. Much of the countryside was secluded, and training camps could be well hidden. Combat UK was, according to intelligence, a spent force, and yet they still carried out terrorist atrocities.

Was Dean away on a training exercise?

The Bretton Sports and Social Club, was that a terrorist hub? The man who had attempted to kill Reichsstatthalter Klarsfeld, Dougie Hardcastle, he'd been a customer of the club. Rhodes too. There was no smoke without fire. Was Flannigan the leader? He couldn't have been. He was so unassuming.

But then, would the leader of a group of terrorists actually look like a terrorist?

"We have to do something," Zimmerman urged. "Imagine if we do nothing and something happens."

Himmler sighed. "You know, Zimmerman, you have this innate ability to create sentences that mean absolutely fuck all." He wafted away more cigarette smoke. "Put that thing out and take us to the Sports Club."

54

Tom Flannigan looked up from the newspaper as he saw something out of the corner of his eye. A car was pulling into the car park, a black BMW M3. He was getting rather used to visits from the Gestapo. Cursing under his breath, he folded up the newspaper and picked up a tea-towel, a barman's weapon of choice, the prop to make him feel less naked, less exposed, something for his hands to play with when he was nervous.

It was 10am, the Club was empty. Even the hardened alcoholics generally didn't arrive much before eleven o'clock. Tom opened the dishwasher and began to take out the glasses, wiping them quickly with the tea-towel before putting them on the shelves.

The door to the Club swung open and two young Gestapo officers came in. He recognized both of them. They'd been here before. The pretty young female was not with them this time. They came up to the bar and Tom smiled at them.

"Morning, chaps, what can I do you for?"

"Herr Flannigan," the older of the two said. Both of them looked around the Club, obviously taking in the fact that there were no customers. The younger man walked over to the door, looked it up and down and then locked it.

"Can I help you with anything?"

"We would like a word, Herr Flannigan."

"I can see that." The younger officer walked back to the bar, walked through the entrance and stood beside Tom. "Staff only behind the bar."

"My colleague," the older one said, "Herr Untersturmführer Zimmerman, believes that you can help us without enquiries."

"I'll do my best," Tom said. He was starting to realize that he was now in a vulnerable and dangerous position. These two Gestapo men, they'd been here before, they weren't stupid. They'd connected him to other suspects. For a moment, he wondered whether Barry Rhodes had cracked under interrogation, whether he'd given away another name, whether he'd given them Tom's name.

Zimmerman, the younger officer, grabbed the back of Tom's neck and forced his head down onto the bar. It was a slow but effective movement, one which Tom could not fight. His cheek was pressed down onto the wood and he couldn't raise his head. His glasses were forced away from his face.

"Easy, tiger."

"Can you tell us where Harry Dean is?" the older Gestapo officer asked.

"He's on holiday."

"Where?"

"Up north, I think," Tom said. "I don't know exactly where. I don't take that keen an interest in the whereabouts of my customers if they're not here." Tom felt his head being forced harder into the bar. Zimmerman's hand was clasped around the side of his neck, the side of his face. A fist caught Tom in the stomach and his legs buckled, but because his head was clamped so tightly against the bar, he didn't slide away. "Leave it out," he protested. "I don't know nothing."

"Oh, I believe you do, Herr Flannigan," the older Gestapo man said. "I believe that you know pretty much everything that is going on around here. Your establishment seems to be at the very centre of everything that is rotten about this filthy town of yours."

"That's ridiculous."

Tom was finding it hard, and very undignified, to talk in his current position. His glasses were being pushed further from his face and his vision, as a consequence, was blurring.

"Just let me up," he said.

Zimmerman loosened his grip and Tom could raise his head. And then the German rammed Tom's face back down onto to bar with such force that Tom's glasses broke and stars dotted his vision. Stunned, he slid downwards, but Zimmerman hauled him back upright.

"Tell us what you know."

"The only thing I know, me old duck, is that you're barred!" Tom said, his voice defiant.

Zimmerman chuckled. "The humour of the Engländer."

"I think you are lying to us," the older German said. "We will take you back to the Polizeipräsidium in London. You will talk to us there, Herr Flannigan."

Tom cursed and wished that he, like Harry Dean, carried a cyanide capsule. They had told him that he would not be targeted by the Gestapo, that he would be viewed as harmless, and indeed for many years that had

nach Schema F

been the case. But Peterborough had become more high profile over the last few weeks, thanks in part to Dougie Hardcastle's attempt on Klarsfeld's life. And the focus of interest had been placed upon the Bretton Sports and Social Club. It was inevitable that Tom would come to the attentions of the Gestapo as a consequence.

He felt himself being dragged by Zimmerman to the door of the Club. The cold air hit him as he was taken outside. They didn't bother locking the door and for a brief moment, Tom worried about the security of the Club, about the profits that could be stolen, but then the reality sank in, that he would never have to worry about the Club's security again. He would never be returning here. The Club would be closed forever, probably razed to the ground. There was a good chance that some Club members would also find themselves being pulled in for questioning, interrogated, tortured, executed.

Tom wondered, as he was cuffed and thrown into the M3, how long he would hold out before the desire to give in, to stop the torture, to succumb to their questioning, overwhelmed him. He wondered whose name he would give up. He knew that the moment it was discovered that he'd been arrested, Harry Dean would disappear, but the Gestapo would not be satisfied if Tom gave them only Harry Dean's name, because they were already looking for him. They would want more from him, another name, more information, something that would encourage them to stop torturing him.

The journey down to London seemed to last forever, even though the M3 was travelling fast, scything its way through the traffic, its siren occasionally sounding, demanding that other vehicles get out of its way. Tom didn't want the journey to end because he knew that once he arrived at the Gestapo's headquarters, the real pain would start.

That was part of their methodology, building up the fear in those they were questioning, making them wait, all the while making sure they knew that far worse was to come. Tom had never felt this terrified in all of his life.

Once the M3 reached London, it slowed somewhat, but still carved its way past cars and buses and lorries, Zimmerman driving, blipping the siren whenever his route was blocked. Soon, Tom could see the skyscrapers of the city centre, the ominous black one belonging to the Schutzstaffel standing out amongst the more colourful ones of commerce.

The M3 drove down into an underground car park, its tyres chirping on the polished asphalt. It pulled into a space and its powerful engine was silenced.

Tom was frogmarched to a bank of elevators, and they rode down a few floors. These were the basement levels. Tom had heard stories of them. The lift stopped and the three of them stepped out into a reception area. The Gestapo men spoke in German and Tom was taken down a corridor and thrown into a cell.

The older Gestapo officer said, "We will return shortly, Herr Flannigan, and I hope you will be more willing to talk."

The door clanked shut and Tom was left in the dingy cell.

There was a single, hard bunk against one wall, a sink in one corner, a toilet basin in another. The weak light cast dark shadows where the unspeakable fears of a fertile and frightened imagination could hide away.

Tom heard a muffled scream from somewhere in the distance.

A shout.

He felt his heart pounding hard in his chest, and again he wished he had a cyanide capsule.

All he could do now was wait.

55

Ellen looked up and through her office door she saw Himmler and Zimmerman wandering into the open plan office beyond. Frowning, she got to her feet, poked her head out. Himmler was sitting down on the desk of the young rottenführer, Raubel. Zimmerman was firing up his computer.

Ellen shouted, "Willi, what is happening?"

Himmler smiled at the young Gestapo officer, gave her a wink, and then came over to Ellen.

"We arrested Flannigan," he said. "We have brought him in for questioning."

"Flannigan? But why?"

"Four days following Dauny and we have turned up nothing," Himmler said. "We have to find out what the terrorists are up to, Ellen. This is the only way. To interrogate somebody. We cannot interrogate Dauny, not without sufficient evidence, even though we all know that he is far more deeply involved in whatever Combat UK are up to."

"Willi, I asked you to keep him under surveillance," Ellen said, throwing her arms out in exasperation. "What the fuck?"

"But all he is doing is going to work, Ellen. Whatever his involvement is, we are not going to discover it just sitting around watching him farting around at work. We have to get some information that we can challenge him with."

"And you think this publican, this *barman*, will be able to give you that information?"

"The whole thing seems to revolve around that sports club, Ellen."

Ellen leant against the doorframe. Of course Himmler was right, but she was still torn in two different directions. On the one hand, there was her previously unquestionable loyalty to the Fatherland, but on the other, she was supposed to be preventing this plot from being uncovered.

She still wasn't sure which side of the fence she was prepared to jump down onto.

"Where is he?"

"In the holding cells," Himmler said. "I thought we would let him sweat for an hour or two."

"Have you told Loritz?"

"Not yet. I was going to ring you first. I did not know you were in today."

"I have had a tough few days," Ellen said. "Women's trouble."

"Of course," Himmler said, but she could tell he didn't believe her. "You want Zimmerman and me to question him?"

Ellen shot Himmler a harsh look. She knew that people thought she was incapable of interrogating and torturing suspects. It was like a slur on her abilities as a Gestapo officer. She looked across at Zimmerman, who was engrossed in whatever was on his computer screen.

"You and I will question him," she said. "Zimmerman can head back up to Peterborough to find Harry Dean."

"He is still away—"

"I am not going to fucking discuss this, Willi," Ellen snapped. Himmler held up a hand and nodded his head.

"Okay, Ellen, take it easy."

"We will interview him soon. Tell Zimmerman what I want him to do and then go and see Loritz." Ellen pushed past Himmler.

"Where are you going?"

Ellen stopped in her tracks and turned to face him. "I am going to change my tampon. Is that okay with you?"

Himmler raised an eyebrow and smirked.

"Meet me in the interrogation suite when you've seen Loritz," she told him.

Ellen went to the evidence room on the fourth floor of the Polizeipräsidium. She signed in with the clerk and then checked the computer system for one of her old cases. It didn't take her long.

The evidence room featured aisle upon aisle of shelves, with numbered boxes containing evidence relating to every current case under investigation. Ellen took down a box from the shelf, opened it, rummaged inside. She found what she was looking for.

She took the elevator down to the basement levels and got off at the holding cells. There was nobody in the reception area. She could hear laughter coming from a room at the back – the rest area. She checked the booking-in sheet and found out which cell Flannigan was located in. The cell doors could only be opened from the outside. There were no keys.

nach Schema F

She stepped into Flannigan's cell and looked at him.

He was sat on the bunk. His cheek was swollen, his spectacles broken. He looked up at her.

"Herr Flannigan." He didn't respond. Ellen poked her head out of the cell door, looked up the corridor. There was no-one there. "We have not got much time."

"You're wasting your time," Flannigan said.

"Wait a second," Ellen said, holding up a hand. "Hear me out. I am sorry that you have been arrested. I tried to prevent this. I was tasked with preventing this." Flannigan frowned. "There is nothing I can do for you now, Herr Flannigan." She reached in her pocket and took out the item she'd retrieved from the evidence room. She handed it to the Engländer. He looked down at it.

It was a small capsule, red and black.

Flannigan looked at her.

"You can either bite down on it," she told him, "or you can let it dissolve in your stomach. The first method is pretty much instant. The second method will take two or three minutes." She paused, closed her eyes. "I am sorry," she said. "Either method will be painful."

He nodded.

"I really am sorry, Herr Flannigan."

"You're doing a good thing," he told her. He rubbed the capsule between the fingers of his right hand, removing her fingerprints. Ellen backed out of the cell. She closed the door and leant her head against it.

Another person sacrificed, and she'd had a direct hand in it.

She walked back to the reception area. As she did, two Waffen-SS officers came from the canteen area.

"Frau Obersturmführer, can we help you?" one of them asked.

The elevator made a sound as the doors opened. Ellen said, "I am wondering why there was nobody on duty at this desk when I arrived." She turned to see Himmler stepping out into the reception. He looked at the Waffen-SS officers and then at Ellen.

"I am sorry, Frau Obersturmführer, we only stepped out for a moment."

"This is supposed to be a secure area!"

"Ellen, cool it," Himmler said quietly.

"Fucking imbeciles," Ellen hissed.

Himmler smiled at the guards and then led Ellen up the corridor to the holding cells.

"Are you okay, Ellen?"

"I am fine."

"You do not seem it," Himmler said as they stopped outside the cell where Flannigan was being held. "Look, there are rumours going round—"

"Fucking rumours."

"Ellen, take a few days annual leave."

"I do not need to take any leave."

"You are becoming ... difficult," Himmler said.

Ellen felt like hitting him. But her anger would help to mask the fact that she knew what was going to greet them on the other side of this cell door. Himmler reached for the handle, twisted it, the door unlocked. He pulled it open and they both looked inside.

56

Tom looked down at the small capsule in the palm of his hand. Its colours, red and black, signified danger. He knew that the moment the cyanide hit his system, he would struggle to breathe. He would start to have a seizure. He would rapidly lose consciousness, but in the few moments before that happened he would feel pain and panic.

He had no idea how long he had left before the Gestapo officers returned.

He didn't want to die. He certainly didn't want to kill himself. But he had no choice. What lay beyond was torture, pain, and betrayal, and he wanted no part in that. It was an easy choice to make, but a difficult one to perform.

He thought about his life, his youth, working as a chef at one of the finest restaurants in London. He had served up food for leading Nazis and he had been paid well for doing so. The Nazi regime had essentially paid for his training, set him up for the future. Back then, he hadn't really cared about politics. He just enjoyed work, socializing with his friends, getting drunk and generally having a laugh with friends. The money came in and the money went out. He even drank in the company of a couple of junior SS officers.

But then things had changed. He'd grown up, he'd sobered up, he'd moved out of London, moved back to Peterborough, where his family were from. By that time, his mother was dead, his father was suffering from dementia and his brother was in custody for fraud. Tom had watched the Nazis come and take his father. He'd been kept in a secure hospital for two months while they'd assessed him, and then then he'd been euthanized under the *Aktion T4* directive.

It wasn't long before Combat UK capitalized on his grief. Some said that they were like a parasitic organization, latching onto targets, using grief and anger as a tool to increase animosity towards the regime, to turn them against the Germans. Tom didn't subscribe to that point of view. As far as he was concerned, the Combat UK people who came to see him, they were talking perfect sense. He agreed with everything they said.

Back then, he was in his thirties, he was more active. They'd taught him how to shoot a gun, and he'd shot dead off-duty SS officers, some of them in front of their families. He hadn't felt guilty. They were Germans, they worked for the security forces, they were the enemy, and the families of those men had to understand that their husbands, their fathers, their sons and brothers were all legitimate targets.

Tom didn't agree with indiscriminate bombing. He believed that the work he did, carrying out targeted assassinations and executions, was the best way to fight against the regime whilst ensuring that innocent people were not killed. More violent splinter groups had come and gone, but their reckless ruthlessness had seen the Nazis hunt them down mercilessly and kill them and their families.

Combat UK had continued to be successful.

Tom had been on the Army Council for a number of years, helping to make decisions which had moulded the future of the organization. He maintained a low profile by working first as a barman, then as a pub manager, before becoming the landlord at the Bretton Sports and Social Club.

His had been a lonely existence, filled with brief love affairs and one-night stands. He couldn't afford to have a deep relationship. Nobody in Combat UK could. If you had a family, if you had a wife, children, they were all potential targets. Tom had decided long ago that he wouldn't place any woman in such a position of danger.

He loved children, but he felt he couldn't have any of his own. The Nazis were not averse to killing children, to shooting babies even. It was referred to as collective punishment. Even criminals risked having their families arrested and sent to concentration camps. Terrorists risked having their families shot in front of them. Their partners, their children, their parents, their siblings, their grandparents, their uncles and aunts. Sometimes entire family trees were eradicated.

So Tom had slept with women, but had not allowed himself to become attached to any of them. More than that, he hadn't allowed any of them to become attached to him. At the moment when he felt any form of attachment, he walked away. He didn't care what the women thought of him. He was saving them. They'd never know how fortunate they were that he hadn't allowed himself to fall in love with them, that he had destroyed the potential for love they had felt for him.

nach Schema F

And now here he was, not just contemplating suicide but actually preparing himself to do it, and what did he have to show for all of the years he'd spent alive? What had he achieved during the time he'd spent on this mortal coil?

He looked down at the cyanide capsule.

He said, "I fought."

He heard the door opening and looked up to see the female officer who had given him the capsule standing there with the older Gestapo officer who had arrested him.

He said, "You'll never take me alive, copper," and thrust the capsule in his mouth, crushing it between his teeth. He felt the liquid flow across his tongue, finding the fine capillaries and blood vessels close the surface, crossing into his bloodstream, poisoning him.

He couldn't breathe. He felt confused. His chest tightened up.

Everything went black. He could feel himself falling.

Then there was nothing.

57

Himmler jumped forwards as Flannigan began to fall. He was cursing under his breath, and managed to catch the Engländer before he slid completely off the bunk. He laid him down and checked for a pulse.

"Fuck!"

"Is he dead?" Ellen asked, though she already knew the answer. She'd have known the answer even if she hadn't supplied Flannigan with the tools to kill himself. She'd seen the consequences of cyanide poisoning before.

"Fuck!" Himmler cursed again. Losing a suspect to suicide was a bureaucratic nightmare.

"Did you search him before you put him in here?" Ellen asked him.

"Of course we searched him!" Himmler began to perform CPR on Flannigan.

"He has taken cyanide, Willi, he is fucking dead."

"This cannot be happening!"

Ellen stepped up to the alarm button and pushed it. A klaxon sounded, and seconds later three Waffen-SS officers came barrelling into the cell.

"Call the Medical Officer," Ellen told them. "He is dead." She pushed past them, stepped out into the corridor and leant against the wall. One of the officers was on a radio, calling the incident in to the control room. Himmler wandered out of the cell. He looked dejected. This would reflect badly on him. She felt sorry for him.

"How the fuck did we miss that?"

"He could have hidden it anywhere, Willi."

"Shit!" Himmler punched the cell door nearest to him. "We searched him, but …"

Ellen held up a hand. "Willi, none of us waste time searching for cyanide capsules. We look for weapons, that is all. He could have hidden that under his ball sack or between his toes. We cannot search everywhere."

"But we sign to say that we have," Himmler said, running his hand through his hair. "Loritz is going to go mad."

"It is not the first time the Gestapo has lost prisoners, Willi."

nach Schema F

"But it is the first time I have lost a prisoner."

"Come on," she said, patting his arm. "Let us go out for a coffee. We can write the report later. I think you and I need to have a chat."

"A chat? What about?"

"Just about stuff," Ellen said. She started to walk and was almost at the reception area when she realized Himmler wasn't following. She turned back.

"We have fucked this investigation up," Himmler said.

"We cannot win each one," she told him.

He started to walk, caught up with her. "You are taking this remarkably well, Ellen."

"What else can I do? We have lost one of our suspects. Shouting and screaming and punching doors is not going to change that. We just have to adapt." They were at the elevator doors. "And do not worry, Willi. I will buy the coffees." She smiled at him. He didn't smile back.

58

Zimmerman wasn't happy being told what to do by a woman. He didn't really agree with women being in positions of authority. They weren't built for command, neither physically nor mentally. The fact that Brauchitsch had been sick for three days was evidence of that.

She'd despatched him back to Peterborough but hadn't even seen fit to give him the order directly. She'd given the command to Himmler (and what the hell was that about, Himmler keeping the surname of one of the Reich's most revered men?) and he'd passed it onto Zimmerman.

And there was definitely something odd about the pair of them. He knew that Brauchitsch and Himmler had been partnered for a year, but they seemed very close. They called one another by their first names, which Zimmerman felt was very unprofessional. Colleagues at work needed those professional boundaries.

But in spite of his annoyance at being told what to do by a woman, he was relieved to be working alone. He felt as though he'd finally been given a degree of responsibility commensurate with his rank, and not before time as well.

He parked the Kripo Audi close to Harry Dean's house and switched off the engine. This fucking country was too cold and wet, and he knew he'd have to switch the engine back on before too long to demist the windows and heat the car up. He wondered how he'd ended up being sent to this State of the Greater German Reich, who he'd pissed off at the academy to be given this assignment.

He looked at Dean's house but couldn't see any sign of movement.

He supposed this was just going to be more sitting down and waiting.

He did that for half an hour, before the chill started to get to him.

"Fuck this," he muttered, and he hopped out of the car, locking it shut with the remote as he walked towards Dean's house. He knew that neighbours would be watching. The arrival of a BMW M3 always caught the attention of the public, but even though Zimmerman was in a less conspicuous Kriminalpolizei Audi, it was still too expensive a car for a regular citizen to own. Right now, they'd be looking out from behind their curtains, wondering whose house he was going to visit.

nach Schema F

Zimmerman knocked on Dean's front door but he wasn't expecting a response and wasn't surprised when he didn't get one. He looked in the front windows, saw a dining room, a sitting room, no signs of movement. He took a couple of steps back, looked up at the upstairs windows. The curtains were open, but they weren't twitching. He doubted whether Dean was hiding away up there.

Round the back of the house he looked through a window, saw the interior of a kitchen. The back door was locked. The garden was slightly overgrown. There was a shed, the wood cracked in places. The door was padlocked shut. Zimmerman looked through the shed window, saw garden tools, a lawnmower, a pushbike.

His phone started to ring and he took it from his pocket. It was Himmler.

"Yes?"

"Zimmerman, Brauchitsch and I are coming up to Peterborough. We have lost Flannigan."

"Lost him? What do you mean? He escaped?"

"In a way," Himmler said. "He poisoned himself. Cyanide."

Zimmerman shook his head. "Damn it."

"It happens."

"What has Loritz said?"

"He is not happy," Himmler replied. "But his words were also, 'It happens'."

"When are you coming up?"

"We should be there early this evening. Can you get us all booked into the hotel?" Zimmerman rolled his eyes. Was he a fucking clerical assistant now? "Have you seen Dean?"

"No. I am at his house but there is nobody here still."

"Okay, well, we will see you soon."

The call ended. Zimmerman shook his head and pocketed the phone. He stepped up to the back door, tried the handle again, as though he expected it to have magically unlocked itself in the last couple of minutes. He reached in his pocket and removed a set of lock picks. It was part of basic training at the academy, but he wasn't particularly proficient at it. It took him five minutes to get the door open.

Inside, the house stank of stale food. Zimmerman saw the overflowing bin, unemptied, and cursed the filthy Engländer who had left it in such a state. He looked quickly through the kitchen cupboards but found nothing of interest. He searched all of the rooms downstairs but they too held no secrets. Upstairs, he looked through both bedrooms and the bathroom. Again, no sign of Harry Dean, no sign of anything suspicious. The spare bedroom had a bookcase, and Zimmerman picked some of the books from the shelves at random. None of them appeared to be on the list of banned literature.

He rummaged through a filing cabinet which contained old correspondence, mostly bills, insurance documents, the registration deeds for his car, guarantee paperwork for electrical items. There were a few old letters, and Zimmerman read a couple, but they seemed perfectly innocuous. He knew, however, that a full search of the house might reveal addresses for contacts. He made a mental note to suggest this to Brauchitsch when he saw her later on.

But after a quick glance through the property, there was nothing to interest a Gestapo investigator. If he didn't know better, he'd have said that Dean was a model citizen.

He was about to descend the stairs when he heard a key in the front door.

nach Schema F

59

Willi put his phone down on the table and looked at Ellen. He had to confess that he found her attractive, and though he'd never admit it to anyone else, he did have something of a crush on her. He'd known when they'd first been partnered that she was destined for better things. She had that way about her, that confidence and arrogance, something he'd berated her for in the past, but of which he was secretly in awe.

Of course, he'd never mustered up the courage needed to ask her out on a date. The rumours – and he believed them to be true – were that she had no time for love, not since the undercover operation she'd been involved in a couple of years ago. She certainly showed no signs of ever warming to his advances of friendship, and so they'd spent much of their time as partners in a cycle of banter and bickering.

They were sat in a coffee shop close the Polizeipräsidium. True to her word, Ellen had paid for their drinks. He'd chosen a table next to the window, where they could see the rain sodden streets and the people rushing along them, umbrellas shielding them from the elements.

Ellen said, "Loritz will not be pissed off for long."

"It made us look like fools," Willi said.

"Yes, it did. But I know for a fact he has lost a couple of prisoners himself."

Willi smiled. "You have done research on our leader?"

"Of course. Did you not?"

Willi shrugged. "I figured it could be traced."

"Perhaps, but believe me, it is expected."

Willi took a sip of the coffee. It was hot and bitter.

"What did Zimmerman say?"

"He said he was at Harry Dean's house but that no one is home."

Ellen stared out the window and for a moment, it was as though she were lost in her own little world. She let out a deep breath. "I think that perhaps Herr Dean has gone on the run."

"I think I agree," Willi said. "I just wish we could find out what they are up to."

"Perhaps we will not. We cannot win them all, Willi."

They were both silent for couple of minutes, both lost in their own thoughts as they sipped their coffee. Then Willi said, "Are you okay, Ellen. I mean, are you really okay? You seem ... different."

"I am fine. Just tired."

"You can be honest with me, you know," Willi said, but he knew that nobody was ever truly honest in the Reich. People were suspicious of others and kept their secrets to themselves. Ellen smiled at him.

"You are sweet, Willi."

"I think a lot of you," he told her. "I mean, as a colleague. I think a lot of you as a colleague." She was still smiling. She reached across the table, patted his hand.

"Thank you, Willi."

"Tell me, have you ever thought about returning to Germania? Or even just to Germany?"

"Have you?"

Willi shook his head. "The strange thing is, I do actually like it here. It rains a lot, yes, and the Engländer, a lot of them hate us. And I do not have your accent, so everyone can tell I am a German, but ... this just seems like home, you know?"

"I know."

"I have not been here as long as you though."

"No, you have not. Do I want to return to Germany? I do not think so. I have pretty much grown up here. This is my home. Germany, it just seems like a foreign place. When I went there with the Reichsstatthalter recently, it just seemed so different, so alien. I could not live there."

"I guess we should both hope that we do not get posted back there on a reassignment."

"Officers in the provinces rarely return to Germany," Ellen said. "We have so much local knowledge, they prefer to keep us here. In fact, I think that most of Germania's officers regard us as backward and provincial."

"And after losing my prisoner, I suppose I should expect to be considered backward and provincial even by the SS officers stationed here."

"Oh please, Willi, stop feeling sorry for yourself."

Willi grinned. "Okay, but tell me, what do you really think these terrorists are up to? Flannigan, Dean, Rhodes, Dauny even. What have they been planning?"

nach Schema F

Ellen was distant. Her eyes narrowed and it was like she was staring into space, gazing into the past. Or into the future. "I kind of feel that this will be something terrible."

"Well, that has cheered me up no end." Ellen glanced down at her drink. She looked like a woman with the weight of the world on her shoulders. "I still think you need some time off, time away from here, from work. Why do you not take a vacation?" She shook her head.

"When this is over, Willi, I am sure there will be plenty of time for a vacation."

"I hope you are right."

Ellen finished her coffee and stood up. "Come on," she said. "Let us see what mischief Zimmerman is up to."

Willi let out a sigh. Something was wrong with her, but it was apparent she wasn't going to open up to him. But she knew that if she did need a friend, he would be there for her.

He couldn't do any more than that.

60

As soon as he opened the front door of his house, Harry Dean knew that he wasn't alone. Some people would call it a sixth sense, but Harry would probably have put it down to the fact that he'd been trained to spot this sort of stuff. His ears, his eyes, they were finely attuned to every small detail, to spot subtle changes, to hear the quietest of sounds.

He reached inside his jacket, took out the Browning Hi Power pistol. A 9mm round was already chambered, the hammer back, the pistol made ready. He flicked off the safety. He didn't actually want to have to fire the pistol. It would make too much noise and someone would call the Orpo.

He had just returned from Scotland, having driven home, and wanted to take a shower to freshen up before making his way to a rendezvous with Marcus Dauny at the Bretton Sports and Social Club. They had a week before the window of opportunity, and Harry wanted to know how close Dauny and his old university friend, Owen Dunne, were to achieving their aims.

Harry cursed himself for not checking the street before he'd entered his house.

He checked the lounge, saw no one. There was no one in the dining room or the kitchen. Looking around, he noticed that one of the drawers was slightly open, and one of the cupboard doors was slightly ajar. Somebody had definitely been in here. He paused, stood still for a few seconds, cocking his head to one side. He wondered momentarily whether whoever in his house was adopting a similar position.

He made his way to the stairs.

He had two options. He could either lull the intruder into a false sense of security by walking casually up the stairs, or he could alert the intruder to the fact that he suspected somebody was in his house by cautiously climbing the stairs. Either option was fraught with danger.

At the bottom of the stairs, he took a deep breath, and then, gun held out in front of him, he began to ascend. He reached the landing. All of the doors were open. The bathroom was empty. He could see that from where he stood. He carefully entered his bedroom, gun first. It was empty, but he could smell something. Deodorant, unfamiliar to him.

nach Schema F

This bedroom was empty.

The intruder was in the spare room. Had to be.

Harry stepped up to the doorway of the spare room. The door was half open. With his gun still held out in front of him, he pushed the door with his left hand. There was movement from inside the room and someone slammed into him, knocking him to the ground. The Browning was still in his hand, but whoever had attacked him grabbed his wrist and proceeded to bang it against the floor. Harry grabbed the person's face with his left hand and thrust it backwards, kicking up with one of his legs.

The intruder rolled backwards, banging his head against the doorframe. Harry moved his gun hand, but the intruder kicked out, this time succeeding in knocking the pistol out of Harry's grip. Harry looked to see where it had fallen, but that gave the intruder the opportunity to throw himself back onto Harry. His hands moved around Harry's neck, the thumbs pushing down on his Adam's apple. Harry punched with both hands on either side of his attacker's head. The attacker's grip loosened and Harry grabbed both wrists and wrenched them free. The attacker started to fall, so Harry thrust a hand upwards and placed it around the man's throat. He squeezed tight. The intruder started to lash out with his fists, catching Harry in the face. Harry pushed him to one side and scrabbled back to his feet just as the intruder was trying to stand. He kicked the intruder in the face a couple of times.

And then the intruder pulled a gun.

Harry leapt to the side as the gun was fired, the report loud in the confined space of the landing. He had to act quickly now. It was possible that his neighbours would call the Orpo to report the gunshot. It was also obvious that this intruder was Gestapo, which meant that it was highly probably more Gestapo officers were in the vicinity. Harry's cover was blown. He had to put this man down and go on the run.

He threw himself down onto the intruder, his knee catching the man in the stomach, winding him. He punched him viciously in the face with one hand, whilst holding the man's gun hand down with the other. Harry was a lot larger than the intruder, and he was finding it easy to overpower him. Once he was happy that the man was subdued, he ripped the pistol from his hand and tossed it to one side.

And then he enveloped his huge hands around the man's neck and squeezed. The German's eyes widened and his hands clutched helplessly out towards Harry, not able to reach him. Harry squeezed his hands as tightly as he could. The German kicked out his legs, but Harry continued to tighten his grip, cutting off the air supply and blood flow. His struggling lessened until finally his hands flopped down. It had only taken ten or fifteen seconds to get to this point, but Harry kept on squeezing the guy's neck for a further minute to make sure he was dead.

He released his grip and searched through the man's pockets. As expected, he found the Gestapo ID. He tossed it to one side. He found two spare magazines for the man's pistol and he pocketed them. He also found a set of keys for an Audi, which he presumed would be parked outside. The Audi would probably ring as many alarm bells as his own car, but at least it was faster. Plus he wouldn't be driving it for long. Just long enough to get out of the immediate vicinity.

He scooped up the Gestapo man's SIG, his own Browning, and stepped into his bedroom. He went to the set of drawers next to his wardrobe, opened the second one down, rummaged through the underwear until he found a pair of brown socks with a red stripe around them. Inside the socks he located RM2,000 which he pocketed. Then he left the bedroom and bounded down the stairs. Perhaps three minutes had passed since the gun had been fired. He opened his front door, looked outside, listened for sirens. There were none. He spotted an Audi parked fifty yards up the road and made his way to it. He knew that his neighbours would be watching his every move. He wondered which of them would be the first to call the polizei.

He pressed the remote on the keyfob and the Audi's doors clunked as they unlocked. He hopped behind the wheel and fired up the engine. The Audi's tyres squeaked as he knocked it into drive and accelerated quickly from his house.

He had no idea how long it would be before the full might of the German security forces would be out searching for him, but he knew he didn't have much time. He had to make one stop, at the Bretton Sports and Social Club, and then he would head for Scotland.

It was always easy to lose yourself in Scotland.

61

Loritz looked down at the corpse of Tom Flannigan and shook his head. This man, he would've wagered, was a key figure in Combat UK. He'd thought that even before Flannigan had bitten into the cyanide capsule in front of Himmler and Brauchitsch. The defiant act of suicide only served to reinforce that view. Regular, innocent members of public did not kill themselves with a cyanide capsule whilst in captivity.

Himmler and Zimmerman had screwed up. Loritz couldn't blame Brauchitsch for this. It had been the other two who had arrested Flannigan and brought him in, and it was they who should've ensured that he had been searched properly. Sloppy police work. That was the problem with the younger recruits. Fast-tracked through the system because of their fine analytical skills, but they had no idea how to carry out the basics.

Loritz nodded at the crematorium worker, who wheeled the body into one of the furnaces. As far as Loritz was aware, Flannigan had no family, no one to return the body to. Under those circumstances, the bodies of dead prisoners were just cremated. The crematorium was on the ground floor of the Polizeipräsidium, to the rear, out of view of the general public.

He made his way to the main reception hall and there he found Schmid.

"Herr Sturmbannführer, may I have a word?"

They found an empty interview room and Loritz closed the door. The pair of them sat.

"So, your truth serum, Schmid? How goes it?"

"He gave me a name."

"A name?" Loritz's interest was piqued, but he wasn't confident this was going to be anything useful in terms of the investigation. He'd read about the so-called truth serums – merely barbiturates given in sufficient doses so as to relax the person being interrogated – and at the moment the current research wasn't particularly promising.

"Schottel," Schmid said. "He said he was a German friend and then he condemned him as a traitor."

"And I am presuming you have searched for Schottels?"

"There are four men with that surname in the DSvG. I am working my way through their files to see what assistance, if any, they could be providing to Combat UK."

"You have them under surveillance?"

"Naturally, mein Herr."

"Good. Let me know what you turn up."

"I heard about Tom Flannigan, the Engländer," Schmid said. "Did he give up any information at all?"

"I have not yet seen the full reports. Himmler and Zimmerman are currently continuing their investigations in Peterborough, but I am led to believe that he said nothing of consequence. It is unfortunate, but these things happen."

"These Engländers are up to something. But they are also very resilient."

"They certainly are. What else can you tell me about Rhodes?"

"His accent has dropped. He sounds less English. More American."

"Well, we suspected this all along," Loritz said.

"Will we be making an announcement to that effect?"

Loritz shook his head. "I would not think so. I have yet to bring this to the attention of the Reichsführer, but I would imagine that he will be more concerned with the trade deal which is currently being negotiated with the Americans." He knew that Schmid would've been expecting such an answer. He also knew that Schmid would not be happy with that answer, but there was nothing Loritz could do about that. The machinations of politics would always triumph over everything else.

Loritz stood up.

"Just see what else you can get out of him," he said. "Once he has outlived his usefulness, dispose of him. We can put an announcement in the press. It will still get back to the Americans."

Schmid nodded. "Yes, mein Herr."

Loritz saluted and left the room. He went up to his office, sat behind his desk and pondered on recent events. The Klarsfeld thing was still bugging him. There was something about it which just didn't smell right. And now there was the death of Tom Flannigan, who was from the same town – and undoubtedly the same Combat UK cell – as Dougie Hardcastle. All of these people, they were connected.

He had one of his brightest investigators in Peterborough, and another working with Rhodes, the American spy, but he was tempted to step from his ivory tower and take over the investigation himself. What were Brauchitsch and Schmid missing?

He leafed through one of the files on his desk, the one belonging to the Engländer, Marcus Dauny. Here was an intelligent man, Party member, a computer software engineer who was working on a government system, but so far no one had discovered which one. Clearly Gerhard Fieseler Werke were playing their cards close to their chest, which was something they were perfectly entitled to do. But Loritz's team had to know which system Dauny was working on in order to proceed with their investigation.

He logged into the secure computer system and sent an electronic letter to SS-Oberstgruppenführer Mittendorf's office, requesting that they give him authorization to demand that GFW reveal the nature of Dauny's work for them. He then read through Himmler's preliminary report on Flannigan's death. It detailed how he had arranged to meet Brauchitsch in the interrogation suite, that he found her in the reception berating the Waffen-SS officers for not being at their post, and that they had then gone to Flannigan's cell, unlocked it, whereupon the Engländer had remarked, "You'll never take me alive," before biting down on the cyanide capsule. Himmler had attempted CPR, but it was apparent that Flannigan was dead. Cyanide acted within a few seconds, and recovery was always highly unlikely. He put the report to one side and collected Brauchitsch's from his in-tray. Hers was almost identical to Himmler's, albeit from a different perspective.

Loritz logged into the CCTV system and searched for the cameras in the interrogation suite. He found the footage from around the time of Flannigan's suicide. He watched as Brauchitsch entered the suite, signed in, and then wandered up one of the corridors. That was where he lost her. She returned a couple of minutes later, just as the Waffen-SS officers came out of the rest room. The cameras did not record sound, but Loritz could tell that Brauchitsch was chewing them a new arsehole. Himmler appeared from the elevators and then the pair of them walked back up the corridor and out of view.

Loritz clicked off the footage and took another look at Brauchitsch's report.

It read, '*I entered the interrogation suite. No officers appeared to be on duty. I signed in. I then went to check on the prisoner, Flannigan. I opened the viewing flap in the door. He was sat on the bunk in his cell. I did not say anything to him and he did not acknowledge me. I returned to the reception area and berated the Waffen-SS officers on duty for deserting their post. Untersturmführer Himmler arrived and we returned to Flannigan's cell. Himmler opened the door. Flannigan remarked that we would not take him alive and then appeared to bite on something in his mouth. He fell sideways, and appeared unconscious. Himmler unsuccessfully attempted to administer CPR on Flannigan.*"

Loritz was naturally suspicious about everything, and though Brauchitsch had mentioned in her report that she had checked up on Flannigan, the CCTV footage seemed to suggest that she had been in the cellblock, out of view, for longer than he would've deemed necessary to merely check up on a prisoner.

He picked up his phone and dialled Brauchitsch's number.

She answered on the third ring. "Brauchitsch."

"Frau Obersturmführer, it is Loritz. Where are you?"

"We are on our way up to Peterborough, mein Herr."

"I will be coming up there," Loritz said. "I will call you again when I arrive. In the meantime, proceed with your investigation."

"Of course, mein Herr."

Loritz ended the call.

Had he been wrong about her? Had Schmid also been wrong about her? It was not unheard of for SS officers, Gestapo officers even, to render support to the terrorists. But Brauchitsch had always seemed to be such a loyal officer.

Surely she hadn't provided Flannigan with the cyanide capsule?

He put a call through to the forensics department, told them he wanted a report on the cyanide capsule. Where it came from, whether there were fingerprints or DNA not belonging to Flannigan. He explained that he wanted the report to come to him and to him alone.

His computer made a pinging sound. An electronic letter had come through. It was from Mittendorf's office. He printed off the attachment. It was authorization for him to demand all information from Gerhard Fieseler Werke pertinent to his current investigation, irrespective of the level of security. With that in his hand, he grabbed his overcoat and left

nach Schema F

his office, making his way down to the car park.
   He would get to the bottom of this.

62

Schmid had dismissed Keitel. He didn't need the big bruiser, experienced in torture, to get information from Barry Rhodes. He had decided that if he couldn't get any information from the American with the barbiturates that Doktor Corcilius was pumping into him, he would terminate the interrogation and Rhodes's life.

He had arranged to meet Corcilius in the interrogation room at 1pm. She had assured him that Rhodes would be suitably drugged by then. As he waited, Schmid sat in his office reviewing the files on the four men called Schottel who lived in the DSvG. None of them worked for the Schutzstaffel, though they were all loyal Party members. One was a lawyer, another a helicopter pilot, yet another was a manager in a factory which produced ladies' underwear and the last was a businessman who specialized in manufacturing and selling fans. Schmid could see nothing of value in the work they did. And yet Rhodes was adamant about the name.

Schmid had all four men under surveillance, but he knew that the junior officers assigned to that duty had uncovered nothing untoward. Similarly, Schmid had read files on the men's wives, but they too offered nothing of interest to a Gestapo officer aside from the fact that one of them seemed to be having an affair with her tennis coach.

Perhaps this Schottel was not in the DSvG? But then, how would Rhodes have come to know of a Schottel in another part of the Greater German Reich? Aside from the fact he hadn't shown up in the Reich before 1990, he also hadn't appeared to have left the DSvG during the intervening seven years. Of course, if he was an American spy, it was also highly likely that he would have access to a whole network of spies. The name Schottel was not an entirely rare one, and within Germany, there would be thousands of them. Schmid needed things to be narrowed down. A location, a job, anything which would make the Schottel of interest more easily identifiable.

Schmid left his office, took the elevator down to the interrogation suite. He entered Room 19, where Rhodes was. Inside, Corcilius was standing over the prisoner. She looked at Schmid, nodded, and took a step back.

nach Schema F

Schmid walked over to the gurney.

"Barry, how are you feeling?" Rhodes looked up at him. "Are you in any pain?" Schmid looked down at Rhodes's shattered legs. The metal framework was holding the bones in place. Rhodes was also on medication for the pain.

Rhodes said, "I feel fine ..." He was blinking slowly. Schmid wondered whether he'd been given too much of the barbiturates Corcilius was administering.

"Barry, I want to ask you about Herr Schottel. You mentioned him the last time we spoke. A friend of yours."

"Schottel ..."

"I would very much like to meet him. Where can I find him?"

"I don't know."

"Is he here? In England?"

"No, he's not here."

"Where then?"

"He's not here."

"In Germany, perhaps?"

"No."

Schmid paused for a moment. "Is he in America?"

"No, he's not in America."

"Are you from America, Barry?" Schmid asked him.

"America," Rhodes said. "Land of the Free."

"Is that where you came from, Barry?"

"My parents."

"Your parents came from America?"

"They had this lovely house," Rhodes said. "By the sea."

"In America?"

Rhodes fixed his eyes on Schmid. He closed his eyes, shook his head, as though he were fighting with his mind. "I am from Fenland."

"Of course you are," Schmid said. "Where is Schottel from?"

"He is from Germany."

"Where?"

"I don't know."

"Where does he live?"

"I don't know his address."

"What is his job?"

"He works ..." Rhodes let out a sigh. "He works for Germany."

"What does he do for Germany?"

"He sits in a room," Rhodes said, and he laughed lazily.

"Where does he do this? In Germany?"

"No."

"No? Where?"

Rhodes shook his head. "I can't tell you. I don't want to tell you."

"It will be between you and I," Schmid said. He smiled at Rhodes. He was convinced more than ever that this man was an American. He knew now that Schottel was not in the DSvG and he was not in Germany, which meant he had to be in one of the provinces. "Is he in France?" Rhodes looked up at Schmid. There was something in the way he'd moved his head, the expression on his face. Rhodes closed his eyes. "France? He is in France?"

Rhodes kept his eyes shut.

"Herr Rhodes, is he in France?" Rhodes didn't respond. Schmid grabbed his shirt, shook the spy. "Rhodes!"

Corcilius stepped up to the gurney. "That will not work," she said. "You have lost it now. He won't talk anymore today."

Outside the room, Schmid leant against the wall. There were interrogations happening behind every door along this particular corridor, which stretched for a hundred metres. Corcilius came out and looked at him disapprovingly.

"When you do that," she said, "when you break the cycle of conversation, when you lay hands on him, intimidate him, threaten him, you have lost the chance to break him. He will see through the haze, he will see you for who you are."

"I know," Schmid said. "But I almost had him."

"This is not something that can be done overnight, Schmid."

"I am starting to realize this." Schmid wanted to punch something or someone. "When can we do it again?"

"Tomorrow. I will keep him sedated. It will help to confuse him."

Schmid nodded and walked from the interrogation block.

In the meantime, he would get to work looking into any Schottels who lived and worked in France. More than that, he would get his whole team on the job. Schottel, whoever he or she was, held the key.

63

Zimmerman had been unreachable for the last hour or so. Ellen had tried ringing him countless times but had just been sent to his voicemail. Himmler had suggested that perhaps his phone's battery was flat, but Ellen wasn't convinced. It would be a schoolboy error to go out on surveillance without ensuring one had a reliable communication device.

They checked at the local Gestapo office only to be told that Zimmerman had borrowed a Kripo Audi, eschewing the BMW M3 in which he'd driven up to Peterborough. Of course, the M3 would stand out like a sore thumb – not very inconspicuous when carrying out surveillance. The Gestapo officer they spoke to also said that Zimmerman had not arranged any accommodation for them, but assured them that he'd sort something out for them himself.

Himmler drove, with Ellen in the passenger seat. It was four o'clock. Zimmerman should've checked in. He should've at least returned to recharge his phone, if the battery was flat. He could've charged it in the car if he'd had the foresight to take an in-car charger. There really was no excuse for him going off the net.

"He must still be at Dean's," Ellen said.

"But what is the point, if Dean has not turned up?"

"Well, I did ask him to keep an eye out for the Engländer."

"All the same, there comes a point where you have to give something up as a bad job."

Himmler pulled up outside Dean's house. It was dusk, but they could see that the Kripo Audi was no parked nearby.

They walked up to the house. The lights were out. They looked in the windows but saw nothing, even with the benefit of the torch Himmler was carrying.

"No one is home," he remarked.

Ellen tried the front door. It was locked. They went round the back of the house, saw nothing of consequence through the windows. Ellen tried the back door. It gave way, opening inwards. Immediately, Himmler drew his pistol. Ellen pulled hers out, took out a small torch and stepped into the house. It wasn't pitch black inside but the narrow beam from the torch helped to illuminate the dark corners of the house.

They found nothing downstairs.

Ellen led the way up the stairs, finger on the trigger of her pistol. She had the utmost confidence in both her quick reactions and her accuracy should she need to shoot. It was dark on the landing so until she swept the floor with her torchlight, she didn't see the body. When she did, she visibly jumped. Himmler came up beside her, saw Zimmerman's face illuminated, his eyes open, staring but unseeing.

The pair of them moved quickly, each of them clearing one of the bedrooms, making sure no one else was in the house. Then Himmler dropped down to Zimmerman, checked for a pulse – an automatic action but one which was wholly unnecessary.

Ellen flicked on the landing light as Himmler looked up at her and shook his head. She was already on the phone, calling the local Gestapo office. She wanted a Orpo unit here and another on standby. She wanted junior Gestapo officers to go door to door. But she already knew who had killed Zimmerman, and she also knew that he was long gone.

She waited outside for back-up to arrive. Curtains were twitching all around. These people, some would've heard and seen something. An M3 pulled up outside the house, its red lights flashing. A man introduced himself as SS-Hauptsturmführer Huber. He despatched three junior officers to start questioning the neighbours.

"What is it?"

"SS-Untersturmführer Zimmerman," Ellen told him. "One of mine. He was supposed to have the occupier of the house, Harry Dean, under surveillance. It looks like Zimmerman was strangled. We found a bullet hole in the wall, which suggests he managed to discharge his firearm. One of the neighbours will have heard that."

"Undoubtedly," Huber agreed. "But you can guarantee that they all had the TV volume turned up and heard nothing. Nobody wants to get involved here. This is not like London. Here, the people have more to fear from their fellow Engländers than they do from the Gestapo."

"This man murdered a Gestapo officer," Ellen snapped. "These people should be dragged from their homes and interrogated."

Huber raised an eyebrow. He was the senior officer here. "Think about this rationally, Frau Obersturmführer. We know who the killer is and we also know that by now he has gone to ground. The only information any of the neighbours can tell us will be information we already know. That Harry Dean was seen leaving his house shortly after the gunshot. Other than that, they have nothing of importance to tell us. We do not need to terrorize them."

Ellen glared at Huber. These SS officers from outside of London were even more provincial than she was. She heard Himmler's telephone ring and turned as he answered it. He spoke quietly into it, then put it back into his pocket.

Ellen had finished with Huber. The man knew nothing about their investigation and she wasn't inclined to tell him.

"Loritz," Himmler said. "He is about thirty minutes away. He says that we should check—"

"The sports club and Herr Dauny's," Ellen said. Himmler nodded. Ellen turned to Huber. "We will leave this part of the investigation in your hands, mein Herr. Myself and Untersturmführer Himmler will pursue other lines of enquiry."

In the M3, Ellen displayed her anger. She felt that she was a Gestapo officer once more, and not a traitor to the Reich. Zimmerman was one of her colleagues, a member of her staff. She took his murder personally.

"We will find this bastard," she said. "And we will kill him."

Himmler didn't respond. He just drove the car. They pulled into the car park of the Bretton Sports and Social Club. There was a light on in the bar, but no cars in the car park. The pair of them hopped out of the M3 and searched the club. There were no signs of life, but it was apparent that someone had just been here, taken a look around. There were signs of a prior search. Drawers opened, the till emptied. A burglary, perhaps, but Ellen was more inclined to believe that Dean had been here.

She looked at Himmler.

"Let us pay Herr Dauny a visit," she said. "And if he does not tell us what we need to know, we will kick it out of him."

As Himmler drove, she rang Loritz to update him.

64

Something had gone horribly wrong in Peterborough after Harry had left Scotland, that much was apparent. Finding the Gestapo officer at his house had been bad enough, but then Harry had visited the sports club and had found it deserted. The door was unlocked. Tom Flannigan was not there. It was apparent he'd been pulled in for questioning.

Harry knew he was on borrowed time. The Gestapo would be looking for him the moment they found the body at his house. He wondered whether any of his neighbours would actually call the police or whether the dead Gestapo officer would be found when someone realized he was missing.

At the club, he emptied the till and the safe, coming up with RM3,000. Tom's car, an old Peugeot, was parked out back and he found the keys in their usual spot on a shelf beneath the bar. The car's fuel tank was full, enough for almost 400 miles, but Harry didn't think he would use the car for that distance.

He drove to Dauny's and parked on the roadside up the street. He was looking for signs of the police or the Gestapo, but in truth if they were looking for him they'd hardly make it obvious. In any case, only thirty minutes had passed since he'd killed the Gestapo officer.

Dauny answered the knock at the door and Harry pushed him aside and entered his house. He locked the door behind him, threw the two bolts at the top and bottom and went into the front room. He drew the curtains, leaving a gap of about an inch, and flicked off the main light. It was almost dusk.

"What's going on?" Dauny asked him.

"You need to disappear," Harry said.

"What?"

"They will be coming for you." He handed Dauny the RM3,000 he had taken from the club. "Pack your gear and leave."

"But why?"

"They've taken Tom. They came for me, but I managed to get away. You have to be next on their list." Dauny looked as though he was going to shit himself. "Marcus, listen to me. The whole Peterborough cell, it's

nach Schema F

destroyed. But you have to complete the mission. Do you understand?"

"But if there's nobody left …"

"Our man in the missile silo," Harry said, "he will proceed with his objectives on the specified date. You have to make sure that he will succeed. You don't need to contact him. You don't need to contact anybody. You just need to complete your own mission objectives. You have four days. Do you understand?"

Dauny looked momentarily confused. Then he nodded. "Yes. Yes, I understand."

"Owen Dunne, nobody has his name," Harry said. "Get in touch with him. Work with him. Complete the mission objectives. And then go up to Scotland. Wait for further instructions."

"Wait where? Further instructions from whom?"

"Marcus, calm down."

"I am calm," Dauny said indignantly. "You're the one who's acting crazy."

Harry sat down, ran his hands through his hair. He could still get out of this alive, if he could get up to Scotland, regroup with Liam Lovett's cell. But before that, he had to make sure that Dauny was safe. Dauny had to survive in order for the mission to be a success.

"I'm sorry," he said. "You're right, I'm not calm. But I have to make sure you're safe."

"Can't I just go up to Scotland now?"

"You have to work with Dunne, Marcus."

Dauny rubbed his face. "God."

"Get a bag, something small," Harry said, getting to his feet. He was urging Dauny upstairs. "Bare essentials."

"I've got a suitcase—"

"No, you're not driving anywhere," Harry said. "You need something light, something you can carry. You'll need your computer, a change of clothes, the money I've given you. You get away from here, run to the other side of town, book yourself a taxi and get to Dunne's house."

Dauny stuffed a few belongings into a holdall together with his portable computer. As they were coming back down the stairs, there was a knock at the door.

The pair of them paused. Harry could see the outline of two people through the obscured glass of the front door. He looked at Dauny, then handed him the Gestapo officer's SIG.

"Run to the back door, get the fuck out of here," he hissed. Dauny pushed past him and darted for the back of the house. The knocking on the door became louder, more frantic. Someone was shouting. Harry saw one of the people disappear from view, probably making their way to the back of the house.

He knew what he had to do. He couldn't let Dauny get caught. He drew the Browning from his jacket and moved to the front door, unbolting it and swinging it open.

65

Nobody answered on the first knock. The lights were out downstairs, but there was a light visible through the front door and a corresponding light in one of the upstairs windows. Someone was in the house.

Ellen banged again on the front door.

Then she saw movement.

"There's someone in there," she said. She took out her gun. She saw a shape moving inside, making for the back of the house. "Round the back!" she ordered Himmler. "Go. Go!" Himmler ran off.

Ellen banged on the door again, and then kicked it furiously, trying to kick it from its hinges. A shape loomed before her in the glass of the front door, and then the door was opened.

Harry Dean stood before, a beast of a man, semiautomatic pistol in one hand. She raised her own gun, but Dean's other hand grabbed her jacket and pulled her inside. She was tossed to the ground and the pistol spilled from her grip. Dean kicked the door shut, locking it, and then aimed the gun at her.

"Might as well be executed for killing two Gestapo scum," he said.

Ellen raised her hands in a surrender gesture.

"Wait," she said. "Wait a minute!"

Dean fired his pistol and a bullet tore a hole in the wall next to Ellen's head. She jumped. He fired again, twice, missing her both times. She frowned. Then she realized that he was trying to draw attention to her plight. She was trying to lure Himmler back to the house.

"Dauny has escaped," she said. Dean nodded his head, a smile on his face. "My colleague will not come back," she assured him. "He will catch Dauny." But she wasn't so convinced. Himmler didn't even know who he was chasing nor indeed whether he was chasing anyone at all.

Dean moved his aim slightly. Now the big 9mm Browning was aimed at her chest.

She shook her head. "You do not have to do this."

"I do."

"You do not. I am on your side." Dean just smiled. "It is true. I work for Reichsstatthalter Klarsfeld. I know what your mission is. I am on your side, Herr Dean." There was uncertainty on the Engländer's face. His aim waivered slightly. "I have my own doubts – this is true. I cannot condone the deaths of millions of people. But I am working for Klarsfeld." Ellen thought about the fact that she had sent Himmler after Dauny, that if Himmler succeeded, the mission would fail. Perhaps that was what she wanted.

"Well," Dean said, "you're doing a piss poor job of helping us. What's your name?"

"Ellen. Ellen Brauchitsch."

"Well, Ellen, your colleagues have fucked this all up for us. I'm struggling to see what help you've offered." The aim was back on Ellen, the pistol aimed right at her heart.

"I could not do anything to prevent Flannigan's arrest," she said. "But I helped him to die."

"You killed him?" Dean frowned now.

Ellen shook her head. "No. I gave him the chance to die before he could reveal any information. I gave him cyanide."

Dean readjusted the grip on his pistol. Ellen could see the perspiration on his face.

"I know Klarsfeld had helpers," he said. "I know Klarsfeld was involved in all of this. I know too much."

"As do I."

Dean lowered the gun. "And will you let me escape?"

There was the sound of a powerful engine revving outside, a car screeching to a halt, the flashing red lights bouncing off the walls of the hallway.

Dean closed his eyes. He knew it was all over now.

He came closer to Ellen, dropped to his knees. He lay her down on the floor, put his pistol down. There was hammering at the door behind him.

He said, "Scream." Ellen frowned. "Scream." His hands closed around Ellen's throat. "Scream," he said again.

Ellen screamed, and then Dean's big hands began to choke the life out of her. She could feel herself losing consciousness as she looked up into Dean's face. He was smiling at her, nodding his head reassuringly. There were shouts, a loud crash, and then a gunshot.

Dean's face exploded, his grip loosened and he fell on top of her.

nach Schema F

66

Loritz lowered his pistol as two Gestapo officers rushed over to the body of Harry Dean, pulling him to one side to reveal SS-Obersturmführer Ellen Brauchitsch beneath him. Blood and brain matter covered her face and her jacket. She didn't seem overly concerned by the gore, but she did seemed stunned to see the corpse of a man who, moments earlier, had been attempting to strangle her.

One of the Gestapo officers helped her to her feet, at which point she used the sleeve of her jacket to wipe away some of the blood from her face. She looked at Loritz.

"Thanks," she said.

"Where is Himmler?"

"He went round the back. After Herr Dauny."

Loritz gestured to the two junior officers to find Himmler, to offer back up if necessary. They rushed from the house. Loritz prodded Dean's corpse with his foot. Naturally, there was no response. The bullet hole in the back of the Engländer's skull oozed blood. He didn't particularly want to look at the mess the 9mm hollowpoint would've made to Dean's face.

"Did he say anything?"

Brauchitsch shook her head. "He pulled me into the house, threw me to the floor and then started to strangle me." She used her other sleeve to wipe some of Dean's brains from her face. "I suppose he was going to do to me what he did to Zimmerman."

More officers came in through the front door. Loritz ordered them to search the house.

"Zimmerman made a mistake," he told Ellen. "He went into Dean's house without back-up and he paid the ultimate price. You almost paid a similar price."

"I had to send Himmler to the rear of the house. I could see that somebody was escaping."

Loritz nodded. The circumstances here were slightly different, and Brauchitsch had had to think on her feet. He placed a hand on her shoulder, squeezed it, gave her some reassurance.

"You were caught out," he said. "You will learn from this mistake. Of that I have no doubt." His radio crackled to life and he plucked it from his pocket. "Say again, over."

The voice on the other end was out of breath. "Himmler here. I lost Dauny. I thought I saw him running down one of the side alleys, but he just seemed to disappear, over."

"Never mind. Return to the house, over."

"How is the Obersturmführer, over?"

Loritz looked at Ellen and then down at Harry Dean's body. "She is slightly damaged, but I am sure she will recover. Get back here ASAP, over." Loritz pocketed the radio. "Rhodes, Flannigan, Dean. The big three for this Peterborough group of terrorists. Dauny has managed to evade capture, but we will find him. We will find out what they are up to."

They returned to the Gestapo offices in Peterborough. He took Himmler and Brauchitsch into a conference room. The three of them sat down. An assistant brought in coffee. Huber, the lead investigator for Peterborough, wanted to join the meeting but Loritz asked him to leave. The further north one went from London, the more stupid the SS officers became.

Loritz handed over the authorization from Mittendorf's office.

"First thing tomorrow, I want you to pay a visit to Gerhard Fieseler Werke. Show them this and demand to know what Dauny was working on. Dauny is now a fugitive, an enemy of the State." Loritz took a sip from his coffee. Even the coffee up north was shit. "I have to say that I am disappointed with the pair of you. This investigation has been a catalogue of errors from start to finish. However, I must take some of the responsibility myself. We should have closed down this Peterborough cell right at the start, when we found out about Dougie Hardcastle. There are also too many connections with too many people, people in positions of authority."

"What people?" Himmler asked.

"Herr Dauny, a so-called loyal Party member. He had been placed under surveillance by the local Gestapo, but it is apparent that these people are incompetent fools. A connection between this Bretton Sports and Social Club, the terrorist cell, and a Party member should have been made. There was the security breach which had been made using Dauny's access. This too should have been investigated in more depth, but it

nach Schema F

would appear as though too many officers were too nervous to arrest a Party member, to interrogate him. That was another mistake." Loritz sighed, stirred his coffee, though he hadn't put any sugar in it. "And then we have the attempt on Klarsfeld's life. An attempt?" He choked back a laugh. "Either Hardcastle was blind or he made no attempt whatsoever to kill Klarsfeld. That bastard has gone native. He is more British than German now. He is not working for the Fatherland. He is working for the Engländers. I believe he knew that the assassination attempt was going to take place. I believe his entire security team – with the exception of you, Frau Obersturmführer – knew that the assassination attempt was going to take place. I believe that Dougie Hardcastle had no intention of killing Klarsfeld. He sacrificed himself to improve Klarsfeld's faltering reputation."

"But Herr Klarsfeld never showed any signs of treachery," Brauchitsch said. Loritz held up a hand to stop her. Of course she was going to protest Klarsfeld's innocence. She had vouched for his loyalty, and if it was proven that the Reichsstatthalter was indeed a disloyal traitor, she could find herself sucked into an investigation. Schmid had absolved her of any guilt, but as far as Loritz was concerned, his whole team had been sloppy. And he, as their leader, had allowed them to get away with it. He had devolved too much power to them, and this was the result. His bright young things had turned out to be rather ineffectual.

"We are all guilty of being blinded by the assumed brilliance of those around us," Loritz said. "But that is all over now. There are three people still alive who can probably provide the key to this mystery. One is on the run, one is currently in an interrogation suite at the Polizeipräsidium, and the other is governing this province. You two will find Dauny. Schmid will continue to interrogate Rhodes. And I will question Klarsfeld. Between all of us, we will get to the bottom of this. If we do not, well …" Loritz gave a smile of regret. "If we do not, then we will all have to answer to a higher authority. And I dare say that none of us will be happy with the outcome of that."

Himmler said, "If Dauny has gone to ground, how will we find him?"

Loritz sighed. "You are an investigator with the Geheime Staatspolizei, Herr Untersturmführer. If you do not know by now hold to trace someone who has gone to ground then perhaps you might consider resigning from the service?" Himmler looked suitably chastised. "Read and re-read every piece of documentation concerning Dauny. Look into each and every one of his associates. Bring them in for questioning. Interrogate them. Torture them." Loritz looked at Brauchitsch. She wasn't up for torturing people. That much he already knew. "I will ask Sturmscharführer Keitel to assist. He might not have the investigative skills that both of you allegedly possess, but he does has strengths which you can possibly use. You will tear this town apart until you find someone who knows where Herr Dauny is."

"Yes, Herr Sturmbannführer."

Loritz drained his coffee and got to his feet. "We will all be carrying out some difficult tasks over the next few days. People will be hurt and they will be incensed. Some may die. But rest assured, we will get to the bottom of this."

And with that, Loritz left the police station.

nach Schema F

67

The taxi pulled up in a street some distance from Dauny's intended destination, but he figured that he wouldn't make it easy for anyone who was looking for him.

The chase from his house had left him exhausted. He was not a fit man but running for one's life generally improved one's fitness, if only momentarily. He was perhaps three hundred yards away when he heard the first gunshot, and he wondered whether it had been Harry who'd fallen or one of the Gestapo officers.

The Gestapo officer – he had to presume that whoever was chasing after him was Gestapo – was determined, but did not know the back alleys as well as Dauny. Dauny entered a back garden, scaled a fence, ran through the garden of an adjoining property, across a road which ran parallel to the road where he lived, down by the side of an unlit house to the foot of the garden, where he scaled another fence and did the same thing again until he was a few streets away. He had no idea where he had lost the Gestapo officer. All he knew was that he could no longer hear footsteps behind him.

He caught his breath in a small wine bar close to the city centre. He sipped slowly from the sauvignon blanc, but it didn't quench his thirst. From the wine bar, he stopped at a newsagents and bought himself a bottle of water which he downed in one go. He walked to the taxi rank and told the driver, an Englishman, that he wanted taking to Leicester. He tried his best not to look suspicious but wasn't sure whether he had succeeded. It was a hackney carriage, so there was no radio call to any base. The driver just nodded and pulled from the rank.

It took almost an hour and a half to reach Leicester. The most nerve-wracking part of the journey was the drive through Peterborough. There were a few flashing lights as Orpo and Gestapo units sped through the town. Dauny wondered whether Harry had managed to take another Gestapo officer down with him. Once the taxi had left Peterborough behind, Dauny started to relax. They were beyond the realms of Orpo roadblocks. He didn't ring Owen to let him know he was on his way. He figured that the Gestapo would have his mobile phone under surveillance. He'd actually ditched it before he'd got in the taxi, before he'd even reached the taxi rank.

The driver pulled up and looked back at Dauny, who paid him and jumped out into the cold, dark night. He slung the bag containing his portable computer over his back and watched as the taxi turned around and headed back the way it had come.

Dauny didn't want to just arrive at Owen's house unannounced. He had no idea whether his old university friend had visitors, or even whether he was at home at all, and there was nothing guaranteed more to draw unwanted attention than a stranger knocking at your neighbour's door when your neighbour wasn't home.

He found a phone booth at the end of the street and keyed in Owen's mobile number.

It went to voicemail.

Dauny said, "Owen, it's Marcus. I will ring back in a couple of minutes." He cradled the receiver, and twenty seconds later the public phone rang. Dauny scooped up the handset. "Hello?"

"Marcus." It was Owen.

"Where are you?"

"I'm in a secret location," Owen said. "Why?"

"I need you to pick me up."

"Where are you?"

"I'm in Leicester."

It took Owen twenty minutes to arrive. He was driving a beaten-up VW. Dauny was in a pub close to the phone box he'd rang from. He was inserting Reichspfennigs into a fruit machine which was situated close to the entrance and a window through which he could see the car park.

Dauny drained his pint and left the pub.

Once in the car, Owen looked at him suspiciously. "What's happened?"

"Everything's collapsing," Dauny said. "Tom Flannigan and Harry Dean have been arrested. I think Harry might be dead. I managed to escape."

"You managed to escape? What the fuck, Marcus? You're on the run? You're a fugitive?"

"Is there somewhere safe you can take me?"

"Well, just my 'secret location'," Owen said. "But it's hardly salubrious accommodation."

nach Schema F

They drove for twenty minutes through moderately heavy traffic, before disappearing down a few deserted side streets. Owen parked the car up and led Dauny down an alley. At the rear of what appeared to be a row of lock-ups, Owen pushed his way through some bushes to reveal a small hatch which was padlocked shut. Owen removed the padlock and opened the hatch. The pair of them scrabbled through and Owen closed the hatch, padlocking it from the inside. He switched on a light and the interior of the lock-up was revealed to Dauny.

Just a desk, a chair, a computer. A cupboard.

"Are you living here?"

"Working here," Owen said. "Though to be fair I'm going to have to bring a couple of camp beds down because if they're after you, it won't be long before they're onto me."

Dauny walked over to the desk, ran a hand along the computer.

"Networked?"

Owen nodded. "Of course."

"Capacity for more than one computer?"

"Definitely."

Dauny handed over the remainder of the cash that Harry had given him. "There's almost three thousand Reichsmarks there. Get whatever you need. I figure we're going to be here until we've completed our objective."

"The next four days."

"Are you on target?" Dauny asked.

Owen smiled. "Are you?"

"My job is significantly easier than yours. Also, if I mess up, nothing happens. If you mess up, we both get caught."

"I am finished," Owen said. "We're just waiting for the deadline." He leant against the desk and folded his arms. "But the thing is, if they're after you, how does that affect our mission?"

Dauny frowned. He'd been contemplating this also. If the Gestapo discovered that he was working on the missile launch control system, they would undoubtedly tighten security. It was possible that all of Owen's hard work could be for nothing. He explained this to his friend.

"It would be easier if we could speak to the guy on the inside," Owen said. "We've been working with the idea that we needed to keep not only our access a secret but the fact that we've updated the software as well.

But the thing is, if we update the software, reboot the system, it would take the security guys a couple of minutes to figure out the system had been penetrated and compromised. And in those couple of minutes, the guy on the inside could launch his missiles." Owen was shaking his head. "We were working to a fixed window of opportunity because we're computer geeks, because we need a plan in place. But we don't need that, do we?"

"I suppose not."

"How long before you've completed your work?"

"All I've had to do is remove a few lines of code, reroute some of the subroutines, amend an array or two. I'm pretty certain it's all in place. I just need to test it, make sure it all works."

"So you've changed the targets, removed the failsafes?" Dauny nodded. "How about alternative access?"

"Until the software is repaired, the only place that will be able to launch nuclear missiles will be Grenoble. No authorization codes from Missile Command will work."

"We have to get this done quickly."

Dauny flopped down onto the chair. He still harboured doubts. He said, "We're talking about killing millions of people, Owen."

"Not us. We're not killing anyone."

"Okay, well, we're helping to facilitate the deaths of millions of people then."

Owen shook his head. This lock-up was poorly lit, the single bulb barely illuminating one corner. A weak draught blew in from the front of the room, through a small gap at the bottom of the door. It certainly wasn't a welcoming place to spend the next few days, particularly for two men who were used to the comforts their elevated status could ordinarily bring them. Dauny shuddered, but he wasn't sure whether it was the cold or the horror at what he was helping Combat UK to do.

Owen said, "It's for the greater good."

"Bloody hell."

"We need to get in touch with their inside man."

"And how do you propose we do that?"

"We know where he is, don't we? We know which bunker he works in."

"There are twenty or thirty members of staff working at each bunker," Dauny said. "Our could be any one of them."

nach Schema F

"Then maybe we need to do some research?"

"And how do you propose to do that?"

Owen smiled. "I know how to access the personnel database for the Schutzstaffel."

Dauny frowned. For a moment, he was silent. Then he said, "Why would you have even attempted to do that?"

"It was a challenge."

"And what good would it do to have a list of names?"

"We can send an electronic letter to every member of staff that works at Grenoble," Owen said. "Something seemingly innocuous, something which only the man responsible for pushing that button would pick up on. The others would just think it was junk and delete it."

"Owen, you're insane."

"With the work I do, Marcus, it helps." Owen moved to the rear of the lock-up, to the small hatchway. He undid the padlock. "Get to work on the software, get it finished, test it, do whatever the hell you need to do. I'm going to get us something to sleep on, a change of clothes, some food and water."

"You're going back to your house?"

"No, I'm not going back to mine," Owen said. He opened the hatch, looked outside. "There's no telling whether the Gestapo will already have me under surveillance." He looked back at Dauny. "I'll be about an hour. When I come back, I'll use the front door. I'll say, 'olly olly oxen free'. If you don't hear that, you leave through this hatchway. Okay?" Dauny nodded. Owen held up the padlock. "Lock it from the inside," he said, and then he was gone.

Dauny put his bag down on the desk, took out the *Trag*, connected it to the network. He took out the pistol Harry had given him just before he'd ran from his house. He looked it over, finding the safety switch, flicking it so a red circle was exposed on the body of the firearm, before placing it on the desk next to Owen's computer.

He had no idea how to shoot a gun, but he figured that if the Gestapo came to this lock-up, he would only need to figure out how to point it at his own head and pull the trigger.

68

Ellen was reading through the interview transcripts made by Obersturmführer Mann after his interview with Marcus Dauny. She'd read everything else she could find about the Engländer, but there was very little worthwhile information. He had no known associates, but that was probably down to the fact that he hadn't been placed under serious surveillance. Had they been back in Germania, there was every chance that a man in Dauny's position would've been closely monitored by the Sicherheitspolizei.

As she scanned through Mann's report, a name sprang out. Owen Dunne. Another Engländer. An old university associate of Dauny's. Another specialist in computers. This man lived in Leicester. The Leicester Gestapo had questioned Dunne briefly to confirm that Dauny had visited him on a specified day.

Ellen leant back in her chair. It was ten o'clock, she was tired, she was stressed. One of her team had been murdered and a terrorist had pretended to strangle her in order that her cover could be maintained and he wouldn't be taken in and interrogated. Though it transpired that Harry Dean had a cyanide capsule on his person. He had no intention of being taken alive.

She'd showered Dean's blood, brains, and skull fragments from her body earlier, before she'd eaten in the hotel's restaurant. She'd told Himmler she wanted to be alone, and he'd walked away without another word.

But now she needed him.

She picked up her phone, dialled his number. His phone rang a few times before he sleepily answered it.

"Ellen?"

"Owen Dunne."

"What?"

"One of Marcus Dauny's friends. From university. They've been in contact with one another recently. And get this. Dunne also specializes in computers. His father owns a business which manufactures computer parts."

nach Schema F

"Where does he live?"

"Leicester," Ellen said. "Get dressed. I will meet you in the lobby in ten minutes." She closed the call, rubbed her temples. Her head was hurting. It was stress. She'd been placed in a difficult situation, and her mind was being torn in two directions.

She knew that if either Marcus Dauny or Owen Dunne were pulled in for interrogation, they would crumble. They would crumble and they would give up Klarsfeld's plan. They might not know that he was involved, but nevertheless his plan would fail and with Loritz determined to question the Reichsstatthalter, it was just a matter of time before he too succumbed to interrogation. And he could point the finger at Ellen.

She tugged on her jacket and left her room. Himmler was already waiting for her in the lobby. Their M3 was in the secure car park at the rear of the hotel. Ellen let Himmler drive.

As they left the lights of Peterborough and hit the main autobahn which would take them to Leicester, Himmler said, "We will get these people, Ellen. We will make them pay for killing Zimmerman."

"Dean killed Zimmerman. Dauny would not have the nerve to kill anyone."

"Well, whatever, we will find out what they are up to."

Ellen sighed. She took her pistol out, checked the action, shoved it back into her holster. She could still smell Harry Dean's brains. She didn't think she'd ever get rid of that stench. It was indelibly etched on her now. She'd smelled the signs of fear, the shit and the piss, that accompanied an interrogation. But the smell of somebody's exposed guts, their brains, the offal of a violent death, that was an entirely different scent.

She knew that she should've phoned Keitel, arranged for him to accompany them. But she also knew that he was very effective in getting information from people. One threat from him and Owen Dunne would confess to every crime he was accused of. Ellen wasn't so sure she wanted that. This, what she and Himmler were doing now, it was more a case of going through the motions.

She phoned the Leicester Gestapo office, spoke to the hauptsturmführer in charge, explained that they were about to enter his jurisdiction. He wanted to know what it was about, but she said it was a matter of national security and told him to speak with Loritz if he wanted to know more.

She said to Himmler, "How do you feel about us losing Zimmerman?"

"I am pissed off."

"That is not what I meant, Willi. I know you two guys worked together in the past."

"We were partners briefly, Ellen, that is all. As you know, it is impossible for a Gestapo officer to have friends." There was a bitter edge in Himmler's voice. Ellen turned away, rested her head against the side window. He said, finally, "I am sorry. It is not easy losing a colleague."

"We all feel it, Willi. But I just assumed you would feel it the most."

"He was an idiot," Himmler said quickly. "The way he died proves that."

"I was almost killed by Dean as well."

"Yes, but you made a mistake. Zimmerman, he was proof that the selection process for the Geheime Staatspolizei is not as stringent as once it was."

"A little harsh."

"But fair," Himmler said. "You know, if Dean had killed you I would have been devastated."

"Why?"

"Ellen, as if you do not know."

"Willi," Ellen said softly.

"Sometimes I wish you would just open yourself up," Himmler said. "Accept that people want to be your friend."

"And that is all you want?"

"Of course. I think a lot of you, I have told you this before, but I have no interest in you in a romantic sense. You are more like my little sister."

Ellen sighed. "I have no time for friends, Willi. None of us have the time for friends. The Reich takes up all of our time, all of our love, all of our attention."

"Do you actually believe that rubbish?"

Ellen didn't answer. She didn't want to answer. She just wanted to close her eyes and go to sleep. They were in a car on their way to arrest and interrogate a man who would reveal a secret plot, one which she'd been asked to keep a secret. But she could not have ignored the evidence which had been right in front of her eyes. If she did that, Loritz would want to know why.

She could only hope that Dunne was intelligent enough to go to ground the moment he discovered Dauny was wanted for questioning. She didn't think she'd be able to engineer his escape if he was still at his house when they arrived.

69

Klarsfeld was in bed reading a book when there was a knock at the door to his private quarters. He looked at the clock on his bedside cabinet, saw it was almost eleven, and wondered what the hell had happened for him to be disturbed so late at night.

Tugging on his dressing gown, he left his bedroom and unlocked the door to his apartment. A member of his night-security team stood there, a concerned look on his face. Behind this man stood SS-Sturmbannführer Loritz and the beast interrogator, Keitel.

"What the hell is this all about?" he said. Loritz gently brushed the security guy aside.

"Herr Reichsstatthalter," he said. "We would like you to accompany us to the Polizeipräsidium. There are things we need to discuss with you."

"You can discuss them in my office in the morning," Klarsfeld said, folding his arms.

Loritz smiled, shook his head. "This cannot wait until the morning, mein Herr. If you would like to get ready, we can escort you there ourselves."

"There is certainly no need for you to drag me down to the Polizeipräsidium, Sturmbannführer. You may wait in my office and I shall be down shortly."

Loritz shook his head again, the smile still on his face. "I am afraid that will not suffice, Herr Klarsfeld."

"I am a Goddamn Party member and the governor of this province, and you will accord me some respect," Klarsfeld said, raising his voice. "You should remember your place, Herr Loritz."

Loritz pulled a document out of his pocket. He unfolded it, handed it over to Klarsfeld. Even before Klarsfeld had the chance to read what was written on it, Loritz said, "It is a communiqué from the Oberstgruppenführer's office. It provides us with the authority to detain you. A protection order for senior Party officials."

Klarsfeld clenched his teeth. That fucking bastard Mittendorf was behind this. He almost tore the Schutzhaft in two. Instead, he handed it back to Loritz.

"Wait here," he said, slamming the door to his apartment. As he dressed, he wondered what possible reason the Gestapo could have for placing him under protective custody. Schutzhafts were reserved for political criminals. There was nothing to link Klarsfeld with any criminal activity, political or otherwise.

Once he was dressed, he met the two Gestapo officers in the lobby of the Amtssitz. His head of security was hovering around but Loritz told him that he wasn't welcome, that he was to stay at the Reichsstatthalter's official residence.

They took him to the Polizeipräsidium in one of their M3s. The back of the car wasn't that comfortable, certainly not like the Maybachs Klarsfeld was used to travelling in. They slipped down into the underground car park and the M3 pulled in alongside a row of other dark M3s. He was escorted to the entrance, entered the lift lobby, and from there they waited for a lift to arrive.

After they stepped into the lift, Klarsfeld watched as Loritz pushed the button for the one of the subterranean levels, and he felt his heart palpitate so violently, he was concerned that the two Gestapo officers would hear it.

"What is this about?" he said, but the anger had gone from his voice. As with most people who were arrested and taken to the interrogation suite, he was practically broken before he'd even arrived.

Loritz said, "We will discuss this shortly."

Klarsfeld had only visited the Polizeipräsidium on a handful of occasions. He did not like the building, and he did not like the purpose it served. More than just the main headquarters for the police service in the British province, it served as the main drop-off point for those suspected of committing serious crimes anywhere within the province. The interrogation suites were impressive, by all accounts, though up until this moment in time, Klarsfeld had managed to avoid seeing any of them. Like all German officials, however, he'd heard the rumours.

They took him to the nearest interrogation room. It just looked like a normal interview room, with a table with three chairs around it. There were two cameras on the walls, both of which appeared to be directed towards where Klarsfeld sat. A door behind him led, presumably, to another room. He figured that the room beyond was where torture took place.

Loritz and Keitel sat opposite him.

"So, I presume now that you are going to tell me what this is all about?" he asked.

Loritz said, "You may recall us speaking a few days ago, Herr Klarsfeld, about the assassination attempt on your life." Klarsfeld nodded. "I am still … puzzled as to why you survived, or at the very least, escaped serious injury. Your assassin came from Peterborough. At the moment, many other problems seem to come from Peterborough. We have two dead Combat UK members – one of whom took his own life, and another who is responsible for the murder of a Gestapo officer. We also have a suspected American spy. And we have a computer expert, an Engländer, who is on the run. We can presume that all of these people are connected, in some way, to Combat UK." Loritz waved a finger at Klarsfeld. "And you, mein Herr, you are also connected, in some way, to Combat UK."

"This is preposterous. I am the Reichsstatthalter!"

"You have been in the *Deutscher Staat von Großbritannien* for a long time, have you not?" Loritz asked. Keitel, the oaf, took out a packet of cigarettes, lit one. The Sturmbannführer seemed slightly annoyed, wafted the smoke aside.

"What of it?"

"It is usual for some people to 'go native'," Loritz said. "I would say that you have sympathies for the Engländers. Would that be a fair thing to say?"

"I serve the people of this province."

"You serve the Führer," Loritz said quickly. He leant forwards. "The Führer and the Fatherland are the only people you serve, Herr Klarsfeld."

Klarsfeld looked down. He realized that he was in a precarious position. Loritz had the upper hand. He had the backing of Oberstgruppenführer Mittendorf. Klarsfeld knew that this man could make him disappear overnight.

He said, "Of course I know that, Herr Sturmbannführer. But to a lesser degree, I am here to lead the Engländers and all of the Germans who live in this province. Your suggestion that I have sympathies for the Engländers is absurd. However, I do have to understand their needs. It is integral to maintaining a level of peace."

"Tell me what you know of Harry Dean."

nach Schema F

"I know no one of that name."

"Tom Flannigan?"

Klarsfeld shook his head. "Should I know him?"

"Marcus Dauny?"

"Not a name I am familiar with."

"Barry Rhodes?"

Klarsfeld showed no emotion. Again, he shook his head.

"Barry Rhodes is an American spy," Loritz said. "He is currently being interrogated not far from where you are sitting. These people, they are strong-willed. Sometimes they give us nothing. But occasionally, they will blurt out a name. One name, it leads to another name, and that name leads to another, and so on, and so on. It is how we eventually work our way upwards through an organization to those who lead the terrorists."

"I understand all about investigative work."

"Tell me, do you know Liam Lovett?"

"I know of him," Klarsfeld said. "Everyone does. It would be impossible to live in this province and not know of him."

"When did you meet Lovett?"

Klarsfeld frowned. What did Loritz know? The pause he gave was telling. Even as he realized that Loritz was bluffing – for if he knew that Klarsfeld had actually met Lovett, he would know when that meeting had taken place – he realized that Loritz had achieved his aim. A moment of uncertainty. "I have never met Lovett."

Loritz smiled. "Of course not." The Gestapo officer sniffed. "Tell me about SS-Obersturmführer Brauchitsch. How did you find her working as your chief of security?"

"She is a good officer," Klarsfeld said. Loritz nodded. "Loyal to the Fatherland."

"She has certainly been tested," Loritz said. "I fear that perhaps I placed too much trust in her. I do not think that she was ready for promotion. She has made … mistakes."

"I can only commend her on her strengths."

Loritz raised an eyebrow. "I am sure you have your reasons for praising her, Herr Klarsfeld." He stood up, as did Keitel. "My colleague will escort you to your accommodation. We will resume our chat in the morning."

"You are keeping me here overnight?"

"Herr Klarsfeld, you are under arrest. I am sure that this was made obvious to you. You will not be released unless our investigation reaches a satisfactory conclusion." Loritz headed for the door. "I would get plenty of sleep if I were you."

And Klarsfeld could only watched as Loritz left the room. Keitel came over and planted a huge hand around his arm. He didn't say anything as he led Klarsfeld to the door.

nach Schema F

70

Dauny looked at the list Dunne had given him. Thirty-one names of SS officers who worked at the missile bunker at Grenoble. Two of them were more senior officers, but in actual fact any one of them would be able to launch the nuclear missiles after Dauny had amended the launch control system.

"I know what you're thinking," Dunne said. "Our contact could be any one of them."

"Quite."

"What do you know of the missile bunkers? The set-up?"

Dauny shrugged. He had never visited a missile bunker. He just supplied the software. He was sat on one of the two camp beds Dunne had brought to the lock-up. There were also now two chairs positioned at the desk. Both Dauny's portable computer and Dunne's desktop computer were switched on. Dauny had yet to run one final test on his software. The previous test had revealed a couple of small bugs that could compromise the mission.

"Each of the individual silos is manned by two junior officers," Dunne said. "They're sealed in the control room of the silo, not accessable from the outside. The bunker commander on duty is located in his own control room. He controls access to the bunker. Nothing happens within the bunker without his knowledge."

"He has to authorize the missile launches, yes, I know that. But my adaptations to the software remove that limitation."

"Think about it, Dauny. If our contact works in one of the silos, he's going to have to kill or disable whoever he works with before he launches the missiles. The bunker commander has access to video feeds of each of the silos. I just think that it'd make more sense if our contact – Combat UK's contact – was one of the bunker commanders."

Dauny rubbed his temples. What had Lovett said on the occasion when they'd met in Scotland? The events of that meeting tumbled through his mind.

"Lovett. He wanted the software to allow the bunker commander to fire the missiles. It has to be one of the commanders." Dauny looked at the list. "Bannhoff or Schottel?"

"Schottel is the more senior officer."

"I think we should contact them both."

"I'm just thinking of reducing the risk."

"We can word something perfectly innocuous, something that most people would discard. We all get marketing electronic letters."

"Yes, and what do we do with them? We discard them. Tell me, Marcus, do you actually read anything that's written in a marketing E-Letter?" Dauny gave a casual shrug. "I'm just worried that our contact, whoever he is, won't read the main body of the letter and our message won't get through."

"You may be right," Dauny said. "But what else can we do? We can't make it obvious, we can't make it personal, and we can't risk contacting both of these bunker commanders with something personal. We either send a hidden message or else we have to target the actual contact."

The two of them fell silent for a few moments.

"We could wait until the predetermined date," Dauny said.

"And in the meantime, the Gestapo could squeeze the information out of Barry Rhodes. Or they could find us and squeeze the information out of us."

"We don't have the information."

"In which case that squeezing is going to hurt a damn sight more."

Dauny shook his head. In the absence of a leader, one of them had to make an executive decision. He said, "We send an electronic letter to each of them. We just have to compose something which entices the contact to reply."

Dunne sighed, glanced at his computer screen.

"It's not going to be easy," he said.

"Nothing about this is going to be easy, Owen." Dauny grabbed a notepad and a pen. "Let me see what I can come up with."

nach Schema F

71

Ellen hadn't expected Owen Dunne to be at home. She could guess what had happened. Dauny had come here from Peterborough, told Dunne he was compromised, and the pair of them – both computer experts undoubtedly carrying out some mission for Combat UK – had gone to ground. They could be anywhere by now. Computer work, she presumed, could be carried out at any location.

Himmler kicked open the door to the house and the Leicester-based search team did their thing. They found nothing of interest on the quick sweep. Ellen ordered them to carry out a deep search, which essentially meant stripping the house down, removing floorboards, checking for secret compartments in the walls.

Himmler came into the garden, where Ellen was standing. He put his hands on his hips.

"What now?"

"We are too late," she told him. "We will not find either of them."

"But what are they up to?"

"We will know more when we speak to that Arschloch at Gerhard Fieseler Werke."

"In the morning?"

Ellen shook her head. "No. We return to Peterborough, we go to his home address and we find out precisely what Dauny is working on. Once we have that …" But Ellen knew what Dauny had to be working on. The missile launch control system. And once that information was revealed to the Gestapo, security measures would be put in place to prevent whatever Dauny and Dunne had planned.

Her phone rang. It was Loritz.

"Mein Herr."

"How is your investigation proceeding, Frau Obersturmführer?"

"We have just arrived at the home of one of Dauny's contacts," she told him. "Owen Dunne. He lives in Leicester. But he is not here. I suspect that the pair of them have gone on the run together."

"That is unfortunate."

"Yes."

"Frau Obersturmführer, I want you to return to London tomorrow," Loritz said.

"But we still have work to do here."

"Himmler can coordinate that part of the investigation from the Polizeipräsidium. I need you here to help me with my current interrogation." Ellen frowned. He had returned to London to question Klarsfeld. Who was he interrogating now? "We have the Reichsstatthalter in custody. I feel that your relationship with him will aid this branch of the investigation."

"If you think it will help …"

"Get a good night's sleep," Loritz told her, "and be down here for nine o'clock tomorrow morning."

"Yes, mein Herr." The call was concluded. Himmler looked at her expectantly. "We have to return to London."

"Fucking hell. And he wants to know why this investigation is so fucked up? We are being moved from one task to another before we have completed our work."

"We are just following orders," Ellen said. "And if it all goes wrong, then we cannot be held responsible."

But she wasn't sure how true that was.

nach Schema F

72

Schottel arrived on shift as normal. He was doing his best to appear as normal as possible. Greeting the security detail, asking his jaded staff about their shifts, signing off the electronic work sheets. Those who observed him would think that he was just a loyal member of the Schutzstaffel, disabled, but carrying out his duties to the best of his ability.

They couldn't know that in four days, he would be flicking some switches which would send five nuclear missiles on their way to Germania, instantly vaporizing twenty million people. He would become the greatest mass murderer in the history of mankind.

He removed the bottle of schnapps from his bag, placed it on his desk. He found the dusty, dirty glass in his drawer, unwashed from the last time it was used, and he filled it. He savoured the scent of the spirit before gulping down a large mouthful. He wasn't concerned with the CCTV camera which was filming him. Nobody ever watched the bunker commanders. He checked each of the video screens in turn, seeing his men, some sleeping, others reading, others drinking. Each silo leader explained that there had been no issues, that everything was fine.

Schottel looked at the control panel in front of him. The most prominent features were the five red buttons marked with a number and the word 'Raketenstart'. The missile launch buttons, one for each silo. How the system worked was that the two guys in the silo would simultaneously press a button marked *Bewaffnet*, which would arm the silo. Once the silo was armed, the bunker commander would then fire the missile by pressing the launch button. The missiles could not be armed without the authority of Missile Command. Three layers of control before a missile was launched.

And the resistance, the people Schottel had betrayed the Fatherland for, were supposed to be removing two of those levels of authority. Which meant that rather than the blame being spread between a number of different people, Schottel alone would be the man responsible for pushing the launch button.

He had no idea what would happen to him after he'd launched the missiles, but he assumed that it wouldn't be pleasant. He knew that he would have to contemplate using his service pistol to end his life.

He logged into his computer system, waited for the operating system to load, then for the system to connect to the wide network. His electronic letter application automatically loaded and the computer chimed as letters were downloaded . He opened up a browser and checked today's news. This normally took him half an hour. Whatever letters there were for him, they could wait. Most of the time they were just junk. Advertisements for stuff he had no desire in buying jostled for his attention amongst memos from his department head.

Finally, he clicked into his letters and began the laborious process of reading through them. The software dictated that a letter wasn't read until he had scrolled through all of the text, and any letter that wasn't read on the day it was received triggered an alert to the computer network team. It was bullshit. He didn't have to actually read the letters – just scroll to the bottom – but it still took time.

The first two were just memos about shift alterations, and he flagged them for further attention. He would read them more thoroughly when he had the time. There were a few junk letters, and those he just scrolled through. He had no interest in buying a new car or a new suit.

There were more tedious departmental letters, some of which he deleted immediately after scrolling through them.

Another junk letter was addressed personally to him. That wasn't so unusual, and he would've dismissed it immediately were it not for the opening paragraph.

> *Herr Schottel, are you preparing to make a party go with a BIG BANG? Then you must get in touch with us at Mushroom Cloud Party Celebrations. We have special things to tell you about your party, and we can assure you that if you place your party needs in our hands it is sure to be a success. Your party will be an instant success, even in somewhere as cosmopolitan as Germania!*
> *If you're the man with the finger on the button, don't delay. Drop us a line now.*

Schottel frowned. He read the letter a few more times. There were

nach Schema F

graphics dotted in various places – balloons, mushrooms, fireworks. He poured himself another schnapps. He was drinking too much, but it calmed his nerves.

It couldn't be a communication from the people who had tasked him with this mission. Surely not.

He closed the letter down, moved onto the next one. More junk, more memos, more reports. He scrolled through each of them, barely taking in what was on the screen. Finally, he was done, and he returned to the letter from Mushroom Cloud Party Celebrations.

It was too much of a coincidence.

They were reaching out to him.

He typed a reply.

> *I am interested. I am arranging a party in Germania, which is taking place in four days.*

He clicked on send.

He turned his attention to a sports page in his browser and read about the weekend's Formula One motor race. He wasn't a huge follower of motor racing, but it passed the time. After that, he checked out the latest football results. He'd barely finished the first match report when his computer chimed. An electronic letter. He opened it. It was from Mushroom Cloud Party Celebrations.

> *When you receive our next electronic letter, you will have a three minute opportunity to proceed. You will receive our next electronic letter within the next three hours.*

The instructions were quite clear. He was to proceed with his mission when he received another communication from them. A three minute window of opportunity. The mission was being brought forward.

Schottel took out his service pistol, checked it was loaded. Of course it was. Not that he had ever expected to use it, not in this job. He jacked a round into the chamber, flicked off the safety. Within the next three hours, he would be using it blow his own brains out.

73

Schmid came into Loritz's office, an excited look on his face. The sturmbannführer looked up from the document he was reading. SS-Untersturmführer Himmler was sat in front of him. Schmid offered a salute.

"Heil Führer!"

Loritz raised a hand half-heartedly. "What is it, Schmid? You look as if you are about to have a heart attack."

Schmid glanced at Himmler, smiled briefly, and then sat down. "Mein Herr, the name Rhodes gave me."

"Schottel?"

"Yes. The last time I spoke with him, there was a subtle implication that Schottel worked in France. As you might expect, there are a few Schottels who work in France. Most of them are industrialists, businessmen, clerical assistants. There are a handful of SS officers, a couple of Gestapo men, none of whom would provide Combat UK with any worthwhile assistance."

Loritz raised an eyebrow. Schmid was building up to something big. He said, "Tell me."

"SS-Hauptsturmführer Schottel. He works for Missile Command. He is one of two bunker commanders at the missile bunker at Grenoble."

Loritz looked down at the report Himmler had given him. He smiled.

"Well, gentleman, between the two of you, you have confirmed what Combat UK's plan is." Schmid raised a questioning eyebrow, and Loritz gestured for Himmler to speak.

"Herr Dauny is – *was* – working on the software for Missile Command."

Schmid said, "They want to take control of Missile Command."

Loritz nodded. "So it would appear."

"Mein Herr, we should give instructions for Schottel to be immediately arrested."

Loritz smiled. He could not fault the enthusiasm of his junior officers, particularly after such an arduous investigation. But they could not react blindly.

nach Schema F

He said, "There is one minor problem."

"What is that?"

"All missile bunkers are secured from within. Of course, they can be unlocked by Missile Command, but if Missile Command has been compromised ... well, for one thing we do not know when the terrorists are launching their attack. We may end up prompting Schottel to launch the missiles prematurely."

"But surely we know whether the system has been compromised."

"The experts at Gerhard Fieseler Werke," Himmler said. "They say that the system could have been compromised weeks ago. They are having to disassemble the computer code, look for unauthorized alterations." Schmid frowned, looked at Loritz, who shrugged helplessly.

"I am afraid, Herr Obersturmführer, that when it comes to computers I have no idea how they work. But we are reliably informed that the system could have been infected by unauthorized changes when the software was last updated."

"Apparently," Himmler said, "the software is updated every few weeks. Errors are rectified, processes are updated, and streamlined It is during this update process that the system is most vulnerable."

Loritz said, "Schmid, I want you to contact Missile Command. We need to know what shifts Schottel works. We can have him arrested the moment he leaves the bunker. If we show our hand whilst he is in the bunker, he could initiate his attack."

Schmid sighed, frustrated. "But what the hell would his target be? These are nuclear missiles. It is overkill to use them to knock out, for example, police headquarters."

Loritz raised an eyebrow. He had his suspicions as to what the terrorists were planning, what – or rather who – their target was. He was surprised that Schmid hadn't already caught on. The younger officer frowned, looked between Himmler and Loritz.

"The Führer?"

"The perfect tool for an assassin. It would kill everyone within a thirty to forty mile range of the target area."

"But there are twenty million people in Germania," Schmid said.

"More if you include nearby towns within the blast zone."

"Just to kill one person? The terrorists would sacrifice more than twenty million civilians?"

It was a ludicrous concept, Loritz had to concede that. It was definitely overkill.

"And this thing, it obviously is not just down to Engländer terrorists. Grenoble is in France. The French Resistance must be involved also." This from Himmler. "Possibly even German terrorists."

Loritz nodded. "Undoubtedly Vierte Reich have a hand in this. I have already notified the Chiefs of the German and French Geheime Staatspolizei. I want you both to provide them all of the information you have. It will be up to the French Gestapo to apprehend Schottel."

"Hardly seems fair," Schmid said. "After the work we have put in."

Loritz could not argue with that reasoning. However, it would be a logistical and political nightmare to send his officers outside their jurisdiction. In any case, the Geheime Staatspolizei was more than just a local secret police force. It was responsible for the entire Reich.

He waved a hand dismissively. "You have both worked well but you have also made errors. I can overlook the errors, naturally, provided that you have learnt from them." Himmler and Schmid both nodded. "Good. Let us hope that we can wrap up this investigation in the next couple of days. I shall, of course, ensure you each receive a commendation for your efforts." He stood up and the two junior officers followed suit. "Heil Führer, gentlemen."

They both saluted and shouted enthusiastically.

"Heil Führer!"

74

Ellen was waiting in the lobby of the interrogation suite. There were half a dozen guards from the Waffen-SS on duty. Two stood at the entrance to the corridor which led to the interrogation room where Klarsfeld was being held. No entrance was permitted without SS-Sturmbannführer Loritz's express approval. The middle-aged officer seemed to delight in telling Ellen that she did not have the express approval from Loritz. She was to wait for him.

She'd been there for almost half an hour before he arrived. He had Keitel with him, which was an ominous indicator of what was to come. Loritz greeted the Waffen-SS officers and then led Ellen and Keitel down the corridor. He stopped at a door, opened it, and gestured for Ellen to enter. She was surprised to find the room beyond empty.

"Take a seat, Frau Brauchitsch," Loritz said. He removed his jacket and sat down on one side of the table in the middle of the room. There was only one more chair at the table and Ellen took it. Keitel leant against the door, lit a cigarette, pretended to look preoccupied with something else.

Ellen felt uncomfortable, but at least she noted that the room did not possess a doorway which led to a torture cell. She was clearly about to be interrogated, but she wasn't going to be tortured.

Not imminently, anyway.

Loritz didn't have any documents with him, but that was not so unusual. He generally worked from his impressive memory and only used documents as a prop with which to intimidate the people he was interrogating.

He said, "You and Reichsstatthalter Klarsfeld. You became close, yes?"

"We had a good working relationship, yes."

"And yet you remained loyal to the Reich when you told me, told the Führer even, what your professional opinion of him was."

It was a question, even if it wasn't couched in such terms. Ellen nodded. "Yes, of course. I like to think that my loyalty to the Geheime Staatspolizei, to you, to the Reich, is proven."

Loritz didn't answer immediately. His grey eyes stared impassively at her. "I had faith in you, Ellen. When you returned to work after the

Führer's assassination, my colleagues, my superiors, they thought that either you were not ready to return to work or indeed that you would *never* be ready to return to work. But I had faith in you. I believed in you, Ellen."

"And I thank you for that, mein Herr."

He smiled tightly. "But yet I am concerned, Ellen. Suspicions have been raised as to Herr Klarsfeld's loyalty."

Ellen frowned. She knew what was coming but she didn't know how this would affect her.

"You were already aware that I had expressed my own concerns as to the assassination attempt on Herr Klarsfeld." Ellen nodded. "And you yourself have been investigating a very active branch of Combat UK in the city of Peterborough."

"We were getting to the bottom of it—"

"That particular investigation has now been concluded."

"Oh?"

"Marcus Dauny worked on the launch control system for Missile Command," Loritz said. "And Barry Rhodes – a man we suspect of being an American spy – mentioned under interrogation the name of an SS officer working at a missile bunker in Grenoble." Loritz smiled. "It would appear as though we have uncovered their plot. Even as we are speaking, Gestapo officers are on their way to arrest the SS officer, and staff from Gerhard Fieseler Werke are endeavouring to correct any sabotage Marcus Dauny may have carried out."

Ellen smiled. She had never wanted to be involved in the murder of millions of innocent people, so her relief was palpable. She leant back in her chair and nodded. "I am glad that we have managed to put a stop to their plans."

"Quite. And yet the involvement of terrorists from Peterborough has been quite spectacular. And I cannot help but suspect that Herr Klarsfeld is, in some way, inextricably linked to these people."

"If he is, mein Herr, then I was utterly remiss in my conclusion of him," Ellen said. Now was not a time for loyalty. Now was a time for saving her own skin. Klarsfeld could easily falter under interrogation. He could so very easily implicate her, and she would not be able to blame him for that. People being tortured would give up their closest friends, their relatives even, if they thought it would save them.

nach Schema F

Loritz smiled but it did not reach his cold eyes.

"I need you to do something for me, Frau Obersturmführer," he said. "Frau Brauchitsch. Ellen."

"Anything, mein Herr."

"I need you to interrogate Klarsfeld." Loritz cleared his throat, looked up at Keitel. "You can take Keitel in with you. I need you to get him to give us names. The names of his co-conspirators. I need him to confess that he is involved in this diabolical plot to launch nuclear missiles at targets within the Greater German Reich. I need him to sign a confession. And then I need you to execute him."

"Execute him?"

"The penalty for high treason is death, Ellen."

"Of course. But what if he is not involved?"

"If he is not involved, then a man with such a weak resolve as Klarsfeld will not confess convincingly." Loritz rested his elbows on the table, clasped his hands in front of him. He pointed at her with two fingers that were perfectly aligned. "The reason I am asking you to do this, Ellen, is to prove to me your loyalty. I am not giving you any bullshit. I am not pretending to mislead you, and I know that you have a certain distaste of torture. This is the truth. At this moment in time, I do not trust you. I need you to convince me of your loyalty. Does this make sense?"

Ellen didn't respond immediately. Even had she not been colluding with Klarsfeld, it would be natural for Loritz to suspect that she had been. It was how she comported herself now which would seal her future.

She nodded. "I understand, mein Herr. I will do this. If Klarsfeld has betrayed the Reich, he deserves to die." Loritz seemed satisfied with this. He looked at Keitel, almost a smile on his face, and Ellen realized that this was the test – the difference between her interrogating and leading the torture of Klarsfeld, and her herself being tortured.

Loritz led her to where Klarsfeld was being held. Outside the door, he said, "I will be watching. I am intrigued as to how you will perform as an interrogator. You have proven to be – in the past – an exceptional investigator. I want to see if you have the all-round skills to make you a leading Gestapo officer."

Ellen could almost smell the duplicity in his words.

75

The report from Mittendorf went directly to Reichsführer-SS Schaemmel and he read it with interest. He picked up the telephone and called through to the head of the Leibstandarte-SS *Führer*, asked for him to prepare the Führer's helicopter together with an appropriate security detail. Then he got to his feet and pulled his jacket on. It was a short walk to the Führer's office.

"Mein Führer, we have to leave."

The Führer looked up from the paperwork he was reading.

"What for?"

"This is serious," Schaemmel said. "We must leave Germania immediately." The look on Schaemmel's face was serious, and the Führer closed the document in front of him and stood up. He was wearing a suit. He opened his drawer and took out a pistol, checked it was loaded.

"The helicopter is waiting for us."

They walked quickly through the Reichstaghalle, and Schaemmel felt a momentary twang of guilt as they passed by secretaries and SS officers, all of whom would be left behind. He smiled at some of them he knew. He could recall meeting their families – their husbands, wives, children – at functions. Schaemmel was good at remembering names and faces. The Führer stopped briefly to chat with one of his typists, asking how her mother was. Schaemmel resisted the urge to drag the Führer away. Time was certainly of the essence, but there was a very good chance this woman would die, and at least she would die with good, positive memories of the Führer.

They took the lift to the roof, where the helicopter landing pad was situated. There was space for four helicopters. Two were Benz-AG Tiger attack helicopters. A third was a Bölkow MB-90 transport helicopter, containing 30 members of the Leibstandarte-SS *Führer*. The fourth was an MB-92 command helicopter – the Führer's personal transport. Already the rotors were turning. An officer saluted, and Schaemmel spoke into his ear.

"We need to get fifty miles away," he said. "At least. And as quickly as possible." The officer saluted and relayed the instructions to the pilot. It didn't really matter where they went, but the nearest military base at least fifty miles away would be an obvious choice. He helped the Führer on board and as the doors were sealed, they put on headphones. In the back of the helicopter, they could talk without the crew listening in.

The helicopter lifted off and Schaemmel watched as the other three helicopters followed suit. They banked to the side and a voice in his ear told Schaemmel which military base they were headed for. Schaemmel closed off the communication to the cockpit and looked at the Führer.

"So, my loyal Reichsführer, are you going to tell me what this is all about?"

Schaemmel paused, took a deep breath. "A plot has been uncovered, one which spreads throughout the Reich. Germania is to be destroyed."

"Destroyed?"

"Terrorists have seized control of our nuclear missiles and they intend to launch five at Germania. We do not know when, but we presume it could be imminent. That being the case, essentially we have twenty minutes to get out of the blast range."

The Führer looked stunned, but seemed to quickly recover. He wasn't as gullible as previous leaders. He was under no illusions that the people adored him unquestionably. He knew that many did not. He read regular security reports, and rather than lose his temper, he asked for resources to be shifted to deal with security issues.

"Is there any way we can stop it?"

"I do not know," Schaemmel said. The report had stated that the French office of the Gestapo were going to arrest the traitor, but would they get it done before he'd completed his act of terrorism? He could not give the Führer any guarantees, any reassurance.

"But if they destroy Germania, millions will die."

"I know. Our men are doing their best to put a stop to it."

The Führer's eyes looked out of the window, dropped to the city below. "Schaemmel, there are twenty million people down there. Men, women, children. I cannot stand by and watch them die."

"What is the alternative, mein Führer? That you should die with them? If the terrorists do succeed, we will need a strong leader to bring the people together."

"Tell me, Schaemmel, how many soldiers are there in Germania?"

"Forty thousand. They will have to be sacrificed. If this information became public knowledge, imagine the unrest." The Führer nodded, but he was still looking at the city.

Schaemmel knew that he'd had the opportunity to seize power, to leave both the city and the Führer behind, to even go so far as to allow the terrorists to destroy Germania. But he was a loyal Party member. And he would stand by his Führer to the very end.

76

Ellen looked down at Klarsfeld. He was a broken man, head in his hands. She sat down opposite him. Keitel leant against the wall next to the door. Ellen tapped her fingers on the table and the Reichsstatthalter looked at her.

"Ellen. How good to see you."

"I wish that I could say the same, mein Herr."

Klarsfeld nodded wearily. "It is not a good place to be."

"Then why are you here?"

"Your superior arrested me." He shrugged. "I cannot say any more than that."

"My superior believes that you are involved with Engländer terrorists," Ellen said.

"He is mistaken."

"Even were you involved, you would not admit it."

Klarsfeld smiled at her. The CCTV cameras would catch his expression and hers as well. She knew that, and she could tell that he knew it also.

"I always knew you were an excellent investigator. Of course, you were also a very observant security officer."

"You have told my superior, SS-Sturmbannführer Loritz, that you are not involved in any terrorist plot. That you are not working with Combat UK."

"Combat UK has been destroyed," Klarsfeld said. He shrugged, leant back in his chair. "The idea that I am working with an obsolete organization is utterly absurd."

"My superior, he also believes that I am colluding with you."

"Really?"

"He believes that I have become corrupted," Ellen said. "That I am a traitor." Ellen rested an elbow on the table, her chin on her hand. "He does not believe the report that I wrote about you."

"I trust it was a good report."

"This is why he does not believe it."

"Ah." Klarsfeld nodded. "Then I see your dilemma." There was a brief glance in her direction, an affirmation perhaps that she must do whatever she could to protect herself.

"I want you to tell him that I have been colluding with you," Ellen said. She knew there was only one way she could save herself from Loritz's accusation. Klarsfeld allowed his face to sink. He shook his head.

Ellen wanted to cry.

"I would not collude with you," he said. "And I am not working with terrorists."

"It would be easier for you if you just confessed," Ellen said. "Told me everything. Told Herr Loritz that you and I were working together."

"What can I say?" Klarsfeld said with a smile and a shrug. "Neither of those accusations is true. I am a politician in a county where we do not need politicians. I am merely a mouthpiece. I was shot at a few weeks ago and I was lucky to escape with my life. And for this, Loritz would question my loyalty, would accuse me of being a traitor?"

"Herr Klarsfeld, this can go one of two ways," Ellen said. She hated interrogations. She hated torture even more. Her eyes flicked to Keitel and she saw him straighten up, readying himself for the inevitable. "Tell us the truth and we can end this thing quite painlessly. Or have us beat it out of you."

"And you, my dear, will you beat it out of me?"

Ellen frowned. Of course Loritz would know that Klarsfeld was fully aware of her reticence regarding torture. This was Klarsfeld challenging her.

She smiled, looked down. "Not me, Herr Klarsfeld. Rather the large gentleman behind you." Her gaze met the Reichstatthalter's. She said, "I want your confession." Klarsfeld shook his head. "And even when you give me that, Keitel will continue to beat you until you tell us that you and I were colluding together, that I am a traitor also."

She glanced back at Keitel and nodded. He moved quickly for a tall man. He grabbed Klarsfeld, pulled him to his feet, propelled him towards the door which led to the torture chamber. Ellen was at the door before them, pushing it open. She followed them into the room.

Keitel worked efficiently. He ripped Klarsfeld's jacket off, then his tie and shirt. Within a few seconds, he had Klarsfeld hanging from the bar. Ellen sat down at the solitary table. She looked away as Keitel tore Klarsfeld's trousers down, tossing his shoes aside. This was interrogation. Dehumanize the person, strip them naked. All the same, the big SS officer looked back at Ellen. She was a female, Klarsfeld was in his underpants.

Ellen gave a solitary nod, and then Klarsfeld was naked.

He gasped, but that was expected when you were hung from a bar with handcuffs holding you in place. They taught investigators at the Geheime Staatspolizei college that people who were militarily trained would try to grip the handcuff chain, taking their weight in their hands rather than allow the cuffs to cut into their wrists.

Klarsfeld, obviously, did not do this.

Ellen said, "Do you know Liam Lovett?"

"Of course I do," Klarsfeld said. "We all know him."

Ellen sighed. She nodded at Keitel, who punched Klarsfeld in the stomach. The old man gasped, struggled for breath. Ellen wanted to close her eyes. She didn't want to see this. But the cameras were watching.

She had to be convincing.

Loritz knew that she hated torture.

"Herr Klarsfeld, I do not want to see you getting tortured. I want us to bring this all to an end. You can see that Herr Keitel is a powerful man. He can do to you things that you would not believe."

Keitel punched Klarsfeld a few more times, as though to prove a point. Ellen had to appear as though she found the torture distasteful, without actually looking as though she were upset. She found that part particularly difficult.

"Herr Klarsfeld, a confession is all I need."

Klarsfeld moved his head, looked at her. "You also want me to condemn you."

"Yes, I do."

Klarsfeld smiled. "That will never happen."

Ellen closed her eyes.

If Klarsfeld cracked too soon, it could be seen as absolving her of any wrongdoing. He had to hold out, hold out because otherwise he could be seen as giving her what she wanted. He had to be hurt.

Hurt a lot.

She looked at Keitel and gave a nod. Keitel pulled a pair of pliers from his pocket. She watched as he reached up for Klarsfeld's mouth, opened it, gripped one of his teeth with the pliers.

She looked away, but she heard the crack and the scream.

Ellen wasn't sure she would ever get over this.

nach Schema F

77

Schottel was startled away by the sounding of a buzzer. Frowning, he looked at the security screens. The buzzer belonged to the main entrance up on the ground. Someone wanted to come inside.

There were two of them, plain-clothed, undoubtedly Gestapo. They weren't alone. Behind them were standing ten armed men from the Waffen-SS. Schottel put down the glass he was holding and pushed a switch on the control panel in front of him.

"SS-Hauptsturmführer Schottel," he announced into the microphone protruding from the control panel. "Can I help you?"

"Herr Hauptsturmführer, could you please open the security doors," one of the Gestapo officers replied.

"I am afraid that is not possible," Schottel said. "You do not have authorization to enter this secure bunker."

"Herr Hauptsturmführer, I am from the Geheime Staatspolizei, and we have a warrant from Missile Command to enter this bunker."

"I cannot see the warrant from here," Schottel said. The Gestapo officer held it up to the CCTV camera. "It is not possible to read it."

"Herr Hauptsturmführer, you must check in with Missile Command, who will instruct you to let us into the bunker."

"I will do that," Schottel said, and he closed the communication. He turned to his computer, found the electronic letter from Mushroom Cloud Party Celebrations. He hastily typed a reply, clicked on the send button, and the communication was gone.

He glanced down at the buttons which would launch the missiles and wondered what would happened if he pressed them now.

The telephone rang.

He let it ring. It would be Missile Command ordering him to open the security doors. He certainly did not feel like talking to them. He looked back down at his computer screen, willing a reply to appear.

Missile Command could open the doors from their end, but it required four different officers from different locations to key in specific codes at the same time. Generally, it was considered that there was no valid reason to open the doors from the outside. Schottel considered that he had perhaps half an hour at most before the exterior doors were unsealed. It depended how far away from Missile Command the four officers were.

He stood up, went to the control room doors, found a lever at the side. He pulled down on it and two iron bolts were thrown across the doors, mechanically sealing the doors from within. This was a last line of defence should the other doors be breached by an invading enemy. It would take an oxyacetylene cutting torch a few minutes to get through.

That done, he looked back at the computer screen. There was still no reply.

The buzzer sounded again, mingling with the ringing telephone. Schottel closed his eyes and put his fingers in his ears.

78

Dauny looked at Dunne and smiled. This had been a rush job, but Dauny liked to work under extreme pressure. It was how he thrived. It did not necessarily mean that the work he did was of a poor quality. But even behind the smile there was the reality. The reality that in testing his new software, ensuring that it would actually perform as expected, he was condemning millions of people to death.

Dunne said, "Are we good to go?"

"It's working."

"So we're good to go?"

Dauny nodded. Dunne cranked up his machine and prepared to log onto the relevant system. Dauny reached out, held onto his wrist.

"We need to be certain."

"Certain? Certain that you've done your job and I've done mine? That we aren't going to massively screw this up at the last minute and it's all going to fail?"

Dauny shook his head. "Certain that we're happy with the consequences of our actions here."

"If we thought about the consequences of all of our actions, Marcus, we'd never do anything. We do what we do because that's what we were born to do. I was born to hack computer systems. You were born to write computer software. Put us together and…"

"And we are easily manipulated?"

Dunne looked down. He was still smiling. His computer was behind him and to the right. He was ready to go. He'd been waiting for Dauny to finish his job for days.

"I like to think I'm slightly more intelligent than that."

"Owen, when you upload this software, which will take no more than a couple of minutes, we'll send an email to this Schottel, whom, incidentally, we don't even know is actually our contact, and he will react. If he *is* our contact, he will press a few buttons and he will kill more than twenty million people."

"More like somewhere between thirty and forty million people."

"Owen, you're not making me feel any better." Dunne laughed. He had absolutely no empathy for anyone. When given a task, he completed it but did not consider the consequences. "I'm being serious. Do we want to do this?"

"Marcus, we already have. Your task was to rewrite software. Your task is complete. My task was to ensure that this new software could be uploaded. My task is complete – though, as yet, unproven, because we haven't actually 'done' it. But I know I've completed my task."

Owen's computer made a sound. He frowned, arched an eyebrow.

"What?" Dauny asked.

"That's an electronic letter."

"And?"

Owen swung round to face the terminal. "And this computer is set up for the Mushroom Cloud account. Which means—"

"Schottel?"

Owen nodded his head. "You'd better take a look."

Dauny stood up behind Owen and read the letter on the screen.

> *I have only a few minutes in which to complete my objectives. After this time it will become impossible. If you cannot give me the go ahead before this time then the mission will fail.*

Dauny met Owen's gaze. "We have to do it now. He's become compromised."

"No more doubts?"

Dauny closed his eyes, ran his hands over his face. This was the final opportunity to stop this. Once they uploaded the software, once they gave Schottel the go-ahead, there was no going back.

But this was the only way to stop the Führer, to prevent another world war, potentially to prevent a nuclear war.

He nodded his head slowly.

"Do it," he said, wondering how he had become the man to make the final decision.

79

Schottel had watched as the Gestapo officers and the Waffen-SS men had made their way into the bunker. They had been at the door to the control room for the last few minutes, but their banging had ceased. They knew what they had to do, and he'd seen them make the necessary phone call.

The monitor showing the gatehouse was on the main screen now. Schottel was awaiting the arrival of another vehicle, one which would bring cutting gear to be used to break through the final door to the bunker. He looked at his service pistol lying on the desk in front of him. He knew that he wouldn't be using it to attack the officers once they entered the control room. He'd be using it on himself. They would want to take him alive, and under no circumstances did he want that to happen.

The protocol for the silo officers should a breach happen was for them to fully seal their doors and let no one in. Schottel knew that Missile Command had been in touch with the silo officers. He'd watched each of them take phone calls, seen the officers look up accusingly at the camera. The doors to the silos were already sealed, but he'd seen the officers throw the bolts across the doors, sealing them manually as he had sealed the control room.

The telephone rang and he picked it up. He didn't want to speak to them, and part of him wanted to rip the phone from the wall, anything to stop it from ringing. But he raised it to his ear.

"Schottel, are you there?"

"What do you want?"

"Open the door, damn you!" It was one of the officers from Missile Command. "You can make this easier on yourself. But in any case, our men will be inside in the next few minutes."

"Perhaps."

"Why are you doing this, Schottel? What do you hope to achieve?" Schottel didn't reply. "There is still time for you to return to us, Schottel. Open the door and we can discuss this. We can forgive your betrayal if you just open the door."

Schottel smiled and looked up at the CCTV camera. He shook his head slowly. He could hear the person on the other end of the line sighing heavily.

"You are leaving us no choice, Schottel."

"Likewise," he said. He cradled the handset and then ripped out the phone's cable. He considered disconnecting the CCTV camera, but decided against it. There was no point. As soon as the Waffen-SS officers had breached the door, he would blow his brains out.

He looked back up at the bank of monitors, in time to see a truck pulling into the complex. Undoubtedly this vehicle held the cutting gear required to breach the control room. All of this was in vain. He hadn't received the message from the resistance fighters.

Then his computer made a sound. The delivery of an electronic letter. Schottel spun his chair round and opened up his mail application.

There it was.

He clicked on it and the electronic letter filled the screen.

All systems go. Proceed.
Godspeed, Herr Schottel.

Schottel smiled. He looked up at the CCTV camera and gave a wave. Then he turned back to the desk, flipped the safety covers off the five launch buttons. The banging on the door became more frantic now, the officers outside alerted to Schottel's intentions.

He poured himself a glass of schnapps, raised it in a toast to the computer screen, the electronic letter, and then downed it in one gulp.

Then he pushed the launch button for Silo 1.

His eyes shifted to the monitor displaying the silo. Already, the silo doors were opening. There was a deep rumble coming from below, somewhere to his right. The ICBM's rocket was firing up. He checked the other monitors. There was panic on the faces of the officers outside the door, and also above ground.

He pushed the button for Silo 2, then Silo 3, then Silo 4 and finally Silo 5. The rumble of rockets firing became louder. He watched as the missile in Silo 1 started to rise out of the ground, getting faster the higher it went.

Schottel started to laugh. The roar of the missiles filled his ears and he watched as each of them rose from the ground, beginning their journey

nach Schema F

to Germania. He poured himself another schnapps and continued to laugh.

80

Ellen looked at Klarsfeld. Keitel had just been beating him with a baseball bat. One of his legs was broken, the bones protruding from his shin. He'd vomited and shit himself. He'd screamed in agony, but now he was quiet. Breathing heavily, but no sound leaving his lips.

"Herr Klarsfeld, tell me about your links to Combat UK." She asked the question, but she wasn't interested in his answer. She didn't want to see him getting tortured anymore. Her heart wasn't in it. She was mindful of the video cameras watching her, but Loritz knew that she didn't have the heart for torture.

Klarsfeld gasped. "I know nothing about Combat UK. I am the governor of the German State of Great Britain." Keitel punched him in the stomach. The big German clearly took delight in torturing people. He turned to Ellen and smiled. She wondered how much he knew, whether he suspected that Ellen was a traitor.

Ellen said, "You can make this stop now, Herr Klarsfeld."

"Please, just make it stop."

Ellen got to her feet. She walked up to the Reichsstatthalter. Her face was level with the lower part of his ribcage. She looked up at him. She said, "You know what you have to do." He looked down at her. Saliva was dripping from his face.

"I cannot tell you what you want to know."

"You can tell me that I betrayed my country. You can say that at least."

"I am not going to help you," Klarsfeld said. His eyes met hers. She was sure that he smiled. It wasn't a big smile, but it was a smile nonetheless. She felt ruined inside. He was giving her permission to continue brutalizing him.

She walked back to her chair and sat down. Keitel looked back at her. She shook her head. Even in a proper interrogation, there would be no point in torturing Klarsfeld any more. He had lasted longer than many other people would have. At this point in an interrogation, there were two conclusions. Either the individual knew nothing or he was going to say nothing. In either case, there was no point in continuing. In both cases, the end result was usually death.

Ellen looked away from Klarsfeld. She didn't meet Keitel's gaze. The Reichsstatthalter could be executed here, or he could be taken away to a court where he would be sentenced and then killed. She didn't want to make that decision. But she knew Keitel was expecting her to give him further instructions.

She said, quietly, "You stubborn old fool."

The door to the interrogation room opened and Loritz entered. His eyes fell upon Klarsfeld, and then he looked down at Ellen.

"He told you nothing." She shook her head. "What do you presume we do with him now, Frau Obersturmführer?"

"We suspect he has been treacherous," Ellen said blandly. "We must execute him."

Loritz walked up to Klarsfeld, looked him up and down. He regarded the shit and vomit on the floor with a curled-up lip. "The Obersturmführer is right, Herr Klarsfeld. You are a stubborn old fool. You could have given us the name of a contact. You could have told us what the plans were. You could have given up Frau Brauchitsch. All of these may have seen an end to your torture. But you remained silent." Loritz glanced at Ellen and then looked back up at Klarsfeld. "As the Obersturmführer said, it is usually at this point – when we realize that we will get no further information from a suspect – that we effectively give up and put the suspect out of his misery." Loritz looked at Keitel, who lit up a cigarette. "However, I think that in this case, that would be letting you off lightly. You must be in pain, Herr Klarsfeld. That broken leg, it looks horrific. Though I have seen worse. Keitel, here, he must be losing his touch." The big German gave a half-smile at that. "Let me tell you something, Herr Klarsfeld. Right now, the French Gestapo is in the process of arresting a German SS officer by the name of Schottel. Schottel works at a nuclear missile silo at Grenoble. The resistance were attempting to launch an attack on Germania, killing more than twenty million people together with the Führer and the rest of his government." Loritz walked around Klarsfeld, looking at the injuries on the man's back where Keitel had beaten him with a stick. He returned to the front. "The plot has been foiled, old man. You have lost. And this, what happens in this room, this is no longer about getting information from you. This is about punishment for your treachery." Loritz stepped back, leant against the wall just behind Ellen. He nodded at Keitel.

Ellen watched as the big German grabbed Klarsfeld's broken leg and twisted it, the exposed tibia and fibula moving apart. Klarsfeld screamed out and retched. Ellen looked away, turning her head to the side. She looked at Loritz who was staring impassively at the torture scene before him.

"You should watch this, Ellen," he said. "This is what happens to traitors."

Ellen stood up and pushed past the Sturmbannführer. She left the interrogation suite, made her way up the corridor to the reception area, where Waffen-SS officers gave her curious looks. She could still hear Klarsfeld's screams, and she sat down and closed her eyes.

81

Schaemmel received a telephone call as the helicopter continued to speed away from Germania. The news was not good. He cut the call, closed his eyes, shook his head.

The Führer said, "What is it?"

"Our men failed, mein Herr. Five missiles have been launched from Grenoble."

"My God."

Schaemmel pushed a button on his headset, got through to the pilot. "How far from Germania are we?"

"We are still over the outskirts, mein Herr. We are twenty miles from the Reichstaghalle."

"We need you to fly as quickly as you can," Schaemmel said. "The Führer's life depends upon it."

"Yes, mein Herr."

Schaemmel turned to the Führer. "This will be the greatest disaster to befall the Reich."

"We will come back from this even stronger, Schaemmel."

"The entire leadership is still in Germania. You will have to form a new government."

"The Fatherland will remember their sacrifice."

"There will undoubtedly be a period of uncertainty."

"Of course," the Führer said. "And it is during that period that we should be tough. This plot involved people from France and from Great Britain, yes?" Schaemmel nodded. "How deep does the treachery run?"

"Without a full and independent investigation, we cannot say."

"I want you to give the command to withdraw our top officers from London and from Paris. Once that is done, I want you to destroy both of those cities. The people of the Greater German Reich will know what it is to lose a capital city."

Schaemmel nodded. Of course there had to be retaliation. But London and Paris were both administrative capitals for two of the Reich's most profitable states. It would take a lot to rebuild both Great Britain and France after such a devastating punishment.

The Führer eyed him curiously. "You doubt my decision on this?"

"I have concerns, mein Herr, but hopefully once we land you will give me the opportunity to express them."

The Führer nodded. "You are a loyal man, Schaemmel. You could have left me to perish in Germania."

"I still feel you have important work to do, mein Herr. And Germany could certainly not survive the disaster of losing another leader in addition to losing its capital."

"How long before the missiles strike their target?"

"Perhaps ten minutes."

The Führer closed his eyes as though in silent contemplation. He said, "History will remember this day, Schaemmel. And the people of Germany will forever remember what we did afterwards. We must be strong. We must be brave. We must be ruthless. We must retaliate."

"The United States of America?"

"They are involved in this. They have to be. And they will not be expecting us to launch an attack against them so soon after our capital has been destroyed. We must appear to the outside world to be weak, but we must intensify our plans to invade America. We must make a move on them as soon as possible."

"I understand, mein Herr."

To Schaemmel, it seemed strange to be talking of war when their capital was about to be destroyed. It seemed wrong to be talking of invading another country when they would have to rebuild Germania. But perhaps the Führer was right. Perhaps this would be good for the German people.

They would rise from the ashes of this act of terrorism and be a stronger nation as a result.

For the next few minutes, they travelled in silence, each of them contemplating the great disaster which was about to occur. Schaemmel looked at his watch. The missiles would be so close to Germania that people would be able to see them in the sky.

He spoke to the pilot.

"We are forty miles from the Reichstaghalle," the pilot said. There was concern in his voice as he spoke. Schaemmel wondered whether they had travelled far enough from the blast zone.

He said, "A nuclear missile has been launched at Germania. It is about

nach Schema F

to strike. We may be caught in the blast. Be prepared."

"Yes, mein Herr!" the pilot shouted.

*   *   *   *   *

In Germania, in one of the many kindergartens, children were leaving the school building. It was a sunny day, and the teachers had let them out to play. Mostly, the children played in set groups with friends they had known since starting school. But as in every walk of life, there were a few loners. Some were loners because for whatever reason they had been ostracized by their classmates. Others were loners out of choice.

Leopold was one such loner.

He was ten. He didn't trust his classmates. He didn't really trust anybody. He kept a watchful and suspicious eye on his teachers, looking for signs of anything untoward, anything un-German, anything disloyal to the Reich.

Leopold was waiting for the day that he turned twelve and he could join the Hitlerjugend. He believed that Germany was the best nation on the planet. The German people were well fed, prosperous, happy. Anybody who said any different was a liar and a traitor.

Leopold was an intelligent boy and he devoured history books, knew everything about Germany's rise to power, how the country had been almost destroyed after the Great War, and how it had risen from the ashes to become the most powerful nation in the world. He excelled in physical education, he possessed an inquisitive and analytical mind, he was already proficient in the use of computers to conduct research for science projects. His head teacher had told Leopold that he could become a great scientist if he put his mind to it.

But Leopold wanted to join the SS. Ultimately, he wanted to work for the Geheime Staatspolizei. He wanted to be an investigator. He wanted to seek out traitors and make them pay. As a young boy, this was not a 'game' he could play with his peers. He couldn't pretend to investigate them. Where was the fun in that? his peers would ask.

So Leopold investigated them without their knowledge. He investigated them for real.

He sat down on a bench and watched his classmates playing, and he took out a notebook and checked some of the previous entries. Which children played together. Who their friends and associates were. Who they argued with. Who they fought with.

It was a veritable intelligence dossier about everyone in his year at school, a document from which could be determined trends and relationships.

Leopold smiled.

His eyes scanned the playground and he felt happy. He was one of the watchers, and he knew that he wasn't the only one. He had seen another boy and also a girl sitting alone, watching the playground, jotting in notebooks. So long as there were people like him, like them, Germany would be in safe hands. The traitors would not be able to hurt the Fatherland.

Something caught his eye and he looked up. In the sky something was flying incredibly quickly. He frowned. It was the wrong shape for an aircraft, and it was travelling a lot faster than any jet he had ever seen.

He shielded his eyes from the sun and watched as the object drew closer. It was long, narrow, but at the same time, it was huge. Easily the same size as the body of an airliner. It was arcing down towards the city, so close now that he could see the small ailerons moving, adjusting the object's course.

Leopold frowned.

This was a missile. He had seen photographs of them in books. Missiles were weapons. This was a weapon, bearing down directly on Germania, on his school.

His mouth fell open. He felt no fear – just wonderment.

For a brief instant, there was a brilliant flash of light.

And then everything went black.

*   *   *   *   *

The shockwave hit the helicopter with such ferocity that Schaemmel was thrown against the side, banging his head so hard that he was momentarily stunned. He could hear warning alarms sounding as the helicopter lurched from side to side, dropping altitude.

He got through to the pilot, but the pilot was shouting at his co-pilot, the both of them too busy to talk to their passengers, no matter how important they were. Schaemmel glanced out of the side window and saw one of the attack helicopters spinning out of control, its tail rotor smashed. He watched as it plummeted to the ground where it was consumed by a fireball.

They were perhaps five hundred feet from the ground and dropping. Schaemmel could see trees, houses, cars on the roads, all of them getting closer and closer. The last few feet seemed to rush up towards him.

And then there was darkness.

82

A klaxon sounded in the Polizeipräsidium. Ellen had never heard it before. From over the loudspeaker a voice demanded that all senior officers go to the conference room on the thirtieth floor.

Loritz rushed into the reception. He looked at Ellen, who shrugged. There was a shout from the rest room at the back of the reception. The shout was joined by others, expressions of shock and horror.

Ellen followed Loritz into the room. The news was on the large TV on the wall. The announcer looked stunned. She said, "Early reports are that five huge explosions have rocked Germania. We are waiting for more information, but eyewitnesses are stating that these were nuclear explosions. At this point in time there is no communication from the capital."

Loritz turned to Ellen. The look of horror on his face was palpable.

"We have failed," he said. All Ellen could do was shake her head. The resistance had succeeded. They had destroyed Germania. They had killed the Führer. Loritz flopped down into a chair and held his head in his hands. "What happens now?" he asked.

"Did you kill Klarsfeld?"

"What?"

"Did you kill him?"

"What difference does that make?" Loritz snapped. "Who cares about Klarsfeld?"

"The people of this state need a leader, mein Herr. Klarsfeld is a recognizable leader, one who can hold us together in this time of uncertainty."

Loritz choked back a laugh. "He is barely recognizable at the moment, Brauchitsch. And he is also a traitor."

"We do not know this for certain," Ellen said. "We should clean him up, get him in front of the cameras. The people trust him. Let us not forget that we are an occupying force in a foreign country. With the Führer gone, what is to stop the Engländers from seizing power?"

"The fact that the SS is a great force—"

"The SS could not stop the resistance from destroying Germania," Ellen said, "from killing the Führer. We need Klarsfeld."

"This is out of my hands," Loritz said, getting to his feet. "There are people many ranks above me who are deciding the fate of this province right now in the conference room on the thirtieth floor."

"Go to them," Ellen said. "I will help to get Klarsfeld cleaned up."

Loritz squinted at Ellen. "You know, Frau Obersturmführer, I still do not trust you. And I will discover the truth."

"Right now, mein Herr, we have more important things to consider," Ellen said. She watched as Loritz left and then she rushed to the interrogation suite where Klarsfeld was being held. Keitel was sat in the interrogation room smoking a cigarette. She asked him where Klarsfeld was, and he gestured to the torture room. "I want you to take him down and help me to clean him up."

He frowned. "Why?"

"Because I am telling you to, Herr Sturmscharführer."

Keitel shook his head and stood up.

The Reichsstatthalter was a mess. His broken leg was bleeding, was twisted sideways. There were bruises and cigarette burns all over his torso. The fingers of his left hand had been broken or dislocated. He was covered in a sheen of sweat and vomit. Once he was on the floor, Keitel washed him down with a hosepipe as Ellen called for a doctor. She wanted to tell Klarsfeld that the resistance had been successful, but she couldn't do that in front of Keitel.

By the time the medical team arrived, Keitel was turning off the hosepipe and Klarsfeld lay shivering in a pool of water. Ellen told the medical team to fix the Reichsstatthalter's leg, to stabilize him. They took him to the medical suite on the floor above. She sent Keitel with them.

And then she sat down on the chair and rested her head on the table in front of her.

*   *   *   *   *

SS-Oberstgruppenführer Mittendorf rushed from his house. He had received the news about the capital, and had been summoned to the Polizeipräsidium where he was due to preside over an emergency meeting.

There was a Mercedes saloon in his driveway, together with two 4x4s containing his security detail. As he walked up to them, two more 4x4s pulled up outside and ten men hopped out. They were carrying MP5 submachine-guns. More security for him.

Mittendorf nodded to his security chief.

"We need to get to the Polizeipräsidium as quickly as possible," he told him.

"Of course."

Mittendorf opened the rear door of the Mercedes and looked at the new arrivals. They should've stayed in their cars, he was thinking.

And then all hell broke loose.

The new arrivals opened fire, cutting down his security team. Mittendorf was thrown into the Mercedes by his security chief, who subsequently gasped as bullets tore into him. The driver of the car fired up the engine, but two of the armed men rushed up to the car, yanked the driver's door open and emptied their weapons into him.

Mittendorf reached for his pistol, but one of the armed men grabbed him, pulled him out of the car and wrenched the gun from his grip, before throwing him to the floor. He looked up at one of the men. He recognized him.

"You are Udell," he said. The man nodded his head. He was holstering his pistol. "You are Klarsfeld's head of security."

"That is correct," Udell said.

"What are you doing, man?"

"Assuming control."

Another man appeared by Udell's side. Mittendorf frowned. The man's face was vaguely familiar. He had a pistol in his hand. He jacked a round into the chamber.

"Who are you?" Mittendorf asked him.

"I *was* SS-Oberführer Scholl," the man said. He aimed the pistol at Mittendorf's face. "But you shall know me as the man who killed you."

Mittendorf felt a tremendous blow to his forehead and then he felt nothing.

nach Schema F

83

The various heads of the SS in the German State of Great Britain were waiting in the conference room on the thirtieth floor of the Polizeipräsidium. The Oberstgruppenführer had not yet arrived. They'd all heard of the tragedy which had befallen Germania, though actual details were still scant.

Twenty minutes earlier, SS-Sturmbannführer Loritz had entered the conference room. To them, he was just a junior officer and had no place amongst them. But he'd told them that Reichsstatthalter Klarsfeld had been injured and was on his way. The most senior SS officer present, SS-Standartenführer Fuchs, had not been impressed.

"This is a security matter," he'd said. "There is no place for a puppet politician here."

"He is a familiar face for the people."

Fuchs had to concede that Loritz had a point.

Now they were still awaiting the arrival of Klarsfeld and Mittendorf.

The doors to the room swung open and Klarsfeld, sitting in a wheelchair, was wheeled inside, being pushed by SS-Obersturmführer Brauchitsch. On either side of him were two armed men. Fuchs recognized one of them immediately. He jumped to his feet.

"Scholl, you treacherous pig! Arrest that man!"

More armed men filtered into the conference room, spreading out, their weapons aimed at the dozen SS officers present. Klarsfeld was pushed up to the head of the table, a space reserved for Mittendorf. He looked a mess. Pale, uncomfortable, a sheen of sweat on his face. One of his hands was bandaged and one of his legs appeared to be in plaster.

He raised a hand. "Please, Fuchs, sit down."

"What is this? Where is the Oberstgruppenführer?"

"Herr Mittendorf is no longer with us," Klarsfeld said. The SS officers began to shout out questions, but Klarsfeld once again raised a hand and they gradually quietened down. "By now I am sure you are all aware of what has happened in Germania. We can assume that the Führer has been assassinated. As Reichsstatthalter of this state, I am assuming control as the Führer's proxy."

"This is a security matter, Klarsfeld," Fuchs said.

Klarsfeld shook his head. "It is a political issue, one of government, and as Reichsstatthalter, control of this state falls to me. It is clearly laid out in the German constitution."

"What is that traitor doing with you?"

"Scholl is the most senior SS officer in the country."

"He is a traitor and has been sentenced to death."

"In his absence," Klarsfeld said. "He did not have the opportunity to defend himself. I am satisfied that he is innocent of all charges made against him."

"This is bullshit!"

Klarsfeld took a deep breath and then he spoke loudly, with a determination that only a handful of people had ever before heard. He said, "You will all pledge your loyalty to me, or you shall be removed from duty and be detained in protective custody. SS-Oberführer Scholl will be placed in overall command of the Schutzstaffel. By now, the people of this state will have heard of the terrible events in Germania. There will be a period of uncertainty, and if we do not retain control we face a potential uprising. With our political leaders in Germania now gone, we must run Great Britain as a separate entity. We are foreigners here, an occupying force. We have to work with the Engländers or face being overrun. You gentlemen here, all of you, have the most to lose if that happens."

Fuchs looked around at the armed men in the room. All of the SS officers sitting at the large table were looking to him for guidance. He knew that if he opposed Klarsfeld, Klarsfeld's men would take Fuchs away and kill him, but he also knew that this was all so terribly wrong.

He said, "We do not know for sure whether the Führer is dead."

"We have to assume he is. Will you work with us or against us, Herr Standartenführer?"

Fuchs looked across at Scholl. This was a man who had betrayed the Reich, who had worked with Reichsführer-SS Von Stauffenberg in a plot against the old Führer. He'd been sentenced to death *in absentia*, and here he was about to become the most powerful SS officer in Great Britain.

Fuchs did the only honourable thing a loyal Party member could do. He stood up and drew his pistol, aiming it at Klarsfeld. Immediately, he

nach Schema F

was cut down in a hail of bullets. He was dead before he hit the ground, and he didn't witness the six other SS officers at the table who pulled their own weapons and died in a similar fashion.

The remaining SS officers looked nervously at Klarsfeld.

The Reichsstatthalter smiled and said, "Welcome to Great Britain."

84

Ellen returned to her office and sat down behind her desk. The whole floor was in turmoil. People were on the phone trying to contact relatives in Germania, others were asking what would become of the SS, of their jobs. What future did they have?

Klarsfeld had smiled at her when she left him, but she knew that whatever friendship they'd had before today could never be rekindled. She'd had him tortured, effectively to save herself. He might be able to forgive her, consider it to be a necessary evil, but she could not forgive herself.

There was a knock at her door and she looked up to see Willi Himmler standing there. She gestured for him to enter. He had a bottle of schnapps in one hand, two glasses in the other. He sat down and poured them both a drink.

"Drinking on duty?" Ellen asked as she picked up her glass.

"I think we need to make a toast."

"To what? We all failed, did we not? Germania was destroyed."

"We make a toast to a new future then," Himmler said. "We have all lost family and friends. But I am guessing that things will be different from now on."

"You did not have a problem with the way things were before," Ellen reminded him.

He just smiled. After a few moments, he said, "We were living in a paranoid society. What could I have said?" He raised his glass. "To the future." Ellen did the same, and they both took a sip. "So, will you be working for our new Führer?"

"Klarsfeld?"

"He is taking over, is he not?"

"It seems that way. But I rather feel he is not intending to be a führer."

"We shall see. But in any case, will you be working with him?"

"I think, Willi, after torturing him downstairs there will not be a place for me within his organization."

"Well, maybe neither of us will ever have to torture another person as long as we live."

nach Schema F

Ellen raised her glass in another toast.

*   *   *   *   *

Marcus Dauny shook Owen's hand. They had succeeded. The news reports were full of the story of Germania's destruction, and the first footage was starting to come out.

The city was devastated, the magnificent skyline flattened. Skyscrapers had tumbled, the Volkshalle was no more. Twenty million people vaporized in an instant. Further out, in the suburbs of the massive city, some buildings were only partially destroyed, but the inhabitants had surely perished under the might of the huge shockwaves that had followed the multiple explosions.

There was no news of the fate of the Führer, nor of his cabinet, but it was assumed that they had all been killed.

"We did it," Owen said.

"Yes, I think we did. I'm just not so sure it's something we can be truly proud of."

"We've brought down the Reich. We've averted another world war."

"But at what cost?" Dauny shook his head and the smile on his face was rueful. "We have become the greatest mass-murderers in the history of humankind." He walked to the front of the lock-up, gripped the handle on the door and opened it. Light cascaded into the place which had been their home for the last few days. Outside, the sky was grey. It had been raining, but now it was just slightly misty.

Dauny stepped outside.

Beside him, Owen said, "Where are you going now?"

"Somewhere safe."

"But you can go back home. You'll be safe here now, in Leicester, in Peterborough."

Dauny smiled and patted his friend on the arm.

"I don't think either of us will ever be safe anywhere in the world."

And with that, he walked off.

*   *   *   *   *

SS-Sturmbannführer Wolf Loritz looked at his Gestapo ID. The photograph of him had been taken five years earlier. It was due for renewal, but he assumed that wouldn't be necessary anymore. He tossed it idly onto his desk, shook his head and then picked up the cardboard box containing his belongings. Framed drawings, certificates, photographs. On the very top were two files – one with Klarsfeld's name on it, the other with Ellen Brauchitsch's name. He knew that he wouldn't be able to complete his investigations into them both now, he wouldn't be able to bring them to justice, if they were indeed guilty of treason, but at least he could ponder over the evidence during his enforced early retirement.

There would no longer be a place for him under the new regime, that much was apparent. He was a loyal Party member, and a loyal Geheime Staatspolizei officer. He could not and would not turn his allegiance over to Klarsfeld and Scholl. There would be a dangerous period of uncertainty, where the Engländers would undoubtedly seek revenge on any SS officers they could identify. Perhaps Klarsfeld would be able to solidify the relationship between the Germans and the Engländers, but it would take time. The irony was that in ditching the Nazi Party principles, Klarsfeld's government and police force would have to continue to adopt some of those policies to end the civil unrest which was sure to follow the destruction of Germania, the death of the Führer.

But that would be someone else's problem.

Loritz took the elevator down to the ground floor. He chose to walk from the Polizeipräsidium, aware that everyone would see him leaving with his box of belongings. He could be targeted, but he wasn't going to hide who he was. If he made it safely to his apartment, there he could hide away. There he could make contact with other disenfranchised SS officers. There he could contemplate his future.

But if he didn't make it safely home, then fate was not on his side.

As he walked up the busy road, people were tearing down the Nazi regalia, the flags, the Reichsadlers, the posters and banners. People were cheering. They were celebrating. Some even tried to get him to join in, but he just smiled weakly at them. He passed a group of men who were kicking another man, and he paused momentarily, looked at them. The man was crying out in German, asking for help.

Loritz shook his head and continued walking.

Let the Engländers have their moment of triumph. Germany was not

nach Schema F

dead. The Greater German Reich had lost its capital, but it was not completely destroyed. And he would forever remain loyal to the Fatherland.

85

Reichsführer-SS Schaemmel opened his eyes. He was in pain, all over his body. He felt hot, on fire, and he looked down to see that most of his uniform had been burned from his body. He cried out in agony.

He could hear voices, shouts, men panicking. He looked around, saw that he was in the wreckage of the helicopter. The smell of aviation fuel was strong, together with the acrid stench of burnt plastic, burnt flesh. He tried to move, but his legs were broken. He shouted out, tried to draw the attention of the men who were closing in on the crash site.

They reached him, Waffen-SS officers from the nearby barracks. He raised a hand.

"I am Reichsführer-SS Schaemmel," he said.

"Mein Herr," one of the officers said. He didn't salute. He dropped down beside Schaemmel. "We have a medical team on the way. They will be here shortly." Schaemmel tried again to sit up, but the officer stopped him. "Mein Herr, do not move. You are injured."

"The Führer. Is the Führer alive?"

"The Führer was travelling with you?" There were frantic shouts now from the other officers. "Where was he?"

"He was sitting next to me."

The officer looked around, shook his head in a confused manner. Schaemmel raised his head, looked to his right. That side of the helicopter wasn't there anymore. The seat where the Führer had been sitting as gone.

"You must find him," Schaemmel said. He could hear sirens now, the emergency services, the medical team. He reached up and gripped the officer's arm. "What is your name?"

"I am Kuhn, Herr Reichsführer."

"Kuhn, you must find the Führer. Do you understand me?"

Kuhn nodded his head, turned to his colleagues and urged them to search for the Führer. He looked back down at Schaemmel, but the Reichsführer had closed his eyes. The pain was too much. His injuries were horrific. In his last moment of consciousness, Schaemmel wondered whether he would survive. He wondered whether he actually wanted to survive.

And then he heard someone shouting excitedly.

"The Führer! The Führer is here!"

And as the blackness washed over him, dragging him down into a pained sleep, Schaemmel nodded his head and smiled.

"Heil Führer," he said, softly.

THE END

Printed in Great Britain
by Amazon.co.uk, Ltd.,
Marston Gate.